I0588244

The Space In Between: A Novel

JULIA'S STORY

TUCKAWAY BAY
BOOK TWO

MADELEINE JAIMES

SAND DUNE BOOKS

The Space in Between: A Novel

Julia's Story

Tuckaway Bay, Book 2

Madeleine Jaimes

Sand Dune Books by Maddie James

www.maddiejamesbooks.com

Copyright © 2024 Madeleine Jaimes

All rights reserved. The unauthorized reproduction or distribution of this copyrighted work, in whole or part, by any electronic, mechanical, or other means, is illegal and forbidden.

Author: Jaimes, Madeleine

Title: The Space in Between: A Novel / Madeleine Jaimes

Description: First edition. Sand Dune Books

Identifiers: eBook ISBN: 978-1-62237-555-4, Print ISBN: 978-1-62237-564-6

Subjects: Fiction / Women's Fiction | Friendships | Relationships| Family | Saga | Beach Book

Editor: Wendee Mullikin, Purple Pen Wordsmithing, LLC

Cover Design by Author Journey Solutions and DALL-E

This is a work of fiction. Characters, settings, names, occurrences, and story elements are a product of the author's imagination and bear no resemblance to any actual person, living or dead, places or settings, and/or other occurrences. Any incidences of resemblance are purely coincidental.

Published by Turquoise Morning, LLC., dba Jacobs Ink, LLC.

PO Box 20, New Holland, OH 43145.

Learn more about Madeleine Jaimes at www.maddiejamesbooks.com

Join the VIP Newsletter List at Newsletter – Maddie James Books

The Space In Between

The day Julia Salinger admits to her girlfriends that she has a drinking problem, she vows to do something about it. Spending time in a recovery center helps. So does attending AA meetings and therapy. But the thing that saves her, day after day, is fixing breakfast for strangers.

It's routine. It gets her out of bed every morning.

While she and her husband, Mark, had dreams of operating their Old Louisville B&B together, her drinking put an end to that dream—and their marriage. And while Mark still shares in the business venture, the running of the inn is Julia's responsibility.

And all goes well, until it doesn't.

Despite therapy, Julia wrestles with the cause of her drinking—her difficulty coping with the loss of their stillborn child, months of bourbon binges covering up her grief. But now that she's sober, grief surfaces in other ways.

Her father pressures her to return to the family law firm. A friend from AA dies of an overdose. She hears a baby crying in the attic and is certain her Victorian era home is haunted. She craves the sweet oaky taste of bourbon and caves to a night of binge drinking.

She doesn't get up to fix breakfast the next morning.

Mark gives her an ultimatum.

That's when Julia decides her best therapy is the beach, and heads to Tuckaway Bay for solace, healing, and her girlfriends. A secluded cottage at the end of the Sea Glass Inn Resort becomes her sanctuary, where she lets very few people into her life for weeks—except for the older man who surf fishes in front of her cottage every day.

Louisville

One

April

"GOOD EVENING. MY NAME IS JULIA, AND I'M 192 DAYS SOBER. For those of you who are new, welcome, and keep the faith. If I can do it, so can you."

Julia Salinger silently scanned the room, absorbing the mood. Six people sat in the circle, plus her. The physical space was as expected, church basement cinder block walls with thick gray-green peeling paint. There were posters of Jesus with children scattered about the walls, covering the bigger peelings, she suspected. A statue of Mary was positioned in a corner—a Madonna, the Catholics called her—eyes downcast. A crucifix balanced the room on the opposite wall.

God grant me the serenity...

Not overly religious, Julia viewed the images and relics in the room as memories, or perhaps reminders, of her past. She'd grown up with Sunday School and Vacation Bible School in a Methodist Church. Her parents still went there. She stopped going during college, much to her mother's distaste. What decent southern girl didn't go to church of some sort?

Well, she didn't. Not anymore.

Her meetings, in this church basement, were about as close as she would get.

She frequented several groups, all with different moods, setting dissimilar tones. The early morning group took place in a Starbucks—an entirely different atmosphere. Her noon group, located in a meeting room at the hospital downtown, was convenient to her office. The evening groups were generally at one of the churches.

She centered her attention on the two newcomers. Homeless, or close to it, she suspected. *Maybe here for the cookies and coffee.*

A woman sat to her right, mid-thirties she'd guess, nicely dressed in a skirt and sweater, heels. *On her way home from work.*

A man sat directly across from her, older, graying, beard—one might describe him as a silver fox. *Attractive and knows it.*

Two regulars, friends of hers, sat side-by-side to her left. Gretchen, a twenty-something, pink-haired server at a downtown eatery battled pills and booze. *You're way too thin, Gretchen. Are you using again?* Larry, a real estate agent from the east side, came all the way downtown for meetings so he wouldn't run into friends or colleagues. *Not a great plan, Larry.* But at least he was there.

...to accept the things I cannot change...

The leader of the group, Bill Martinez, stood silent with a coffee mug outside the circle, listening intently. Carefully observing. Part of Julia's growth was stepping up and taking a leadership role occasionally. That's what she was doing tonight. Bill was her sponsor.

They locked gazes for a split second, then she refocused, zeroing in on the woman to her right, who fiddled with a small object in her lap—a child's pacifier. *Shit.* Julia's gaze rose to her profile, where a tear begged to spill over a lower eyelid.

...courage to change the things I can...

Julia turned back to the group. "My story is exactly like yours and nothing like yours," she began. "While how we got here is different for each of us, we've all followed the same repetitive, addictive, hopeless, and hopeful process, time and again, before we stepped through that door—or through any AA door anywhere."

All eyes were on her, except for Working Woman, who stared into her lap.

The look on Silver Fox's face was overly intent.

She blinked away.

Gretchen's troubled gaze caught her eye, and Larry heaved a sigh.

"My story involved a horrible personal tragedy, then bourbon, lots of bourbon, and kicking my husband out of the house. In between, there was much more. So much more. I'm still there, now," she told them, glancing about the group, making brief eye contact with anyone who would make it back. "I'm in that space in between. I could be here for a while but that's okay because that is where I will grow and heal. And so will you."

...and the wisdom to know the difference.

"My advice to you tonight, for anyone who needs to hear it, is to find joy in the dark moments, if you can. That might sound odd but try it." She paused, glancing about. "Tonight's topic is patience. But first, let's do some introductions. Would anyone like to share?"

Two

May,
    213 days sober

I SHOULD HAVE PAID MORE ATTENTION TO THE MUFFINS.

Julia glanced at the sideboard and grimaced at the slightly burnt edges of the blueberry muffins. They weren't perfect but they would do. Tomorrow she'd try eighteen minutes rather than twenty. Eventually, she'd get the hang of the new gas oven.

Perhaps she should have baked a practice batch yesterday.

I can do that this afternoon.

While she had loved the vintage look of the old electric, stacked wall ovens, Mark had not. He'd insisted on new appliances, and of course, that's what one does when renovating an older home for a bed-and-breakfast. She had balked then, standing her ground and being difficult, cherishing the retro look-and-feel of the older double unit. A new refrigerator, she was all in for—dishwasher and microwave too. And she'd be lost without her premium, restaurant-grade, six-burner gas cooktop with griddle and grill combo.

But the health department wouldn't pass inspection until they replaced the unit. No choice. She had guests booked and breakfasts to serve.

Damn Mark for being right.

Overruled twice, a new premium gas oven unit now graced her kitchen—the reason she had burnt muffins.

While she couldn't deny the new appliances were literally awesome, convenient, and safe, there was something about the old-fashioned ovens that she'd liked. Predictable. Familiar. Authentic.

No, not authentic. The house was well over a hundred and fifty years old. Why would she want to hang on to a 1970s avocado, double-stack wall unit?

Not getting rid of old stuff was a bad habit.

Welcome to my life.

Separating from Mark hadn't been easy either. Fortunately, he no longer had a say over how she ran her bed-and-breakfast. While he technically remained as a partner in the endeavor, the bottom line rested with her.

The upside to the muffin fiasco was that most of the breakfast spread looked delicious, if she did say so herself. She was getting the hang of this daily domestic ritual. Fresh-squeezed orange juice, sausages, a baked egg dish, coffee, and assorted teas.

And the muffins, of course.

It would do.

The clock struck eight. Let the morning begin.

Glancing through the open pocket doors of the dining room and into the foyer, she looked at the elegantly carved Victorian newel post and spindled banister at the base of the massive stairs. Funny, she half expected her guests to come bolting down the curved stairwell like they were kids late for school. They never did, of course. That was her own bit of private humor.

Smiling, she headed back to the kitchen. One step inside and the phone rang. She picked it up. "Good morning. Old Louisville B&B."

It was routine.

It was a good thing.

It got her out of bed every morning.

"How long did you say you've been here?"

Julia peered up from the flower bed, setting her trowel and a flat of pansies aside, and shielding her eyes with a forearm. The sun was unusually bright this morning. "Mr. Kelley? That you? Hello." The glare silhouetted his body. She straightened, angling to get a better look at him.

The older gentleman had arrived yesterday, requesting the Four Roses Suite on the second floor. Four Roses, like the bourbon—the sleeping rooms were all named after local distilleries. She'd done it as a joke at first, a dig at Mark, since he despised her love for bourbon, but her decorator thought it was a great idea, and it actually fit with the history of the house.

The idea stuck.

There was the Woodford Reserve Room, her favorite suite in the house, located on the first floor. It was the only bedroom unit there. Their goal was to make it handicapped accessible and ADA compliant. The second floor housed the Old Forester, Heaven Hill, and Wild Turkey rooms, in addition to the Four Roses Suite. The third floor, which used to be the attic, was her personal space—a bedroom, bathroom, and another small room she didn't use. At one time it would have been the nursery. Not now. When she finished the rest of the attic renovation across the hall—which wouldn't be until next year—she'd name that the Pappy Van Winkle Suite.

Kentucky loved its bourbon. There was a time she did, too.

"Only a couple of years," she replied.

"You've done a fine job with the place."

That made her smile. "I've lived here that long, but the B&B has only been open a few months," she admitted. "Since New Year's. But I think you already knew that."

"Well, it's beautiful."

She glanced about. "It's getting there."

"I'm sure it's a lot of work."

Not work. Therapy.

She nodded and fully stood, peeling off her garden gloves and tossing them onto a stack of mulch bags. "Let me show you the carriage house. If you are interested? You might want to stay there sometime with your grandchildren."

He beamed. "Oh yes. I'd love to see it."

"It's not quite ready yet for public consumption."

"I can already see the potential," he offered.

She liked this older gentleman. This was his second stay with her, and she was already getting accustomed to his warm smile and kind heart.

They ambled toward the back of the property. "I had hoped you would give me a tour back here," he told her. She smiled and grasped his elbow to steady him as they stepped onto a brick walkway.

"Watch. Some of those bricks are uneven," she told him. "Be careful with your cane."

He stopped and looked up at the two-story structure. For a moment, he was silent. "Did I tell you I worked here as a child? It was a stable then. I might have been ten years old." He paused, silently staring. "It was not long after World War II. The Mulvaney's, the owners then, still had horses. I mucked the stalls."

Julia watched as his gaze played over the structure. "No, Mr. Kelley, you didn't. I would love to hear more about that. I'm very interested in the history of this place. I plan to do some research when things slow down with the renovations." That was one thing about living in Old Louisville, the place smacked of history and stories. Some of them rather sultry and others, a bit on the eerie side of things. The home next door was supposedly haunted, she'd heard, and she'd even wondered a time or two if her own home had spirits.

He dropped his head in a nod, and they moved forward. "Another day. I'd like to just look around now if you don't mind."

"Absolutely." She gripped his arm a little tighter. "The door should be open. Let's be mindful of things lying about on the floor." To be honest, she was second-guessing her decision to bring him inside today. She didn't want him to trip over loose boards, piles of old plaster.

Turning, she took his arm and pushed the carriage house door inward. "Now, the house was built in 1866," she started. "But the carriage house wasn't added to the property until 1872, or so the deeds and other paperwork indicate."

Mr. Kelley nodded, listening intently.

"But you may have already known that."

He smiled and nodded again.

"We've gutted the thing, basically. The plan is to keep the exposed brick inside and those lovely heavy beams up above. I just love the old features, don't you?"

He patted her hand tucked into his elbow. "I do. Tell me more."

"Well, there will be two bedrooms, a kitchenette, living area..." They headed into the center room, which would eventually become the large great room.

The older gentleman gave her his undivided attention, listening intently, and holding on to her every word.

"One bedroom will be down, the primary suite. The other bedroom will be in the loft, with a bathroom up there, too."

"Sounds perfect."

"I'm excited to see the finished project."

"As am I." He grinned and patted her hand.

Thirty minutes later, she waved at Mr. Kelley as he rode away in his daughter's car. She'd called to pick him up, and Julia instructed her how to pull around—via the alley behind the house—and had whisked him off for lunch. She found it interesting that the older gentleman didn't live in Louisville, where he'd grown up, but his daughter did. He lived in Chicago, for some reason. Maybe she'd ask him about that one day. He had to be eighty years old or so, and she wondered why he didn't move closer to his children and grandchildren.

Likely family dynamics. She could understand that.

Rounding the carriage house, she spotted Pamela, her assistant, and halted. The younger woman—younger than her forty-two years, anyway—pushed a wheelbarrow full of topsoil toward another flower bed.

Julia called out. "Can you finish the flowers, Pamela? If there are plenty, let's put some in the urn on the front porch too."

Pamela nodded. "There should be plenty. I'll take care of it."

"Great." Julia smiled. *This is a good day.* "I have some lawyering I need to take care of this afternoon—a meeting downtown—after I shower and get lunch."

"No problem, Mrs. S. I've got this."

Smiling, she headed toward the house, then turned back. "Oh, before I go. I want to make sure we are clear on the plans for next week? They are still tentative, but I should know more later today. You can still come by Sunday night and stay through Thursday morning?"

She'd been looking forward to getting away next week. While the trip to North Carolina was for her friend Maggie, it also felt like she was clearing her soul of something. What? She wasn't sure yet. There were a few things to choose from.

Straightening, Pamela grinned. "Yes. I'm looking forward to it. Thanks for letting me bring Caleb, too."

"Being a single mom isn't easy, I'm sure."

Pamela nodded. "He'll be in school during the day, and here only at night. I'm so thankful you trust me."

"Hey, I trust you with the pansies and petunias. I can trust you with breakfast and making a few beds and dusting."

"And laundry."

"There is that."

"And the guests."

They both laughed. "Right. Is it too much?"

"Absolutely not," Pamela quickly replied.

Good. This woman is a godsend.

Julia took a deep breath, and quickly blew it out. "By the way, I didn't book the downstairs suite next week, so stay there. Make yourself at home."

Pamela smiled. "Thanks. We will."

This would be a test, to see how well Pamela handled things while she was gone. She needed a backup and hopefully, this would work out perfectly. Selfishly, she wanted Pamela to get the routine down pat long before August—and beach week—rolled around.

Beach week was non-negotiable. If she didn't feel comfortable with Pamela taking over by then, she'd close down the inn for the week. Nothing interfered with beach week with her best girlfriends.

"All right. I need to get to my meeting. Oh, and I made pimento cheese this morning so help yourself. And there is a cucumber and onion salad in the fridge." She looked back to catch Pamela's eye.

"That sounds good on a day like today."

"Well eat up. And thanks. You always do great work."

Pamela stabbed a bag of soil with her trowel, splitting the plastic. "I love working here with you, Mrs. S."

"Don't you think it's time you called me Julia?"

Pamela grinned. "All right. Thanks, Julia. And call me Pam."

The girl focused on her work.

Julia stood there for a moment, pondering why she'd not previously asked if she preferred to be called Pam or Pamela. Well, she knew now.

Glancing about the courtyard and garden, situated between her Victorian home behind her, and the carriage house facing her, she felt a keen sense of accomplishment.

All hers. It was all hers. To run with as she pleased.

That thought halfway scared the shit out of her.

Julia rushed from the elevator, glanced at the Salinger & Salinger sign to the left of the double glass door, and pushed through to the outer office. Granting Jayna Lindon, their receptionist, her brief attention, she breezed by her desk. "He in?"

"Yes."

"Good."

"He has a meeting in five minutes."

"I'll be brief."

No doubt about that. She was always direct when it came to conversations with her father. To the point, no beating around the bush. She'd learned that before she was six years old.

Don't waste time, Julia. Get it done. Don't dally. Say what you want. Don't sugarcoat.

She knuckled two knocks on his office door and pushed inside.

Nick Salinger looked up from a spread of paperwork on his desk. The silver streaks at his temples caught the sunlight steaming in the window behind him. She glimpsed a coal barge drifting down the Ohio River out the window, fifteen floors down.

"Julia? Nice surprise."

"It's Wednesday. I always work on Wednesday."

He slid his gaze to the clock on his desk. "It's one o'clock in the afternoon. Short day?"

"I'll be working more than a day next week. That's why I'm here."

She and her father had an agreement. While she was getting the B&B off the ground, she'd still log billable hours at the firm—just in case things went south with the inn, and she had a desire to get back into lawyering full time again.

He still had hopes.

She had her doubts.

He sat back, studying her. She settled into a chair on the other side of his desk.

"I'm likely running down to North Carolina for a few days early next week. The Oliver case. That is if I can get in touch with her this afternoon to confirm. Just letting you know."

Leaning forward, he held her gaze. "Maggie's divorce? This is all cleared with the board, right?"

"It's all good, Nick. I've handled it. Reciprocity, and all." She'd always called him Nick. At first, it was just at the office when she started working for him right out of college. Seemed easier that way. But as the years rolled on, she called him by his given name all the time.

"A few days is a lot of pro bono work."

"It's Maggie."

He shifted. "I get that, but you have to start pulling your weight soon, Julia."

"And I will. I have a bit on my plate right now, with the renovations and...the other things. Maggie's case is helping me get my lawyer legs back underneath me." It had been a couple of years since she'd done much lawyer work. After she'd lost the baby, well, she'd also lost herself....

Her father raised an eyebrow at that. "You okay?"

She jerked a quick nod. "I'm fine."

"Good."

She continued. "I am also putting in hours on the Bledsoe case. That's billable. I have a call with Jillian at two. Besides, Maggie needs me."

"Good on Bledsoe. Helluva mess Ralph got himself into." He stood, towering over her. "I'm fine with you helping Maggie—she's practically family and that husband of hers is an ass. But I need you, too. Since your brother baled on the business—who knows where he's gone off to now —you have to step up. Sooner rather than later or I'll have to change the name on the fucking sign."

Salinger & Salinger.

Today was not the day for the partner discussion.

She had to admit, the past couple of years had not been easy on her father. While she rolled around in the muck of her life, he'd had to deal with a daughter who was too hung over to get out of bed in the morning to practice law, and a son who had gone rogue. Her older brother, Nathan, had ditched his partnership to sail off on a catamaran near Cabo, or some other place south of the border. Both incidents left her father stranded, and the business failing.

She had to wonder if Nick sat around and contemplated how he'd produced two fucked up children?

Or previously fucked up. She was better now. Who knew about Nathan.

And she'd agreed to come back one day a week—it was actually good for her, the sobriety thing and all. She'd had to alter her strict routine for the day, but change was also good, and of course, she had Pam. Handling change appropriately was even better.

Her dad specialized in estate planning, social security disability, and tax issues. She focused on family law, divorce, and domestic violence. Nathan had practiced real estate law—they dropped that wing of the business a year ago.

That's when she knew Nick had given up on her brother and was expecting her to step up.

Damn you, Nathan.

Squaring her shoulders, she stood in a feeble attempt to match his stance. Thank God he had a meeting. She did not want to hash this out today with him.

"Nathan has nothing to do with what I need right now. I'm rusty. I've been out of the game and Maggie needs my help. She can help me get my chops back. I can get her out of that abusive hellhole. It's a win-win."

He exhaled and gathered up a file of papers on his desk. "Fine. I've got to meet with the Barnards."

She smirked. "That should be fun. Want me to sit in? I have thirty minutes I can spare."

He waved her off, circling his desk. "No. You have plenty to do. Take care of Maggie and Jillian Bledsoe and let me know how it goes." He headed toward the exit, then turned back. "And would you please call your mother? Take her to lunch or something before you go out of town. She bugs the fuck out of me every day about how you are." His glare meant business.

She nodded. "I'll set something up this afternoon.

"Do that." He bustled out of the office.

Julia saluted the closing door. "Aye aye, captain."

Three

Her call with Jillian Bledsoe started late and ran longer than she had intended. Still, billable hours. Right? Her father would be pleased.

"Make him pay," Jillian bit out. "Squeeze every dime you can out of that perverted son-of-a-bitch. I want the college funds, the house paid for and in my name, and half his retirement. More if you can get it."

"I'll do my best." Glancing at the clock, Julia noted the time. She needed to move this along so she could catch a meeting downtown before heading home. "I think I have what I need. Touch base in a week? You have my cell phone should you need anything before then."

"Yes. That's perfect."

"I'll transfer you to Jayna to schedule the next call. Or, if you prefer to come to the office, let her know that. Talk soon."

Julia grinned inwardly and transferred the call. Rubbing her temples, she massaged away a potential headache. While Maggie's divorce would be challenging, and exactly the type of case that got her juices going, the Bledsoe case promised to be a slam-dunk.

Jillian Bledsoe was a prominent real estate agent who married up, maneuvered her kids into all the right private schools, traveled all the right social circles, and enjoyed her highfaluting, southern rich bitchiness lifestyle. And while Julia didn't subscribe to such a life herself, and in fact had never really cared for Jillian, or wanted to be part of the Bledsoe's circle—even if her parents did—Jillian was not at fault in this divorce.

Ralph Bledsoe liked his extracurricular flirtations young and innocent. Unfortunately, several months earlier, he'd ventured into off-limits territory seducing a fifteen-year-old server from the clubhouse, resulting in statutory rape changes. Some local groups were calling him out for pedophilia—which was not a great thing to be called out for when one worked as an administrator in the local Catholic private school system.

Ralph claimed the girl presented herself as older, and that she came on to him. But the girl, who got pregnant and subsequently suffered through a botched abortion—unknown to her parents at the time—denied his accusations and described Ralph as a perverted old man. Why would she be attracted to him?

Her parents—both local attorneys—sued the hell out of Ralph, and rightfully so.

Julia's only worry with the Bledsoe case was whether Ralph's money would run out before Jillian and the kids got any of it. A challenge, but she was on it.

Of course, the entire gamut was the last straw for Jillian, who had suffered his infidelities for years—*but how dare he ruin her reputation, too?* She was ready to throw in the towel and call in her cards.

All her cards.

Logging off her computer, Julia gathered the Bledsoe and Oliver files, slipping them into her leather bag. She'd review a few things tonight and be ready to touch base again with Jillian in a week. In the meantime, she had to focus on Maggie.

Speaking of which....

Scrolling through the text messages on her phone, she realized it had been a couple of weeks since she'd chatted with any of her girlfriends. She typed a quick message to the full group—Lia, Alice, Maggie, Wren, and Willow. The six of them were close and had been for over twenty years since they lived together in college.

They never excluded Wren and Willow from texts, even though no one had heard from the twins since last August. While that made them all uneasy, they had to trust that the sisters knew what they were doing and promised each other they would be patient.

And Maggie? Her communications were sporadic, at best. Occasionally, they had to add a new cell number to the group text because she kept switching out burner phones. While Maggie claimed that Max, her husband, hadn't forbidden her from talking with her girlfriends, she risked using the burner phones on occasion so she could communicate more freely.

That was her story, anyway. The thing was, Maggie had been pretty closed mouthed about her home situation for several months.

Julia: *Hey. I know it's only April but any decisions yet about beach week? Same week? Location?*

She drummed her fingers on her desktop, staring out the window over the traffic on I-64 by the river, thankful she didn't have to fight that mess on the way home. Living close to downtown had its advantages, and traffic was high on the list.

Lia: *Hey back! Tequila Sunrise is unavailable for the summer, renovations. Don't think it will be ready by beach week. But we left two cottages open for the last two weeks of August—the Pelican and the Gull. That work?!*

Julia: *Ok by me. You and Zach are working so hard on the properties. Too bad about TS.*

Lia's happiness seemed to ooze through the text messages. She and Zach had inherited Sea Glass Inn Resort at Tuckaway Bay last fall when Zach's Aunt Grace passed away. At times, Julia had experienced a few pangs of jealousy that the newly married couple had accomplished so much in such a short time. Meanwhile she and Mark had floundered in their attempts to get the B&B renovated and open.

Lia: *You too! On yours, I mean!*

Alice: *The cottages are lovely. Next to each other. Right?*

Lia: *Yes!*

God, Lia loved her exclamation points.

Julia: *I like the sound of that. Works for me. Maggie?*

Lia: *Wren? Willow?*

The message string lay stagnant for several seconds while they waited. Of course, nothing from Wren or Willow, but she'd been hopeful a message from Maggie would pop into the conversation.

Alice: *I'm sure it's fine with the others. I hope everyone can make it this year.*

Alice was hopeful, but Julia didn't share her friend's enthusiasm. Maggie's life was hanging in the balance, so to speak, and Wren and Willow were just fucking AWOL. She wished she knew where they were so she could figure out how to help them.

God, Julia, you can't fix everyone.

Julia: *I can't wait to see you all. <smiley emoji>*

Lia: *Same!*

She had to wonder if Wren and Willow ever saw the texts. Were they covertly monitoring their friends from a distance? There'd been trouble in their lives when they left beach week abruptly last August, and while she had expected to hear from them before now, after so many months, it bothered her.

Where were they?

Did they escape whatever it was they were running from? Or did they run head-on into it?

Her phone binged again. This time, a private message.

Alice: *Heard from Maggie lately?*

Julia: *Two weeks ago. Plan to make contact later tonight.*

Alice: *Good.*

She waited through a pause, sensing Alice had more to say. After a minute, the three dots started jumping: *Alice is typing...*

Alice: *Sort of worried. She's quiet.*

Julia: *Yes. Too quiet.*

Alice: *Let me know if you talk to her. Okay?*

Julia: *Definitely. Heading out. Meeting. Talk soon.*

She was five minutes late—something she strived never to be—so Julia covertly slipped down the basement stairwell of the Catholic church and pushed the swinging door into the meeting room. She paused, standing in the doorway, and let the heavy door bump against her backside, preventing it from slamming against the metal frame. Nothing could break a mood faster than a *slap-jolt-bang* from behind when one finally mustered up the courage to bare their soul during an AA meeting.

There were several people in the circle, and she didn't stop long enough to peruse who was there, but instead, spotted an empty seat off to the left and headed for it. As unobtrusively as possible, she lowered herself onto the seat and stared at the floor. Bill sat across from her—that was his usual spot—but he was not the one speaking.

She purposely didn't make eye contact—with anyone. That was her usual M.O. when in a meeting and others were talking. Not that she had anything to hide, or felt shame for them, but that she could empathically feel their pain and looking into anyone's eyes not only hurt her gut, but she worried it made the other person nervous. Especially for anyone new to the group.

She also tried hard not to disrupt the flow of the meeting. She didn't want to pull Bill, or anyone else's attention, from whatever was going on with the woman talking at the moment.

Listening intently, she kept her gaze downcast, staring at the dark spot on the dull tiled floor. Coffee, perhaps. Or maybe ground-in mud. What did it matter?

The woman droned on, speaking in short quiet bursts, pausing, sniffling, and then speaking up again. She'd not long been sober, Julia could tell. Maybe even had relapsed. Funny, she heard the woman's speech, but hadn't really absorbed her words.

Too much on her mind?

Perhaps you've become numb to all of this, Julia? Maybe a bit desensitized?

Maybe. But that wasn't fair to everyone else in the room, all of them likely going through their own crises—however big or small.

Lifting her gaze finally, she slowly looked toward the woman speaking. Familiar. Yes. The young woman from a week or two ago. Working Woman.

Julia's gaze fell to her lap, where yes, her fingers fiddled with a pink pacifier.

Her gut clutched with nausea.

Suddenly, the woman snorted and sobbed. "I can't do this anymore," she wailed. "I give up. I need to feel numb just so I can get through the day. How do I do this? I can't function with or without a drink. I don't know where to turn."

"You turn here, just like you did." Julia quietly rose and went to the woman. Kneeling in front of her, she took the woman's hands, softly folding them and the pacifier in hers. She side-glanced at Bill, who sat watching her. This was probably going out of protocol, but what the hell. The woman was in pain.

"Hi," she said. Though she kept her eyes downcast, Julia persisted, and spoke softly. "I'm probably the only other person in the room who could say I know how you feel." She paused and the woman sniffled again. "I know that's cliché. I know you are in pain. And I know as you do how it feels to make the hurt go away by dulling the pain in our brains and bodies with booze."

The woman lifted her gaze slightly, making eye contact. "You don't understand."

"Maybe not." Julia gave her a half smile and whispered. "Tell me your name?"

After a sigh, she said, "Marsha."

"Hi, Marsha. It's tough. One day at a time. Remember?"

The woman squeezed her eyes shut briefly, tears escaping, then opened them again to look at Julia. "I lost everything."

"I know. I did, too. It hurts."

"My husband left me."

"I pushed mine away because I could."

"It was my fault, you know, that the baby died. I don't know if I can live with that for the rest of my life. I don't know how to live anymore, knowing that my baby is dead."

Oh, shit. Was this a hint at suicide? This was going deeper than she had anticipated. One thing she'd learned from Bill was to recognize when things were escalating beyond what an AA meeting could handle. "Marsha, I'm so sorry."

Suddenly, the young woman looked up and glanced about, the terror in her eyes rising as she made eye contact with several of the others in the room. "I've already said too much. You all will hate me."

Julia grasped her hands tighter. "No one hates here Marsha. We help each other."

"So, I'm supposed to admit what I've done, right? Okay, so I killed my daughter. I left my baby girl sleeping in the hot car. I was late and busy and I had a hundred things on my mind and I forgot about her—forgot about my baby, who does that?—and went to work. All day."

Abruptly, Julia recalled the news reports from several months back —so this was the woman? "Marsha, that is a lot to handle."

"I'm a terrible person."

Julia stood, knowing things were rapidly accelerating beyond her capabilities. She held out a hand and sidled a glance Bill's way. He didn't stop her, so she continued. "Let's go chat. There's a room over there where we can talk, just you and me. How about that?"

Marsha jerked and took Julia's hand. As she led the young woman to the private room, she caught Bill's eye. He gave her a shallow nod.

She had no clue if this was the right or wrong thing to do. Going with her gut seemed her only choice at the moment. They entered the private room and Julia shut the door behind them with a soft click.

Thirty minutes later, after she had convinced the young woman that she might need more support than Alcoholics Anonymous could provide—*in addition to AA, she emphasized*—Julia scribbled the suicide prevention hotline on the back of one of her business cards, then added her therapist's number on it as well, and placed it in Marsha's hand. With a hug, she asked her to join the group again, if she was ready.

Marsha refused, and said she preferred to slip out the back door, if it was all the same to her.

She had to let her make her own decisions, so Julia didn't stop her. After Marsha left, she sat there for a while, absorbing the silence of the empty room, then she rejoined the group.

Bill stood by the snack table, talking with an older gentleman. The ending part of the meeting was always social. Glancing about, Julia looked for Gretchen and didn't see her. Larry sat in the circle, talking with an attractive woman about his age. Realizing she was exhausted, she decided to head home.

She finger-waved at Larry while she passed. He grinned back.

Bill appeared engrossed in conversation, so she bypassed him and headed for the door. In the parking lot, she was about to push the button on her key fob to unlock the door, when someone called out behind her.

"Julia! Wait."

She turned. Bill.

He jogged up to her. "You okay?"

Was she? She wasn't sure, to be honest. "I just feel a little numb. That was more than what I bargained for tonight."

"You did fine."

"She needs help. I'm hopeful she will be back, but I'm not sure."

"That's not on you."

"I know that. Still...."

Bill grasped her hand. "Julia, how are you? Really?"

With a sigh, she squeezed his hand back. "I'm busy. Tired. There's a lot going on with the inn, plus picking up work at the office. But I'm fine. Maybe I helped Marsha a little, I don't know, and that feels good. But I'm not desperate, Bill. And I'm not going to drink." She was rambling, several thoughts exiting her mouth in that one brief speech.

He grinned. "I didn't think you would."

"But you just wanted to know how I was feeling."

"Yes. Emotions can be crazy things."

"Tell me about it." Stepping forward, she laughed a little and hugged him. "Thank you. I'm fine."

Pushing back, he held her at arm's length for a moment. "Good. See you soon."

"Will do. Thanks, Bill."

He turned and headed back into the church, not saying the unspoken words. *Call if you need me.*

Heaving another sigh, Julia unlocked the car.

WHILE HER PRIVATE SUITE WAS HER FAVORITE AREA OF THE bed and breakfast, the first floor was Julia's second-best place to be. She often spent afternoons in her sunroom, looking out over the courtyard garden. Or later in the day, in her office, after the guests had either settled into their rooms for the evening or were out and about seeking downtown nightlife.

The nice thing about Old Louisville, where the inn was situated across the street from Old Louisville's Central Park, was that it was just off of the downtown business and entertainment districts. While she never recommended walking to downtown—there were some shady streets and blocks along the way—it was a quick drive if one wanted to pay for parking, or better yet, grab a speedy Uber or Lyft ride.

One could seek out a concert at the historic Brown Hotel in the theatre district, or dine at the Gatsby-era Seelbach Hotel, or at many other popular restaurants along Fourth Street Live. A visit to the museums and Whiskey Row never disappointed. Baseball fanatics came to see the Louisville Slugger Museum or take in a game at Slugger Field. The Mohammed Ali Museum and Kentucky Center for the Arts were huge draws as well. Ghost and garden tours were offered in Old Louisville seasonally, and paddleboat dinner cruises on the Ohio River via the Belle of Louisville were available some evenings.

Make reservations in advance, she always told potential guests when they called. *As far ahead as you can.* While she loved knowing that the inn would be full and bringing in the income she needed, she also knew the city was fast becoming a destination getaway spot. One didn't lack for authentic Louisvillian experiences when visiting the city.

Of course, the bourbon trail and thoroughbreds were unique draws of their own. For many, they were the primary destination. Kentucky Derby season and the festival had proved to be extremely profitable the past few weeks—the inn fully booked for the month of April through mid-May—with no sign of letting up. Next year she would plan better and have the carriage house and the attic room ready for guests.

That's a fantastic goal, Julia. You could double your income by next Derby season if you can make that happen.

Pulling her thoughts away from the inn, she settled her gaze on the open notebook on her desk, and the flickering screen of her laptop.

Generally, her afternoons involved taking care of the rooms and linens, evenings spent doing paperwork, planning breakfast menus and grocery lists for the coming week, reviewing and filing the receipts from the construction firm, and keeping track of the financial ledger.

Tonight, she was doing just that, trying to get ready for her week in North Carolina.

If she could get in touch with Maggie.

Looking up from her menu book, she drummed her fingers on the desktop. Having tried Maggie twice in the past week with no answer, she was concerned. The last time she'd spoken with her was two weeks ago by text message. She'd not seen her since last August, when Julia and her girlfriends had watched Maggie leave their beach house with her bastard husband and her smug, bratty teenage daughter.

Maggie hadn't wanted to go with Max. She'd told him earlier that week she wanted a divorce. When he arrived though, along with their teenage daughter whom Maggie had thought was missing, he gave her no choice. She went home with him because of his threats to take away her children—and to be honest, Julia was unsure how Maggie could support them on her own. No doubt she loved her kids, and they were well taken care of, but she'd not worked in years, and had no money to her name.

And that's the way Max wanted it.

Typical, classic, control freak, abusive husband—*if I can't have you, I will see to it that no one else can either*, he'd said. That worried her. She'd heard those warnings too many times in the past, and sometimes, the outcome was not good.

She didn't want that for Maggie.

While Julia was a top-notch divorce attorney who catered to women in impossible situations, Maggie's case was slightly different because of their close friendship—and because she also knew the kind of manipulative ass a man like Max could be.

She had to tread carefully.

To say Maggie was up shit creek was an understatement.

And now, Julia was concerned. Too long since they'd had any kind of meaningful contact.

She'd promised Maggie last summer she would handle her divorce. However, nearly nine months had passed and only the preliminary work had been done. While she had filed the necessary reciprocity paperwork to practice in North Carolina, and she and Maggie had talked extensively once after the first of the year, their communications were brief. That's why a few days with Maggie next week was so important.

Of course, Julia had been somewhat to blame for the delay in getting started.

After she'd returned to Louisville from Tuckaway Bay late last August, Julia had checked herself into Healing Hope, a live-in detox and recovery center located on the outskirts of Louisville. She'd stayed a month, gotten herself clean and sober, and her head on semi-straight, before heading back to the inn. Healing Hope is where she met her therapist, Melinda, who specialized in grief and addictions, and where she was introduced to Alcoholics Anonymous.

While she was gone, Mark had supervised the work on the bed-and-breakfast, putting the construction efforts on a better path, with enough of the renovations finished to plan an open house for the week after Christmas—starting the new year off with guests on New Year's Eve.

Consequently, Maggie's divorce was on hold until she got her shit together. Meanwhile, Maggie wasn't ready to separate from Max, and was trying to figure out how to cohabit with him in some sort of cordial manner, while shielding the kids from the issues and protecting them from any potential violence.

Julia could only guess that Max was making Maggie's life a living hell—but she had no clue how she could help her, until she got a handle on her own life.

Flipping over her cell phone, which had been lying face down on her desk, she scrolled for Maggie's last text and typed in a quick message. *Hello. Checking in. Still on for next week?*

Immediately, the words "undeliverable" flashed beneath her message.

"What the hell?"

She checked the number she'd texted again. It was Maggie's latest burner phone, she was certain. Impulsively, she called the number.

The person you are calling is not accepting calls at this time, or this service has been disconnected.

She clicked off the call. "Fuck. What does that mean?" Maybe she got a new burner and just hadn't had time to get the number to them. That would make sense.

Maybe.

Standing, she jerked open a desk drawer, searching for an old Franklin planner she'd kept which had an index of phone numbers from years past. She flipped through the pages until she found Maggie Oliver's name, and the number for her house landline.

Quickly, she dialed that number, hoping it was still workable. She didn't care how late it was.

"Hello." It was a kid, a girl. Carol, the teenage daughter. Maggie's other daughter was too young.

"Hi. I'm calling for Maggie Oliver. Could I speak with her please?"

A sigh came from the other end, then she heard the girl shout out. "Da-ad. It's someone for mom again."

She heard some shuffling, then a man's gruff voice spoke into the phone. "Yes."

"Hi. May I speak with Maggie, please?"

"Who's calling."

Immediately Julia wished she'd not called from her cell phone because of caller ID. Maybe she should get a burner too. She had to make a split-second decision whether to fake the call or actually say who she was. Max would be an ass either way.

"It's Julia, from Kentucky. Just calling for Maggie. We've not spoken in a while."

"Yes, well, I doubt that."

"Excuse me?"

"Maggie can't come to the phone right now."

"Is she okay?"

Max paused. "I'll tell her you called."

"Right." Julia bit her lip. "Please do and thanks."

He hung up before she could utter another word.

Didn't take her long to process that something was wrong.

Again, she scrolled her phone, this time for Alice's number. Pacing now across the creaky wooden plank floorboards, she traveled the short distance from the desk to the window several times, finally pausing to stare out the window at the street. A couple stood under the streetlight across the street at the park, kissing.

"Julia?"

She wasted no time. "Alice? When was the last time you talked to Maggie?"

"Well, hello to you too. Didn't we just talk about this?"

Julia shook her head, although that was ridiculous since Alice couldn't see her. "Not really. Just wondering how long it's been since any of us have actually heard her voice."

"She called, not texted, about a month ago, I think. We had a long conversation while she was getting groceries. Why?"

"Just tried her cell. Disconnected. Called the house number too. Carol answered and handed me off to Max, who said she was unavailable."

"Damn. You talked to Max? Was that wise?"

She huffed out a breath. "Probably not but I panicked when my text didn't go through. Carol said to her dad something like, *it's someone for mom again.* Again? What the hell does that mean?"

"Maybe she is taking a nap?"

"Alice," Julia's voice raised. "You know goddamned well that something is wrong if Max won't let her come to the phone."

"Don't go borrowing trouble, Julia. When we talked, she said they were trying to make a go of things. That they were working on their marriage. I imagine there is a simple explanation."

"No. Max doesn't do things simply and Maggie doesn't want to make a go of anything. It's all a front she's been playing to keep the kids safe, and frankly, herself."

"Are you sure about that?"

Shit. Alice and her Pollyanna attitude. "What the fuck, Alice? Not every couple should try and save their marriage. You certainly aren't planning to save yours so why are you pulling for Maggie to save hers?"

Alice didn't immediately respond. "Well, the kids are young, and Maggie has no means of support...."

Julia impatiently paced away from the window. The couple across the street had left now. Sometimes it seemed that the world was full of couples. She turned away.

"Then Maggie will just have to find a job, get skills. It's what people do."

"You're right."

"Damn straight, I am."

"Are you working on her divorce?"

"Covertly. In a way. It's been difficult to get Maggie alone on the phone for any length of time. That's why I need to go down there and see her face to face."

"Do you think Max somehow found out that you were coming? Talking to her? Maybe read her text messages? Cut off her phone?"

Julia shook her head and leaned her backside against her desk. "I don't know. Next week was to get things started. Supposedly Max was going to be out of town. But honestly, I want to know that she is okay. Seeing someone can be a lot more telling than texts and an occasional call. Now, I wonder...."

Another sigh from Alice. "You want me to go check on her. Don't you?"

"Can you?"

"Oh, Julia. I don't know."

"You're closer."

Alice didn't say anything.

"Alice? Please?"

"I can't, Julia. I've got things here I'm dealing with. Ella is about to graduate. George and I are trying to figure out the next phase of our lives. Marilyn wants me to go on the campaign trail with her and frankly, I'm about at the end of my rope trying to juggle it all. You understand. Don't you?"

She didn't. Not really. Alice was two hours away from Maggie, and Maggie was in trouble.

Julia was convinced. Sensed it. Maggie and Alice were two of her oldest friends, and they always took care of each other. While Alice was close, it would take Julia a day to get down there, ten hours at the minimum driving straight through.

But maybe she should.

"Fine," she said. "No problem, Alice. I understand."

"Julia?"

"It's good, Alice. I'll handle it and let you know." She didn't care if Alice sensed her frustration.

"It's just that... Well, things are a bit cockeyed here, too."

Of course, they are. Your perfect life is taking a dive.

Alice was juggling a husband and a lover and a family about to implode.

We all have our problems, don't we? Shit. "Got it. I'll let you know if I talk to her."

"Okay, call me."

Julia clicked off.

Sure. The minute I fucking know something. Not.

But she would. They all stuck together—the six of them. Even with the odds stacked against them. Even when some of them were AWOL.

She'd figure this out.

Tomorrow was Thursday—if she could get Pam on board, perhaps she could leave a few days earlier.

A message notification sounded from her phone.

She glanced down.

Nick: *Call your mother. Lunch tomorrow.*

"Crap." Why the hell couldn't her mother communicate this herself? Well, that was Denise Salinger, for you.

Her fingers flew over the small keyboard. *Will set something up with mom soon. May have to go to North Carolina tomorrow. Will be in touch.*

Nick: *Lunch tomorrow. Jeff Ruby's. I made a reservation.*

Julia: *Sure.*

Just ignore what I fucking said, Dad.

Nick didn't respond.

Fine.

All the better.

With a sigh, she scrolled and pressed to make one more call.

Pam answered. "Hi Julia."

"Sorry to call so late. Look, I might have to leave earlier than expected for Rocky Mount. We can discuss tomorrow, but just for my peace of mind, I wanted to touch base tonight. Can you take over a few days earlier? Something has come up. We can go over all the details in the morning."

Pam hesitated slightly. "I'm sure you forgot. I'm off tomorrow, Julia. And Friday through the weekend. Remember? My parents are in town."

Oh, that's right. Shit. "Of course. Listen, don't worry about it. I'll figure out something else."

"What about Mark?"

Fuck me. Mark? "Oh, no. That won't work."

"He's the only other person who knows the routine."

True that. Hell. "I'll think about it. Thanks."

"I can be there Sunday night late, or Monday morning early."

"Got it. Pam, sorry to interrupt your evening. Have a great weekend with your parents."

"Tell Mark to call me if there's an emergency."

"Sure." Like, she'd already decided to call Mark.

Hell, she had to call Mark. *Fuck a damn duck.*

Four

December, five months earlier
  92 days sober

"JULIA, WE NEED TO MAKE A DECISION."

Shoving a tray of cookies into the top oven, she set the timer, checked the temperature in the lower oven, and side-glanced at Mark. Why the shit was he bugging her about this now? "Mark, I have a thousand things to do today. Can we talk about this later?"

Returning to the kitchen island, she wiped her hands on a dishtowel then tossed it aside. Puffs of flour wafted into the air. Stacking measuring cups and spoons, a rubber spatula, and the rolling pin into a large mixing bowl, she carried it all to the opposite counter and set it in the sink.

Mark followed her. "We really need to figure out some things, Julia. The separation agreement, the business partnership and what that looks like going forward, and more."

"Not now. Not today." She ran a steam of water into the mixing bowl.

"I know this is a busy weekend."

She whirled. "Busy? Mark, the grand opening is in two days. The open house is in less than forty-eight hours—two days before Christmas. All the rooms and suites are booked for New Year's weekend. There are still cookies and cakes to bake, pastries to fill, beds to make and rooms to decorate. Plus, Pamela's kid is sick and she's not sure she can help at all, let alone be here on Sunday."

"For the open house?"

Turning, she met Mark's gaze, and sighed. "Yes. For the open house."

"I'll work it with you."

Shit. No.

"That's not necessary." She turned back to the island, yanking the flour container toward her, and pulling down another set of mixing bowls from the cupboard to her right. "I can handle this."

He didn't say anything, but his gaze fell heavy on her—she could practically feel the stifling weight of it. She always knew when he was staring at her, or assessing her. Probably because they'd lived most of their lives together.

"What?" She looked at him.

"You don't have to do this alone."

"Oh," she huffed, "I most certainly do. That's what I do so well—be alone, right?—isn't that what you told me a few months ago?"

He grimaced. She'd intentionally hit a nerve.

"Well?"

"Touché."

She opened another bag of flour and emptied it into the cannister. "I don't need your help, Mark. I'm fine."

"Should I remind you that we agreed I'd still have a stake in the B&B? I've invested time and money, and even though I know you don't want me underfoot, I can still help. This is only one of the reasons why we need to work out that partnership agreement."

With a sigh, she looked up at him. "Fine. I'll talk with Craig Paulson next time I'm downtown. He's good with business contracts and partnerships."

He nodded. "Great. If you can get that rolling, then let's talk about therapy."

"I'm already going to therapy. You know that."

"I'm talking about us, not you."

She measured out two cups of flour and poured them into the large mixing bowl. "Mark, there is no us."

"Put the measuring cups down, Julia. Look at me."

After a moment, she did, turning. "What?"

He stared into her eyes. "There's been an us for over twenty-five years. I've said it before, and I will continue to say it. I don't know how to do life with no 'us.' I know you are in therapy to deal with all that's happened the past couple of years—but I also want couples therapy —for us."

"We're not getting back together, Mark."

"The divorce papers are still not signed."

"And who's signature is missing?"

"Mine, of course. I can't bring myself yet. Then there must be a reason."

She glanced off, staring at the mess she'd made with the cookies on the island. Flour everywhere. Sugar sprinkles, too. Open jars of spices and a bowl full of cracked eggshells. Had she made the same kind of mess of her life? Their lives?

It wasn't all her fault. Was it?

With a sigh, she lifted her gaze. "One condition." Hells bells, it was Christmas. She could give him that, couldn't she?

"Anything."

She made eye contact. Oh, how she had loved doing that when they were younger. Gazing into his brown eyes. They were just kids but didn't know it. That was then.

This was now.

"We do this so we can learn how to live without each other, Mark. Not to get back together. That ship has sailed."

"Has it?"

"God, you're relentless." She dug the scoop into the sugar cannister. "We need to learn how to be friends, and evidently, business partners. Let's just do that."

"Before we can become lovers again?"

She turned away, dismissing him.

He rounded the island. "Sorry. I'm dropping that. I'll take friends."

She lifted her gaze and took in his sincere expression. For a moment, her heart ached for him, for all they'd been through. She supposed she owed him couple's therapy.

"If you're free on Sunday, and even tomorrow, I could use your help." Bill would be happy with her for that concession—one of her biggest problems with battling alcoholism was reaching out for help. She wondered what Melinda, her therapist, would say about it all.

A slight grin spread across his face. "You can count on me."

The thing was, even after all the shit she'd put him through, she knew that she could.

<hr>

MAY, PRESENT DAY
214 days sober

AFTER SHE GOT OFF THE PHONE WITH PAM, SHE DECIDED NOT to call Mark.

Morning will be better.

With nothing resolved—with Maggie, asking Mark for help, the woman in the AA meeting—it was time to say fuck-it to all and let it go for the evening. Not a damn thing she could do about any of it at this moment.

Especially where Mark was concerned.

Besides, it was late, and the last thing she wanted was to send the message that she was desperate, or something. Calling him. Asking for a favor. Hell. Maybe she couldn't even do it.

There I go again. Refusing to ask for help.

Shit.

Of course, she should reach out to him—business partners and all, even if they had agreed Mark would be mostly a silent partner.

With all the guests tucked in for the night, she locked up downstairs and moved to her third-floor suite. Her brain too wired for sleep, she showered instead, hoping the warm water would relax her mentally and physically—and that the steady stream would help ease the tension of one long damn day—and contemplate the next steps with Maggie.

While her body was tired, her thoughts raced like a thoroughbred chasing the last leg of the Triple Crown.

The shower helped somewhat but not as much as she would have liked. Suddenly, she wished she had some of Willow's weed. Smiling, she closed her eyes and thought of her free-spirited, CEO friend. Such a contradiction—in life and in everything she did. They could always count on Willow to do the unexpected.

Julia sure as hell hoped she was okay.

But weed was out of the question—and she'd never been a big partaker anyway.

She couldn't deny, however, that this was the kind of day when, months earlier, she would have reached for a bourbon nightcap to settle her anxiety and help her get to sleep. This was the time of evening when she felt the most vulnerable, and alone. Even when Mark was living in the house, she'd often felt alone.

Abandoned.

Lost. Useless. Lonely.

In those days, she'd kept a bottle of bourbon and a tumbler in her dresser drawer, ready to pull out. She had her favorite—Woodford Reserve Double Oaked, her poison of choice—but to be honest, any bourbon or whiskey would do in a pinch.

And there'd been a lot of pinches.

At her worst, she didn't even hide the evidence.

She glanced at the dresser and the drawer.

"No. Not tonight. Not any night."

Besides, she'd long rid the house of any alcohol. And she'd promised Bill.

She sat on the side of her bed, brushing out her hair, her bathrobe gaping at her chest. She was thinner, she could tell by her prominent clavicle. Removing the booze from her diet had eliminated a lot of consumed calories, but she'd feared gaining weight now that she was eating more, so had switched to a largely plant-based diet—even though there were days she craved meat. She also walked at least two miles every morning. Besides keeping her blood pressure under control, walking was an important part of her daily routine.

While she felt good, healthy, she knew she was too thin, and staring into her face in the mirror, she wondered if she needed to find ways to get more protein into her diet.

Maybe fuck the plants and eat some cow tomorrow. A hamburger sounded like a good plan. Smiling, she studied herself some more.

At least her hair looked better.

Her light auburn locks had grown out since she'd whacked off the length last summer, right before beach week, during an impromptu, self-imposed, hungover pity party. She wasn't sure what she'd been thinking at the time.

She stared, further inspecting herself.

She wasn't thinking. That was the problem back then.

That desperation was behind her now. The week she'd spent in Tuckaway Bay with her girlfriends had helped. It had been a wild, over-whelming, and life-changing week for all of them. Lia had found her one true love. Alice finally came clean about her lesbian lover. Maggie, of course, had the issues with Max. And who the hell even knew what happened to Wren and Willow, and where they had ended up?

While she worried about them all, she knew she couldn't forget her own issues.

Keeping sober was a struggle. Every. Single. Day.

She blinked, staring into her face in the mirror again.

"I can't take on Maggie's problems too. Can I?" *Am I strong enough?*

But the bastard husband hit her. Maggie had confessed as much. Julia had seen the black eye and knew she couldn't let that go on, but what could she do?

"Fuck." The word hissed through her teeth. She texted Mark.

Do you have a minute in the morning? I need to talk to you about something.

Talk to him, not ask him anything. She still had a difficult time asking for his help, even after all these months, years. After therapy.

She waited but he didn't respond. Probably asleep.

Standing, she pulled back the covers on her bed and slipped out of the robe, placing it at the foot. In between the covers, the sheets were cool against her warm, showered skin. Her hair was still slightly damp, so it would look like hell in the morning, but she didn't care.

Turning to her side, she reached to shut off the bedside lamp, glancing at the rose wallpaper on the wall. Quickly, she switched the lamp to darken the room before she started counting those fucking roses.

As she closed her eyes, the woman from the AA meeting burst into her head.

"It was my fault. I killed my baby."

Julia rolled over, away from the roses, and covered her head with her pillow.

Darkness wasn't necessarily her friend. She prayed sleep would come soon.

———

AUGUST, SEVEN MONTHS EARLIER
  0 days sober

"JULIA!"

Jolting at the slam of the back door downstairs and curling tighter onto her side—her back to the bedroom door—she stared at the rose-patterned wallpaper on her bedroom wall. She'd stared so long that the petals were all meshing into small pink masses, and then for some odd reason, burst into a single rose blossom popping from the wall. A life of its own.

She studied it. The rose. The minutia of its petals. The delicate lines and curves of each one, shaped differently, like snowflakes. The rich, succulent blush of pink that bordered on purple, and nicely complemented the ivy green vine and leaves winding up the wall and over the window.

She loved the simplicity—yet complicated delusion—of the old Victorian wallpaper.

Which was an apt description of her, lately.

Complicatedly delusional, yet simple.

Mark's footsteps pounded the staircase as he ascended. "Don't you think it's time to get out of bed and do something? My God, Julia, look at this place."

She swore she could smell the bloom's fragrance. No, what she smelled wasn't a rose.

Lilac. Yes. That was it. She smelled lilac.

She'd told Mark once, just before falling asleep—back when they still slept together—that she smelled lilac in the room. He'd mumbled something about her being crazy. They'd cut the old lilac bush down when they demolished the side porch to rebuild it. Removing it was unavoidable, he'd told her back then. She'd begged him to get a landscaper to move it to another spot in the yard. He didn't.

She'd mourned that old lilac bush ever since.

And she'd kicked herself repeatedly for not getting it done herself—why couldn't she have picked up the phone and made a call or two? But that was months ago, when they were starting the renovation work on the historic home in Old Louisville, and the eradication of the lilac was only a minor problem.

Her only defense was that she was eight months pregnant and on bedrest—preeclampsia, the doctor had said. Most likely due to her high blood pressure. Maybe she shouldn't even have tried getting pregnant at her age.

Was that it? Was it her fault?

Her fault the baby was born not breathing?

She assessed Mark's footsteps as he ascended the stairs, each foot striking the tread heavily and more slowly as he climbed. His labored footfall was a clear sign of how tired he was—of her, of life, of all this shit—until he pushed through the open door of her bedroom.

"Christ. Did you not get up this morning?"

Leave me alone, Mark. Leave me the fuck alone!

He crossed the threshold.

My baby is dead. Give me a freakin' break.

"God, Julia. You are a mess."

"Don't start with me," she mumbled.

He sat next to her. "You didn't let the workers in."

"Didn't feel like getting up."

"We are paying them. Every day you don't let them in, we lose money, and we're one more day behind in opening."

Money. It's always about money. She burrowed deeper into the covers.

"Julia."

She threw back the comforter and half-sat up. "I'm sick, Mark. A stomach bug or something. Leave me alone."

"You're not sick."

"Yeah, well, maybe I don't feel well today."

"You don't feel well every day."

She got up and stumbled away from the bed, pushing past him with a steadying hand on the garden roses on the wall, and picked up a pack of cigarettes from the dresser. She fished her lighter out of her pajama bottom pocket and, avoiding looking into the mirror on the dresser, lit the tobacco end of the cigarette while sucking in a shaky breath.

Facing Mark, she blew out a healthy stream of smoke.

"You're drunk," he said.

"No." She glared, cigarette hanging from her lips. "Hungover. There's a difference."

Mark rolled his eyes and scowled, looking at the floor. "Remind me to search for the bourbon you've stashed in here somewhere before you go to bed tonight."

"Now why would I do that?"

"Please don't smoke in the house, Julia. We agreed."

"And you agreed to leave me alone."

"Give me a break. That was nearly a year ago."

"I need time. I'm not like you." She stared straight at him.

He winced and hung his head. "Just because I go to work every day doesn't mean I'm not hurting too." He gave his shoulders a quick shake and Julia wondered if he was trying to grasp the reality of his statement; wondered if he realized how those words really sounded. Rising and changing the subject, he faced her. "I'll fix dinner."

"I'm not hungry."

"I am."

He moved toward the bedroom door. A twinge of sympathy skittered through her, then disappeared. The dysfunction was difficult for him, she knew. And she was a fucking pain in the ass. Not making it any easier. Well, so be it.

"It's different for me," she burst out.

He half-turned, his gaze skimming hers. "How so? Because you were the one who gave birth? I lost a child too, Julia, and I hurt just as much as you."

Logically, what he said was true, and the way it should be, in a normal world. But she didn't live in a normal world. She lived in Julia-World, where she made the rules.

I gave birth to a dead child, Mark. Just say how it was. "My baby came out dead."

"Our baby."

How dare you? "No." She stepped closer, the cigarette dangling from her fingertips. "No. It doesn't work that way, Mark. I hurt more. I need more time. You pushed your hurt away. Put it behind you. Abandoned me when I needed you. Well, I can't forget, Mark. I won't forget. And I'm still trying to deal with it. So fuck off and get over it. Your hurt is not the same as mine."

She kicked at the comforter, now slouched onto the floor. "I'm allowed to have my own fucking pain."

He stood there for the longest moment. She tried to picture what she looked like, from his perspective. She'd not bathed in a while. Her long, auburn hair, caught up in a messy ponytail, needed brushing days ago. Likely, there were bags under her eyes from last night's bourbon binge. Her flannel pajama bottoms and ratty twenty-year-old sorority T-shirt had seen better days.

"I'm not responding to that. Get cleaned up and sober, then we'll talk." He headed down the stairs.

Shit. Why fight it? Why prolong the inevitable? Maybe she should make it easier on the two of them.

"Mark!"

He turned, frowning. She took another drag from the cigarette and blew the stream of smoke his way. He'd aged ten years in the past six months. She'd done that to him.

"I want a divorce."

Five

May
 215 days sober

THE BABY IS CRYING.
 No.
 No.
 I killed my baby.
 My baby came out dead.
 Everyone here will hate me.
 You don't get to feel my pain.
 I left her in the hot car. Who does that?
 But she's crying. Can't you hear her? Go get her!
 I shouldn't have tried to have a baby. I'm too old.
 I'm a terrible person.
 My hurt is worse than yours.
 Go get the baby. The baby is crying!
 No.
 No.
 It was my fault.

My fault.
My fault.
The baby is crying.
THE BABY IS CRYING!

JULIA TWISTED BENEATH THE TANGLED COVERS AND HASTILY tossed them away from her body.

Her heart pounded, striking her ribcage, painfully so, rapidly sucking in air and exhaling. The back of her neck was sticky hot. Sweaty. Had she worked herself into a sweat during her dream?

Had the furnace kicked on in the night?

Maybe. Good Lord, she didn't need that thing to go out. She'd turned it down for the spring weather, to knock the chill out of the old house when the temperature got too low and the rains had set in—they still needed heat occasionally this time of year. But was it malfunctioning? Out-of-whack? Overheating? Were her guests too hot?

Angling toward the bedside lamp, she flipped the switch and sat up, her back against the headboard.

"Stop making excuses, Julia. The furnace is fine."

You're the one who is out-of-whack.

The time on the old digital clock on her dresser said two-seventeen in the morning. Closing her eyes, she tried to slow her breathing. She inhaled, held that breath for a moment, then let it out slowly through pursed lips. And again. Her heart rate slowed. Her head stopped spinning.

But the words in her head started rolling back in, behind her darkened eyes.

The baby is crying.
I killed my baby.
It's my fault.

Her stomach ached with a pent-up wail she so very much wanted to let loose—but she wouldn't. Couldn't. That would certainly turn her guests away, wouldn't it? A lone pensive guttural cry in the night?

She supposed she could lay blame on a ghost or otherworldly specter. There were many stories of paranormal activity in Old Louis-

42

ville—gargoyles that trip over the rooftops, sightings of ghosts and apparitions, the witch's tree, and other strange and interesting happenings.

It could happen, she supposed.

Like a baby crying from out of nowhere.

A viselike swell of panic gripped her heart.

Did I hear a baby cry?

She had heard a baby crying once. Hadn't she? In the attic?

Or thought she had.

That was months ago when she was on a bourbon binge. She'd thought it was coming from the attic room they'd not renovated, and had even ventured over there, hadn't she? She remembered telling someone about it at the beach—it was the only time she'd talked about it.

Was it Lia? Alice?

Can't remember. Had probably been drinking.

Her gaze traveled to the far wall, imagining what was on the other side of the layer of lathe and horsehair plaster. She'd rarely been in the attic room—once, right after they bought the place, with Mark. She recalled it full of cobwebs and hadn't stuck around for long. She knew Mark had poked around, time and again, when he still lived there. She saw it with the contractor, too, when they had looked around to see if the space was suitable for renovation. Odd but she hadn't remembered the webs that time. Had Mark cleaned up the space?

And then...she'd gone again...that night when she'd thought she heard the baby...saw a rocking cradle?

Or was all that a hazy, delusional by-product of copious amounts of Woodford?

THE ALARM SOUNDED AT FIVE—JUST AS IT DID EVERY morning.

Julia was up, dressed, and in the kitchen at five-thirty, brewing coffee. Rarely were guests up this early unless they were headed to the airport, but just in case, she always wanted caffeine at-the-ready. No one was due to leave today, however, so she expected breakfast to be relatively normal.

Routine was a good thing.

She pulled two casserole dishes from the refrigerator and set them on the counter to bring to room temperature. She'd pop them both in the oven in about an hour—one dish of baked oatmeal, and the other the inn's signature breakfast casserole made with eggs, smoky gouda, bacon, chives, and day-old croissants. She'd prepared them the previous evening.

Variations of the oatmeal dish was a daily given.

The protein menu items changed often depending on her mood and the number of guests. Some days she preferred quiche to a casserole, and if there were only a couple of guests, she'd make custom omelets with bacon or sausage.

Today was casserole day.

Moving into the dining room, she pulled out plates and flatware and set them on the buffet, along with a platter for the pastries, and a basket for bread. She fetched a stack of fresh linen napkins and set them at the end of the buffet with the flatware. Then, she arranged the iron trivets in the center, so they were ready for the casserole dishes when they came out of the oven. Finally, she checked the toaster shelf for crumbs.

All good.

Three rooms were booked for the night—Mr. Kelley, a middle-aged couple on a getaway from their kids, and another couple with a toddler —a total of six guests for breakfast, five adults and the child. That thought in mind, she moved back into the kitchen to fetch several individual boxes of kid cereal for the buffet too, in case the child didn't like oatmeal or the egg dish.

Over the next couple of hours, she'd readied the buffet with the hot dishes, coffee, juices and milk, pastries, and bread for toasting, and all the condiments one could ask for. Stepping back, she perused the dining room, and sighed.

Another morning off to a good start.

Routine. The repetitive process was good for her. In fact, she lived for this moment of accomplishment every single damn day.

Her phone buzzed in the side pocket of her yoga pants. Retrieving it, she glanced at the message.

Mark: *Got coffee?*

She typed: *Yes.*

Mark: *I'm at the front door.*

Turning, she exhaled forcefully. At least he had stopped using his key. Meeting him at the door, she let him in. "It's early."

"Got your message from last night. Everything okay?"

Her gaze met his and held for a split second. "Yes. Maybe. It's Maggie and—"

"Good morning!"

Turning, Julia smiled as Mr. Kelley leisurely made his way down the stairs. "I'll tell you one thing, as soon as you have that carriage house finished, I'll be booking there. I like the idea of a bedroom on the first floor."

Oh dear. She rushed forward and helped him down the last few steps as he maneuvered them with his cane. "I wish the first-floor suite had been available for you, Mr. Kelley. I'm sorry about that."

"Well, that's great for those people who need it, but that's not me." He winked.

Julia inwardly laughed. She sort of loved this older gentleman.

He settled on the landing and Mark stepped up too, grasping his elbow on the other side. Stopping briefly, Mr. Kelley caught her eye. "It's my own damn fault. I thought I could do the stairs and most days I can, but this morning Old Arthur is creaking into my bones something fierce."

Julia nodded. "Let's get you seated at the table. You just point and I'll get your food for you."

He patted her arm. "You're a sweetheart." He glanced at Mark. "She's a sweetheart. You know that young man?"

Mark grinned and caught her eye. "I do. Now, how about this seat here?"

"That works."

"Great."

Giving Mark a quick glance, she headed off to the buffet while Mr. Kelley called out what he wanted. She scooped and toasted while Mark poured the older man a cup of coffee and a small glass of juice. In short order, they had him set, while the remaining guests filtered in and began filling their plates.

Julia stepped back, as was her custom, to let them take care of themselves. The last thing anyone needed in the pre-caffeine hours of the morning was a hovering host.

"Enjoy, everyone," she told them, smiling. "If you need anything at all, I'm right through the door in the kitchen. Just give me a shout."

"We will."

"This is a beautiful spread. Thanks, Julia."

"Just point me to the coffee."

Again, she flashed a smile at her guests, then, grasping Mark's elbow, led him into the kitchen. Once inside, she dropped his arm and began cleaning up the kitchen island.

Mark stood there, watching.

She waited a minute. "You're staring at me."

"I'm so proud of you."

Her head jerked up. "What?"

"You are amazing."

She huffed, turned to grab a damp dish towel from the sink, and wiped down the counter. "Clearly, I am not amazing, Mark. I've been a major screw-up for a very long time." She avoided eye contact.

"Not true." He moved closer. "You've had a bit of life thrown at you, Julia. You screwed up, yes. I did too. But you got through it and so will I. The fact remains that from where I stand right now, looking at all you've accomplished over the past seven or eight months, you are exactly what I just said. Amazing."

She put up a hand. "Stop."

"Julia." He caught her hand and pulled her closer. "Last summer you couldn't get out of bed. Today, and every day since New Year's, you've gotten up, fixed an incredible breakfast, and sent your guests on their way. You greeted them, fed them, and smiled all the while. If that's not a remarkable accomplishment, I don't know what is."

"Smoke and mirrors. That's all it is."

"I don't believe that for a minute. Maybe early on, but now? You're in your element."

Mark had always been her cheerleader. Through college and law school. When her parents were impossible, especially her father when she'd decided to leave the firm. Throughout the tragedy with the baby, followed by her days of endless drinking, the depression....

"I'm still a work in progress."

Progress, not perfection. It was Bill's favorite AA mantra.

She contemplated Mark's words, unsure how to respond. Perhaps there was something to what he was saying? Had she morphed into a better version of herself because of this old place? That had been her plan—hadn't it?

Find something to get you out of bed every morning. Melinda had told her last fall, early on in her therapy.

Like what? Julia had joked. *Breakfast?*

Sounds like an excellent plan to me.

And so, breakfast became her daily mission.

It gave her a reason to get out of bed.

It gave her purpose.

One day at a time.

Her gaze dropped, fixed on a vein of marble in the kitchen island. She and Mark had been through so much together. Dragging her finger along the irregular pattern, a jag here, a sharp edge there, she couldn't help but compare it with their own unique path.

There were times she wondered if she was wrong to discard all that history.

Lifting her gaze, she looked directly into his eyes. *Okay, if you want to give me a compliment, I'll own it.* "Thanks, Mark."

"You're welcome." He squeezed her hand.

She shifted her body, pulling her hand out of his grasp. "I know you need to get to work so I'll get to it. I need to ask a favor. It's a big one."

"Name it."

"I have to go to North Carolina earlier than expected. It's Maggie. Can you run the inn starting tomorrow for a few days? Pam's parents are in town. She will be back at work on Monday. It would just be Friday and the weekend."

Mark's head bobbed up and down. "Yes. I can rearrange a few things. I can do it."

"You're sure."

"Absolutely."

"I'll make casseroles this afternoon."

"You know I can cook, Julia."

"I do, but I don't want to take advantage of you."

He rolled his eyes. "Good Lord, woman. Stop. I can handle it all. When are you leaving?"

"Tomorrow morning, very early. Too much to do today. I have a session with Melinda—but can we meet later to go over things?

"I can. Will you be back by four o'clock?"

"Sure. That works."

"Good. Tell Melinda hello."

She would, of course. Melinda was the only other person in the world who knew all their issues, good and bad.

TWO HOURS LATER, AFTER THE KITCHEN AND DINING ROOM were cleaned up, the sleeping rooms freshened and beds made, Julia pushed through the heavy wooden door to Melinda's office. She'd walked the few blocks over to the Second Street residence, the morning breeze crisp and biting against her cheeks.

Dr. Melinda Karnes was a one-woman show. Her practice was small, and she was the only employee. No partners and no receptionist. She'd told Julia once that by keeping her overhead low, she could also keep her clientele numbers small, with increased focus on the needs of her patients.

A native Louisvillian, Melinda had inherited the Italianate Victorian home from her parents. The tall and narrow three-story brick home sat on the edge of Old Louisville, on a street with mixed properties where businesses and residential structures cohabitated. The front two rooms of the circa 1870 home were Melinda's office—one room her main office and waiting area for patients, and the second room, the private area where she held her sessions. The rear of the first floor held a kitchen, bathroom, and storage area. Her father and grandfather—both local physicians in their day—had also used the first floor for their practices.

With her residence located on the second and third floors of the structure, Melinda had shared once that she liked keeping business and personal life separate.

Curious, Julia asked how she felt about having the front door open all day long when she was in a therapy session behind closed doors. Didn't she ever worry that someone would come inside and breach the private areas of her home?

Melinda smiled, patted her hand, and said calmly, "Barriers are a wonderful thing, my dear. I have lots of locks."

It was then Julia knew that she loved this woman. Barriers were exactly what she, herself, had needed at that moment. Barriers and controlled boundaries had been her salvation when she'd been convinced she couldn't get through the day without a drink. Setting boundaries had helped her feel in control. The routine, the repetitive drill, day after day, was the only thing that kept her sane. Today, she wondered if she needed to work on breaking through some of those barriers she'd erected months ago.

Could she? She wasn't sure.

Were they holding her back now?

Were they keeping her isolated from the real world, making it easier to handle her problems? Or more difficult?

Maybe something to talk to Melinda about.

The waiting room to her left was empty, she noticed, stepping into the foyer. Polished oak floors with the same oak woodwork greeted her. High ceilings drew her eyes up to the ornate chandelier overhead. She never ceased to look up and marvel at the thing, with its dripping glass baubles twinkling overhead in the morning light. The stained-glass window on the first turn of the staircase added a muted colorful twinkle effect to the area.

The sign on the door to her right showed that Melinda was still in session, so as was customary, Julia settled into the waiting area across the hall. The settee was situated away from the door, where one couldn't easily see who was leaving the session room. She perused the Victorian era furnishings and paintings, always spotting something new she hadn't noticed before, and then picked up a year-old architecture magazine. She knew she was early, so took a moment to breathe before the session.

Her eyes fluttered and she found herself drifting, trying to stay awake, while thumbing through the magazine pages. She'd had little sleep after she'd woken in the middle of the night, and what sleep she did get, was restless. Now, after the flurry of breakfast and her brisk walk, her body was beginning a slow unraveling. Unsure how to describe her mood other than tired and sad, she didn't try to name it— but simply closed her eyes and tried to feel the mix of emotions swimming inside her head and gut.

When the door opened across the entry hall, she startled, jerking her eyes open and sitting up a little straighter. Had she slept for a few minutes? Voices echoed against the tall ceiling then faded as they headed toward the front door. Melinda's heels clicked against the wooden planks, then halted when she popped her head into the waiting room.

"Julia? Hi." Her smile broke through Julia's melancholy.

She rose and greeted Melinda, then followed her across the hall into the session room. After the two of them had settled in their usual seats —Melinda in a wingback chair situated in front of her desk, and Julia on the overstuffed sofa opposite her—they started the session.

"So how are things?" Melinda always began with the same question. Julia sometimes wondered why she used the word 'things' and decided that perhaps it was intentional—things could refer to a multitude of items to discuss—real, imaginary, emotional, physical, tangible, random, unrelated, new, stupid, life-altering....

"Things are fine." Julia smiled.

"And Mark?"

She nodded. "He seems to be fine and says hello. We have a session soon, right?"

"I believe we do. You've seen him?"

"Yes. We spoke this morning."

Melinda shifted, crossing her legs. "Do you want to share how that came about?"

She didn't. Not really. Could she just cut to the meat of it, and leave out all the minutiae? Her brain scrambled for the best response, but in the end, opted for the truth. Hell, it was why she was here. Wasn't it? "I'm leaning on Mark again."

"Tell me about that?"

"I hate it, actually."

Melinda nodded and studied her face. "Given your history and what I know about you, I think that's understandable. Tell me more?"

"It's the inn. I need to go out of town and Pam, my assistant, is not available."

"So you reached out to Mark?"

"I did. At Pam's suggestion." That sounded like an excuse and Julia wondered if she should have said that.

"How did that make you feel? Asking Mark for help."

Honestly, she wasn't sure. "Weird, in a way. Relief that he agreed. Guilt that I had to ask in the first place, and that he had to change his plans. Fear that he would read into it something he shouldn't."

"Like?"

"Like, that I *want* to depend on him."

"Do you?"

Julia rose, ambling toward the window. She often did this during their sessions—difficult for her to sit still for too long, especially if she were antsy or agitated. Melinda once said that perhaps her walking away, pacing the room, was a way of coping physically with the stress or anxiety. Julia wondered if it was avoidance, sometimes—but mostly, she did it to force a pause, so she could mull over her response.

She stared out into the street, her arms crossed over her chest. Suddenly, for the first time in a long time, she wanted a cigarette. "I don't know."

"Is that a problem? Depending on him?"

"In my head it is."

"Why?"

"Because we aren't a couple any longer."

"But you are business partners."

That was true. Yes. "Because I don't want to lean on him, depend on him."

"Does he mind?"

Julia shook her head. "No, I don't think so. I think he enjoys it, actually."

"Then he's okay with it."

"Apparently."

"And that worries you?"

Did it? It did, in some ways. Didn't it? "I think so."

Melinda leaned closer. "Tell me more, if you like."

Julia didn't know if she liked. She paused, thinking.

"Julia?"

"I wonder if I need to put up some sort of barrier between Mark and me. So I won't think I can lean on him. Is that wise?" She watched the traffic heading toward downtown, and wondered if it was a little busy for this time of day.

"We've had this discussion, Julia. Do you recall?"

Of course, they had. You put barriers up, and then you work to take them down. When they are down, you wish you had them back up. How to find that happy balance? Suddenly, she realized she wasn't ready to fuck with any barriers she'd constructed or walls she'd built. It wasn't time yet.

"I'd like to talk about something else."

"Oh? All right."

"I heard a baby crying." She turned and headed back to the sofa, deflating into the soft cushions. After a minute, she met Melinda's gaze.

"Go on."

"I woke from a dream last night. I was in that never-never-land space between sleep and awakening. I heard a baby crying."

She held Melinda's gaze, who said nothing, and simply waited. That was Julia's cue to keep talking.

Fuck.

"I've heard it before—when I wasn't sober. I can't remember if I shared that."

Melinda gave her a noncommittal nod. *Jesus.*

"And I dreamed I was in my bedroom, ripping down the wallpaper."

"Ah. That's understandable, given the months of construction on your home."

"This was different."

"How?"

"The wallpaper is old. Remember I told you once, I think, that I used to count the roses on the paper when I was drunk or hungover? When I was bored out of my gourd laying in that bed but lacked the initiative to get up and do anything about it?"

Melinda nodded slowly. "Yes. I remember. So in your dream, you were tearing down the wallpaper with the roses?"

"Yes."

"Interesting."

Julia studied her. When Melinda used the word 'interesting' that meant she was thinking, pondering her words. She'd been in therapy with her long enough to realize that.

"What?"

Uncrossing her legs, Melinda shifted in her chair and leaned forward. "Do you think there may be any connection with you starting our conversation about removing barriers, and your dream about tearing down the wallpaper that has annoyed you for months."

Blinking, and staring at Melinda, she considered that. Was there a connection?

"I don't know. Maybe."

"Let's park that idea for a moment." She jotted a few words down on her notepad. "We can explore that as we move forward. So, the baby was crying in your dream?"

"No. The baby came later, after I woke up."

"I don't understand."

"The baby was crying in the house and woke me up. I was dreaming about the wallpaper, but the baby woke me up."

"Hmm. Interesting."

Julia swallowed, feeling like she'd been talking forever. Her jaw ached.

"Is there more you want to say about that?"

"No."

"Did you go to the crying?"

She shook her head. "No, I stayed in bed. I...."

Melinda waited.

"I was afraid if I got up, I would want a drink."

"But there is no alcohol in the house."

"Right."

"I feared if I got up, I'd walk out the door and down to the corner drug store, where there is liquor."

Melinda exhaled. "Are you still going to AA?"

"Yes. Religiously."

"Good."

Melinda studied her and Julia stared out the window. "I really want a cigarette. You know, I quit that too when I quit alcohol. I used to wonder if my smoking early on during my pregnancy had contributed to the baby dying. Then when I started drinking, I figured fuck it, I wasn't going to have another baby so why not smoke? But I realized it was another addiction I needed to get rid of." She turned to Melinda. "But I really want a cigarette right now."

She rose again, walking toward the window. She needed to see the daylight, the sun bouncing off the concrete, people alive and milling about on the streets. Normal people? Or were they half-crazy like her?

"I'm not going to tell you to smoke, or not to smoke, Julia," Melinda said. "I'll leave that to you and your AA sponsor. Bill, isn't that his name? But I will say this, from my own perspective and somewhat from the clinical perspective—one addiction does not necessarily beget another. Yes, people often smoke more when drinking. But that doesn't mean that people drink more when smoking. The official verdict is out, of course, but I will tell you that I would much rather see you smoke a cigarette than down a fifth of whiskey."

Maybe she'd ponder that on her walk home. "Thanks, Melinda." Maybe she'd smoke on the way home too.

"You're welcome."

She glanced at the clock over the fireplace mantle. "The time is almost up."

"Yes." Melinda set her notepad aside and stood. "Julia, a couple of things. All right? The next time you hear the baby crying, I want you to follow the sound. Go to it. Just to satisfy your curiosity and perhaps eliminate an unknown."

"I know where it's coming from."

"You do?"

"Yes. The attic room."

"Are you comfortable going there?"

"Maybe. In the day. Not at night."

"I see. There could be an explanation. Maybe visit the attic now, soon, before you hear the baby again. That way the place will be somewhat familiar and less daunting."

"Perhaps." Her phone pinged in her pants pocket. Evidently, she'd forgotten to turn off notifications. She ignored it.

"How are you feeling right now?"

"Better. In the night, I wanted to scream. I still feel like there is a scream pushing at my throat, and that if I can let it out, I'll feel better. But I couldn't scream in the house, I had guests. I thought about going to the park, but that would be weird, and I'd wake up the entire neighborhood."

Melinda reached for her hands. "Are you driving home?"

"No. I walked."

"Okay, then take a drive sometime today. Go to the cemetery. Sit in your car. Scream your head off. No one will hear you."

"Seriously?"

"Oh yes. I'm dead serious."

Julia laughed out loud. Melinda did too.

"To recap." She tucked Julia's hand in the crook of her arm and led her toward the door. "We can explore more, of course, but I feel like the crying baby may have something to do with your grief process. Go to the crying sound if you can. See what you find. Smoke a cigarette if you want and don't feel guilty about it. A cigarette is not going to make you reach for an Old Fashioned. Scream like hell on the way home. And perhaps, if you feel it will help, call Bill and have a chat with him. Can you do that?"

She gave Melinda a half-hearted smile. "I can."

"Good. Then I'll see both you and Mark next week."

Next week. Shit. "Oh, we may have to move that out a week. I may be out of town. I'll have Mark call."

"Leaning on him again?"

Julia grinned. "No. Delegating."

Melinda chuckled. "Good. See you soon."

Six

"I understand you're helping Maggie with her divorce. Is that wise, darling?"

"I made a promise, Mother. I don't back down on promises."

"Yes, you always were like that."

And you're not.

Julia wished she had heeded Melinda's earlier advice and visited the cemetery. She also wished she'd ignored the text message that had come during her session. Because right now? She could use a damn good bloodcurdling scream.

Lunch with Denise Salinger rarely came without complications.

But Julia had promised her father, and she readily admitted she was still having difficulty not striving to please her father, even after all these years—so here she sat, across from her mother in a swanky downtown restaurant, attempting conversation and lunch.

Jeff Ruby's was *the* place these days for lunch, her mother had relayed—*if one wanted to be seen.* Which Julia didn't.

The entire escapade was an event she had very little time for today, of all days.

Denise fiddled with the stem of her vodka martini glass and sighed. Her mother would never get that alcohol was poison for Julia. Once she'd told her, "...that's your problem, not mine. I'm still enjoying my Grey Goose."

So be it.

Studying her sixty-years-old-plus mother—perfect makeup, shoulder-length blond waves softly framing her face, botoxed lines and lips, tinted and waxed eyebrows—Julia wondered, at times, if the two of them were indeed made of the same stock. She was so entirely different from her mother it was difficult to understand that she came from the woman's womb.

Julia was a no-nonsense, straight-shooting, tailored businessperson who went to college and earned degrees. Or, more accurately, she had been that woman, before the B&B and the baby. Back then, she was a plucky, hard-ass, no-holds-barred attorney who showed no mercy when she fought for her clients.

Her mother, on the other hand, was more debutante and Derby Princess, and preferred being taken care of, rather than taking care of others.

Denise went to college to find a husband—which she did. Nick Salinger. Her mother was her polar opposite, a woman who sugarcoated and whitewashed just about everything—and did it in three-inch heels while dripping zirconia. She wouldn't go so far as to say that her mother was fake, but she did marry up. And once some women got a taste of a finer life—the country club, the horse races, the charity social events, and the like—they learned to play the part perpetually.

Nick tolerated it. Julia wanted none of it.

"But it seems so wishy-washy. Are you sure Maggie truly wants a divorce? I mean, goodness, one can withstand a whole lot of things, if one has too. Besides, Max Oliver has provided well for her and the children, and how dare she leave him and rip those children from that kind of lifestyle. She needs to think of their future."

"I believe that is what she is doing, Mother. And let me remind you that we are living in the twenty-first century, so just because she and Max divorce doesn't mean he will not take care of the children. That's my job—to see that he does and does it well."

"And you're so good at doing that, aren't you? Sticking it to all the men who wrong their wives?" Denise gave her a good stare. "Like Ralph Bledsoe?"

"Ralph is a pervert, and he broke the law."

"He's not a bad man though, family wealth of course, and Jillian might be wise to remember that."

Good Lord spare me, please.

Julia closed her eyes and pictured an Old Fashioned on the table in front of her. She wished Melinda had not mentioned the drink during their session, because right now, lunch with her mother, was going to drive her to drink again.

"Max hit her, Mom. And he has a history of doing so. Maggie was worried he was coming after the kids too, if she didn't go back to him. Now, she's trying to get out."

"Well, she needs to get control of that situation."

Julia rolled her eyes and glanced off, perusing the restaurant crowd. "And how do you propose she does that?"

Her mother leaned closer and whispered. "Blow jobs, darling. They are power."

"Good God, mother. This isn't the 1960s. There are more powerful things out there than blow jobs."

"You're sure about that?" She leaned back and arched a brow. "When was the last time you administered one to Mark?"

"Oh, holy fuck."

"That's what I thought."

"Mark and I are divorced."

"Separated. Correct?"

"Fine. The divorce isn't final yet. And believe it or not, Mother, I've administered plenty of blow jobs for his pleasure over the years. We didn't separate because things were lacking in that department." *How superficial can one get?*

"And did he reciprocate?"

Julia folded her napkin, laid it beside her plate, and stood. "Good gracious, look at the time. Speaking of Mark, I'm meeting him shortly and need to get back to the inn. Thanks so much for lunch."

Bending, she aimed a whisper of a kiss toward her mother's cheek.

"Tell Maggie hello for me?" Denise lifted her martini glass to her lips.

"Of course."

Time to get the fuck gone. Her lungs ached for that scream.

SHE HAD TIME TO SPARE BEFORE MEETING WITH MARK.

It was barely two o'clock in the afternoon, and for whatever reason, the idea of heading for Maggie's this afternoon struck her. As she exited the parking garage upon leaving the restaurant, her brain spun with the possibilities.

Maybe she needed an escape, of sorts, from her regularly scheduled life.

Should she just go ahead and go, to see what was up with Maggie? Make sure she was okay?

If she left within the hour, she could put a lot of driving time behind her tonight, grab a few hours' sleep, and be at Maggie's by nine in the morning. Her need to get some resolution with Maggie—to understand exactly what Maggie wanted, where she was with all this divorce shit—was strong, and she didn't want to ignore that.

Mentally, she ticked off a few things in her head that would have to happen soon, to make that happen.

Call Mark.

Casseroles.

Pack a bag.

Call Bill?

She pulled out of the parking garage and turned left, stopping at the traffic light. Quickly, she called Mark.

"Hi Julia. What's up?"

"Hey. I've had a brainstorm. Can you stay at the inn tonight? I may need to leave this afternoon."

"When?"

"In an hour or so, if I can."

"Everything okay?"

That was the question, wasn't it? "I'm not sure. Maggie is evasive and Max was an ass on the phone. My intuition is telling me to get down there."

"If there is one thing I never mess with," Mark chuckled as he spoke, "it's your intuition. Come on home. I'm already making casseroles."

The light changed to green and Julia moved forward. "What? You're at the inn?"

"I had vacation time coming and took the rest of the week off. It's not a problem, Julia. I'm already here."

"You're sure?"

"Positive."

"All right. See you in a few."

Damn. The man needed to stop making himself so accessible.

Well, that was two items checked off her mental checklist.

Easing through the downtown streets, she maneuvered her way down 4th Street and toward 2nd, then headed home. Her cell phone parked on her dash, she scrolled for Bill's number. He answered quickly.

"Julia?"

"Hi Bill."

"Everything okay?"

That seemed to be the question of the day.

"Yes. Just want to pick your brain."

"Shoot."

Bill didn't beat around the bush, and she sort of loved that he didn't. It was a good characteristic for him to have, being her sponsor. She didn't like being fed bullshit.

"Can I smoke? I really want a cigarette."

At that, Bill let out a guffaw. "Seriously?"

"Yes, goddamn it, I'm serious. Am I going to fuck up my sobriety if I smoke a damn cigarette?"

Bill fell quiet for a moment. "Does the thought of smoking make you uneasy? Like, if you reach for the cigarette, you'll want a shot of bourbon to go with it?"

That was it. Wasn't it?

"I think so. I think that's my hesitation."

"Then I'm sorry I laughed. You just caught me off guard. I shouldn't have done that."

She was a little annoyed but tried not to show it. "I know it's just a cigarette, but I don't want it to trigger me. And I don't want to trade one addiction for another."

"It's not like it's pot, Julia."

Abruptly, she thought about beach week, and how every year they could count on Willow scoring some weed somewhere. "Would pot be a problem?"

"It could be. Alcoholics Anonymous doesn't recommend it, even though it's legal in a lot of places now. But of course, alcohol is legal too. That fact doesn't prevent addiction."

"True. I realize that. So, no weed. Got it."

"Probably not a good idea. When was the last time you smoked regular tobacco?"

"Right before I walked through the doors of Healing Hope. I tossed my last one before I entered the facility."

"I see." Bill inhaled loudly, then let the breath out slowly. "While generally I don't like to lump smoking and alcohol addiction or cessation in the same ballpark—many of us still smoke while remaining sober —I'd caution you to consider, given your history. If you are associating one crutch with the other, then don't throw out the baby with the bathwater."

"Not throwing out any babies, Bill."

"Damn it, that was a bad analogy, metaphor, whatever. I'm sorry."

"It's okay. Look, I'm almost home. Thanks for picking up and no cigarettes for me. No use picking that back up again."

"Good plan."

"I'm heading out of town, Bill. I'll be back in a few days."

"Be safe." He clicked off.

Julia pulled into the alley and parked next to the carriage house and Mark's Honda sedan. Looking up at the back of the main house, she blew out a breath, easing a bit of tension from her chest.

She could do this. Talk to Mark. Pack a bag.

Get on her way.

There was just one other thing she had to take care of first, before she imploded from the inside out.

CAVE HILL CEMETERY WAS TRULY ONE OF THE MOST beautiful sites in the city of Louisville—if not the entire state of Kentucky.

Located just off downtown, the garden cemetery hosted statuesque and stately monumental art, ornamentally landscaped settings, mausoleums, lakes, a cave and stream, and an arboretum. An afternoon spent in the cemetery could be a delight for the eyes as well as healing for the soul.

The historic burial grounds had always fascinated Julia.

Originally farmland bought by the city in the early 1800s, the acreage was leased for decades to local farmers, then eventually became the site of the Pest House, a home for people suffering from infectious diseases. Death became a frequent visitor, and subsequently, graveyards were built.

During Louisville's Victorian era the residents became increasingly wealthy, and the graveyards took on a new life. Louisvillians spared no expense to send their loved ones off to the afterlife with marble sculptures, exotic trees and flowers, and ornate memorials. Over time, the garden-style cemetery became known as a place to visit—not only for locals with family members resting there, but a tourist stop for travelers. A number of celebrities, such as Colonel Harlan Sanders and Muhammad Ali, were laid to rest there.

Julia had always found the acres of graves and trees and flowers and buildings so peaceful and joyful—more so than any other cemetery she'd ever visited.

This was why they chose to lay their baby to rest between two dogwoods and a weeping willow tree, a short walk from the creek.

As she drove through the cemetery, heading toward the place she'd not been to in some time, her chest began a slow tightening. Her breathing grew shallower because of the tension settled there, and she knew she would need to get a grip before leaving the car, so she wouldn't hyperventilate and grow dizzy—and hopefully not pass out at the grave.

That would be inconvenient.

She wound through the property, taking her time, trying to inhale deep when she remembered to, and let her breath out slowly. Instead of focusing on the task ahead of her, she allowed her gaze to drift right and left, absorbing the flora and fauna of the cemetery. Besides the beautiful May flowers and trees wearing fresh green leaves, several chipmunks and squirrels skittered across the asphalt road before her, birds fluttered up when she passed, and a pair of swans floated on a lake.

A hawk circled lazily above, silhouetted in a robin egg blue sky, probably searching for prey, or perhaps, simply enjoying a warm updraft.

As much as she had avoided coming here, the place offered a sense of peace. Even gutted with pain and turmoil, she knew her child rested there forever beneath the dirt.

No pain. No stress. No tears.

Blinking back her own tears, she took the last turn and parked her car. She sat for a moment, closing her eyes against the madness rooted in her heart. There were times she had indeed felt mad—crazy with pain and longing and fear—although those days had mostly gone the way of the bourbon and cigarettes. Still, insanity lurked around the corner. She'd seen it, felt it. Pushed it away. Times like these—when facing something she didn't want to face—the repulsiveness liked to rear its ugly head.

Tempting her.

Not today, Satan.

Without another thought, she lifted the door latch, exited the car, and strode toward the gravesite.

They'd placed a bench there, facing the small headstone, about a year after the service. She knew Mark came here often although she'd never come with him. She'd not been here since the memorial.

As she approached, she imagined Mark sitting there, looking down at the block of granite with etchings laced across its façade. She imagined him staring into the sweet face of the cherub statue he'd bought along with the headstone and had placed there, too.

Standing behind the bench, Julia glanced left and right, where there were plots ready for both her and Mark—the baby in between them.

Apropos. The baby was what came between them—inadvertently, of course—and now they'd never rest there, the two of them, she was certain, beside their child.

How horrible.

The ache that had pressed against her throat for hours now, the scream daring to erupt from her chest, escalated its existence. The pressure was almost nauseating, and she needed to find some sort of relief soon.

Dizziness sneaked up on her, the lightheadedness causing her to stumble. Rounding the concrete bench, she sat, her eyes closed. Leaning over a little and hanging her head, she tried to catch her breath and slow her heart rate. When she lifted her head and opened her eyes a few seconds later, her gaze landed upon the headstone.

Infant Salinger-Shepherd
June 12, 2020
Child of Julia E. Salinger and Mark L. Shepherd

At that instant, a thousand images ripped through her brain. Haunting and heart wrenching memories she'd not allowed herself see or imagine or feel in quite some time.

The bleeding. The ambulance. The flashing lights that made her disoriented and frantic.

The excruciating pain that stole away her every sense of awareness.

The doctors mumbling, avoiding her questions.

Mark was frantic, crying in her ear next to her. Whispering. "I don't want to lose you. I don't want to lose our baby. God, save them."

Am I going to die?

Are we going to die?

The baby.

Coming out. The baby is coming out.

The baby.

Not crying.

The baby.

Her baby. Their baby.

Not breathing.

Dead.

I'm so sorry, your baby did not make it.

Mark hit the floor. She remembered the sound of him falling into a lifeless heap against the tile. She'd screamed and clutched for him but couldn't reach him. A nurse tried to calm her, contain her battling arms and fists. An orderly attempted to rouse Mark, get him to his feet. The scene was panic and chaos and well....

Pure hell.

Without warning, the scream begging to exit her body curled up from a place deeper than her chest, from someplace low and guttural and primal and painful. It burst upon her without warning, and she thrust back her head and howled. She dropped from the bench to her knees, her body propped up on all fours, her back arched like a frightened cat, and her head hanging like that of a wounded animal.

Involuntarily, she inhaled deeply, a second scream on the verge of ripping from her throat. She had no control over it, as if she had dry heaves and couldn't stop vomiting. The scream hurdled into the peaceful existence of the sanctuary and the hallowed grounds. An ugly, snotty sob created by a gasping of breath and an overwhelming sensation that she couldn't breathe split the afternoon calm and pierced her soul. The cry coiled up and away from her body, into the trees and beyond, and giving wing to her suffering, the agony of her loss.

Her body spent, she fell onto the cool grass and rolled onto her back. Tears streamed down her temples as she inhaled—exhaled and attempted to gain some semblance of composure, to slow her heart rate, to calm her erratic breaths.

Gradually, the pain in her chest dissipated. Her rib cage expanded and deflated, repeatedly. Faster at first, then slower.

Exhausted, she watched the sky. Stared into the heavens. Inspected a few wispy clouds drifting away.

The hawk circled. Soaring in the updraft. He screeched, as if calling out to her, and she wondered if he was.

I caught your scream. Let me take it away. I'm here if you need me.

Seven

Rocky Mount, North Carolina
  216 days sober

JULIA PARKED DOWN THE STREET, ABOUT THREE HOUSES away from Maggie's home. Waiting. Her ignition off, she rolled down her window to catch a breeze and perhaps a bit of conversation, if she were lucky. The temperature in Rocky Mount was several degrees warmer than at home.

She'd left Louisville around three-thirty yesterday afternoon, after a candid and pleasant conversation with Mark. In fact, they were getting along so well lately, that sometimes she wondered what she was doing divorcing him. Fortunately, she'd had miles of empty highway ahead of her to work through those emotions, and determined that she was, indeed, doing the right thing by setting him free.

She drove straight through for about six hours—with only brief stops for bathroom breaks and fast food—and had checked into a hotel outside of Asheville, North Carolina by ten o'clock.

She left the hotel at five that morning, before the breakfast coffee in the hotel lobby had finished percolating, and headed toward Rocky

Mount and Maggie's country club estate community. She'd been there several times previously, before Maggie confessed that Max was both emotionally and physically abusive to her. They all knew Max was an ass —boastful, bossy, abrupt, and often critical of Maggie—but until they saw her black eye and the bruises, no one had suspected he was hitting her.

The thought made her stomach grip with anger.

She had to get Maggie out of the situation.

Watching the house, she wondered if they had already left for the day.

Her goal had been to be there early enough to catch Maggie before she ran out for errands, or something, perhaps taking the kids to school —but late enough to miss Max. Of course, Julia really wanted to see her, to make sure she was okay and functioning in her life. Julia's brain often took her to places she really didn't want to go—like that Max was holding her prisoner, controlling all her wants and needs, like the evil husbands in some of those terrible B movies.

She really wanted to get Maggie alone.

At a quarter before nine, Max stepped out onto the sweeping front porch of the two story, half-million-dollar home with the children following. Maggie, looking fresh and all made up, dressed in a floral summer dress, a sweater draped over her shoulders, with matching sandals and purse, scurried along behind the children. Max stopped by the driver's side door of his black Escalade. The kids scrambled to get in the SUV—Carol, the teenager, claimed the passenger seat up front, the younger two children in the back—while Maggie hung back waiting for them to get settled.

She handed a backpack to the youngest child, a girl named Chloe, and a lunch box to Jason their middle child, a boy.

Max turned to Maggie and grasped her playfully around the waist. He tugged her up close to him. Maggie turned her face up and smiled. Julia could almost hear Max's predatory growl and fought off a bit of nausea because of it. Given Maggie's sexual proclivity, Julia figured she was probably already wet just looking at him. She and Max had always shared an explosive sex life, and Maggie had made no bones about telling them all about it.

Sometimes, Julia had wondered if the sex was what kept Maggie with him for so long.

And now, well, she still had to wonder....

Max took Maggie's lips in a lengthy and rather inappropriate kiss—particularly in front of the children—then slapped her on her ass and sent her on her way.

Son of a bitch.

Maggie giggled loudly and headed to the Toyota Camry parked beside Max's SUV. "See you tonight, honey!"

"What the ever-loving fuck." Julia started her engine and idled while sitting there, watching Max back out of the driveway and head down the street, away from her.

She remained in the car watching Maggie, who took a moment to scroll through her phone. Apparently, she had a phone that worked. What the hell?

When she laid the phone aside and started the car, Julia scooted down in the seat as Maggie backed out and angled the car her way. Ducking lower as she passed, as if she were retrieving something from the floor, Julia waited a few seconds then lifted her head and glanced behind her.

Maggie's car turned right at the end of the street.

Wasting no time, Julia cut a quick U-turn on the narrow street and followed her out of the subdivision, staying far enough behind hoping Maggie wouldn't spot her.

When she became a lawyer, Julia hadn't expected to be covertly spying on people, tailing them, or stalking them—but there had been times, she'd have to admit, that she'd resorted to such things.

Today was one of those days.

"Where the hell are you going, Maggie Oliver, and what the fuck are you doing?"

She followed her into the downtown area of Rocky Mount, then wound through a business area by some side streets. She slowed when Maggie turned on her blinker and pulled into the parking lot of a rather shabby looking restaurant and motel combo in what appeared to be a questionable part of town—*but what do I know about Rocky Mount?*—and parked her car beside a very large pickup truck with Alabama plates.

Julia eased into the lot too, backing into a parking space near the road. Facing the hotel and the vehicles, she slid down into her seat a little and waited, watching over the steering wheel.

Within seconds, the driver's side door of the pickup swung open and a tall, stocky man wearing jeans, boots, and a cowboy hat rounded the bed of the truck.

Simultaneously, Maggie pushed her car door open and rushed toward him.

The cowboy caught her up into his arms, her flippy dress swaying around her hips, and planted a sultry, sexy, and oh-so-wicked kiss on Maggie Oliver's lips.

That kiss appeared even more passionate than the one Max planted on her just thirty minutes earlier.

The hussy. "What the fucking shit, Maggie?" Julia uttered.

The couple broke the embrace, and Julia caught sight of Maggie's smiling face. Radiant. She had to admit, she wasn't sure she'd seen Maggie look that happy in quite some time. Fifteen years or more, perhaps.

Maggie hooked her arm into the crook of his, and they headed toward the motel. The tall cowboy paused at a nearby motel room door, pulled a key out of his pocket, unlocked the door, and with his hand in the small of her back, escorted her inside.

SHE WAITED, KNOWING THAT MAGGIE HAD KIDS TO GET home to eventually, and a husband to account to long before that happened—if Max was anything like he used to be. Julia recalled days at the beach when Maggie had to field calls and texts all day long from him wanting to know what she was doing, who she was with, where she was going, and all that shit.

Maggie Oliver always had a penchant for sexy, down-to-earth guys—which was why every single one of her friends had rolled her eyes and uttered, "That won't last long," when she and Max got together all those years ago.

But it did.

Maggie was the one who, early in their college days, they'd had to pull out of pickup trucks of the local farm boys who came to town looking to bang a college girl. She'd always been pleased to oblige. Julia swore back then that the girl oozed more testosterone than most men—and Maggie wore it like a badge of honor.

Her sex drive was insatiable.

She was fine being known as the Slut of Simmons Hall during their first year at Eastern Carolinas University.

She and Max met a few years after graduation, when he was traveling for business and Maggie was a flight attendant on one of his trips.

Max was all about suits and appearance, a model of wealth and accomplishment. While Maggie was okay with all that, money did have its advantages—and also its trappings—but what she really liked about Max was what he willingly offered, his studly package built to please.

And what she had sampled the night their flights were delayed, and they'd ended up at the same hotel, pleased her immensely.

Suddenly, the fumbling farm boys were forgotten.

The two met and fucked around their flying schedules for months.

Then Maggie got pregnant—and reluctantly for them both, they got married.

Maggie figured he had money.

Max figured she was as good a fuck as any. Better than most.

They married with one stipulation—Max wanted an open marriage. Initially, Maggie agreed. As time went on, however, she came to regret that decision. By then, they were so deep into the marriage charade it was difficult to dig out—three kids, mortgage, social standing, no career for Maggie....

Julia knew all this, and the facts ran helter-skelter through her mind as she stared at the motel room door. Room 116. She glanced at the sign over the office. Room 116 at the Starlight Hideaway Motel.

Sounded like a sleezy pulp fiction mystery novel.

She glanced at her cell phone. An hour has passed. How fucking long did it take?

She contemplated calling Alice to pass the time, then thought better of it. She didn't want to be into a long conversation, explaining every detail of what she knew so far, when she didn't have nearly enough details to share. She knew Alice only too well. The woman would get in the car and drive the two hours to get here—speeding, more than likely —and maybe arrive before Maggie and Cowboy Dude had finished up roping and wrangling.

Julia didn't need Alice underfoot right now.

So, she'd wait. And she did.

Just before noon, the couple emerged from their motel cocoon and after a steaming-long kiss, parted ways. The cowboy left first. Maggie fiddled with her keys in her purse while watching him drive out of the parking lot. By the time she had unlocked her Toyota and looked up, Julia had exited her vehicle and was standing in front of it, leaning against the hood, arms crossed.

Maggie's gaze locked with Julia's.

Lowering her hand with the keys, she strolled toward her, not breaking eye contact.

"Julia. What are you doing here?"

"I came to rescue you. Seems you've already been rescued. Yee haw, ride 'em cowboy?"

Maggie glanced back to the empty spot where the pickup truck had sat. "What are you talking about?"

Pushing away from her car, Julia took a step. "What in fuck's name are you doing, Maggie?"

Her friend inhaled, then pushed out the breath. She fiddled with the keys in her hand. "Want to get lunch? I have about an hour."

"Great. Get in my car."

She shook her head. "No. I'll drive. I don't want to leave my car here."

Julia stared, understanding. "In case Max sees it."

"Something like that."

"Fine. Let me get my bag and lock the car." Julia slowly turned, keeping an eye on her friend. She retrieved her purse and keys, locked up, then followed Maggie.

They got in, buckled up, and backed out of the parking spot.

"Mexican?"

"Sure."

"Good. I need a margarita."

Julia stared at her.

Maggie rolled her eyes. "They have soda, too. And coffee."

"Just drive, Maggie."

She accelerated and then braked quickly when a text popped up on her cell phone. Maggie glanced at the dashboard where her phone was parked. "On second thought, how about you follow me to the restaurant? That was Max. I may need to leave earlier than I thought."

"Sure." Julia unbuckled her seatbelt. "All hail King Max. Give me two seconds and lead on. Heaven forbid we leave Max hanging."

THIRTY MINUTES LATER, JULIA STARED DOWN AT HER HALF-eaten chimichanga and glass of water, listening to Maggie's babble—her margarita almost gone, her chatter escalating. She'd let her carry on for a while longer, because she was finding out so much more intel than she would have had she asked interrogating questions.

Besides, her friend was always less prickly when she controlled the situation.

Just let her think that.

"So," Maggie continued, "after we met online in that dating app, we chatted for a couple of months and it was really kind of fun, you know. Something sort of secret and sexy at the same time. And then suddenly, he tells me he's taken a new contract job and is moving to North Carolina."

"From Alabama?" Julia lifted her gaze.

"Yes. How did you know that?"

"License plates."

Maggie nodded. "Oh. Gotcha. Yes, from Alabama."

"And how is that working out for you?"

"He's only been here a month. He lives in the next town over, but we try to get together once or twice a week when he can sneak away during the day. He is the boss over a construction crew so he can get away from work easily, most days."

Julia gave a wobbly nod. "Of course. Interesting."

"And the sex? Oh, come to Mama. Mind blowing."

Julia cocked her head a little, pretending to be interested. *How long has it been since you've had sex, Julia?* "Wow."

"Oh, yes, and...." Her phone pinged. "Crap. Just a minute."

She watched as Maggie read the text, typed in a few words, sent the message, then looked back up, smiling.

"Cowboy dude?"

"No." Maggie shook her head. "Max."

"I see." She really didn't, but she wasn't ready to go there yet. "So, about the phone. I see you have one."

Maggie glanced at it, lying beside her plate. "Sure. I always have a phone."

"So, is that your regular phone, or your burner phone, or the one you don't answer or respond to when your friends call or text?"

Maggie blinked and stared, holding eye contact. "What?"

"We haven't been able to get in touch with you, Maggie. You don't respond or answer. Our text messages say *undeliverable,* and your phone indicates it's out of service. We've been worried."

"We?"

Closing her eyes briefly, Julia huffed out. "Yes. We. Alice and me. Lia's too busy I guess to notice, and the twins, well, you know all about that."

Maggie swallowed and ran a tongue over her lower lip, like it was suddenly parched.

"I called the house the other night. Carol answered and handed me off to Max."

Her eyes went rounder. "Oh? No one told me you called."

"Max said you were unavailable."

"When was that?"

"Night before last."

She glanced off, staring into the restaurant, a blank look crossing her face. "Oh yeah. That."

"That?"

Maggie met her gaze again. "I had a headache, migraine, went to bed early with meds."

Julia narrowed her gaze. She was lying, dammit. "I've never known you to get migraines."

"Well, I've started."

"Stress?"

"Maybe."

"Maggie, what the fuck? How are you really? I mean seriously, the makeup, the clothes, and happier-than-ever smile on your face, kissing Max on the street like he is your long-lost love of your life, and now this affair with the Alabama cowboy—what the fuck gives? You're not seriously happy with this situation. Are you?"

"What do you mean?"

Julia leaned closer. "Good God. You're not that gullible, are you? Are you seriously playing up to Max, acting like you want to be married to him?"

"Julia.... It's not easy. Nothing is ever easy."

"True that." She slapped her hand on the table and sat back, eyeing Maggie. "I'm living proof that life is not easy, but you still have to face the music and deal with it. You're not dealing, Maggie. You're avoiding shit."

She bristled. "So what if I am? I'm not hurting anyone but me."

Julia leaned in. "That's the point. You're the one who is going to get hurt. You're bending over backwards to please Max, and the kids, and now cowboy lover. What's next? Any stray animals or kids you want to adopt? Who the hell is bending over backwards for you?"

Maggie's eyes flew wide and round, as if she'd not really thought of things in that way. "I... Julia, you don't understand."

"I understand more than you know. So, are you getting a divorce, or not? I sort of need to know since I am your attorney."

Maggie sat there, not saying anything. Julia let her stew for a moment.

"You don't want a divorce?"

She reached across the table for Julia's hand. "What I want is for my kids to be happy, with both parents. For them to have everything they need in life. To keep the family intact."

"Even if you are miserable."

"I'm not miserable."

"Because you have a cowboy on the side? How long can you maintain that, Maggie? Hmm?"

She squeezed her hand. "As long as it takes. If I can keep Max happy, not second-guessing me, giving him all the attention he wants and catering to his needs, then we all are happy."

"Really."

"Yes."

"And how does that work—the juggling the two relationships thing? Fucking them both. Do you ever do that twice in the same day? I mean, fuck Max in the morning and the dude in the afternoon? I swear, you and your sex drive..." She looked off into the sparse lunch crowd of the diner.

"I can handle it."

"And for how long?"

"As long as it takes."

Julia leaned forward. "How old is Chloe? Five?"

"Four."

"So, you really want to play this game, navigate this charade for another fourteen years or more? Good God, Maggie. No one can do that."

Maggie glared. "I can. I will."

"How's the backhand? Are you dodging that bullet too? What about the first time Carol makes him angry enough to slap the shit out of her? Or little Chloe? Then there's Jason, who adores his father— what about the first time he decks him because his mouth got smart?"

Maggie stilled and paled, withdrawing her hand. "That will not happen. I won't let it."

"You think that, until it happens."

"Julia, stop. I don't want to talk about it anymore."

"Of course, you don't."

"Please don't be mad at me, Julia."

"Let me ask you this... How is Max taking this news about your new friend? I assume the marriage is still open?"

Maggie rolled her eyes. "You know the marriage has never been open for me. Just for Max."

She took a quick, deep breath and squared herself. "Then what in the fucking shit are you doing, Maggie?"

"I'm just trying to keep it all together, Julia. I'm doing the best I can."

The server came with the check, and she put her hand over it. "I'll pick this up."

"No," Maggie shook her head. "I will."

"Nope. I got it." Julia stood. "I need to go. But before I do, tell me one thing. Am I to move forward with this divorce or am I holding?"

Looking up at her, Maggie sniffled, and Julia thought her eyes were a little misty. "I'm thinking no..." she whispered.

"You're making a mistake, Maggie."

"I'm protecting my kids."

"You're going to get caught, you know, with the cowboy. You can't maintain that kind of deception forever, and when Max finds out, there is nothing you can do to protect yourself, or the kids. You realize that. Right?"

"I'm not going to get caught."

"You think that now. You will."

"Julia, please..." Maggie stood and took the check out of her hand. "I'm getting this check. Please don't be mad at me. You don't understand everything."

"Then tell me what I don't understand."

Maggie walked away and Julia didn't stop her. Lunch check in hand, her friend headed toward the cash register counter. Slowly, Julia ambled toward the door, waiting for her to pay, thinking. When Maggie met her there, they took a few steps outside then Julia stopped her with a hand to her elbow.

"Look at me."

Slowly, Maggie turned. Julia drew on some deep-seated lawyer skills at that moment coupled with a few insights she'd learned from AA. She couldn't leave without saying what was on her heart, her mind. "I can't make choices for you, Maggie. I'm not you. I'm sure this guy makes you feel great. Kind of like how bourbon used to make me feel. Happy. Invincible. Maybe even loved. I'm also sure the sex is fantastic, or you wouldn't be risking everything to get it. Please, please think about what you are doing, though. The thrill will not last forever."

Maggie held her gaze. "Are you saying I'm addicted to sex? Is that it?"

"Are you?"

"Heavens no."

Julia squared herself in front of Maggie. "Maybe you should look into it. You've never been able to totally rid yourself of Max because you loved the rough sex. Now you have the dude on the side, so you're getting a double whammy. Maybe you should go to an AA meeting."

"I'm not a drunk, Julia. I'm not like you."

That stung. So deep that she didn't want to acknowledge it. Pushed it aside. "Like it or not, my friend, you *are* like me," she bit out. "Substitute sex for booze. Just go and get the concepts. Addiction is addiction."

"I'm not going to AA."

"Well, you need to do something. I guarantee Max will find out, sooner or later. He may already know. Don't trust him. You hear me? Do not let yourself get caught up in all the mystery and sizzle of an affair that you lose all common sense and let your guard down." She paused, watching Maggie's face.

"I'm still here. I'm a call away. Please get a fucking burner phone that I can contact you on and let me know the number. I'm not mad, I'm worried. This fantasy world you are building around yourself cannot be sustained. And when it's over, you are going to get hurt. The kids are going to get hurt. You could lose them, emotionally and physically. And then, I won't be able to help you, Maggie. There will be nothing I can do. You understand?"

Maggie exhaled, like she'd been holding that breath for Julia's entire speech, then nodded a little. "I understand."

"But you're not ready to do anything about any of it. Are you?"

"No." She shook her head. "I'm not."

Staring into Maggie's eyes, she let that sink in for a minute. "I want you to be clear because honestly, you haven't. You've been evasive and avoiding saying the words I need to hear. Maggie, do you want a divorce?"

Maggie set her jaw, then said, "No. I don't want a divorce."

Great. Then why the fuck am I here? Why did I drive all this way and do all that goddamn paperwork for you? Her stomach jumped in queasiness, and she broke eye contact, stepping back.

"Okay then. Fine. Your case is officially dissolved."

She turned her back on Maggie and took a few steps toward her car.

"Julia, wait." Maggie stopped her with a hand to her arm. "Wait."

Slowly, she angled back and met Maggie's dark-eyed gaze. She wanted to rip her eyes out, truth be told. Or slap her across the face. The anger inside had jolted her entire body, coming from somewhere out in left field. She hadn't expected that.

Sucking in a lengthy breath, then exhaling, was a near futile attempt to calm the chaos erupting inside—but she managed to quell it long enough.

Julia grasped her around the shoulders and gave her a tight hug. "Get ready," she whispered. "Don't let your guard down. Call occasionally and let me know you are alive."

Maggie's shoulders shook a little.

Julia stepped back, gave her one last look, then headed for her car.

One less thing....

Eight

July, two months later
   279 days sober

LEAVING HER OFFICE AT SALINGER & SALINGER, JULIA PEEKED at her phone for the time and rushed toward the elevator. It was Wednesday, which meant a full day of work with Nick, followed by her mid-week AA meeting, then finally home to prep Thursday breakfast.

That was her schedule.

She pushed the elevator call button.

The day was long enough, and fortunately her father was busy most of it. Yet again, she had avoided the partner discussion—but she knew she couldn't sidestep it much longer. Nick had been pressuring her for a decision.

"I need to know something soon, Julia," he'd mentioned casually a couple of weeks ago.

"Nick, I just can't decide on a whim, but I am working on it. We have a good routine going on at the inn, and I don't want to disrupt that yet by taking on additional work and having to spend more time downtown."

"But you have that girl, right?"

"I do and she's fabulous, but I don't want to turn over the day-to-day to her yet. Maybe in a year or so." She paused, almost uncertain whether to say the next part. "But I also need to make sure I'm in the right headspace before I take on more clients."

She averted looking at him and took his silence as either avoidance or indifference. She wasn't sure which.

"And Mark?" he eventually asked. "Didn't you two come to some sort of business agreement about the inn?"

They had. Seemed they could work out the business agreement easier than the dissolution of their marriage. But supposedly, that was a first step, according to Melinda. "We did."

Do I really want to get into those details with you? No, I don't.

"Then things are settled?" He paused, hesitating a few seconds before adding, "Sounds like things are good with Mark. Is there hope for you two as a couple again?"

That thought sent a panic into her gut that she hadn't anticipated, nor wanted to acknowledge.

"No, Dad. Things are not settled." He'd looked up from his desk when he heard her call him "Dad", which she rarely did. "And Mark and I are not reconciling."

He studied her. "Are you well, Julia?"

You mean, am I sober? "I'm good. Over nine months now."

Her father nodded. "I'm proud of you."

"But I have a lot to handle," she added.

"At least Maggie is off your plate."

"Right."

Enough said. Nick went back to his work. Neither had spoken of it since.

Maggie. She hadn't heard from her in a month, and honestly, she was really ticked with her friend. She should reach out to her, and all the girls, very soon. Too much time had passed.

The elevator pinged, signaling its arrival. The doors swooped open, and she stepped inside, along with four workers from other offices also likely heading home at this hour. A thought struck her as she rode the elevator to the basement parking garage, and she quickly set a reminder to bring it up later with Pam.

"Thank God for her," she uttered, leaving the elevator, and heading for her car.

She couldn't have asked for anyone better than Pam. While she'd had doubts about her son coming to work with her for the summer, it turned out that the guests adored him, and he was an angelic child. Never a problem. Smart too, for a six-year-old.

She knew Pam was having difficulty juggling the bus route from where she lived in South Louisville to the inn, and also connecting with Caleb from school, or after school day care. Having him come to the inn solved the problem for the summer. Come fall, when school started, would be another story.

But Julia didn't mind him coming. It made Pam happy, and Julia wanted her to love her job.

Mark had seriously stepped up his game lately, too. Truth was, they had both made her life easier, things running so much more smoothly the past couple of months than previous, and she was grateful.

At times, she worried she was leaning on them too much. But isn't that what people do in real life? Maybe that was a lesson learned—she'd always hated relying on others.

But was it such a bad thing?

Maybe she'd bring it up next time with Melinda. Shit. She should make a fucking list.

How could she present the appearance of being put-together on the outside, and feel so utterly chaotic on the inside?

Several minutes later, she descended the steps into the church basement. The meeting hadn't started yet so everyone was milling around with cups—Styrofoam for coffee or red cups with Hawaiian Punch. Someone brought a large platter of bakery cookies—different from their usual store-bought variety. Occasionally, group members would contribute, so this was a lucky night. Stepping toward the table, she had to admit they looked delicious, but she'd pass, trying to keep to her no sugar rule.

"Coffee?"

She glanced up and smiled. "Absolutely. Thanks, Bill." She took a cup from his hand.

"How's your day?"

"Good. Yours?"

"Splendiferous."

Julia smiled at that.

Bill liked to use unexpected words.

"Glad to hear it." She glanced about. "Seems a bigger crowd than usual."

"With one person AWOL."

"Oh?" She glanced about, scanning the gathering.

"She wasn't here last week either."

Pinpricks of panic shot into Julia's gut. "Gretchen?"

Bill nodded. "Seems no one has heard from her for a while."

"Not Larry?"

"No, and he's worried."

Julia scanned the room for her friend and decided to chat with him before the meeting. "Such an unlikely friendship," she whispered.

"Outside of these walls, the two of them would never have met, let alone forge a relationship."

"Addiction makes for strange bedfellows."

"Indeed. More ways than one."

Larry turned and caught her eye. "I'm going over and talk with him."

Bill nodded, then touched her arm. "Julia? I know you've got a lot on your plate right now, starting back to work at the office more, the business at the inn picking up, plus the issues with your friend down in North Carolina. Just wanting to make sure you are okay."

Grinning, she patted his hand. "I'm good, Bill. Thanks."

"Are you?"

She stared. "Why do you ask?"

He hesitated, as if measuring his words. "Your body language."

"What?"

"Usually you stand stall, confidently. Lately, your shoulders are slumping."

"Good God, Bill. I'm juggling a lot. Just tired."

"You're sure?"

"Positive."

He reached for her hands. "You're fidgety, too. Glancing about nervously."

She pulled her hands away from his and shoved them into her pants pockets. "It's just stress. I'm fine. Promise."

He nodded.

"Seriously."

"You know you can call me."

"Yes." She searched for Larry again. "I know that."

"Still going to therapy?"

"Of course." She paused. Was there more to this interrogation? "Sometimes with Mark."

"That's great."

Is it? I'm on the fence. "Look. I need to find Larry. Talk to you later."

As she approached Larry, she felt uneasy. Why was Bill giving her the third degree?

But Larry's distress made her forget all about that as soon as she started chatting with him. He was visibly upset. Something, somewhere, was wrong—her intuition on high alert. His concern for Gretchen was genuine.

Apparently, she had called him a week or so ago, her speech slurred and lazy, not making sense, but she wouldn't tell him where she was, or if she was with anyone.

Tears rimmed his eyes as he spoke.

"We met the first night I came," he said. "I'm like, who is this chick with the pink hair and why am I here sitting by her? I'm not like her. Then she shared some things about her addiction, and I realized we are more alike than not."

"The things we uncover when we're at rock bottom," she whispered.

"I'm worried for her."

She searched his eyes. "I am too. I'm also worried about you."

His nod told her he understood—he didn't need to fall off the wagon, too.

"Be strong." Julia leaned closer and gave him a hug. Generally, she was not a huggy person, especially with men, but she made an exception this time. "Call me," she whispered, "if you need to talk. Or if you hear from her."

He nodded and wiped his nose on a handkerchief. "I will."

"You have my cell?"

"I do. Yes."

"Great."

He paused, not making eye contact at first, then met her gaze. "I'm going to find a seat."

Julia watched him amble off and after a minute, found an empty chair herself in the back of the room. She listened intently during the meeting topic, but while the others shared, her mind drifted. She knew she should put everything out of her head—that was her thing when coming to AA meetings, to push everything else in her life aside for an hour—and focus on the addictive part of her personality.

She couldn't tonight.

Lately, the underlying currents of her reality repeatedly teased into her thoughts and were at their heyday tonight—the voices in her head popping in and out, leaving bits of conversation behind like litter for her to mull over. Often it was too much.

The voices crowded each other, like they were jockeying for position in her head.

It's like she disappeared, totally AWOL.

You can't sustain this, Maggie. Call me and let me know you are alive.

The baby. How to stop the crying baby?

You're the drunk, Julia. Not me.

We need to have the partner discussion, Julia. Soon.

Your problem, not mine. Give me my Grey Goose.

I don't know how to do life without you.

I killed my baby. Who does that?

Stop.

Just stop.

Obviously, she had to either get some things settled in her life or learn how to let them go. Sounded like another Melinda discussion.

The words in her head co-mingled with the words tossed about in the room. *God, I can't take their problems on as my own too.* Glancing at Larry, she felt his concern across the room. He sat staring at the floor, listening as Bill talked.

Maybe she was just too damn empathetic, or something.

Or maybe, subconsciously, if she tried to solve other people's problems, perhaps she didn't have to work on her own.

Shit.

She did that. Didn't she?

She'd done that with Maggie. Hadn't she? When Maggie told her no divorce, she'd had an actual physical reaction—she'd felt gutted, lost even. Without purpose, temporarily. Like, what did she have to live for now? Which was ridiculous, of course, but that's the way she'd felt at the time.

And she'd been extremely concerned about Gretchen for a while now.

Slowly, Julia rose, gave Bill a quick nod, and left the room. Right now, she couldn't take anything else onto her shoulders. What was it she had said to Maggie a few weeks ago? You can't sustain this?

Is that what I am doing?

Trying to maintain and sustain the status quo while inside, I'm still reeling in self-doubt and pain and grief—and like suddenly, after all these months, I don't know how to, or can't, handle the hurt?

Will I ever shake this?

LATER, IN THE KITCHEN AT THE INN, JULIA COVERED TWO casserole dishes with foil—one baked oatmeal with strawberries, and the other, an egg casserole with sausage, cheese, green onions, and mushrooms—and slid them into the refrigerator until morning. Cooking always relaxed her and tonight, making the casseroles, was just the thing to keep her hands and mind busy.

Somewhat.

Pam worked beside her, having just put two tins of orange marmalade muffins in the oven, and was now tidying up the kitchen island and slipping dishes into the dishwasher. It had also been great to have her there too, just chatting about normal things and working together.

She felt more relaxed now, at this moment, than she had all day.

"Those look great, Julia. I admit, eating your breakfast leftovers for lunch is one of my favorite things."

"Me too!" Caleb grinned.

Julia smiled. "I'm glad the two of you enjoy them, and equally glad the food isn't going to waste." She'd always let Pam take whatever leftovers she wanted. While Julia paid her a decent wage, she knew it likely wasn't enough to support both her and a growing boy, so she was happy for her to take the food.

"You're here late tonight. Is there a reason?"

Pam settled onto a stool at the kitchen island. "Not really. Well, yes, I want to ask you something." She sighed.

"Oh, I forgot. I wanted to ask you something, too." She caught Pam's eye while she swiped the granite countertop. "Everything okay?"

"I think so." She glanced at Caleb, who sat coloring on some art paper at the kitchen table. "Can we talk in the living room?"

Sensing something serious, Julia laid the dishtowel on the island. "Of course."

Pam called out to her son, "Caleb, you stay there. I'll be right back."

"Okay, Mommy."

As they moved into the living room, Pam seemed to tense up. Julia faced her. "Oh my God. You're leaving me."

Pam burst into tears, covering her face with her hands. "I love this job. I don't want to. But...."

Julia angled to look into Pam's face. "Look at me. What's going on?"

Slowly, Pam lifted her gaze, and the words tumbled out. "Caleb's dad is nowhere to be found. He's stopped paying child support. Plus, the rent on my apartment is going up September first and I have to give them a thirty-day notice if I'm staying or moving. I either have to find another job where I make more money or find a cheaper place to live— which means it will probably be further out and a longer bus ride. I wanted to ask if I could have a couple of afternoons off so I could look around and figure things out. Could I? I would work around your schedule."

"Oh, good gracious." Julia leaned in and gave Pam a hug. *There I go again, hugging.* "You'll never believe what I was going to ask you."

Pam blinked and met her gaze. "What?"

Smiling, Julia's heart felt full. But how could she spin this to make Pam feel like it wasn't a handout? Because truly, it wasn't. For once, she could help someone because she had the means to do so—and besides, it would work out best for everyone.

And, the bottom line was, Julia needed her.

There I go again. Leaning.

Suddenly, it felt okay.

"My father is nagging at me to become a partner at the firm and take on more clients, which means more responsibility, which also means I may have to be downtown more. I really wasn't sure I could handle it, and then I had an idea."

Pam stood silent, looking at her. Waiting.

"I was thinking. The carriage house will be finished in a couple of weeks. While the income from those rooms would be nice, you're much more valuable to me. How about if you and Caleb move into the carriage house?"

Pam shook her head. "Oh, I could never afford that."

"Rent free. I forgot to add that."

Her face froze in surprise. "What? Julia, I couldn't."

"You most certainly can. Let's say it's part of your salary. Also, I've been wanting to give you a raise. You deserve it. There is one stipulation though."

Pam's hopeful expression fell a little.

Julia smiled. "No worries. This is nothing you can't handle."

"What is it?"

"You'll pretty much be on call at times. We will set regular hours, of course, but I may need to go out of town occasionally, and perhaps Mark can't be here, and you'll need to manage things 24/7 on your own. We can work out the details and of course, you would have scheduled days off. Think you can handle that?"

"Oh, Julia. I can. I don't know what to say. I feel like I've just been given the world. I can't believe you trust me that much."

Pam hugged her again.

"I trust you that much and more." She pulled back. *Enough hugging for one night.* "Besides, having you here on the property will be extremely helpful to me, and easier for you and Caleb. Win–win."

"He might need to change schools."

"Right." She hoped that wasn't a dealbreaker. "Let's research that tomorrow. So, what do you say?"

Pam exhaled, grinning with tears running down her cheeks. "I would love to. I don't know how to thank you, Julia."

Her heart felt full. "Just be here for me, for the guests. Continue to do the wonderful work you are doing. Perhaps we'll work out a job description together."

She nodded. "Oh goodness. I never imagined I could live someplace like this."

Again, Julia grinned wide. "Do you think Caleb will be okay with it? New school and everything?" That worried her a little. Kids hate changing schools.

"I'm going to talk with him right now."

"Good. I'll give you two a moment before I head back in there."

Pam grabbed her and hugged Julia tighter than she believed she'd ever been hugged. "Thank you so much," she whispered. Then she ran off to the kitchen. "Caleb! You'll never guess...."

Julia smiled, her heart full. One good thing this day.

But she was tired, mentally and physically. Her body and brain needed rest. Soon as she could swing it, she would head for her suite, a hot shower, and her bed.

With a sigh, she sat for a moment, glancing about the living room.

Offering the carriage house to Pam and knowing she could take on more responsibility had given her an unexpected and indescribable sense of peace. A long sigh escaped her lips.

HER RINGING PHONE WOKE HER FROM A SOUND SLEEP.

Julia jerked, grasping at the nightstand, and snatched it up. She glanced at the caller's name before answering, then sat straight up.

"Larry? What's wrong?"

"Oh God, Julia. She's gone."

"What?" She stood, twisting the switch on her bedside lamp. "Who? Oh my God. Gretchen?"

"Yes. On the news. Just saw it."

She rushed to the small television on her dresser and turned it on. A glance at the time told her it was just after eleven. "Where are you?"

"I'm home."

"Do you need company?"

"No, no. Just talk to me."

"Of course. I have the TV on now. What did the news report say though?"

"They didn't say it was her yet, but I know it is. Someone found her in the restroom of the restaurant where she works—the needle was still in her arm, and they said she was deceased."

"Shit."

"I feel like my insides are breaking apart."

"Larry," Julia warned, "that's normal. It's a shock to your system. But no booze, you hear me?"

"I'm not sure I can guarantee that."

"Larry, seriously. That's not the answer."

"Of course. No. I won't."

"Do you want to meet somewhere?"

"No. My wife. She doesn't get it. I'm outside right now on the deck. I just wanted to talk for a second."

She understood. "You can call or text anytime. You know that."

"I do."

"Listen, after we finish talking, I'll make a few calls downtown. I know some people at the station and the morgue. Let me see if I can get a positive I.D. and more information."

"I'll let you go do that now. I need to get back inside."

"I'll call if I find out something."

"Text me, if you would. My wife...."

"Sure."

"Julia?"

"Yes?"

"Thanks for being there. I appreciate it."

"No problem, Larry. I'm so sorry. I really liked her. She had a good soul. Just a troubled one."

"I know. Me too." He sniffled. "Yes, you're right."

He hung up. Julia tossed her phone aside and sat on the edge of her bed, hanging her head. Threading her fingers through her hair, she sat there for a moment, just breathing.

In. Out.

Easy.

Not rushed.

She made her calls to the morgue while she still had her shit together. No information. Call back in an hour.

"God damn it, Gretchen!" She jumped up and whirled about frantically. "Why did you go and fucking do this? We would have helped. I would have been there for you!"

Exhaling deep, she paced back and forth at the foot of the bed for several minutes, her arms clutching her abdomen. Her gut hurt. Something twisty was going on inside. She wanted to cry. Scream. Wail.

For Gretchen. For her. For Larry. For anyone she knew, or lives she'd touched.

"What a fucking waste. Oh, you sweet girl."

Tears came then, and she sobbed, unable to hold them back.

Sucking in another breath, she held it for a moment, and stared out into the street. The streetlamps along 4th Street created misty halos every few feet along the sidewalks, lending an almost creepy, eerie ambiance to the night.

"Oh, Gretchen..." she whispered. "Why?"

The cry came, at first, small and weak. Barely there. But she heard it.

Julia jerked and cocked her head, pointing an ear toward the sound, and waited.

The second time it came, the cry was stronger, a bit louder. Longer.

It was a choppy, hiccupy, cranky baby cry. And then....

And then the cry was followed by a...a cooing.

A hushing sound, like that of a mother soothing her colicky baby.

Good God, Julia. You're going insane.

And then it stopped.

She waited.

Still standing near the window, she closed her eyes, and waited. Listening.

Nothing.

Maybe it was a cat. There were a number of strays that roamed the area at night.

The scent of lilac drifted beneath her nostrils.

Shit.

Abruptly, she rushed to her dresser, jerked open the top drawer, and pulled out the bottle of Woodford Reserve she'd bought a couple of weeks ago.

That was the first thing she'd done wrong. Bought the damn bottle.

But she'd just wanted to smell it. Inhale the sweet oaky aroma. That wouldn't hurt, would it? Get the smell of fucking lilac out of her nose.

She was better now. Stronger.

She could handle a drink now and then. Right?

She was in control. Wasn't she?

She could stop any time she wanted. After all, it was just one drink.

And right now, she needed to numb the pain for a minute. The confusion. The self-doubt.

Nothing wrong with that. People do it all the time. And then they go back to their regularly scheduled lives.

With trembling hands, she twisted the lid, unleashing the sweet scent of corn mash and spicey rye. Her nose above the opening, she inhaled, pulling the essence of the bourbon past her tongue, down her throat, and deep into her lungs.

"Oh, my God..." she whispered.

She was smart. In control. She could do this.

Gulping in another deep breath, she shuddered.

No.

I can't do this.

You know you can call me.

Gretchen is gone.

Shakily, she put the cap back on the bottle—spilling a bit of the bourbon on the back of her hand—and placed it on the dresser. She thought about licking the bourbon away and for a moment, savoring what it would feel like on her tongue.

But she didn't, and stood motionless, eyes closed, head tossed back, and just breathed.

In.

Out.

And again.

Twisting back, she wiped her hand on her t-shirt, dove for the bed, and rifled through the sheets for her phone.

Found it.

Scrolled and dialed.

He answered.

"Mark," she said quietly. "I need you."

Nine

280 days sober

SLOWLY BLINKING AWAKE, JULIA FOCUSED ON THE BEDSIDE clock, but the face and the numbers were blurry—her eyes hurt, her head groggy. Had she overslept?

Shit. Breakfast.

Anxiety stabbed at her heart. The numbers came quickly into focus. Ten minutes until five... And then the alarm would sound. She was fine, not late.

Breathe, Julia.

Rolling over, she yawned and stared toward the window. Still dark outside, of course, but even three floors up, the streetlights cast a few rays toward the window.

Looking closer, away from the window, she fixated on the pillow beside her head, and a familiar profile slightly illuminated by the filtered light. Panic gripped her.

The fidgety feeling in her gut was back.

"Shit!" she hissed, pushing at Mark.

She shot up on the opposite side of the bed and switched on the overhead light. Mark lazily rolled toward her.

"Get up!"

He squinted. "Ow. Not fair. Eyes."

"Quit being a baby."

"Wondered when you would wake up."

Jerking her robe about her naked body, she belted it tightly, her hands shaking. "If you were awake you should have either woken me or left. Leaving would have been the decent thing."

He shrugged, sitting up straight in the bed. "Thought maybe you'd need help with breakfast."

"No. I don't need your help."

"You needed me last night."

"That was different."

Mark stared.

Julia didn't look at him. Instead, she paced. "Are you just going to lay there and watch me?"

"I've always loved watching you."

She stopped and faced him. "Well, don't."

Pushing himself up and off the bed, Mark reached for his jeans and shirt, and started getting dressed. His back to her, he said, "We have to talk about last night."

"No, we don't."

He turned. "We do. And if you want me to leave, then we have to talk first."

"I didn't take a drink, Mark. I'd had nothing to drink when you got here. I swear it."

Fastening his fly, he took a few steps closer, a serious expression on his face. "I'm not talking about the bourbon being out on your dresser. I know you didn't drink. You didn't smell like alcohol."

She shrugged. "Then what?"

"Seriously, Julia?" He came closer, standing just a couple of feet away. He pointed to the bed. "We need to talk about what happened in this bedroom last night. I've not been in your bed in over a year. But last night..." His voice grew softer, and he reached for her. "Julia, last night was...."

She jerked her arm away and stepped back. "Last night was a mistake, Mark. I shouldn't have called you."

"Oh, yes, you should have called me and I'm glad you did. Because if you hadn't, you'd be shitfaced this morning, hungover in your bed, with guests downstairs waiting for breakfast. Not that I expected to end up in your bed, mind you, because I didn't. But because I knew when I heard your voice on the phone, and when I saw the desperation on your face when I got here, that you were not in a good place."

Closing her eyes, Julia huffed out a breath. "Fine. All true. Sorry I called so late and roused you from your bed but... Well, thank you."

"I'm not sorry. I'm glad you called. I want you to call me."

She blinked, studying his face. Yes, Mark had always been there for her. Probably always would be, whether or not they were married. But was this leaning on people thing going too far now? For months she didn't want anyone to lean on, to help her solve her problems—she knew she had to do that on her own. But lately, leaning on both Pam and Mark—was that a good idea?

Asking for help is never a bad thing, Melinda once told her.

Reaching out to others for support is perfectly acceptable, Bill reminded her on occasion. *It's not a weakness.*

Was that her issue? Did she feel strong when she could handle things on her own? And weak when she couldn't? Was that a Nick thing? He'd been tough on her as a child, wanted her to grow up to be a strong, independent woman—unlike her mother, she supposed.

Funny, she'd not put two-and-two together until this moment.

Interesting.

"Julia..." Mark's voice invaded her thoughts.

Slowly, she lifted her gaze. "What?"

He moved closer. "We have to talk about this."

"Oh, please. Aren't we a little too old for the 'what does this mean' or the 'what comes next' discussion? We know what it means—I was weak and needed you—and we also know there is nothing coming next."

"I want you to need me, Julia. And you are stronger than you think."

"Evidently not, or you wouldn't be in my bed this morning."

She glanced away from the semi-pained expression that crossed his face.

Suddenly, the bedside clock wailed and a second later, her cell phone alarm buzzed, too. She pushed Mark away with a hand to his chest and silenced both alarms. "We will have to talk later. I have to get breakfast started."

"Breakfast can wait five minutes."

"No." Rushing to her dresser, she pulled out a pair of yoga pants and a T-shirt, panties and a bra, stripped out of the robe, and quickly dressed. "No, that conversation will take longer than five minutes, so let's wait." She pushed past him and headed for the bedroom door.

He grasped her arm, stopping her. "Five minutes, Julia."

"No, Mark. I have to get downstairs."

"That's part of the problem, isn't it? You always rushing off? Avoiding the issue at hand? Not wanting to talk about anything of importance only to hustle off to something that can easily wait?"

With a sharp inhale, she whirled back and planted her feet. "Fine. Not rushing off. Let's talk. Except we don't need five minutes. In fact, we barely need a minute. You want to talk? Great. Well, here is what I want to say. Go home, Mark. Leave. This is never happening again."

He didn't say a word, just stared into her eyes.

"Say something."

"Are you finished?"

"I've said all I'm going to say."

"Great. Because I have at least four minutes coming to me then."

She broke eye contact, glaring at the door.

Mark grasped her biceps and shook her a little. "Julia, look at me. We made love last night for the first time in months and it was beautiful. You cried. I cried. We held each other until we both fell asleep. And I slept more soundly than I have in months. Maybe you did, too. The answer is not to tell me to go away and that it can never happen again. The response from both of us should be that we need to talk about how we got there, and how we felt when it was happening, and how we feel now."

"Jesus, you sound like Melinda."

"Well, so what. We probably need to talk to her about it too."

Rolling her eyes, she headed for the door. "Oh, hell no. We are not analyzing what happened here last night. I know what happened. I was vulnerable and in a bad place, and I reached out and called you because...."

She stopped, looking toward the bed. Why had she called Mark instead of Bill? Bill was the one she should have called. Right? He was her sponsor. Why hadn't she?

Slowly she lifted her gaze. Mark made eye contact and held the beam between them. Strong and steady Mark. He'd always held them together until he couldn't. When she couldn't. Until she went a little mad. Hell, a lot mad. And then, even he couldn't save them.

"Because of what, Julia?" he asked softly.

"Because I knew I could trust you," she said. "Because you've always been there for me."

His head dropped into a slow nod. "That's right," he whispered. "That hasn't changed, and I doubt it ever will."

I wish I could say the same, Mark, but I can't.

Steadying herself, Julia took a breath. She glanced at the clock—five minutes after five. "Mark, I need you to leave right now. Please? While I agree we need to talk about last night, even if I don't want to, what I need more is to get on with my morning routine. Last night I fell apart. I nearly screwed 280 days of sobriety. Today, this morning, I need to get back in step. It's the thing that saved me once, and I need it badly this morning. So, if you can slip out the front door quietly...."

Mark leaned forward and softly kissed her forehead. "I'll talk to you soon."

She watched him walk out the door, took a minute to pull herself together, then headed downstairs to the kitchen to make coffee and pull out the casseroles.

Her safe place. Her kitchen. *Maybe I should never leave it.*

THE NOON AA MEETING WAS AT THE UNIVERSITY HOSPITAL downtown. Early in her sobriety journey, she'd pop in during the day to boost her confidence and get a fix of support so she could carry on for the remainder of the day. But lately, she'd not gone to day meetings unless she really needed to.

Today, she needed to.

The uneasy feeling in her gut was still there but it had stopped jumping around. Now, it was laying on her abdomen like a weight she couldn't remove, getting heavier by the moment.

The room was clinical, clean, sparse, and antiseptic. She'd not attended a meeting in this location before—they used to hold the meetings on a different floor, but it seemed someone new was in charge. Thus, the change in venue.

She didn't recognize anyone sitting in the circle, either—a diverse gathering of men and women, white, African American, Hispanic, young, middle-aged, and old.

The leader, a woman who said her name was Queetha, talked about anger. Julia listened with interest—had she been angry with Mark earlier? Or with herself?

Queetha's tone appeared to resonate with the others in the circle. They nodded in agreement, some of them—the others stared into space or at the floor.

Her phone buzzed in her yoga pants pocket, but she ignored it. Usually, she turned the thing off but had forgotten. Glancing about, she realized that one of the men in the group had started sharing. When he finished, Julia hesitated, then jumped into the fray.

"Hi. I'm Julia. I usually go to a different meeting. I'm 280 days sober. Last night, I came close to taking a drink. Things have been piling up lately. Work. Family. A friend died yesterday, and I spiraled. I should have reached out to my sponsor, but I didn't. Instead, I called my ex-husband."

"And you didn't drink?" Someone from her left called out that question.

"No. By the time he got to my house, I had mostly pulled myself together."

"And he talked you down the rest of the way?"

She chuckled. "No, we had sex."

"Then you're good," someone else said.

Julia smiled and shook her head. "No. Far from it. I lean on him too much. I need to learn how to handle these things by myself. At least that's what I keep telling myself."

Queetha leaned closer. "Handling things by ourselves is sometimes what gets us into trouble. You know?"

She did know and needed to hear that. "Yes." She nodded, meeting the woman's gaze. "Thanks."

Her phone vibrated again on her hip.

No one spoke for a moment, then Queetha said, "No problem. We're happy you stopped by Julia. Do you have more you would like to share? I hope you can stay after and chat for a while."

She shook her head. "Thank you. I'm good."

It felt good to say what she'd said.

A woman across the way scooted to the edge of her seat. "Then I'll jump in. My name is Cora, and I did fall this week, for no apparent reason, I guess, other than I wanted to. I feel like crap and am so disappointed in myself."

Queetha reached for Cora's hand. "Let's say the words, child...."

Cora gave her a hesitant grin. "God grant me the serenity...."

The rest of the circle chimed in.

Julia chanted the prayer along with the group, then quietly excused herself and left. On the way to her car, she pulled her phone from her pocket.

Two text messages.

One was from Bill. The other from Lia, a group text to all the girls. She glanced at it, promising to fully read it later. The group message made her think of Maggie, and that caused her nervous stomach to jump a little.

Sitting in her car, she called Bill first, who wanted to give her an update on Gretchen, and also Larry. They arranged to meet tomorrow. Then she called Melinda and made an appointment—for her, and not with Mark. She had to get the Mark discussion off her chest.

She sat in the parking lot for several minutes, her brain wandering over all the parts and pieces, the dribs and drabs of her life. Then she re-read Lia's message and added her responses.

Lia: *Where is everyone? So quiet here.*

Alice: *Hi. Missing all of you.*

Lia: *I'm ready for beach week!*
Alice: *Just a month away.*
Julia: *A month seems like an eternity.*
Alice: *It will fly.*
Julia: *Maybe.*
Her phone fell silent for several heartbeats, then....
Lia: *We've had a few cancellations, so if anyone wants to come early, just let me know. I have rooms at Sea Glass and the cottages.*
Alice: *I wish. I'm so tied up with this campaign.*
Lia: *I know. But anyone, just let me know. Okay?*
Maybe getting away early was not such a bad idea. Julia pondered that.
Julia: *Sure thing.*
Alice: *Maggie? Are you listening?*
Nothing from Maggie. That worried her. Immensely.

---

281 DAYS SOBER
"I slept with Mark."

Melinda nodded. "I see. So, is that why you called yesterday checking for a cancellation?"

Julia sank onto the puffy sofa, but sat on the edge, not leaning back. Instead, she slanted toward Melinda, and watched the therapist wiggle into her chair and turn back the cover of her steno pad. Who still uses steno pads? Julia wondered. She guessed therapists did—or at least Melinda.

"Yes. That, and other things. I feel like things are piling up."

Melinda leaned forward a little too, mimicking Julia's position. "Okay, so let's take one thing at a time. Do you want to start with Mark?"

She thought about that. "No. I need to start before that."

"All right."

Julia exhaled. "So, here is the thing. I've been having these feelings lately that I'm leaning too much on others and not relying on myself. I know we've talked about this before, but the self-doubt is sort of getting to me. That's one thing."

"Okay. Go on." She sat back, crossing her legs.

"Then I learned that Gretchen, one of my friends from AA, died of an overdose. I wanted to drink that night. So, I called Mark."

"Not your sponsor?"

"No. That was a mistake."

"Why? Mark was your husband. It's okay to call him for help."

"Was my husband. Not now."

"Oh, so you've signed the papers?"

She shook her head. "No. We haven't."

"So he's still your husband. Is that the confusion?"

Was it? She wasn't sure. Biting her lower lip, she stared at the shelves of books behind Melinda's desk. "It's confusing because I don't want to lean on him."

"Or anyone else, it sounds like."

"I guess."

"But Mark is more...personal?"

She stood and took a few steps away from the sofa. "I'm afraid I'll get used to leaning on him."

"And that would be a bad thing?"

"If I'm dependent on him, how can I leave him?" She paced back and forth in front of the window, her arms crossed over her abdomen, hands tucked under her arms.

"Ah. I see."

"Do you?"

Melinda shifted in her seat to look fully at Julia. "You know, many divorced couples find they can still be very close friends with their exes, and even lean on them for support occasionally. Not saying that you and Mark should strive for that, but it's perfectly legit if you end up heading that way."

She faced Melinda. "I don't know."

"Then perhaps that's what you need to figure out. Eventually. There is no rush. Julia."

"Maybe."

Returning to the sofa, she sat again, this time with her back against the fluffy pillows. Maybe if she sat there long enough, she could simply sink into the soft cloud of cushions and disappear.

"So what else is happening in your life? You said things were piling up."

Laying her head back against the pillows, she closed her eyes, letting her mind drift. After a moment, she responded. "Nick wants me to increase my hours at the firm. I'm considering it but it doesn't feel right, for some reason I can't pinpoint. I did offer Pam, my assistant at the inn, to live in the carriage house so she could be around more and take over should I start to work more."

"Does that feel like leaning too much on her?"

She hesitated, then raised her head and said, "Actually, no. It felt good to offer it to her. She was in sort of a bad place too with her landlord, and her kid's dad, so it worked out to both of our advantages. Besides, I'm paying her."

She caught Melinda's smile.

"I'm sure Pam is appreciative of your support. You are helping her, you realize. Not all leaning is one-sided. This sounds like a win-win."

Nodding, she said, "Yes."

"What about the alcohol? Your friend's death triggered the response to drink?"

Julia sat up straighter. "I think it was the last straw. It had been a long couple of days."

"Have you talked with Bill about it?"

"I did. Yesterday. We are having lunch tomorrow. I also went to a meeting earlier today. I'm good."

Melinda smiled. "I'm glad about that."

Silence fell about the room and Julia wondered if Melinda was simply letting everything settle in for a moment. It wasn't like they had resolved much of anything—she'd just let her talk. And then the pause, for her to think. Julia noticed she didn't feel as anxious as she had when she stepped into the room, so maybe just talking was a good thing.

Melinda cleared her throat, drawing back her attention. "I'm wondering if I can bring up something else."

Julia focused on her expression. The woman never showed emotion during their sessions and was very good about being neutral. At times, it drove Julia crazy. Sometimes she wanted Melinda to show something—other than an occasional smile—to let her know how she was doing. "Sure. What is it?"

"Tell me more about the smells and sounds you were experiencing a few weeks ago. Have those remained?"

Julia blinked, studying Melinda. "You mean in my bedroom?"

"Is that where it usually happens?"

Suddenly she felt like they were talking in circles. "Yes." She paused.

Melinda waited.

"I have had the dreams."

"Dreams?"

"The one where I'm tearing down the wallpaper."

"You've had it more than once?"

"Yes." She met Melinda's gaze. "The last time, I ripped a lot of it down. Guess what was underneath?"

"I don't know."

"Lilac wallpaper."

Melinda leaned forward, scribbling something on the steno pad. "Really."

Julia nodded. "Weird, huh?"

With a nod of agreement, Melinda asked, "Have you ever looked to see what's behind that wallpaper in your room?"

She shook her head. "No, actually, I haven't."

"Are you still smelling lilac?"

"Not for a while." She lied. She'd smelled it the other night. Right?

Melinda sat back in her seat, glancing off, as if thinking.

This time, Julia waited.

Turning back, Melinda asked, "Do you believe in paranormal activity?"

That came from left field. "What do you mean?"

Melinda shifted, uncrossing her legs. "It's not my area of expertise, of course, so I'd have to refer you elsewhere, but you know that Old Louisville is supposedly ripe with supernatural activity and spiritual occurrences, right? I'm just thinking out loud."

It was something Julia had pondered in the past. "I'll have to think about that. I'm not sure."

"Just a thought."

Her head bobbed in acknowledgement.

"We haven't talked about the baby in a while," Melinda continued. "Since your visit to the cemetery. Have you heard the baby crying lately?"

"You mean in the attic?"

"Is that where it is coming from?"

"You think it's in my head, don't you? That there really isn't a baby crying in my attic."

"Julia, I think you hear what you hear. I'm not making judgements, simply wondering if you've heard the crying again lately... Or perhaps, you have resolved that issue?"

Issue? My baby is now an issue to be resolved?

She turned slightly away from Melinda and stared off into her bookshelves again. All those books. She wondered if the therapist had read them all. "I've not heard it."

But she had, hadn't she? The other night, when she had pulled out the bourbon bottle?

Why am I lying to her?

"No wait," she added. "I did hear it. The same night I called Mark."

"It?"

"The baby." She looked at Melinda. "The crying baby."

"Not your baby."

"No! The crying baby." *Why am I getting flustered?*

"The thought of two babies sounds confusing." Melinda paused, letting the conversation sink in. Letting her play over their words and ponder them momentarily. Then, she added, "Julia, this may be sensitive and if you don't want to respond, that is okay—but I recall that you told me months ago that you had an abortion in college. Do you think all of this is related?"

Julia didn't know what to say. Did Melinda think she was mentally confused?

Well, shit. She was.

She hadn't thought about the baby in college for some time. She'd never told Mark she was pregnant back then and had handled it all on her own. Alice went with her to the clinic. It was true she'd felt guilt occasionally for aborting a healthy baby back them—especially when her body couldn't keep the other baby alive long enough to be delivered breathing.

"When will you give your baby a name, Julia?"

"What?" Stunned, she opened her mouth to speak, then closed it again. "What?"

"Your baby. Your little girl. When will you name her?"

She pushed the memory of the aborted baby aside—blocked it like she'd done twenty-some years ago. Panic settled over her chest and shoulders, thick like a sheet of ice covering the car windshield after an ice storm, freezing her in place. "I... We...."

"Did you and Mark name her?"

"The baby never lived, Melinda." *Shit. What is her point?*

"Of course, she did. She lived inside of you for nearly nine months. She died just before you gave birth. Remember? Her heart beat inside of your belly for weeks. She was as close to you as any person could get. You always refer to her as 'the baby,' or 'it,'—impartially, like you refer to the other baby, the one crying in your attic. It *is* another baby, isn't it? Or do you think the crying baby in the attic is yours?"

Melinda focused on her, staring, and all Julia could do was glare back. No words.

Melinda continued, "Honestly, I'm curious as to why you and Mark never named her, or if you would consider naming her now. Soon. I think it may help."

Her. It was true. She'd kept "the baby" neutral, just like Melinda's facial expressions. She'd never referred to the baby as her daughter. As a "her." She hadn't wanted to give the baby a name on the headstone because then it felt too real. She hadn't wanted to call out her child's name, because the reality of her child's death was too painful.

Really, Julia? How could things have been more painful than they already were?

Had she made things even more painful by ignoring them? Not acknowledging her child's existence?

"Julia, do you want to tell me what you are thinking?"

She breathed in, and out, and tried to focus on Melinda's noncommittal expression. "Caroline," she finally said. "Her name was Caroline."

———

LATER THAT EVENING, JULIA SAT ON THE SIDE OF HER BED, alone, staring at the rose wallpaper. An unsettled, jittery feeling had swallowed up her body for over a day now. It had started not long after Larry called and had accelerated over the past twenty-four hours. At first, it was a nagging jumpiness in her abdomen. Then earlier this morning, she'd noticed a shakiness in her hands while fixing breakfast.

At times, it fell into her gut with a thud, laying heavy on her being. At other times, she felt like she might jump out of her skin.

Things had to get back to normal. Soon.

Her day was done. She'd kept to her schedule and had accomplished most everything she wanted to do that day. Guests were in for the night —the breakfast lined out for morning. Pam and Caleb had moved a few small things into the carriage house—things they could carry with them on the bus. Julia had arranged for a moving van to get the rest of their belongings on Saturday and gave Pam Friday off to prepare.

Pam. *Check.*

Plus, she'd met with Melinda. *Check.*

And talked to Bill. *Check.*

Shared at AA. *Check.*

Had avoided Mark. *Check.*

She couldn't, wouldn't, avoid him forever, she knew. He deserved an explanation or at least discussion. She deserved to give herself time to figure out why the hell she had called him in the first place, and subsequently led him to her bed.

Make no mistake, it was she who lured him into her lair. Of course, he needed very little convincing.

She had a bit of soul-searching to do.

There was always tomorrow. Right? Or the next day? One can't solve all their problems at once.

Ten

Julia's gaze followed a trellis of faded pink roses and spring green leaves up to the corner of the room, where she spotted a slip of wallpaper curled down from the edge, just under the painted crown molding. Standing, she moved closer, then picked up the bedside lamp to angle the light more directly at the peeling paper.

Have you ever looked to see what's behind that wallpaper?

Curious, she parked the lamp back on the stand and moved a chair into the corner. She rummaged around in her top dresser drawer for a flashlight, turned it on, and shined the beam upward. Yep. Undeniably peeling.

Climbing up on the chair, she moved to her tiptoes and stretched to grasp the edge of the wallpaper.

She jerked it.

The paper splintered away, crackling as she tore it.

She reached for another ragged spot and tugged. A larger chunk of paper came down, along with years of dusty wallpaper paste. Then more. As she ripped more paper, scattering the remnants over the bedroom floor, her breathing escalated.

Purple. Faded purple flowers. Lilacs?

Yes. There was lilac paper underneath. Just like in her dream.

She gasped, amazed at her discovery.

Ripping another section away, she revealed more of the floral pattern, and the sweet essence of lilac itself.

Sweet. Soft. Tender.

The scent of lilac. Like a baby's breath.

The cry came soft then, as if drifting in the window on a breeze. Like a whiff of baby powder. Or perhaps, wafting on the scent of the elusive lilac.

Transfixed, Julia followed the sound. *Next time follow the cry,* Melinda had suggested.

I'm going now.

Flashlight in hand, Julia scurried across the third-floor hallway toward the attic room. The door creaked softly as she opened it, choosing to leave it open as she took the first step inside. The baby's cries grew louder with each step. Her flashlight illuminated the room until she pulled a bulb string, throwing a triangle of light into the darkened room.

The baby's cries stopped as she moved further inside. The illumination from the single bulb didn't reach the far corners, so she flashed the light around, bouncing it off boxes and random pieces of furniture that she knew weren't theirs, and could only have belonged to previous occupants of the home.

The ceiling above her head was open to the rafters—large wooden beams were visible, holding up the roof, she suspected. Wide planks of wood graced the floor and the slanted interior of the roof. To her left stood the brick chimney for the fireplaces they didn't use any longer. Three of the walls were wood paneled, and the fourth plastered.

Odd.

The cradle—the one that she'd seen before, months earlier—sat unmoving in front of the plastered wall. Alone. Singled out. Like she was meant to lay her eyes upon it, and it alone, and go to it.

So, she did. For the longest moment, she stood and stared, listening.

No crying. No rocking. No cooing.

She caressed the old wood, running her fingertips along the smooth but dusty edges. Oak, perhaps, she thought. The wood was soft and timeworn beneath her touch.

They'd talked of getting an antique cradle like this one, she and Mark, when they'd first discovered they were pregnant. Then, they'd read all the safety warnings about older furniture—lead paint and choking hazards—and had nixed that idea. Funny, how they thought of all the things like that, took all the safety precautions, but didn't see the health hazard coming abruptly there at the end, particularly the one that took her baby from her.

Caroline. Her baby had a name.

Caroline.

Looking beyond the cradle, Julia swallowed back a lump in her throat, and noticed some scratches on the plastered wall—like someone had marked off days, or time. Single lines, side by side, with every set of four including a slash mark across the set. Mentally, she counted the sets. Five. Ten. Fifteen.

She stopped at one hundred but there was more than that. Lots more.

Moving closer, she touched the hashmarks, running her forefinger down one then another, as if she were making the marks herself. She realized then that the marks were scratched into the plaster, not written as with chalk or a pencil—but etched into the crumbly surface, likely with something sharp.

Who had made these marks? What did it mean?

She glanced about again, tossing the beam of the flashlight on an adjacent wall. There, in the corner, sat a twin bed with an old wooden headboard. She moved closer, shining the light over a faded quilt laced with webs. Someone used to sleep here, she was certain, close to the cradle.

Close to the baby?

The cradle creaked then, swaying ever so slightly, yanking her attention to it.

Julia froze, trying to feel a draft—a breeze perhaps—coming from one of the old windows. That could explain it, couldn't it? The rocking cradle?

She lowered her gaze. The gentle sway continued, almost as if an invisible hand were rocking it. Then suddenly, it swung one more time, this time hard enough to hit the wall behind it.

Julia jumped.

A square piece of wall plaster fell to the floor beneath the hash-marks, revealing wood lath, and sending dust and bits of plaster flying. The cradle sway halted.

"What the...?" she whispered.

A hole in the wall, where the plaster had once been, called to her. Curious, she shoved the cradle out of the way and shined the flashlight into the space. The rocking cradle had knocked out a piece of the wall revealing a hidey-hole, of sorts.

She moved closer and peered inside.

Something in there.

Reaching beyond the broken plaster and behind the wood lath, she grasped an object and pulled it out, staring momentarily at a leather-bound book, dirty and covered with sticky webs and bug carcasses.

A diary?

Brushing the debris away, she ran her hand over the outside. The brittle leather crackled as she turned back the cover and revealed the first page.

The Private Life of Veronica Mills
August 1872

IT *WAS* A DIARY, OR A JOURNAL. PERHAPS THE WRITINGS OF A woman who had once lived in this house?

She looked at the bed. *In this attic?*

Turning the page, Julia began to read.

That day was the last day of my life. At least that was how it seemed then. For losing my child was the death of me. Of that, I am certain.

Pain and grief clutched at her stomach and Julia gulped in a sharp breath.

For a moment, she closed her eyes against the words.

Someone else living in this house lost a child?

She closed the diary and clenched it to her chest, holding it tight against her as she left the attic and shut herself up in her bedroom for the night.

The Private Life of Veronica Mills
   August 22, 1872

That day was the last day of my life. At least that was how it seemed then. For losing my child was the death of me. Of that, I am certain.

I shall write in this book, this diary, because I must. I have no one to talk to, no one to share my hurt and anguish, no one to wallow in pain with, save myself. I write because it is what I can do. It is what I do. My husband stole my writing world from me years ago when we married. No reputable married woman writes for a newspaper, he had said. And that was that.

But I shall tell my story here, within these pages, until I cannot. And then. Well. Then it will be done, I suppose.

While my story began long before, I shall start with the day we set out for Lakeland.

Fear filled my heart and dread bit into my throat as we approached that shadow of death, the specter known as Lakeland, an asylum for the deplorables. Or so they say. Lurking over us, its black windows bore down with the same vacant stare as its inhabitants. I could only suppose that, for I had never known anyone who resided there. Its twin turrets spiked into the clear August sky, as if they could prick open a bit of Heaven in a fruitless effort at escape. Because death, I was certain, was the only way to elude the asylum's clutches.

This atrocity, this cold dark place beckoned. This horrible place where I was about to do a cold dark deed—a deed that I did not want to do.

The horses carried us closer, and the carriage shimmied with every step. We drew nearer to the thing that would devour what I treasured more than life itself. This cavern of insanity, which represented greed and indignity and all that is wrong in my world, would snatch life from my very soul and hold me hostage for the remainder of my days.

I knew this. And I was as certain of that fact as I was of my husband's obsession with power, wealth, and greed.

I remember turning, looking at him. Studying him.

The brim of my hat sheltered my face from the hot afternoon sun slanting through the covered carriage, but I could see him clearly, staring at him covertly as he drove the horses.

I looked past his nose and fixed my gaze on the fringes hanging from the roof, shifting back and forth in rhythm with the clippety-clop of the massive horse's hooves. Transfixed, I found it odd that I would study those glittered strings so closely at a time that moved me toward impending torment and a potential life full of pity and regret.

I suppose having something mundane to concentrate on was normal, under the circumstances.

I realized that I truly did not know my husband. Does a woman ever know the man she betroths? Married six years, he swept me off my feet, promised me the moon and then some, and now—

Now, looking at him staring straight ahead, his gaze trained over the horses' heads as they made their way up this desolate dirt road, I knew that I hated him.

And would always.

He was all business. Approaching our life, and this encroaching selfish act, as though it were a contract to be signed or a purchase to be made. My stomach roiled and I shifted my gaze away in disgust.

Little James, our son, whimpered from the back, nestled in the arms of, Matilda, his nursemaid. I glanced behind to stare upon his angelic face, fixing my gaze upon him much like my husband's resolve to complete the quest laid out before us.

"Give him to me," I had told Matilda, my voice soft. I had not wanted to disturb my husband. His head jerked at my request but he said not a word. He would not deny me this, surely?

Matilda nodded and asked if I was certain.

"Absolutely. Let him come here." I reached for my child.

She scooted closer to the edge of her seat, and we moved him over the back to the front while the horses clip-clopped on. He was a heavy child for four years of age, but we managed, and I cradled him in my arms—my gaze playing over his bright blue moon-shaped eyes, plump cheeks, wide forehead, and hair a soft golden sheen upon his damp head.

Oh, how I loved this boy with all my being….

August was brutal in Kentucky and the humidity on this day, so close to the river, was horrid. Little James fussed and squirmed, drool pooling in the corner of his mouth.

"Muh…muh."

My heart clutched, taking in his little voice, remembering the ring of how it echoed in the stark hallway of our home, rebounding off the hardwood cherry floors, pealing off the polished wood, bouncing up to my ears. How many times had I heard that same "muh…muh?" And how many times had my dear husband cringed at the sound, turning his head, and instructing me to deal with whatever nuisance had to be dealt with at that time.

No more.

But the child was not a nuisance. Not to me. Only to my husband. And besides, we had Matilda.

Little James reached for my hat. I let him drag it from my hair, pins falling, my locks tumbling loose and settling around my shoulders. I did not care. It was not a problem.

My husband barked my name in warning. *Veronica.*

My gaze rose to him and met his with a sneer. I did not care what he thought. Not at this time, not this day. Not anymore. He would not control this, this one last small mess our son was making. "It is fine," I said to him. "I will not embarrass you."

Without a word, he looked back to the horses.

"Nor will he," I added.

He grunted.

I never wore my hair down. It was not acceptable at this time in my life nor in my circles. I did not care. Who would see me this day? No one, save the insane. Save my husband and the nanny.

Save little James, my love.

I did not care.

Precious boy. I bent to place a kiss upon his innocent head, my heart growing increasingly heavy with sorrow as the distance grew shorter. Blood hammered within my veins, pooling inside of my chest, pounding against the inner walls of my being. Lancing me with fear, trepidation, and guilt.

I squeezed him. I squeezed my boy, and the tears came.

I held him so close. I breathed in his gentle, sweet musk. I ran my lips over his baby-fine hair. I kissed the tender sweet spot behind his ear.

I took him all in. Tasted of him. His smell. Willing my senses to imprint on every detail. The feel of his chubby wrists between my thumb and forefinger. The sweaty mess of hair at his temples and nape.

I held him so close that he whimpered and—

The horses cut to the right. We clipped toward the structure, dark and unseemly and massive. People milled about. Slowly ambling. Staring. In various stages of dress, or undress... Some dirty, some crying, all watching....

We stopped and my husband touched my arm. *It is time.*

I had never before experienced the kind of terror I felt at that moment. My throat ached to scream, my soul wretched from inside my body, my heart pumped wildly in my chest. It beat so violently I feared it might burst, killing me dead on the spot—and perhaps that might have been welcome—as the pounding raced up and into my ears, my head, causing dizziness and nausea all at once.

"No," I said to my husband. The word came from somewhere low and guttural and didn't sound like me at all.

"Now, Veronica."

"No!"

I screamed and clutched my baby tighter. I recall the words rushing out of my mouth in desperation.

"No, please. Herbert, please..." I begged. "I cannot do this. I cannot give him over. I will care for him, like I always have. I can keep him, and no one would know. We can build a better space in the attic. An entire suite. Matilda will stay and care for him there. She said she would. No, please Herbert, do not make me do this. He is my one, my only child. There will be no others, you know this. Herbert, my heart is breaking apart inside of me. If I am forced to do this, I will from this day never be the same. I beg of you, my husband. I beg of you...."

His finger went to my lips. A soft touch, but firm. Silencing. A message. His eyes bore a solid glare into mine. "You will do this with dignity, Veronica."

Dignity! How dare he?

The man has ripped the last shred of dignity from my very existence.

I sniveled, echoing the soft cry from the boy in my arms. This was not a puppy, chosen on a whim! Decided to be a nuisance and turned into the streets! This was a baby. *Our* baby.

My baby.

My gaze fell to James' sweet face, bloated now from the heat and the long ride into the country. Soft. Innocent. Four years old and still such a babe. But smart. Oh yes, he was smart. I could tell that. A mother can tell these things.

My baby. Mine.

"Take him, Matilda," he barked.

I clutched James tighter to my chest. *No, no, no, no, no...* Tears ran hot down my cheeks. I rocked back and forth, his sweaty chubby forehead flush against my damp chest.

"Muh...muh...."

My soul cracked.

"Mum... Let me."

Matilda. At my side, outside the carriage. I look up, the terror in her deep brown eyes matching the heartache in mine. My leaden arms lifted the child. My brain spun, my head tight, my thoughts incoherent.

"I will do it, Mum. Let me. You stay here. I will take care of him."

And then she was gone. He was gone.

My baby. My little Jimmy....

He was out of my hands, my arms. My soul.

My life.

My love... Gone.

Matilda took him. *Took him*. And Herbert followed her up the mountain of steps, and through the closing double doors, swallowing them into the black depths of the asylum.

They took him. My baby, she...he...took him.

An otherworldly scream curled and wrenched from my mouth, my throat, and echoed off the monstrosity of brick and wood and staring, glassy-eyed, windows.

Mocking me.

We have him, the house said. *He is ours now. Ours. You won't see him again. He belongs to us.*

Glancing about, I saw the people. Still there. Watching.

Staring at me.

He is one of them now. One of them.

Make sure they know his name. His name is James.

Eleven

Louisville
  283 days sober

SHE HATED FUCKING FUNERALS.

Her grandmother died when Julia was seventeen. She'd refused to go to the funeral. All she could remember of funerals when she was younger were people lying in coffins, looking pasty and plastic, like mannequins at the department store—or worse, like those wax figures she'd seen once on vacation in a museum in the Smokey Mountains.

She didn't want to remember her grandmother that way.

So, she didn't—rebelling against her mother's ultimatum and preferring instead to memorialize her grandmother in her own way, in her own head and heart. She didn't want to remember plastic Gran, she wanted to remember the alive and vibrant person whom she loved, and who loved her unconditionally.

When she was barely six years old, Denise had forced her to look at her dead uncle during the viewing, which had not only scared her, but scarred her for life. Good God, her mother was an idiot. She'd only been a child.

And today, she didn't want to see Gretchen laid out in the coffin like she was, either—but here she was, staring down at her, Larry at her side holding her hand. Whoever worked behind the funeral home scene to make dead people look pleasant, had done a really nice job with Gretchen.

"God, she was pretty," Julia muttered. She was way too thin, of course, but she could see how pretty Gretchen likely was when she was younger. How old was she anyway? Mid-twenties, perhaps? The drugs and booze had aged her. She could have been younger.

"Yes, she was," Larry said. He sniffled and she looked over at him, studying his profile. His eyes were red-rimmed and swollen. He'd cried all morning since they'd met for coffee. He shared how Gretchen had introduced herself at his first AA meeting, teasing him about loosening up, and making him feel comfortable.

Finished with their coffee, they headed into a meeting, and not long after that, the service. Larry's wife hadn't wanted to come, saying she didn't see how it was necessary for him to go either. That dead girl couldn't possibly mean anything to him, could she?

Obviously, Larry's wife was part of his problem.

"I'm glad they put long sleeves on her." The words were out of her mouth before she realized it, but those were her thoughts. At least the sleeves covered the tracks in her arms, giving her a little dignity.

"I don't know why she started using again. I wish I knew." Larry leaned closer, almost resting against her. He was a tall man but not heavy. Still, the weight of his body on her shoulder was a little pressing and somewhat annoying. She wanted him to stand up on his own two feet, buck up and be strong.

Like she was trying to do.

Hell, it's hard, Julia. Cut the guy some slack.

"Let's go," she whispered. "There are people in line behind us." She lied, in a way, because there were only two other people in the entire room, a man and a woman. And while they were, indeed, both standing behind him, she wasn't sure there was any sort of line, or if they were waiting.

Larry glimpsed her way and agreed. She put an arm around his back and led him toward the exit. Geez. Why the fuck did she always have to be the strong one? The nurturer?

When the hell would someone nurture her?

Good God, Julia. Mark had always been that someone. Don't you get it? You pushed him away, forced him and his caring spirit to leave you, citing that you wanted to be alone and do things on your own...and now you want the comfort of someone to lean on back in your life?

She shoved her inner voice away and concentrated on leaving.

"Thank you for coming." A thin, female voice called out. Julia halted and turned. A woman, one of the pair standing behind them at the casket, stepped toward her, smiling. "Her friends all disappeared over the past few years. How did you know my daughter?"

Gretchen's mother? Julia immediately grasped the resemblance. Same body build, high cheek bones, wide-set eyes. Dressed casually in denim jeans, a black scoop-neck sweater, and black sandals, the woman's long brown hair was swept back and caught up in a messy ponytail. Julia guessed the woman was not much older than herself.

Shit. Am I old enough to be Gretchen's mother?

Turning, she fully faced the woman, holding out her hand. "I'm Julia, this is my friend, Larry."

She shook Julia's hand, her grip weak. "I'm Bernice Holder."

"We met Gretchen at an AA meeting." She watched Bernice's eyes. "Several months ago."

"I see."

Larry cleared his throat. "We don't know why she did it. I thought she was better."

A long sigh exited Bernice's throat. "She's been off and on clean for the past ten years. Since she was about fourteen. It's been a long road for her." She glanced at the casket. "But her journey is over now."

Julia grasped the woman's hand again and squeezed. "Bernice, I am so sorry for your loss. We cared for her. Truly, we did. And she was trying."

Staring off, Bernice blinked a couple of times and bobbed her head. "She could be very determined in the beginning, but something always got hold of her. Depression, I think. I tried everything. I'm sort of numb, to be honest. I don't know what to do next."

"Do you have other children?"

"Yes. Two. One older, one younger than Gretchen."

"Then focus there."

"I have grandkids too."

"There you go."

"I'll never forget her."

"No, of course you won't. We won't either."

Larry stood silent beside them but gave Bernice a smile. Julia could tell he was about ready to fall apart. "We will be on our way. Again, we're so sorry."

Bernice didn't say anything else but lowered her gaze and headed back to the man waiting near the casket. Then she stopped and looked back. "Thanks for being kind to her. I honestly don't know if you were, or not, because I'd not spoken to her in over a year, but you're both here now and that is kind—so I'm assuming you were nice."

Tears burst into Julia's eyes, and she whispered, "She was kind to us."

Larry choked back a sob.

"Let's go," she whispered, grasping him by the elbow and moving him forward. When they passed over the threshold of the funeral home and stepped out into the fresh air, she said, "Time to get the fuck out of Dodge before we both lose it."

AFTER SPENDING AN HOUR TALKING WITH HIM IN THE CAR, she dropped Larry off at his downtown office, and drove straight to Cave Hill, winding her way through the cemetery toward the baby's grave. Funny how one death made you think of others.

She searched for the hawk as she drove, not finding him. Maybe he'd soar by later, or perhaps, that time she'd seen him, was the only time she would. Maybe he wasn't there any longer. Do hawks migrate or stay in one area? She didn't know.

Besides, it was summer. Migrating doesn't usually happen in the summer. Right?

Seeing him might have lent comfort, in some curious way.

Locating the willow tree ahead, she parked a few grave sites away. The day was hot, humid, and the late afternoon sun beat down on the headstones, reflecting off the shiny surfaces. Julia stepped up to the baby's grave and sat on the concrete bench, facing the grave marker. Perspiration ran down her nose.

August was brutal in Kentucky and the humidity on this day was horrid. Veronica's words, from the diary.

Horrid. Indeed.

It was all horrid. A fucking nightmare, to be exact.

She stared at the engravings in the stone for several long minutes, pondering....

Infant Salinger-Shepherd
June 12, 2020
Child of Julia E. Salinger and Mark L. Shepherd

"FUCK, MELINDA."

Abruptly, she stood, sprinted back to her car, grabbed her purse and rummaged through it, then returned to the grave marker with a sharp permanent marker in hand. Without hesitation, she scribbled across the headstone, striking out some words and adding others on the slick stone.

Infant Caroline Emilia Salinger-Shepherd
June 12, 2020
Child Daughter of Julia E. Salinger and Mark L. Shepherd

SHE STOOD BACK, LOOKING AT WHAT SHE'D DONE.
Mark will be furious.

It didn't matter. What was done was done and she didn't do it for Mark, she did it for herself.

"There you fucking go, Melinda. The baby has a name. Are you proud of me yet?" A name. An identity. She was a person, a child. Their child. And she had a name.

She wasn't sure whether that made her hurt more or helped.

Make sure they know her name. Her name is Caroline.

SHE RECALLED VERONICA'S WORDS.

Even though she'd only read one passage, Veronica's writing had haunted Julia for several days. She felt the woman soul deep. Reading her words conjured up emotions she wasn't sure she wanted to face head on. Yet, the passage, while horrible, was almost a comfort.

Someone else living in my house felt the same pain as me—more than a century earlier.

Abruptly, the call of the hawk overhead caught her attention and drew her gaze upward into the pale blue sky. There. Soaring and circling overhead. Calling out.

To her?

For prey?

What did it matter? He was beautiful, and for some reason, she longed to be like him. Soaring above everything else. Free and unencumbered. Not a care in the world, except, perhaps, snagging prey and finding a meal.

Wouldn't that be a lovely existence? To simply meet the basic needs of life and be done with all the rest? Is life ever like that for humans?

She was certain it was not.

Maybe in death, yes.

But in life, we create our own stressors. What have we done to ourselves?

Gretchen was free now, wasn't she? And Caroline. Her baby was free too.

Neither of them will face the horrors of living any longer—whatever those horrors may be or would have been.

Had Gretchen intentionally taken her life? Had she needed to soar? Like the hawk?

Sometimes bearing life's burdens is simply too much.

Like Veronica— *...losing my child was the death of me. Of that, I am certain.*

Had losing the baby—losing Caroline—been the death of her too?

Was her life—or the life she once knew—over? Was *that* the death that had proved difficult to get past? The death of the future she'd wanted? The future she and Mark had planned together?

Was that what she was mourning now, and not the loss of her child?

While she knew that loss would always be inside her, the grief would continue to take its toll occasionally—suddenly, the loss felt altered.

Her future, while not what she'd planned, perhaps, would be different.

The hawk cried out once more with a lengthy squawk, then dove toward the ground. As he descended, growing closer to his prey, claws flexed and stretched, he snatched up a screaming chipmunk.

Nailed it.

And soared back up into the sky.

Life would never be so simple. And perhaps, it wasn't meant to be.

ONCE HOME, JULIA WAS GLAD TO FIND THE HOUSE EMPTY. She was not in the mood for peopling.

There'd been only one guest the night before—a woman who stayed frequently when she had work in town—and she was gone for the day. Pam had left a note on the kitchen island saying she'd gone out for a few groceries.

Setting her keys and purse aside, she ambled through the house, stopping briefly at the bottom of the massive staircase, looking up, then slowly made her way toward the third floor. Perhaps a nap was in order.

As she moved onto the third-floor landing, she focused on the door at the opposite end—the door to the attic room. With a sigh, she closed her eyes briefly, and remembered that night a few days ago.

She had avoided reading the journal since the night she found it, not yet ready to learn more. Julia had experienced every word of Veronica's account of losing her boy, felt every terrifying emotion. The parallel between her life and Veronica's—both losing a child—was too coincidental to ignore though for very long.

She needed to find out more.

Who was Veronica Mills? When had she lived here? Was Julia sleeping in Veronica's bedroom? Was Veronica's ghost, or spirit, still hanging around, waiting for someone to communicate with? Continue to tell her story?

Was she that person?

Perhaps she should do some research—she and Mark had talked about that when they first bought the home. They'd thought it might be interesting to put the history and some stories of the house together for guests to read—or perhaps it would make good content for the website.

She wasn't sure that this day—the day of Gretchen's funeral—was the right day to read more. Seeing the girl laid out like that had shaken her. Larry's reaction worried her almost as much. She wasn't sure he was going to make it.

Be strong, Julia. Be strong for him. He may need you.

But what about her? Who was strong for her?

Her insides churned with the reality of what substance abuse can do to a person, how it can change and alter the brain chemistry. Bernice, Gretchen's mom, held the look of a parent in shock—blank, hollow eyes, filled with disbelief—and she wondered if her parents ever looked like that thinking about her, when she was binging and out of control.

Of course, she hadn't died. And she hadn't abused alcohol for years. Gretchen, according to her mother, had had a problem for over a decade. Julia wasn't like that. And, she had conquered her evils—at least the ones related to bourbon and tequila.

She had plenty of other evils to conquer, but she would get there.

Wouldn't she?

THE PRIVATE LIFE OF VERONICA MILLS
August 23, 1872

That day I died a thousand deaths.

I recall clutching at my hair, pulling out fists full of strands, sobbing and fighting toward... Something. I know not what. Or away... Away from the anguish, the turmoil running amok inside my chest.

I rocked, thrashed, the carriage jostling with my thrusts. My screams, piercing.

The horses nickered, side-stepped, once and again.

My baby. Gone.

God, what have I done to deserve this?

The carriage shook with Herbert's weight as he slid back inside and picked up the reins.

I rotated my body to look at him, my gaze boring straight through him, my stomach churning. I feared my bowels would give relief and I would soil myself. I willed control. I knew if I could look back at my own face at that moment, it would be wild-eyed with fury.

"It is done," he said, and slapped the reins on the horse's rumps.

My screams went mute. The people stopped staring. They went on about their useless days. Wandering. Was that the course of my life now? To simply go on with my useless day? Mute and dumb and obedient?

My stomach roiled again.

As the horses led us away, I recall a bell whispering in the distance. There was a church on the edge of town closest to Lakeland. Perhaps the peal of the bell was wafting over the barren fields that surrounded this monstrous place, keeping people out and people inside. Its soft ringing lent a subtle contrast to the noise and chatter colliding in my head and my heart, and I held onto that sound, my eyes closed as I listened, trying to place myself somewhere other than where I was at that moment.

It was then I registered that Matilda was no longer with us.

Herbert nickered to the horses, and they picked up speed, turning back out toward the long dirt road that brought us to this horrid place. The fringe on the surrey resumed its swish-swash, keeping time with the clip-clop of horse's hooves.

I asked my husband about Matilda.

He uttered not a word.

"Matilda?" I queried again.

I wanted to look back at the place, at the front steps that I saw before. I wanted to look to see if my boy was there, waving back at me, saying, "Buh... Muh muh...."

I wanted. But didn't.

Where was Matilda?

I grasped Herbert's forearm. "Matilda." I said her name again, and with more force.

"She stayed. She will take care of your boy."

My boy. Yes, James was never your boy, Herbert.

My heart lit on fire. Matilda stayed. I left.

She stayed and I left.

She stayed.

And I left.

What kind of woman am I?

I have forever lost my boy, leaving him behind like some useless, broken piece of existence that no one wanted. Except me. And obviously, Matilda.

I still want him to this day, and that will never cease.

"I gave them a good sum of money," Herbert told me, interrupting my still-frenzied thoughts. His eyes locked, once again, on the horse's heads. "They usually don't take them that young, but the funds were convincing enough, plus Matilda. He will be fine. This is best."

My child—my only child—was left behind because my husband was worried about the neighbors' opinions, about the cost of caring for him, about how the image didn't fit for a fine businessman of his caliber. A nuisance child. A man of his prominence, a banker, didn't need a nuisance child underfoot.

Left him behind because with him, we were not the perfect couple, the perfect people.

Matilda.

Oh, God save her. She stayed.

JULIA LIFTED HER EYES FROM THE YELLOWED PAPER AND LET go of a long pent-up breath. It was as if she'd been holding it the entire time she read the passage. While her heart ached for Veronica, she wasn't sure if she could read more. Yet, she felt compelled to know more about this mysterious woman of over a century ago, who seemed to be the only other person who understood her pain.

Was that odd? Of course, it was.

Still, she settled back against her pillows and turned the page....

SEPTEMBER 24, 1872

I don't remember any more of that fateful day, other than the torturous ride home, sitting slack-faced and slack-handed in the carriage, my brain spent and my heart devoid of everything as we headed back to our lovely home, and lovely life, in a lovely city....

And the hell I would put Herbert and myself through for years to come.

For you see, this all happened weeks ago. I'm finally able to put words to paper because I have resigned myself to my fate. I know how my story will end.

In time.

For many days after my cruel husband forced me to hand over my baby, I lay in my bed in our suite, curled into my side, staring out at the floral pattern of the wallpaper on my bedroom wall. I stared so long that the lilac petals meshed into small lavender-colored masses, and then for some odd reason, all at once, a single blossom would pop out from the wall, like it had a life of its own. I'd study it. The fine details of its petals. The delicate lines and curves of each watercolor brush stroke.

I promise that I could smell its fragrance.

I would lay there until my husband came to get me, barking up the stairwell. Forcing me to get dressed and look presentable in case we had callers.

I hated him then and I hate him now.

But no matter. I shall have the last say.

JULIA SUCKED IN A BREATH AND HELD IT UNTIL HER LUNGS hurt.

I can't read any more.

Words dodged the tears in her eyes, unable to focus any longer. Her heart broke for Veronica—and for herself. They'd both suffered. Hadn't they? In the same way.

I have resigned myself to my fate.

I know how my story will end.

I shall have the last say.

What the fuck did Veronica do?

Closing the journal, she tucked it into the drawer of her nightstand, beside her bed. The emotion of the passage weighed heavy on her heart.

"I can't do this anymore," she whispered.

She stared blankly at the wall opposite her bed. The one with the curls of ripped rose wallpaper falling from above, revealing the lilac paper beneath, unleashing the subtle perfume of lilac—even if it was only in her head.

It was the same wallpaper Veronica stared at when she was in just as much pain as she had been.

If only the chaos in her head, her heart, in her gut, would go away.

Had Veronica felt that way, too? Of course she had.

The aroma wafted beneath her nostrils, then, and she closed her eyes, savoring the sweetness. It called out. Felt like home. Comfort. Luring her to a place where she didn't have to think of crying babies and overdosed friends and ghosts of grieving women.

Of babies taken away before their time.

Of husbands who didn't understand.

She inhaled, taking the scent deep into her lungs. She could taste it, feel its warmth.

It wasn't lilac.

It was bourbon.

Twelve

Hours later, Julia woke with a repetitive sharp pounding on her bedroom door and a man's voice yelling through the thick wood. The jackhammer inside her head rivaled the banging on the door.

Where the hell was she? Oh, the bedroom.

"Julia! Open up or I'm breaking the damn lock."

Grimacing, she pushed herself up from laying on her stomach and into a semi-sitting position, hair falling over her face, her brain spinning. "What?" She could barely speak.

The door came crashing inward and Mark lurched into the room.

She looked at him, unflinching. "What...the fuck?"

He took one look at her and shook his head. "Good God, Julia. You look like hell."

"I had a shit day yesterday."

Pam peered into the room, standing in the hallway behind Mark, looking worried.

Realization crept over her. Gradually she angled her gaze toward her bedside table. The time was seven-fifteen. "Shit. Breakfast."

She tried to stand, then fell dizzily back into the bed.

Lifting her gaze, she noticed the half empty bottle of Woodford Reserve on her dresser, standing like a lone soldier facing the dawn, and reflecting a stream of sunlight in the amber liquid. Alongside the bottle lay an empty highball glass, tipped on its side.

Mark took a step toward the bed. "No. Just stay there. Don't go downstairs. Take a shower and get sober if you can. Stay the fuck out of sight until we get the guests taken care of—Pam and I will handle it and we only have forty-five minutes to pull it off. Then after breakfast, you and I, sweetheart, are having a long talk. I'm not going to let you run this business into the ground."

The business. Sure, Mark. Great. But what about me?

With that, he left the room, slamming the door behind him. The brass doorknob rattled and came loose, dangling from the door.

"Shit." Julia closed her eyes, exhaled, and fell back onto the bed. "Fuck, fuck, fuck."

Tuckaway Bay

Thirteen

Late July
Tuckaway Bay, the Outer Banks
10 days sober

"Hi. I'm Julia, and I'm an alcoholic, only ten days sober right now. I recently relapsed, so I'm happy to join your group today."

It was six o'clock in the morning and she had driven all night to reach Tuckaway Bay, but wanted to stop in for a meeting before she headed over to the Sea Glass Inn. Fortunately, a quick Internet search on her phone, and her GPS led her to an AA meeting at a church and this group. She'd arrived about an hour early, so she'd napped in the car, waiting until it was closer to time and other people had arrived.

"Welcome to the Sunrise Group, Julia. We're glad you are here."

She flashed a fake grin and bounced her gaze about the room. "Thanks. I was 283 days sober until a couple of weeks ago. I had one bad night—a very bad night—followed by a difficult week. My home is in Kentucky, but I have friends here, so instead of rehab, which I have done before, I'm opting for beach therapy."

The group leader, a young man, likely in his early thirties, smiled. "The beach cures a lot of ails for some, and for others, makes things worse. For most, the salt, sea, and surf can be healing, I think we'd all agree. Regardless, we're here if you need us. Are you staying on the island long?"

She nodded. "At least until the end of the month. Or as long as it takes."

"We look forward to getting to know you better," he said. "I'm Bill, by the way. I'm also the pastor of this church and a recovering alcoholic myself."

"Oh, that's funny." She laughed a little, then explained. "Sorry. Not laughing at you. My sponsor back home is named Bill, too."

"Well then, it's all good. Isn't it? Just like home." His gaze skipped over the people in the room. "Anyone else have anything to share?"

Several people took turns and while she heard them, she really didn't comprehend a word they were saying. The drone of their voices, however, was comforting. She needed this. Needed grounding. Staring at the floor, she closed her eyes momentarily and just listened as Bill launched into the day's topic—freedom through sobriety.

Freedom. Isn't that what she longed for in a way?

She had a month to get her shit together. Mark had given her an ultimatum.

Fourteen

Sea Glass Inn Resort
13 days sober

THE PORCH OF GULL COTTAGE FACED THE OCEAN, AND FROM where she sat, watching the tumbling surf and the drifting clouds, a few sun-soaked beachgoers and a lone fisherman, the porch was a damn good place to be. There were six cottages attached to the Sea Glass Inn Resort, with the Gull situated closest to the ocean at the far end of the property. It suited her needs—quiet, off the beaten path, and a short walk to the surf—the most isolated of the cottages Lia had to offer.

Perfect.

The waves, whether in the early morning or late at night, were her salvation. Her constant.

A cup of coffee and the sunrise started her morning—a glass of sparkling water with a wedge of lime ended her day.

Everyday. Routine.

And she needed it.

While she'd had her Louisville routine—which had been her salvation—this was unlike the habits she'd created there. While the home regimen was rigid, the beach day was laid back and well, lazy. It only took her a day to fall into it, to give into it.

Wake. Coffee. Take a walk. Lunch. Nap. Dinner. Lime spritzer.

In between, she spied on her world from the Gull's porch.

Except for Wednesday, the day she went to her morning sunrise meeting.

Truth be told, her beach routine—which was likely no different than most anyone else's beach vacation day—was perhaps better described as a frivolous period of time seeking sun and surf, a temporary getaway in the late summer.

Or was it an escape?

Am I running away?

Of course, I am. In some respects.

Or am I running toward something?

She wasn't sure, but would ponder that later. While she was still in that space in between, she strived to find out what was waiting for her on the other side.

She'd slept, walked the shore, looked for shells and rare pieces of sea glass, but didn't venture too far from the cottage. In fact, she'd become a bit of a hermit, staying within the confines of her temporary home. But right now, she had little tolerance for other human beings—she was not in the right frame of mind for peopling with strangers.

Her AA meetings were the only exception—the only reason she left the resort.

At Lia's insistence, she'd arranged for daily room service. Late every afternoon, one of the staff placed a covered picnic basket full of goodies on her porch. Besides dinner, the basket held pastries and juice for breakfast the next morning, and a sandwich and fruit, or veggies and dip for lunch. Lia was a good friend.

Pampering was probably the last thing she needed, though—what she likely needed was a good swift kick in the ass—but she let Lia have at it. Thank God she'd had the wherewithal to ask her not to tell Alice that she'd arrived early. Beach week was three weeks away, and she needed the time alone before being with the girls. Their week together had historically been a week of drinking and bitching—beach therapy, they called it

—and right now, she wasn't prepared for either. She needed solitude to work through everything inside her head.

Alice always mucked up the waters, and she didn't need her mother-henning right now. And then, of course, there was Maggie. If Maggie even showed up. The twins were a lost cause—since no one had heard from them since last summer.

Regardless, the chatter in her head had mostly calmed. The all-consuming clutter of advice-giving voices, telling her what she should do, had dissipated. The time to decompress was essential—the doubts and nagging questions silenced. For the time being, at least.

She hoped.

Since her arrival three days earlier, she'd slept with the windows open, daring the universe to interrupt her co-existence with the sea, refusing to put even a pane of glass between herself and the pounding pulse of the ocean. Subliminally, she absorbed the repetitive tempo, and likened it to some sort of tribal drumbeat—perhaps designed to put her thoughts on a steady course, and her mind on an even keel.

Whatever, it was working.

She should have done this long ago. She loved the feeling of being free and unencumbered—like the hawk at Cave Hill—and oddly, she also felt safe and secure.

Was that it? The feeling of no responsibility that made her so relaxed?

Why had she waited so long to get back to Tuckaway Bay?

It wasn't that Lia hadn't urged her to come anytime she wanted, or that Alice hadn't invited her on numerous occasions over the past year. They both had. The problem had been then, and still remained, that she had shit to do.

One can't live the carefree beach life forever. Can one?

Tell that to Lia.

The fact remained, however—that she'd had work to do in Louis-ville. Still did. At the inn. With Mark. On herself, of course. The AA meetings. With Melinda.

Maggie had tested her resolve. Gretchen's death had shaken her. And Nick and her mother? They meant well, but....

And then, of course, Veronica.

The thought of the elusive Veronica sent a shimmy into her gut. The passages she'd read the night of her binge had shaken her. Taken its toll. The one that made her reach for the bourbon, consciously knowing she would suffer the consequences later.

She hadn't slipped. Drinking the bourbon was intentional and she had relished the taste and the aftereffects.

And while the world she'd left behind in Louisville would remain, would probably never really be done—and maybe it shouldn't be—she had to focus on just one thing.

The work she had to do now, here, at the beach, was inside her head. *Time to get that screwed on straight.*

The waves helped.

"Julia?"

Pulling her bare feet off the top rail of the porch, she sat up in the wooden chair and turned toward the voice. Lia rounded the cottage next door and walked up the path toward her, waving and smiling.

The beach life suited her friend and Julia had to grin back. Lia had taken her time figuring out her life, and it had ended up nothing like what she'd thought, but Julia knew Lia was exactly where she needed to be. Owning and running the Sea Glass Inn with her husband, Zach, and her college-aged daughter, Belle, must literally be a dream come true.

She looked happy.

Julia wanted that kind of happiness, too.

Standing, she gave her friend a smile.

Lia stepped up onto the porch and out of the sun, swiping her forehead with the back of her hand. "Whew. It's hot already and it's barely ten o'clock. Looks like this week is going to be a scorcher." She cocked her head toward Julia. "You doing okay? Need anything?"

"Actually, I think I want something cold to drink. You? Let's go inside."

"Fine by me."

They went inside and Julia headed toward the kitchenette. "Water or soda?"

"Ice water would be perfect."

"Coming up."

She retrieved crushed ice from the refrigerator and topped it off with ice-cold water, handing Lia the glass. She repeated the process for herself. Lia wandered into the living area and after setting her water on the coffee table, plopped onto the sofa. "It's been a morning already. I had to escape for a little peace and quiet. I hope you don't mind."

Julia smiled. "I never mind spending time with you. You're the most normal of all my girlfriends."

Lia laughed. "I'm not sure about that."

"Well, I am." She chuckled too and sat in a rattan chair facing Lia. "So, a bad morning?"

"Just busy."

"Does Zach help?"

Lia sat up and grasped her drink. "Oh, he's a great help. He manages the restaurant and oversees the maintenance of all the properties—that's the resort and all the rentals too—which is a full-time job for anyone. Belle oversees the hotel staff, cleaning, and such. And I manage the rest, things like reservations and event booking—you know, all the peopley stuff."

"Which means you pick up the slack everywhere."

"Basically."

"We had a snafu in the kitchen this morning—some of the staff didn't come in—and Zach was out with the renovation crew at Tequila Sunrise. I managed to get enough staff in on their day off to cover but it took me a couple of hours of calling to find them. Some days...."

Julia studied her. "Would you rather be back in Chicago securing ancient pottery for a stuffy old museum that no one goes to for a meager salary and no hope of advancement?"

"Or advancement I didn't want?" Lia laughed. "Oh, hell no. Been there, done that. And give up the beach? Not a chance."

"You love it here, don't you."

"I simply love it, Julia. I never dreamed my life could be so full."

Her heart swelled with joy for Lia, and she almost choked up. *Could my next chapter be as happy?* "I'm delighted for you, my friend."

Lia grinned and held her gaze. Reaching out, she grasped her hand. "Your life will be good again, too, one day soon. I'm sure of it."

"Well, I'm not so sure, but thanks."

"You want to talk?" Lia searched her eyes. "I'm not rushing you by any means."

Julia fixed her gaze on her friend. While Lia knew she'd needed to get out of Louisville, and wanted to be left alone, Julia had not shared the details. "I do have a confession to make."

Lia lifted a brow. "Oh?"

"I broke one of your rules. I've been sleeping with the doors unlocked and the windows open."

Her face screwed up. "Julia! I told you not to do that. While it's relatively safe around here, you just never know about people these days."

Lia always erred on the side of caution, which made Julia smile.

She, on the other hand, occasionally liked to take a risk.

If someone wanted to get her, so be it.

"I'll keep all that in mind, but I seriously doubt the boogie man is going to get me."

Lia stared toward the window. After a minute she rose and stepped closer to it, looking out. "Julia, are you okay?" Her gaze darted back and forth as she scanned the beach. "I'm worried about you."

Are you avoiding eye contact, my friend, to make it easier for me? Or you?

Lia was her fair-minded friend—and always the friend who was available. Scooting to the edge of the chair, Julia leaned forward. "Yes, well, not exactly okay, but things will get better."

"Mark called. He wanted to know if you had arrived."

"I see." She stood, nervous energy getting the best of her.

"He's worried."

"And what else did he say?"

Lia turned, facing her. "Just that you needed the getaway."

Nodding, she agreed. "Well, he got that right."

Lia took a couple of steps, maintaining eye contact. Her voice softened and she asked, "Are you drinking again?"

Shit. "Okay, look. I'll tell you but please keep this between the two of us. Especially not Alice. Not yet. All right?"

"Of course."

"I'm thirteen days sober, Lia. I came here instead of going to a recovery center like I did the last time. I can heal myself here. I know I can. I only need time and solitude. There was too much happening in Louisville, and I got overwhelmed."

"Oh, Julia." She rushed closer. "What happened? Seriously, we can talk about it. Are you still going to therapy?"

Lia's caring expression almost made Julia cry. "I am. I have a call with Melinda, my therapist, soon, and I'm already going to meetings here."

"Good." With a sigh, Lia grasped Julia's shoulders and gave her a tight hug. "I'm here for you, whatever you need. I hope you know that."

"I do. Right now, I need quiet, space, and no people. Except for you." She pulled back and smiled.

"I won't pry. Talk to me when you are ready. But I am a little curious about who is manning the ship back in Louisville."

That's a safe enough subject. "Mark is taking over for the month. Pam and her son, Caleb, had already moved into the carriage house. They will handle things while I'm gone."

"How long do you think you will stay?"

Julia shrugged. "As long as it takes or until you kick me out?"

"Are you serious? I would never do that."

"Kidding. I think I'll be here for the month. And I'm paying rent so charge me whatever."

Lia shook her head. "I will do no such thing."

"Then half rent? I have to pay you something. Seriously. Or I will feel rushed to leave."

Lia blew out a breath. "All right. I get it. I'll check the books and make sure this cottage is yours until you tell me it's not. Half price is fine."

"Good."

"Now, as much as I hate to say this, I need to take care of some things back in the office. You okay for now? Need anything?"

Julia smiled. "Nope. I have everything I need. I'm good."

"I hope so." Lia was still concerned, she could tell.

"I am."

Lia gave her another quick hug, softly kissed her cheek, and left. Julia stepped out onto the porch and watched her weave around the cottages and head back to the hotel. With a sigh, she sat in the wooden rocker on the porch and stared ahead at the roiling ocean.

Must be a storm offshore.

She hoped it wasn't coming for her.

She'd had forty-some days to go for a full year of sobriety—and she had been determined to get there—but had screwed that up royally.

Failed.

Best laid plans and all.

She supposed starting over wasn't that bad. Was it?

Who was she kidding? Starting over was hell.

But the beach, as they say, can be therapy.

Work your magic, beach.

SHE WOKE BEFORE SUNRISE THE NEXT MORNING, BREWED A pot of coffee, filled her travel mug, then headed for the surf. A few overhead lamps from the resort provided enough light to make her way toward the water, dodging a few ghost crabs on the sandy path between two very low dunes. With the tide heading out, she stood in the wet sand, and watched the waves break offshore. A stripe of pink-orange light eased up from the far horizon and after a moment, she decided to sit there in the sand, as close to sea level as possible, and wait.

Quietly.

Unmoving.

Waiting. Watching.

She could have spent the time contemplating her life and her circumstance—but she didn't. She simply sat and absorbed her presence in that moment.

The storm brewing last night had apparently swept out to sea. This morning, the surf was calm.

The orb gradually made its appearance, and she took it all in, the sunrise stinging her eyes so that she looked away and closed them for a minute. She knew better than to stare for long. But the colors remained, a continual altering kaleidoscope of pinks and oranges and reds and grays and purples behind her eyelids.

When she opened them again, the event was nearly over, with faded colors lingering over the horizon as if to say: *I'm gone for today but come back tomorrow. I can't promise you the same view, but I can promise it will be exceptional.*

As always.

Standing, she remained for a moment longer, looking out across the waves, then resumed her head-down stroll up the beach, looking for shells and an elusive piece of sea glass. She walked until she saw people heading her way, then reversed course, and started back toward the Gull. Occasionally, she'd stoop to pick at a small shell or fragment buried in the sand, examine it, and either tuck it into her belt bag—she refused to call it a fanny pack—or toss it back to the sea.

"Find anything interesting?"

Stopping, she looked up at a fisherman sitting in his chair, the Gull in the background. He had a couple of poles in the sand and was waiting for something to bite. She literally knew next to nothing about fishing but that's how it appeared to her.

"Not particularly, unfortunately."

He nodded. "Best shelling is in the spring, after the storms. The beaches down around Hatteras are good."

She pondered that, glancing at the sea and back again. "That makes a lot of sense." She knew there were less crowded beaches down that way.

"Ever been here in the spring?"

She studied him before responding. It was difficult to see his face in the shadows of his sunhat. "Yes. A long time ago. When I was in college."

"Ah. A college girl."

For some reason, that made her smile a little. She'd not been called a girl in a long time. He stood and reached for one of his poles, reeling in the line.

"Catch anything?" she asked.

"Just the sunrise."

Nodding, she glanced back at the horizon. "Spectacular. Wasn't it?"

"Every day."

Julia smiled. "Yes."

Angling away, she took a couple of steps toward the cottage. "Have a good day."

He ticked his head her way. "And you."

WAKING WITH A START, SHE BOLTED UPRIGHT IN BED, gasping for a breath, her heart pounding against her chest wall. She sat still for several minutes, gathering her bearings, and concentrating on slowing her breathing. The room was dark, save the beam of moonlight shooting through her window and landing across the foot of her bed. There was no sound, save the surf.

She absorbed that sound—the comfortable cadence of the sea—and attempted to align her breathing, and slow her heartbeat, to the steady pulse of the waves.

Throwing back the sheet, Julia stood and walked to the window, standing slightly off to the side, and peering out at the beach. *Ah, the moon is getting fuller.* It floated over the surf, round and gray-white, illuminating the sands in front of the cottage. The waves were kicking up, the tide rolling in, and she closed her eyes against the familiar rhythm.

Just listening.

She should go back to sleep—but the dream lingered on the fringes.

The baby crying. Swirls of floral wallpaper. The scent of lilac and bourbon intermingled. Luring her. Tempting her. Testing her?

What did it all mean? Why do these things haunt her?

Slowly turning back toward the bed, she paused, clicking on the bedside table lamp. Opening the drawer in the table, she removed the old diary, running her fingertips over the crackled leather, and sat on the edge of the bed. She'd not read from the journal since the night she'd relapsed and wasn't sure if she would read any more—still, she'd not been able to leave the thing behind.

"You and I are connected in some way," she whispered. "I can feel that, Veronica, even if I don't understand it. But right now, I don't have

THE SPACE IN BETWEEN: A NOVEL

the energy to focus on you. I have to figure out my own shit first. Then maybe...."

But what if her shit is your shit?

Her gut clutched a little at the thought. Shaking her head, she tucked the diary back in the drawer and closed it.

Out of sight, out of mind.

Fifteen

15 days sober

She watched him for three mornings straight from the shadows of her porch. She supposed he'd been out there the other days since she'd arrived, but she'd slept later then. Besides the one encounter during her walk, they'd not crossed paths again.

He arrived early, just before the sun peeked over the horizon, and set up his gear on the beach close to the water line. He accessed the area from the south, coming over from the public beach side. Since the part of the beach in front of her cottage was private and owned by the resort, she wondered if he realized he was trespassing.

Was he a local or a vacationer?

A local, she determined. His gear was well-worn, his clothes too casual, his skin too tan. He should know he was trespassing.

Her cottage was the last one in the string—the resort property ending somewhere across the dunes not too far away. And since everyone knew that climbing over the dunes was prohibited, she presumed there must be a path nearby between them for access.

Of course, there was also a line of dune fences, separating the properties, that he would also have to navigate.

Curious, she stood and leaned into the porch post, watching. He set his fishing poles upright in the tubes he'd spiked into the sand. He had one chair, a bucket, and a small cooler. Dressed in shorts and a T-shirt, he also wore the wide-brimmed hat—for sun protection, she assumed.

He'd cast his line already, the long fishing poles tossing the bait far into the surf. Once he had both baited lines in the ocean, and his poles securely positioned in their tubes, he'd lower himself to his chair, and retrieve what looked like a large coffee thermos from a side holder on the cooler.

Legs outstretched, he'd sit and scan the horizon, waiting for the jerk of his line that told him he might have a fish—and when that happened, he'd jump up, grab the pole, reel in the line, and wave the pole back and forth, while pacing forward and backward at the surf, until the fish was landed. Or not.

Most of the time, he released the fish back into the ocean.

He'd stay for a couple of hours, until the vacationers at the resort started venturing out to the sand to claim their spots for the day. Then, he would methodically gather his belongings—like he'd done it a thousand times before, and likely had—and head south again between the dunes.

On the fourth day, her observation of the angler was brief because of her sunrise AA meeting. Still, he arrived, like clockwork, and went about his business. As she left the cottage, the screen door slammed behind her, and the fisherman startled a bit and glanced her way.

He tossed back his head and threw up a hand in greeting. She gave him a nod back.

"So, you've been there nearly two weeks now, is that right? Tell me how things are going."

"Ten days." Julia adjusted her laptop screen so that the video focused on her and away from the sun streaming through the window. She could see Melinda more clearly. "It's lovely here, of course. How could it not be?"

"So, you're comfortable with not going to someplace like Healing Hope again? Or would you like for me to look for a similar recovery center near where you are staying?"

That was the last thing Julia wanted. "No. I'm fine. This was a slipup, and it won't happen again. I need rest and no responsibility right now, save taking care of myself. I promise."

"Good. I'm happy to meet with you like this as long as you like. I've counseled clients in the state before, so my license extends to North Carolina."

"Oh, that's great, Melinda. Thank you."

"Not a problem. How are you feeling?"

"Relaxed, which is good. I felt a bit discombobulated at first, with so much time on my hands, and then I decided just to go with the flow."

"Instead of being so regimented?"

"Yes."

"How does that make you feel?"

Julia thought about that. "Peaceful." She laughed. "And surprised at that."

"Not uneasy?"

"Not now. I'm used to it."

"Good." Melinda paused, jotting a few notes on her steno pad. "I assume you're not working at all. Of course, not at the inn, but what about with your father?"

Julia shook her head. "Oh no. Before I left Louisville, I called Nick and told him what happened and to either take over my two cases or hire someone. He was reluctant, insisting I could work from the beach, but I held my ground. I do not want that hanging over my head."

"That's good progress. I like the way you stood up for your needs."

That small bit of praise did her a world of good, and Julia felt a grin cross her face. "Thanks. Maybe I'm getting there."

Melinda smiled back. "What about AA?"

Julia sat back on the sofa. She could still see herself in the little window on the side of the screen. "I found a group before I got to the resort and have been going weekly. In fact, I just got back from my third meeting. It's good."

"Great. Have you been in touch with Bill?"

Julia laughed. "Turns out the guy who leads the group here is also Bill, but he's not my sponsor. Still, I think I should tag them Louisville Bill and Beach Bill."

"Good idea. Do you think you need a sponsor there?"

She shook her head. "No. Louisville Bill is on call should I need him."

"But you didn't call him the night you relapsed, did you?"

Inhaling deep, she eased the breath out slowly. "No, I didn't. I chose not to."

"I see."

"Well, I don't really."

"Do you want to talk about what happened?"

She did. But not everything. Not yet. "I felt so overwhelmed, Melinda. So much was coming at me, and I suppose I needed an escape. I thought I had a grip on it all—the inn, working for Nick, Mark—it all went to hell in a handbasket when Gretchen died, and Larry was leaning all over me for support, and then the thing with Veronica."

Melinda's head rose and she peered into the monitor. "Veronica?"

"Oh, yeah. We haven't talked about Veronica, have we?"

"I don't believe so." Melinda flipped back through her pad. "I don't see her mentioned."

Julia contemplated whether she should even go there. Why had she mentioned Veronica at all? Would she think her crazy?

"Julia?"

Again, she huffed out a breath, as if in resolution to the discussion. "I found her diary in the attic. Veronica lived in the house in 1872, I gather, and I suppose before and after."

"A diary?"

"Yes."

"Did you read it?"

"Some of it. Not all yet."

"And something about the diary disturbed you?"

Julia stared at the screen and waited. "Yes. Veronica lost a child too. In a different way but she lost her son."

Melinda didn't have an immediate response, but looked away, as if thinking. Finally, she asked, "Are you feeling a parallel in your lives?"

"Somewhat. I think that remains to be seen."

"Do you think the baby crying and the lilacs are connected?"

"I do. But I need to read more."

"Then why don't you?"

A spur of panic shimmied up her spine. "Because the last time I did, I opened the bourbon bottle and drank half of it."

"I see. I'm sure we'll need to discuss more." Melinda glanced at her watch. "We're almost out of time. Are you feeling okay with our discussion today?"

She nodded.

"Why don't you think about how you might feel if you chose to read more in the diary. Perhaps anticipate those feelings and consider what you might do...how you might counteract them. Cause and effect, in a way. If the words trigger a particular emotion, embrace it, and contemplate, then decide how to react positively."

"I will do that."

"Oh, and when is beach week with your girlfriends?"

"Last week of August. In two weeks or so."

"Are you ready?"

She shook her head. "Hell no."

"Then perhaps that's the first priority."

"Perhaps."

Melinda stared at her through the screen. "Julia, are you getting out of the cottage? Among people? Or keeping to yourself?"

Julia wondered if she could see into her head. Her expression looked like she already knew the answer to her own question. "I'm in most of the time, except for the meetings, and strolling the beach."

"I see."

"It's good for now," Julia added.

Melinda gave a nod.

"I'm sure you'll gradually expand your world, see more people. It's okay. Give yourself time and do what's comfortable."

That's what I'm doing.

"Let's talk more about that and beach week on the Friday morning call. I'll see you at nine sharp."

Julia clicked the red button to end the call. Friday, it is.

<hr/>

AFTER HER CHAT WITH MELINDA, SHE STEPPED OUT ONTO the porch, and headed for the hotel. Maybe the therapist was right. Expanding her little world here and there was probably not a bad idea. Baby steps. Right?

Besides, she was starving, and while Lia's basket had held pastries and other goodies she could have eaten this morning, she craved something hot and more substantial. Besides, she was feeling stronger and perhaps it was a good idea to get out among people, a little at a time.

As she approached The Sandcastle Restaurant, located on the first floor of the Sea Glass Inn, she sucked in a breath, and pushed the restaurant door inward.

Zach looked up from the counter and greeted her.

"Julia! So good to see you."

It was good to see him too. "Been a while, hasn't it?" She grinned and scanned the half-empty restaurant. "I thought I'd venture out for a good breakfast this morning. I hear this is the place."

"Best on the beach." He grabbed a menu and nodded to a server. "Let's get you seated. Jenn will get your coffee."

"Thanks, Zach. Wow, what a cozy atmosphere."

He smiled back. "Thank you. We love being here."

They stopped at a table with a beachside view and Zach pulled out a chair for her. "Lia seems so happy," she said.

"We're both happy." He laid the menu on the table. "I can't believe how things finally worked out."

"Well, I suppose all good things come in time. I'm just so happy for all of you."

"Me too."

The server came with a glass of ice water and coffee, then stepped back. "I'll give you a minute to look over the menu, ma'am."

"Oh, I know what I want, if it's okay with you."

"Of course. What can I get you?"

"Just two eggs scrambled. One sausage patty. And two slices of wheat toast, butter on the side."

"Coming right up. Is there anything else I can get for you now?"

Julia grinned. "No, I'm good. This black coffee is perfect." She watched the young woman head off toward the kitchen. "She's cute and very polite."

"Local girl." Zach met her gaze. "I like to hire local when I can. She's friends with Belle."

"How is Belle?"

"Flourishing. Swims every day in the pool. Her leg is getting stronger."

"Will she compete again? Perhaps in the future?" Julia realized she'd not talked with Lia lately about Belle and her accident, which had ended her college swimming career.

He shook his head. "Probably not but she seems content with that. She's pursuing other avenues." Some clatter happened in the kitchen, and he glanced that way. "I should check that out. Please let me know if you need anything and enjoy your breakfast." He headed off.

"I will. Oh, and Zach?"

He turned back. "Yes?"

"Probably none of my business but do you know about the man who fishes over by my cottage every morning?"

"Sam?"

"Is that his name?"

"Older guy? About sunrise most mornings?"

"That's him. Is he trespassing?"

Zach smiled. "No. That's Sam Watters. He knows he's welcome. Aunt Grace gave him permission to fish there years ago. He lives across town on the sound, so he drives over. Most days he's gone before anyone else hits the beach."

"Okay, well, as long as you know."

"It's all good, Julia. But thanks for asking." Shouts emerged from the kitchen. "I should see to that."

"Hope it's not my eggs."

Zach laughed.

Julia picked up her coffee and took a sip. She watched the waves and the people for several minutes until her food came, content with the easy normalcy of it all.

Sam. His name is Sam.

Sixteen

Sam Watters pulled into his driveway and parked his Silverado beside the house in its normal spot in front of the screened in carport. He'd converted that space for cutting bait, cleaning fish, and storing his fishing gear not long after he'd bought the place.

It suited him, and he was the only one he had to please.

He left the truck, retrieved his poles from the tubes attached to the front grill, put them in their place in the carport, and then moved to the truck bed for the cooler. He still had bait left, so he quickly stashed it in the refrigerator inside the carport.

Reaching further into the refrigerator, he pulled out a bottle of Corona Light and twisted the top. He liked a light beer during or after fishing because it was more refreshing. In the evening, though, he generally opted for something crafty, like an IPA.

Opening the screen door to the house, he twisted the doorknob and pushed the inner door forward.

"C'mon, Gunner."

The hound lay on the kitchen floor looking at him. He stretched, then pushed himself up and ambled toward Sam.

"You lazy bones dog, you."

Gunner panted and grinned.

Sam scratched behind his ears for a minute. "Let's go."

Gunner perked up and led him out the door.

His home faced the sound on the quieter side Tuckaway Bay, away from the hustle and the summer crowds. Rounding the house, he sauntered toward the wooden lawn chair in the yard, about halfway to the water. Easing himself into it, he exhaled, his bones creaking more this year than they did last, and took a drink of beer. Gunner sprinted off to relieve himself, sniffed around some trees along the perimeter of the property, and sauntered down to the dock to lay in the sun.

"Lazy dog." Sam laughed and tipped the bottle.

He appreciated living in an older section of the island, where the lots were larger, and the homes were older. *More established*, the real estate agent had told him when he'd inquired about the area. The one-story cottage, built in the late fifties, sat off the ground on pilings. A typical Carolina style beach house, it had unpainted cedar siding and a shake roof, plus a partially screened porch that wrapped the front and side. He had two bedrooms, a kitchen, a living room, a single bathroom, and a utility room.

All he needed.

It wasn't what he was looking for at first, but the price was right, he had access to the sound and a place for a boat, and truth be told, the nostalgia of the place had grown on him. He'd learned a lot about the historical aspects of the area and had grown to appreciate the long-time locals, too. He was as happy here as he could be. The best parts were that it was quiet, and no one bothered him.

The yard was shaded where he sat, and if he let himself, he might doze for a few minutes, although he didn't like to do that early in the day. Still, the quiet provided a napping kind of morning, especially with the shade cooling the day and the sun glinting off the gently lapping waves against the dock.

The hound was already asleep in the sun. Sam chuckled. The short-hair had been with him for about a decade now and was getting older. He slept most of the day. But he'd already earned his keep. In his younger days, Gunner loved to run and point birds with the best of them. They didn't hunt anymore, now that they were living on the coast, but the dog tolerated the boat and always went with him when he fished the sound or ventured into the Atlantic.

The dog was a good companion—and one he cherished.

His eyelids heavy, he figured he'd give in to a short cat nap. As he closed them, he thought of the woman he'd met on the beach. The one who had been watching him from the cottage for a few days now. It had been quite a while since a woman had caught his eye, and he wasn't sure why this one had.

What puzzled him more was why he'd caught hers.

Didn't matter. Nothing in the cards pointed to a potential relationship for him. Not at this point in his life. Like Gunner's hunting days, those days for him were long gone.

HE'D BE GLAD WHEN THE SUMMER TOURIST SEASON WAS over.

Two more weeks, maybe three, and things would slow down for fall. School would start back up—for the little kids and for the college groups—and families would head home for their long winter's nap. At least that's how it seemed, sometimes. Of course, come late September, the fishing parties would start heading in, but he didn't mind them. Always interesting people to meet when fishing the coast.

Sam pushed his cart along the grocery aisle in search of green chilies. It wasn't something he typically bought but lately he'd had a craving for enchiladas with green sauce—a nod to the year he lived in Albuquerque. Weaving through the carts and strangers, he could pick out the tourists in two seconds flat. Locals didn't give two hoots how they dressed to come to the grocery—whatever they had on was fine. Swim trunks and no shirt. T-shirt and bikini bottoms. Always flip flops or maybe well-worn deck shoes and sometimes even barefoot. Tourists generally wore their best vacation clothes, the ones they bought just before they came, or while they were vacationing.

The locals were also tan. Tourists were pale or red.

Rounding the corner, he glanced down the aisle at the canned goods. Maybe he'd find the chilies there. Pushing onward, dodging a kid talking his mom into the bag of candy clutched in his fists, he spotted the salsa and taco fixings and stopped, gazing at the shelves. There, small cans of green chilies on the top shelf, and right next to it, cans of green enchilada sauce. He snagged two cans of each.

Success.

As he studied the cans and contemplated what else he would need for the enchiladas, someone to his right crowded closer, also looking. He sidestepped, as the person was getting dangerously close. He didn't like people in his space.

"Tacos, enchiladas, or an egg dish?"

Good God. Conversation was the last thing he wanted this morning. He slowly angled toward the voice, ready to come back with some snarky old man quip but stopped himself.

He stared at the woman. *College Girl?*

"Well?" One corner of her mouth drew up.

"Enchiladas. But the idea of eggs and chilies is tempting."

"It works." She reached for a can of chilies. "These aren't bad, pretty much standard fare for this part of the country, but if you can get them, Hatch chilies are better."

He knew Hatch chilies well. "I've never seen them around here. Only in the Southwest."

She grinned. "I special order and have them shipped."

Squaring himself, he faced her. "Well now, isn't that an idea."

She shrugged. "It is." She fumbled with her can of chilies then reached for a can of green sauce, too. Meeting his gaze, she said, "One can of each—sauce and the green chilies—add some sour cream, a few chopped jalapeños for extra heat, a handful of Jack cheese, and you have a great sauce for just about anything. I often serve with omelets or an egg casserole."

A grin tugged at his lips. "You a chef, College Girl?"

"No. But I do cook a lot of breakfast."

"I see." But he didn't.

She put the chilies and sauce in her cart and grinned. "I'll leave you to it. Have a good day, Fisherman."

He watched her walk off, gave his head a slight shake, and let that grin have its way with his lips.

AUGUST WASN'T THE BEST MONTH FOR SURF FISHING ON THE Outer Banks coast but for Sam, any morning spent fishing was better than any morning not fishing. He'd claimed this part of the beach the day Grace Allen, the owner of the Sea Glass Inn Resort back then, had approached him while he was casting out a line.

"You know this is private property," she'd told him.

Sam had looked at her, studying her up and down. He remembered thinking that in her younger days, she was probably a looker. He imagined her to be about ten years older than him. "I didn't realize," he said.

"Well, it is." Her fists perched on her hips.

Sam put the pole in the tube. "Then please accept my apologies. I moved here a few weeks ago and I'm still getting a lay of the land."

"Retired?"

"Something like that."

She eyed him. "Well, you know how to handle that rod and reel pretty well, so I'm guessing not a banker or stockbroker."

He laughed. "No. Military."

She nodded. "Well then. Thank you for your service, and as long as you stay in this area and are gone by nine o'clock, you're fine."

"I'll take that deal." Sam smiled.

Grace smiled back. "And if you happen to catch a nice drum, I wouldn't mind one once in a blue moon."

"I can make that happen too."

"Great." She gave him a wave and turned, walking back toward the hotel.

Sam warmed at the memory. He and Grace had become friends and he missed her now that she was gone. Her nephew, Zach, ran the place with his new wife, Lia. He was still getting to know her, but she seemed nice enough.

Not much had changed with the resort since they took it over and he was glad about that.

He wasn't one for change, most of the time.

Glancing behind him, he examined the cottage directly to his rear. He'd not seen her this morning and wondered if she had left the island.

It was Friday, so maybe. Some vacationers like to get off the island early and avoid the Saturday morning traffic.

He supposed he'd let his chance get by him—not that he'd had his heart set on anything.

"Time to head home." Standing, he reached for his pole. His cell phone buzzed in his shirt pocket, stopping him.

Retrieving the phone, he glanced at the face. *Text message from Hannah*. Immediately, his attention diverted, and his emotions elevated.

Swiping at the phone, he shakily entered his passcode with a forefinger, then clicked the text message icon.

Hannah: *Your gift arrived yesterday. Thank you.*

Sam: *So glad you got it.*

The phone fell silent and he waited. Then didn't.

Sam: *Thanks for letting me know it arrived.*

Hannah: *It wasn't necessary.*

What did she mean by that?

Sam: *The gift or letting me know?*

Another pause. He could almost see her eye roll in his head.

Hannah: *The gift wasn't necessary but thank you.*

Sam: *Of course, it was. I'm proud of you.*

There was no response after that.

Resigned, he slipped his phone back into his pocket. Hannah was hit or miss, and right now, their relationship was a huge miss. He wasn't quite sure what to do to get past that, had never been able to, so he'd do what he'd always done—let her take the lead.

Which was unlike him, in any other aspect of his life. But when it came to Hannah, he'd take the back seat every time.

Glancing toward the cottage once more, he wondered again if the woman was gone. He also wondered what the hell her name might be. No matter.

Gathering his gear, he pushed both women out of his mind as he crossed over the path between the dunes. They both lingered in his head though, of course, and would until he had a couple of beers in him later this afternoon.

Seventeen

Sunday, a week before beach week,
19 days sober

JUST LIKE AT THE INN, SHE MADE THE BREAKFAST CASSEROLE
the night before.

It felt good doing something she did well, something familiar she
hadn't done in a while. She'd nearly forgotten how much cooking
relaxed her—the process, the measurements, the start-to-finish accomplishment—although she supposed she was plenty relaxed these past
days, anyway.

Hard to believe she'd been here two weeks and hadn't thought
about getting up and making breakfast even once.

Of course, she didn't *have* to make the casserole. She'd wanted to.

Up early the next morning, around five o'clock, she pulled the dish
out of the refrigerator to come to room temperature—also like at
the inn.

While she waited, she made coffee and sipped it out on the cottage
porch in the semi-dark, anticipating the sunrise. After she'd set the casserole to bake in the oven, she had another forty-five-minute wait, so she

ambled down the sandy path toward the shore to see if she could spot any large shells washed ashore with the tide. None. And also to see if Sam was there yet.

He wasn't.

Maybe he wasn't coming today.

Not likely. To her knowledge, he'd not missed a day of fishing since she'd been here.

With about fifteen minutes to go, she headed back to the kitchenette to make the green sauce—the one she'd shared with Sam at the grocery store the other day. She hoped the combination actually worked, having made it up on the fly, trying to impress.

Look at me, trying to impress a man. What gives?

It sounded good at the time.

Smiling, she pulled the ingredients out of the refrigerator and cabinet.

Using the canned enchilada sauce as her base, she warmed it and stirred in the sour cream. Next, she scraped away about half the seeds from two jalapeños, then whirred the peppers and the canned green chilies in the blender until smooth and added them to the saucepan. She'd discover soon enough if Sam were a hot and spicy guy, or milder. For some reason, she thought spicy.

Time will tell.

With the sauce warming, she added a handful of shredded Monterey Jack cheese, giving the sauce a perfect consistency for topping the casserole.

She peeked out the window again and caught a glimpse of Sam, spiking the tubes in the sand, going about his regular routine, getting ready to put a line in the water. She wondered what he was fishing for— of course, she knew nothing about fishing.

Maybe time to learn?

She also wondered about this man, who seemed to need routine and habit in his life as much as she did in hers. What stories hid beneath the shadows of that wide brimmed sun hat?

Is that what draws me to him? The unknown?

The oven timer went off and she retrieved the casserole. It looked delicious, nicely browned, and cheesy. She was hungry but decided to wait and eat later. After. She was perfectly fine with her coffee for the time being.

Letting the dish cool on the cutting board, she found a container with a lid large enough for a healthy serving of the casserole. She cut and lifted a nice portion, topped it with sauce, and snapped on the lid. Steam immediately clouded the container. Gathering the warm dish, a fork wrapped in a napkin, and her coffee cup, she headed for the door, wondering if she should take him more coffee.

No. He always seemed to have plenty in his thermos. She'd wait and see and could always offer to get more, if needed.

She didn't want to sneak up on him but didn't want to act indifferent either. She was purposely doing what she was doing this morning. Not the side-eye thing while looking for sea glass or picking at shell fragments. This was intentional—she wanted more conversation from this older gentleman. For some reason, she liked him. And she liked the idea of him fishing in front of her cottage.

Coming up behind him, she stopped. "Morning."

Turning, he glanced over his shoulder. "Well, hello there, College Girl."

She thrust out the container and fork, stepping up beside him. "Breakfast?"

"Are you serious?"

"Dead serious. I made one of my famous casseroles this morning. Thought you might want to try it."

"Famous, huh?"

"In some parts."

He grinned and stood, facing her. The brim of his hat flipped up in the wind and Julia saw that grin reach the sparkle of his blue eyes. Older eyes, with stories, and tiny crinkles around the edges. She imagined he might be at least a decade older than her.

"With green chilies?"

"Of course."

"But not Hatch."

"Ah, no. No time to ship. Maybe next time."

He eyed her. "Oh? There's a next time?"

She winked. "Why not?"

Still grinning, he reached for the dish. "I never did get my enchiladas made," he confessed.

"Well, that's a shame. These aren't enchiladas necessarily, but a casserole made with eggs and tortillas and some cheese with the green sauce on top. Hope the sauce isn't too hot for you."

He fiddled with the lid, holding the fork and napkin. "Doubt it."

"Here." She reached for the container. "You hold the fork. This thing is tricky." She unsnapped the four sides of the lid and handed it back to him. "Have a seat and eat that while it's warm. If you want more, let me know."

"Well, that's nice of you," he said. Settling back down into his chair, he looked up. "You got an ulterior motive here, College Girl?"

"Naw. Just curious."

"About me?" The twinkle was back in his eye.

"You fish every day. I never see you take home fish. Do you fish for food or just for the fun of it?"

He laughed. "This time of the year it's mostly for the fun of it and practice. The better surf fishing happens in the spring and fall. Whatever I catch, I catch, and most of the time I release."

"I see."

"You fish?"

"No, never."

"Ah, college girls don't fish?"

"Oh, I don't know about that. I'm sure there are college girls who fish. I just never have."

He took a bite of the casserole and eyed her, slowly chewing. "Got some heat."

"Good?"

Jabbing his fork back into the container, he lifted another bite. "Excellent."

Julia grinned. For some reason, seeing people enjoy her cooking gave her a lot of pleasure. It was a simple thing, but a very real thing.

"So, if you didn't learn how to fish, what did you learn how to do in college?"

"Besides drinking, partying my ass off, and smoking a little weed, you mean?"

He raised a brow. "Sounds like me before I went into the military. But did you study anything?"

"Oh sure. Law."

"Seriously?"

She nodded. "I was an attorney. In my father's firm, no less. How convenient is that?" Well, largely challenging, to be honest, but that was a different story, and not one for today.

"Was?"

She toed a hill of sand, looking down, realizing she needed a pedicure. "I'm taking a hiatus, exploring other avenues. I haven't practiced much in the past couple of years."

"Oh?"

"Yeah, you know, one of those things."

"I get it. Not a subject we are going to talk about."

Not today, Fisherman.

The conversation fell into a lull and Julia looked out over the surf while he ate. After a moment, she said, "Well, I'm going to head back in and get a bite of that casserole for myself. I hope you have a good morning fishing."

He stood, settling the container with half the casserole left in it on his chair seat. "I do thank you for the breakfast, hospitality, and conversation." He pushed out his hand. "Name's Sam. Sam Watters."

She caught that flicker in his eye again and grasped his hand. It was warm. Big. Slightly rough. And comfortable. "Nice to officially meet you, Sam. I'm Julia. Julia Salinger."

MONDAY,
   20 days sober

LIA CALLED AROUND TEN O'CLOCK THE NEXT MORNING, asking if Julia would like to go out for lunch, possibly with Alice, too.

"Oh, I don't know." She'd need to shower and put on something decent to leave the cottage. Was that too much effort? "Have you called her yet?"

"No. Checking with you first."

"I see." Julia strolled to the other side of the porch, looking toward the hotel. "Are you talking about at the Sandcastle, or somewhere else?"

Lia sighed. "I was thinking maybe we'd go into town. There's a cute cafe close to her office. Are you up for it?"

"Eating out or seeing Alice?" Julia chuckled.

"Both."

"Goodness. Not really, but okay." After all, she'd been here two weeks. Seeing Alice was inevitable. Only one week stood between today and beach week, and she'd see Alice then anyway. Besides, Melinda had hinted that maybe she should get out. She just wasn't looking forward to the confessional conversation with the mother hen.

But better now than later. When Maggie got there. If she got there....

"Great. I'll call Alice. Meet me at the hotel office at noon."

"Will do."

They hung up. Julia didn't let herself think about the potential lunch disaster and headed straight to the shower, mindlessly getting ready. With plenty of time before meeting Lia, she took some extra effort in the grooming department, which was needed, as she got ready. She chose a sundress and sandals, grimacing when she slipped her unmanicured toes and still scruffy heels into the strappy shoes.

Nothing to do but apply lotion and keep people looking up, not down. One trick she'd learned in law school from an older female professor, was when one was on display, make sure people are looking at your face and not where you don't want them to look. Draw the eye up.

She'd have to turn on some southern wit and charm to make that happen. Was she up for it?

We will see.

She entered the hotel by the side door and headed down the hallway. Lia burst out of the office. "Julia! You look fabulous."

"Well, it's lunch with Alice, right? The all-important assistant to the mayor of Tuckaway Bay? It's a local celebrity event waiting to happen."

Laughing, Lia took Julia's arm and steered her down the hallway. "Come on. Let's go get some food. I'm starving."

The cafe was two blocks down from the Town Hall and Municipal Building which was where Alice's office was, according to Lia. "Street parking is terrible this time of day," she said. "So, we'll park in the community lot. Alice is on her way out. We can walk to the cafe from here."

Julia couldn't remember paying much attention to the government offices of Tuckaway Bay. Apparently, everything from the mayor to maintenance services were housed there, according to the sign out front.

When Alice stepped out of the building, her face lit up and she rushed forward. "Julia! Oh my God. When did you get here?"

"You didn't tell her," Julia murmured, giving Lia the side-eye.

"No. Surprise!"

Alice caught Julia up in a hug that jarred her. "You came early!" Hooking her arm in Julia's elbow, she led her down the street.

Julia glanced at Lia, then back to Alice, trying to follow her chatter.

"Oh, I'm so glad to see you. We can spend a little time together before Maggie gets here. You know how she's going to dominate every-thing, right? I mean, she always has so many issues and I don't expect things are going to be different this year, than last. Remember what a shit-show that was? Well, let's hope it's not that bad. By the way, have you spoken with her lately?"

Alice stopped and Julia stared at her. "Who? Maggie?"

"Why yes, of course. That's who I was talking about, right?"

Lia stepped closer. "Let's go on inside and get our table so we don't lose it. I called ahead."

"Oh sure," Alice said.

Julia followed the two women inside and immediately wondered if she'd made a mistake. Suddenly, the crowd and the tight spaces between tables in the small cafe were a tad overwhelming. Sucking in a breath, she moved forward, behind her two friends.

They sat, and menus and water glasses were placed.

Julia glanced about, gaining some leverage on the restaurant layout. Should she feel a panic attack coming on, she knew there was an exit to her rear, but also one up ahead to the right—according to the sign above the hallway. The restrooms were down that way too.

She wasn't planning on anxiety ruling her lunch, or her life, but just in case, she needed a plan. Suddenly, she let out the breath she'd been holding.

"That was a deep sigh." Alice smiled at her.

"Yes. I suppose."

Alice's gaze narrowed. "You okay?"

"I am. Look at this menu. So much to choose from. What's your favorite here, Alice?" Julia didn't miss a beat turning the conversation. She glanced at Lia then back to the menu.

"The crab cakes are excellent."

"Good."

They chatted about the menu, then ordered.

"You never answered my question, Julia." Alice leaned closer.

"Oh?"

"About Maggie. Have you talked with her?"

Julia decided to bite the bullet and divulge a little. "You mean since she fired me as her attorney?"

"What?" Lia fixed her gaze on Julia.

"She replaced you?" Alice asked.

Shaking her head, Julia quickly replied. "No. The divorce is off. She's not leaving Max."

"What the hell?"

"How long have you known?"

"Since late June. I didn't tell either of you because it wasn't my place to do so. I've not spoken with Maggie since then, and I didn't know if either of you had. She's living in her own little fantasy world, so who am I to disrupt that? If she's happy, then so be it."

Alice frowned. "She's not happy."

"How do you know?" Julia shifted in her seat as a man squeezed between her table and the one beside them. "Did she tell you that?"

"No." Alice took a drink of her ice water. "No. She's not been happy in years. What would make her happy now?"

Sex? Lots of it? With lassos and leather?

She wasn't ready to go there yet with the girls. Besides, that definitely was not a story that was Julia's to tell. Maggie could disclose that tidbit when she was good and ready.

The server interrupted with their lunches. All three women got the crab cakes salad special and a glass of raspberry iced tea. The conversation paused for a moment while they ate, until Lia changed the subject.

"I've been thinking about beach week. Since Tequila Sunrise is still in renovation mode, where do you all want to stay? I held a couple of cottages back for that week, but do you think we'll need two?"

"Which cottages?" Julia forked through her salad.

"Tortoise and Pelican."

"Why not have everyone stay at the Gull? It's the largest cottage, right? It's secluded and quiet, and there are two king bedrooms. We've all shared bedrooms before so we surely can again. Don't you think it will be better for us all in one place? Otherwise, it's not really beach week."

"I agree with that," Alice said.

"If you're sure, Julia?" Lia's eyes questioned more than her words.

She was, much to her surprise. Perhaps she was ready to have people around her—her friends, around her. "I'm sure. It will be fun. Besides, I have this week to prepare myself."

Alice chuckled. "For what? Us?"

Julia stared, for a moment. "Actually, yes."

"Oh please, Julia. We're not that bad. I mean, we can get into some disagreements occasionally, but in the end, we always make it work."

She caught Lia's gaze across the table, then turned to Alice. "Look. I fell off the wagon almost three weeks ago. I've been here for two weeks and yes, I didn't tell you. I'm trying to get my head screwed back on straight before going home end of the month. I need to make some life decisions soon and I don't need advice coming from three different ways. I also don't need alcohol in the cottage during beach week, so if you all want to drink, there is the Tiki Hut Bar, okay?" Pausing, she looked at Lia. "I suppose I should have said that earlier, so if you want to change your mind about where the others stay, that's fine. I can stay in the Gull by myself."

Lia set her napkin aside. "Julia, do you want us to stay with you?"

She did. Suddenly, she realized how much. "I do. I need you both. Maggie too, if she's coming. And dammit, I miss Wren and Willow."

Silently, Alice reached for Julia's hand and dragged it over onto her lap. She caressed the back of her knuckles with her thumb. "We're here, Julia. Whatever you need."

Tears stung her eyelids. "I need my friends," she whispered. She wondered if they knew how difficult it was for her to say that. "Wanna get pedicures after lunch?"

TUESDAY,
21 days sober

WHEN SHE LOOKED OUT AT THE SURF EARLY THE NEXT morning, she saw two chairs sitting in the sand at Sam's spot.

"Good Lord." Julia rounded the post, stepping off the porch. "If someone has taken his spot, there will be hell to pay, I'm certain."

But as she looked past the dune, she saw Sam casting his second pole into the ocean and returning to the chairs. He looked up, spotted her, and waved as the pole went into the spike.

Waving back, and with a smile breaking over her face, she lowered her head and watched her red toenails appear and disappear into the sand as she ambled his way. Would he notice?

Did she want him to notice?

Good God, Julia. You're acting like a twelve-year-old girl.

"Hey!" She approached as he was closing the cooler lid.

"Hey yourself. Have a seat," he told her.

She eyed him curiously, then rounded the chairs and sat. He followed her lead, sitting in the one beside her.

"You didn't bring your coffee," he said.

"I hadn't expected to come all the way down here." She gazed out over the ocean. Sitting so close to sea level, the waves rolling in from that angle were mesmerizing. "I saw the two chairs and thought someone had stolen your spot."

"Ah. Protecting me from squatters, eh?"

She laughed and met his gaze. "Maybe."

He sat the plastic container from yesterday's breakfast on the sand beside her chair. "Thanks, again. It was excellent."

"There's more if you want. I can't eat it all."

"Oh, I don't want to wear out my welcome."

"Didn't I just invite you?"

"I suppose you did."

"Well, it's there if you want. Just say the word." She stretched her legs out in front of her and scooted down in the chair. Leaning her head against the chair back, she watched the waves again. "This is nice. Did you bring this chair for me?"

"You see anyone else?"

She looked his way. "Nope."

"Well then."

A grin raced across her face. She couldn't stop it. "Well then, I thank you."

"You're welcome."

Julia settled back in to watch the surf.

Sam pointed. "That one there, closest to you, is yours."

Looking to where he pointed, she said, "What?"

"That pole. That one's yours. Keep a watch on it."

She sat up straight. "What am I watching for?"

"Movement, basically. Is the line pulling out from the reel? Is the tip of the rod jerking downward? If so, jump up and grab the pole and hold onto the reel."

She stared at him, knowing her eyes had flown round as they could go. "That's a lot of pressure for a girl who doesn't know how to fish."

"Really? I figure a girl who's a hot shot attorney from Kentucky knows how to handle a little pressure."

She stood. "What? How did you..." *Damn, did he Google me?*

"Your rod."

"What?"

Sam stood too. "Grab it!"

Julia jumped up and grabbed at the rod. She fumbled it, the reel spinning. She could feel the tug on the pole.

"Reel it in some!"

"How? Like this?"

Sam was behind her now, barking instructions. Suddenly, she felt like she was seven and her dad was trying to teach her how to hit a softball with a bat.

"Walk toward the water a little and give it some play. See if you can tire the fish out."

"How in the world?"

"Haven't you been watching all week?"

"Yes, but I wasn't taking notes. I didn't realize this was going to be a performance exam!"

Sam laughed. "Here."

He reached around her, his left hand on the rod, his right on the reel, her back cradled against his chest, hugging her from behind. Immediately, she relaxed and together they reeled in the fish.

"Well, I'll be. That's a keeper."

"What is it?"

"Bluefish. You do know how to fish."

She laughed. "Sam Watters. I do not. But this was fun as shit. Now, show me how to bait up that hook and let's do it again."

"One condition, College Girl."

"What's that?"

"If we catch 'em, we're going to eat them."

She arched a brow. "You cook?"

"Even a man who lives alone has to eat, right? Yes, I cook."

"Good. Because I can't do fish. I always over cook."

"Even if I clean them?"

"You clean, I cook. But fair warning you might get rubber fish. However, if you want to cook, then it's all good."

"Deal. Let's catch some fish."

Eighteen

"BREAKFAST BURRITO?"

Julia rounded the beach chairs and handed him the burrito wrapped in waxed paper.

Sam looked up, giving her that semi-serious, no-nonsense look of his that was sometimes difficult to discern. "Depends on what's in it."

"Eggs, sausage, red peppers and onions, cream cheese, a couple dashes of hot sauce, wrapped in a tortilla, then grilled."

"Gotta love that you grilled the thing." He took the package. "And like hot sauce."

"I don't. But I figured you might."

Unwrapping one end, he said, "Got that right, sweetheart." He took a bite. "Excellent, as always."

"Good." She sat, glancing at the poles already in the spikes. "What are we fishing for today?"

"Anything that bites."

She glanced his way. "I'm up for that."

He choked a little on his burrito. "You're later this morning than usual."

He noticed? "Yes. I have a standing thing on Wednesday mornings, early."

"Oh?" He gave her the side-eye, then took another bite.

"Yeah."

"Breakfast date?"

She laughed. "Hardly. Besides, you're my breakfast date. Eat up."

THURSDAY,
23 days sober

"WAFFLE BREAKFAST SANDWICH?"

"Now what do you have there this morning?"

"Sausage patty, a fried egg, melted Jack cheese, and hot honey between two toaster waffles."

Sam looked up and smiled. "What? No homemade waffles?"

"No waffle iron here. Best I can do."

He grinned and reached for the sandwich. "Where's yours?"

"I had one earlier. Had to test it out."

"Well, stop that. I hate to eat alone, and in front of you."

"All right. Fine." She sat in her chair and looked at the poles. "What's on the agenda today, Fisherman?"

"Mackerel. Heard they are running a little south of here."

"So, they might be running this way?"

He chuckled. "Maybe."

"Bait?"

"No, lures."

"Show me."

"Yes, ma'am. After my sandwich."

FRIDAY,
  24 days sober

"BACON, SCRAMBLED EGG, AND AMERICAN CHEESE ON A biscuit?"

"What? Fast food?"

"Naw. Made the biscuits myself."

"Seriously now. You're a good woman to have around."

Julia smiled. "And don't you forget it." She sat beside him and unwrapped hers.

"I see you took my advice."

"And what's that?" She took a bite, then pinned him with her gaze.

"About eating with me, rather than alone."

Several quick comebacks jumped into her head, and she had to contemplate which one to say, which was probably a mistake. "Alone is overrated at times."

Nodding, Sam sat back in his chair and looked out over the ocean. "You got that right."

He unwrapped the sandwich and took a bite. "Best biscuit I ever had." He grinned while chewing.

"Liar."

Jerking back and widening his eyes—a bit animated if you asked her —he pretended taking offense. "No, sweetheart. I'm as honest as they come. And that's the truth."

Julia didn't doubt for one second that he was an honest man. She glanced past him at the poles. "We're not baited up yet. What are we catching today?"

"Oh, probably a bit of sunburn and maybe a flea bite."

"Not a good day, huh?"

"One of those days when it's hit or miss. See what's in that cooler and let's try a bit of everything."

She tugged the cooler closer and flipped back the lid. "I see mullet, shrimp, minnows...."

"Any of that will do."

"So, I'll bait and you'll cast?"

Sam's eyes twinkled. "Today it's all you, College Girl. Casting lessons in five minutes, after I'm done with my biscuit."

"I think my skill set is better left to baiting hooks."

Stuffing the last bite of biscuit in his mouth, he stood. "Get some of that shrimp on the line, woman. I want to see what kind of an arm you have."

She found the shrimp in the cooler. "Oh, and why is that?"

"Because when I take you out in my boat, we're going for bigger fish."

"You have a boat?"

"I do."

"Like, for the ocean?"

"I think we'll start with the sound."

She squinted, looking up at him. "You know, I've never been over on that side of the island?"

He studied her. "Seriously?"

She nodded.

"Well, let's take care of that. How about a late afternoon boat ride? No fishing, just a pleasure ride. You can meet me at my place if you want. The boat's at my dock behind the house."

Good God, should I? Is this a date? Tomorrow was the start of beach week. The girls would roll in around noon. This might be her only chance to take a boat ride with the handsome fisherman named Sam. "I can do that."

"Great. It's a date. We'll iron out the details later. Now, let's get those lines in the water."

SAM WASN'T SURE WHAT THE HELL HAD GOTTEN INTO HIM. *It's a date?* Jesus.

His fishing gear stowed, and the fish they'd caught today cleaned and packaged for the freezer, he was ready to relax for a minute with his beer and contemplate what the hell he had done this morning.

He'd gotten caught up in all the hoopla, he guessed.

It wasn't that he didn't like spending time with her, he did. He just

180

didn't want to start something he couldn't finish. He was too old for her —must be at least ten or maybe fifteen years older—and he was too much of a loner, a social hermit these days, to be any good to anyone. Besides, he had issues he didn't need to bring into a friendship, let alone a relationship.

And, according to Google, she was married—or at least had a husband at some point. She didn't wear a ring. He'd found nearly a dozen articles about her, the law firm, accolades about a few cases she'd won, and so on, and some of them had mentioned a husband. Last thing he needed was to get involved with a woman who wasn't available.

Plus, he couldn't get a good read on her. Maybe she wasn't even interested. Maybe it was a non-issue.

Put it out of your mind, Watters.

The early morning fishing routine with her was one thing. The flirting was fun. And truth be told, he liked her company. A lot. But dammit, he had to invite her to his home? For a ride in his boat? He hadn't done that in....

Never. He'd never done that.

No woman had graced his doorstep since he'd moved there. He'd never taken a woman fishing.

They'd agreed to meet at four o'clock and Sam had texted her his address. Now, he had her phone number, and she had his. Was that a good or bad idea? Is that the way they do things these days? He'd not been out with a woman in so long he wasn't sure of the dating protocol any longer.

"Not a date." He kept telling himself. She's a friend. Pleasant company. A fishing buddy. That's the extent of it.

He settled himself into his chair on the lawn and watched Gunner make his rounds.

"I suppose I should pick up the house a bit. Probably need to check on the boat too. Take a shower."

This dating shit was almost too much effort.

Hell, maybe he'd leave his dirty underwear on the floor and the dishes in the sink. She'd turn-tail and run then. Wouldn't she?

But do I want her to run?

With an exhale, he perused the sound, watching the gentle lap of waves against his boat and the dock. It was a good day for boating. Gunner had found his spot in the sun and was already asleep. He wondered if she liked dogs. That would be a test. Any woman in his life needed to like dogs.

If she didn't, then maybe they'd just call this off. If she did, well then....

"Shit."

Standing, he downed the remainder of his Corona, took another deep breath, and exhaled. He glanced at his watch.

"Five hours." Plenty of time to clean the place up and himself, too. "Better get crackin'."

<hr />

LIA PICKED UP AFTER THE THIRD RING.

"Hi, Lia."

"Julia! Good morning. I haven't talked to you in a few days. Everything okay?"

She moved back and forth across the porch, watching the people gather on the beach with their umbrellas and chairs and colorful towels and coolers. "I'm good. I wanted to touch base about tomorrow. What time is everyone coming? Still around noon?"

"Well, you know about as much as I do. I'll send a group text in a couple of hours. I'm swamped at the moment."

"I'll let you go then...."

"No, wait. I'm glad you called. I was going to. Anything you need?"

Julia stopped, watching a couple of kids toss a beach ball back and forth. "Actually, I was wondering if you could get housekeeping over here later this morning or afternoon. I have a call with Melinda in an hour so it would need to be after that."

"Of course. What all do you need. Beds? General cleaning? Bathrooms?"

"All that would be perfect."

"I'll see to it."

"Thanks so much, Lia. I thought I'd pick up a few groceries in the morning."

Lia paused, and Julia could hear her whispering something to someone in the office. "I'm back. Sorry. That would be great. I'll pick up a few things too."

"Oh, and I'll be gone for a while this afternoon late, from about three o'clock for a few hours."

"Oh? Hot date?"

Now why in the world would she say that? "No. What do you mean?"

Lia sighed. "I've seen you fishing with Sam in the mornings. Are you seeing him?"

Well, shit. "Do you think that's a mistake?"

"Why would it be? Sam's a great guy. Quiet and laid back, but a good human being. Zach's known him for years."

Julia blew out a thin breath. She wasn't worried about Sam being weird or anything. Generally, she was a good judge of character. Lawyering had taught her that. "It's just rather strange. I don't date."

"Oh, so it is a date?"

"No. It's just a ride in his fishing boat. He wants to take me sound fishing one day. Isn't that ridiculous?"

"Why would it be? Looks like you enjoy surf fishing."

"Have you been watching me?"

Lia laughed. "Our apartment overlooks the beach. I've seen you most mornings. I think it's great, Julia."

"I have no clue what I am doing." *What am I thinking, anyway?* "I don't even really know the man. We just sit on the beach and fish, eat some breakfast together. Should I really do this?"

Lia fell silent for a moment. "Do you want to?"

She did. Didn't she? "I suppose I do."

She could almost hear Lia's grin coming through the phone, as if that were possible. "Have fun, Julia. If anyone deserves it, you do. Just relax and have a nice boat ride."

Good advice. Relax, Julia. "You're right. Nothing to be nervous about, right?"

"Not a thing. Sam is well respected around here. He's safe. Now, I have to go. I'll group text later. Bye!"

And she was gone.

FORTY-FIVE MINUTES LATER, SHE WAS ON THE VIDEO CALL with Melinda.

"Are you ready for beach week?"

She adjusted the screen. "As ready as I'm going to be."

"What have you done to prepare? Are you getting out more?"

Julia stared at Melinda. "Both those questions are loaded. Let me take one of them at a time."

"Of course."

"What have I done to prepare? I had lunch with Alice and Lia a few days ago. We talked about alcohol in the house. I've told them both I would prefer if they want to drink, that they go to the Tiki Hut, or the restaurant. Not in the cottage."

"Are they staying in your cottage?"

She nodded. "Yes. It just made sense. The house we usually stay in is unavailable." She thought about that. "And to be honest, it really doesn't feel like beach week without staying there, so it's going to be different anyway."

"So maybe with the change in venue, it will be easier for everyone to make the adjustments about drinking."

"Maybe. There's Maggie though, and she's not surfaced in a while. We don't even know if she's coming."

"Are you prepared to see Maggie again?"

To be honest, she'd not thought about it. "Probably not. But I'm not going to worry about something that might not happen."

Melinda gave a thoughtful nod. "Still, having a plan for seeing her might not be a bad idea."

"I've never had any issue with telling Maggie exactly what I think, so I will be okay. Plus, the other girls understand and have my back."

"About the drinking?"

"Yes."

"Excellent."

"It might be a good idea to share with the entire group what you and Alice and Lia talked about. If everyone has the same expectation coming into the week, it may be easier."

Julia nodded. "That's a good idea. Lia said she was going to send a group text out later. I can respond to that."

"Good plan. Now, about you getting out?"

"I have. I've been to the grocery and I'm learning how to fish. Been fishing every morning with a guy who fishes in front of my cottage. He's teaching me."

"Fishing! Now that's different."

"I know. So unlike me. Right? But it's fun."

"I'm proud of you. That's quite an accomplishment. Making new friends and learning something new."

She shrugged. "It just sort of happened."

"Good for you, Julia."

She pondered whether to tell Melinda about the late afternoon boat ride, then decided she'd shared enough today. "Thanks, Melinda. I feel really good this week."

"I'm glad." She glanced at her watch. "We said thirty minutes this morning to touch base, so time is about up. Anything else you want to talk about?"

She scanned her brain for a couple of seconds. "Surprisingly, no. I'm good."

"Great. Then I'll talk to you next week. The regular time."

"See you then."

A FEW HOURS LATER, AS SHE HEADED OUT THE DOOR TO MEET Sam, her phone pinged—the group text from Lia.

Lia: *Hey ladies. Beach week is upon us! What time is everyone getting here tomorrow?*

Julia noticed she'd sent the text to the entire group, including Wren and Willow, even though it was unlikely they would respond or show up. But with those two, you never really knew.

Alice: *I'm excited! I'll be there around noon. Where are we meeting?*

Julia: *I'll be at the Gull. Come straight here if you want.*

Alice: *Sounds good.*

Lia: *We can have lunch at the Sandcastle. It's on Zach.*

Alice: *I'll take you up on that.*

Lia: *Maggie? ETA?*

Silence.

Alice: *Maggie, you are coming. Aren't you?*

Julia thought about tossing in the same question and decided against it. She wasn't sure how Maggie felt about her right now, even though it had been a couple of months since she'd spoken with her. Their last encounter wasn't exactly pleasant.

Lia: *We can't wait to see you, Maggie. Just come when you can. If we're not at the Gull, then try the restaurant or the beach. See you all soon!*

Julia: *I did want to say one thing, girls. I've had a bit of a setback with the drinking, so I'd appreciate it if you all not drink at the cottage. That work for you?*

Lia: *We can go to the Hut. No problem.*

Alice: *Or the restaurant.*

Julia: *Thanks so much. I really appreciate it. That way I can walk away if it gets too tempting.*

Lia: *You know we are not going to let you drink. Right?*

All that was for Maggie's benefit, and now at least it was all out there. Julia was suddenly grateful for her friends.

Julia: *Yes.*

Alice: *I'm excited. Can't wait.*

Julia: *Me too.*

But honestly, she wasn't looking forward to the week. Nothing would be the same. And she secretly wondered if the entire week was going to be the shit-show from hell.

Nineteen

Her cell phone GPS led her to Sam's house without difficulty.

As she wound through the narrow streets of this area of Tuckaway Bay, Julia remembered telling Sam she had never been to the sound side of the island. It was true she'd not been to this particular location, but she had been to Alice's many times.

Alice's house was sound side as well, situated near the more populated area of downtown. Her home was one of the earlier ones in the area, a larger beach-style house built in the early 1900s. Hers was a typical four-square style originally—four rooms down and four rooms up with a stairwell in the middle—framed with cedar clapboard siding and a sweeping porch that wrapped around to one side. Alice's parents had added an addition to the east side of the house when she was a child, and they painted the entire house a rich yellow with white trim. After her parents passed, the home became Alice's. She upgraded with a new roof and added decks on the back, plus a new dock.

Alice, her husband George, and daughter Ella had lived comfortably in the old house for years. The bay sunset views were a definite plus and one of the best places in town to enjoy an Old Fashioned or Margarita on the deck with friends.

Well, that's not happening anymore. Both bourbon and tequila were gone from her life. *Not going back there.* She had to find some kind of substitute for liquor that she actually enjoyed drinking while others imbibed. Something special that she drank only on those occasions.

I'll dive into that another day.

As she turned down the street toward Sam's, she noticed a visible difference in the architecture and home styles. The waters of the sound played peek-a-boo with an abundance of trees as she drove through. She noted the houses were smaller, perhaps built in the 1940s or 50s, but the lots were larger—more space and trees between houses, unlike at Alice's. The homes were also set closer to the water than the street and were not as manicured as in Alice's area.

The outside décor of the homes sported nets and buoys and other fishing paraphernalia. Fishing boats were parked in driveways or under carports, if not berthed at docks behind the houses. Obviously, this little village within a village was largely a fishing community.

Apropos, Sam!

She smiled. Not sure what she had expected, she suddenly realized the laid-back, casual place was exactly spot-on Sam's demeanor. Easy going, relaxed, functional, and real.

That was nice, in so many ways. Immediately, she was drawn to the lifestyle.

Louisville was so...formal, pretentious at times, and in the circles her parents ran in, a bit snobby. She and Mark had always tried to avoid the status quo but honestly, she knew it was baked into them both, probably at a cellular level.

And I'm rather tired of keeping up the appearances.

Her GPS indicated a right turn in a hundred feet. She spotted his house number on a lighthouse mailbox and turned onto his property.

She cautiously traveled the sandy drive and parked behind a pickup truck. Her gaze landed on Sam coming out of the side door of the house. A large dog, some type of hound, she thought, ambled out the door behind him and sprinted off into the yard.

Sam stood at the edge of the carport.

Sucking in a breath and quickly exhaling, she got out and approached.

Sam waited, smiling.

"I almost didn't recognize you without your hat, Fisherman."

He ran a hand over his bald head. "Gotta keep the sun off this bowling ball. Not fond of skin cancer."

"I understand that." She stopped in front of him, then glanced about inside the carport. "Wow. This place is neat." And she wasn't just blowing smoke up his ass, either. "Look at all this fishing gear."

Sam laughed and scanned the area too. "I may be a bit obsessed."

She took several steps into the carport, her gaze dancing from wall to wall in the three-sided structure. One wall was full of poles. There were drawers and boxes full of tackle and lures. A refrigerator and freezer stood on one side. Another wall had hooks for hooded rain slickers, wader boots, sun hats, and other types of outdoor clothing. There was a shelf for different kinds of shoes and boots.

"Sometimes obsession is a good thing?" She turned back, smiling. "I might be a bit preoccupied myself. I saw a bait and tackle shop on my way over and had a difficult time not pulling into the parking lot."

Sam laughed out loud.

"You going to teach me about all of this stuff?"

With a lazy grin, he stepped up beside her, looking straight ahead. "It may take me a while."

She looked up at his profile. "I'm not going anywhere."

"Oh? I thought you were leaving end of the month."

She shrugged. "I'm flexible."

Slowly, Sam angled his gaze to meet hers. A current of something foreign but rather exciting jetted between them for a split second. "I guess that's a good thing."

Shit. This flirting thing is getting out of hand. My damn cheeks are hot.

Suddenly, she had butterflies in her stomach. That was a foreign feeling, for sure. How long had it been since she'd had butterflies for a man? Pulling away, she took a few steps in reverse. "So where is this boat you talked about?"

"Behind the house. But before we go there, let's do a safety check. Let me get a look at you."

"At me?"

"Yes." He squared himself in front of her, placing his hands on either shoulder, straightening her angle with his. He looked her up and down. "With a few exceptions, you'll pass."

"Excuse me?"

He stepped away, toward the shelf with shoes and such. "The sandals won't work. Try these."

She took them and looked over the practically new pair of deck shoes, then lifted her gaze. "So, old girlfriend? Ex-wife?"

He eyed her back. "Neither."

He didn't offer an explanation and Julia figured she'd leave it at that. "I see. Well, they look like they might fit."

"Try them." He walked away again and plucked a sun hat off the wall. He positioned it on her head. "This too. You happen to bring sunscreen?"

"I actually did." She patted the tote bag slung over her shoulder.

"Good girl."

One thing she'd hated when practicing law was being called a girl. She was an attorney, not a school child, but there were men in her circle who loved to demean the feminine gender by cutting remarks. Usually, they were subtle, and sometimes not. Either way, she despised it, and the reference always made her shudder a little inside.

But Sam's words—*good girl*—didn't have the same affect. In fact, they called up a totally different response from somewhere deep inside. Warm, cozy, friendly. She loved the banter between them and was growing quite accustomed to it.

Slipping out of her sandals, she set the deck shoes on the concrete floor and slipped her feet in them. "Perfect," she said.

"Great. I think we're almost ready to go."

Julia bit her lip. "Could I use the bathroom before we do?"

"Of course." He pointed toward the house. "In that door, through the kitchen, down the hall, second door on the left."

"Gotcha. Thanks."

"I'll get a few things ready and meet you at the dock, just around that corner." He pointed.

"Okay." She headed for the door, then turned back. "Should I lock up before I come down?"

He turned. "Why? No one bothers anything around here."

Well, that's different from home too, and kind of cool. Of course, I've not been locking my doors lately either. "Okay," she repeated. "See you in a few."

Inside Sam's house, she paused for a moment, letting her eyes adjust to the lower light in the kitchen. Then, she found the hallway and traveled about halfway down, pausing at a grouping of pictures on the wall —school pictures of a girl, about a dozen of them, she guessed, from the early grades through high school.

Sam has a daughter?

She looked at her feet. Might explain the shoes.

Leaving the pictures, she headed to the bathroom, did what she needed to do, and then hurried back to the carport.

Sam was still there, gathering a few things.

"Hey," she said.

He glanced up. "That was fast."

"I don't mess around." She smiled.

Straightening, he handed her a pole. "Here. Take this one, Speedy Gonzales."

"Awesome. But I thought we weren't going to fish this afternoon. Just taking a cruise in the sound."

He stared directly into her eyes. "Lesson number one, College Girl. A fisherman is always prepared."

"Got it." She saluted. "Aye aye, captain."

That grin again. God, he could melt her down to her red toenails.

"And don't you forget it," he said. "This way."

He passed her, brushing her arm as he did. She followed him on a worn path around the carport to the back of the house. Immediately, the trees opened up in front of her and a wide expanse of water sparkled in the late afternoon sun. The backyard sloped down for several yards toward a dock, where the dog now lay sunning himself, with the boat berthed at the end.

Julia had to stop short. "Wow. This is impressive."

Sam stopped too, also watching the water. "Not bad."

"I'm not sure I would ever leave this place if I lived here."

Laughing, Sam headed toward the water. "Only time I leave is to go fishing," he called over his shoulder.

She jogged forward, catching up with him. "And to look for enchilada sauce?"

Again, stopping up short, he turned and smiled. "God, woman, but you do make me smile."

Julia stared. "Is that a bad thing?"

He shook his head. "No. Not at all. Come here."

In a quick motion, he put his arm around her shoulder and tugged her closer, pulling her into his side. She leaned in a little, tucked into the cradle of his body, and relaxed. *This is going to be fine, Julia. Just be smart.*

They walked toward the dock, his arm still around her. "Come on, Gunner. Get in the boat."

The hound jumped up and ran in front of them, leaping up into the boat.

"Gunner?"

"Yeah. A throwback to my past."

"Oh?" Julia looked up at him, her teasing smile also questioning.

"Military man."

She didn't say anything, just studied him, staring.

"The dog loves a good boat ride," he continued, setting a small tackle box and another pole in the boat. "Hates fishing though. He has a hard time reeling them in."

Smiling, she said, "Good thing I'm around then."

He hugged her a little tighter, took the pole, and then helped her into the boat. "Yep."

Julia glanced about while Sam busied himself with the poles and gear. "This is quite the boat, Fisherman."

"Yep. She's a beauty. An Albemarle Express, if you want to get technical. Made for fishing. Has a few years on her but I baby her. Bought her from a guy over in Manteo not long after I moved here." He handed her a life vest. "Here, put this on."

She took the vest and slipped it over her head. "You take her out on the ocean?"

"I do."

"This beauty have a name?"

Sam stared into her eyes for a couple of seconds, his expression immediately somber. "Yes. Her name's Hannah."

SAM DROVE AND JULIA STOOD BESIDE HIM, HER GAZE skimming out over the water. As usual, Gunner lay at his feet.

He was keenly aware of her presence, and it was all he could do to keep from stealing glimpses of her profile as they moved through the water. She stared straight ahead, then looked from side to side as she observed their surroundings from the mainland to the barrier islands. Her demeanor was almost childlike, in awe and wonder of all she saw.

"You can sit there if you want," he told her, motioning to the seat beside him.

"I want to stand right now so I can see everything."

Sam grinned, more inwardly than externally. She certainly did make him smile.

She'd said nothing when he'd told her the name of the boat—and he hadn't offered an explanation, either. He supposed at some point he'd tell her about Hannah but now wasn't the time. The moment had passed, and he wasn't ready to dig up that can of worms. Enjoying her smile as she faced the wind, her hair blowing back from her temples, was all he needed.

Had she ever been on a boat before?

"Your first trip out on the sound?" He shouted.

"Yes!" She glanced at him. "It's marvelous."

"On a boat?"

"Unless you count the Belle. Nothing like this."

Sam thought for a minute. "Ah. Steamboat. Ohio River. Docked at Louisville. Right?"

Julia eyed him. "Yes. That's where I'm from. I'm surprised you know about the Belle."

He'd already known where she lived but he wasn't revealing that yet, either. "I like boats."

"I see." She fell silent again, gazing out over the water. "How did you know?"

"What?"

"First time on a boat like this."

His gaze met hers then, and he absorbed the wonder in her eyes. "Lucky guess." Smiling, he turned back to look ahead of him. "Hold on."

She leaned in closer and draped her arm over the back of the chair. Immediately, all his senses were heightened.

Good God, this woman....

He sped up and they cruised up the sound side of Tuckaway Bay, then north toward Kitty Hawk Bay and Colington Harbor. They eased under the Wright Memorial Bridge and then traveled further north to Duck and Corolla. He pointed out some of the sights along the way, such as a few wild horses and the Corolla lighthouse.

"Sure looks different from this angle," she said.

"Yep. Everything looks a bit different from the water."

"I like it."

He made a wide swath, turning the boat around, cruised for a while, then cut off the engine. They drifted out in the middle of the sound, the waves gently lapping against the boat's hull.

"The sudden quiet is almost unsettling," she finally said.

He took her hand. "Let's head back here and sit. Relax." He pointed to a seat near the back of the boat, pulled the cooler closer, and popped the top open. Gunner ambled over, plopping down between the two of them.

Julia stroked the top of his head, smiling as he pressed into her fingers. "He won't jump out?"

"Naw. He's not fond of the water, but he does get excited when I pull in a fish. You should see him."

"I hope to one day."

"Me too." Reaching into the cooler, he plunged his hand into the cold, icy water and pulled out a Coors Light. He tipped it toward her. "Beer?"

She didn't reach for it. His gaze lifted to meet hers.

"No thanks," she said.

"Trying to quit?" He grinned.

She smiled at the old joke. "In a word, yes."

Sam pondered that and returned his attention to the bottle. He twisted the top off, tossed it into the open cooler, then started to take a drink. Stopping, he turned back to look at her.

"You mind if I have one?"

"Not at all."

"You just don't like beer or is it something else?"

She glanced off and sighed. After a few seconds, she turned back. "Well, you might as well know. I'm an alcoholic. Twenty-four days sober at this point. I was sober for two-hundred-eighty-two days before I fell off the wagon. I'm here, at the beach, to get my shit back together."

He didn't say anything.

She didn't either, just held his gaze.

The expression on hers was stone cold and steady. Determined. He gave her words a moment to sink in, then said, "Well, since it's confession time, my demon is PSTD. I fish because it calms me. I have night terrors that would curl your toes if you were lying in bed beside me."

Her look held steady as she studied him, then one corner of her mouth turned up into a half grin. "So, we're both flawed."

"Totally fucked up." Sam belted out a chuckle. He took a drink of the beer. "There's more but I have to save some of my story for another day."

Julia shook her head, smiling. "Oh Sam, you don't know half of my issues yet. I'm fucked up from way back."

"Let me guess. You mother or your father?"

"Can I just say both?"

"Ah, double whammy."

She nodded. "What about you? Family issues?"

"No. Best family in the world until I lost them all. The military took its toll on me after a while."

"Marines?"

"Navy SEAL. Retired. Sniper. But once a SEAL always as a SEAL, as they say."

She stared. "Hence love of boats and the dog's name."

"Yeah."

"For how long?"

"I retired after thirty years, almost ten years ago. Saw my share of special ops missions and headed up a few too. Killed too many humans and much to my regret, a few kids. Those are the ones that get you. One in particular... I can still see his eyes through the scope when he looked my way at the last second. Those flashbacks cause me the most pain and trigger the night terrors. I take anxiety meds most of the time, but honestly, a few beers in the afternoon generally does the trick."

He paused, observing her face. "But if drinking beer around you causes a problem, I won't. I can set it aside and never reach for one again."

Julia grasped his hand. "It won't. You do you. I know how to take care of myself. Besides, beer was never my drink of choice and I'm not even tempted. Now, bourbon? Tequila? That's another story."

"I don't keep either of those around."

"And I take anxiety meds, too, just so you know. My alcoholism is a relatively new thing, the past couple of years. I experienced some trauma that threw my world into such a chaotic shit-hell of a mess that I couldn't handle it."

Sam felt his heart swelling with concern for her. "I'm so sorry, Julia. Do you want to talk about it?"

She glanced down at their intertwined hands. "I usually only talk with my therapist and at AA meetings... Or sometimes with friends."

He rubbed her palm with his fingertips. "Well, this friend is a good listener, if you decide to share."

She shifted her gaze, meeting his. "I think maybe I do if you are sure. I swear, Fisherman, I can be a lot to handle." She grinned slightly.

Sam leaned in and touched her face, tracing a finger along her jawline. "Sweetheart, I'm sure. And I'm not going anywhere either."

JULIA STARED AT THE FLOOR OF THE BOAT. WHERE TO BEGIN?

After a minute, she made eye contact again with him. He'd put his sun hat on earlier and there was a slight shadow over his eyes, but she could still make out the steel blue color.

"Take your time," he said softly.

"I'm trying to figure out where to start."

"Just say what's on your heart, Julia."

She liked hearing him say her name. Although it was cute when he called her College Girl, and her heart warmed when the word sweetheart slipped from his lips, him calling her by her name felt even more intimate. His slight grin also gave her encouragement. Squaring her shoulders, she sat up, and just started talking.

"I went to law school. We talked about that. And I practiced law for several years. I married my high school and college sweetheart after passing the bar, which took a while, and we settled down and decided we wanted to start a family."

"So, you're married?"

"No. Divorced now."

"I see."

She nodded. "I pushed him away, made him leave. You see, we got pregnant. She was a little girl, and we named her...Caroline. For the longest time, I couldn't say her name. All I could do was refer to her as *the baby*. Therapy has helped with that. I carried her full term, and everything seemed perfect, but she was... Well, she was stillborn. They told me why—some placental problem with blood flow and lack of oxygen—but I never really comprehended how that could happen. I'd done everything right. All the classes. Ate right. Vitamins. Exercised. I even quit my job so I could nest and get ready."

She studied him and he sat and listened. "They also said it could have been my age. I was in my late thirties then, pushing forty. God. Where does the time go?"

He squeezed her hand. "You don't look forty."

"Forty-two. I look old as hell." She laughed. "The bourbon took its toll but being here the past few weeks has put some color back in my cheeks."

He grinned. "I think you're beautiful. You know I'm almost sixty?"

Her heart swelled a little. No one had called her beautiful in quite some time—but she wasn't ready to acknowledge that. "You're well-preserved for sixty."

"Pushing sixty. I still have a couple of months to go."

She laughed with him and then fell silent. He didn't interrupt her thoughts, as she rolled over where to go next.

"We bought a big old Victorian house in Old Louisville early in my pregnancy. The plan was for me to eventually quit the firm—my dad's firm—and turn the place into a bed and breakfast. In fact, I opened the business earlier this year, it just took me a while to get there."

"That's why you make a lot of breakfasts."

"Yes."

"It's coming together."

"But after we lost Caroline, this was while we were still renovating the place, I slowly unraveled. I couldn't cope. I was sad and crying all the time. I wouldn't get out of bed. Probably some insane combination of postpartum depression and grief. My head was not screwed on straight. My husband didn't know what to do with me, so we fought all the time. I blamed him. I blamed me. I wouldn't let the contractors in to work on the house. And I started secretly drinking just to get through the day. I kept a bottle of bourbon and a shot glass in my bedroom. Another one hidden in a kitchen cabinet. This went on for months."

"What made you stop?"

"I told my husband I wanted a divorce. Then last summer, I came out here for beach week with my girlfriends. We come every August and have since college. I drank too much here, too. I was trying to figure out what to do with my life. When I got home, I could see the stupid path I was on, and I picked a random rehab center and checked myself in. That's where I also got hooked up with Alcoholics Anonymous. I thought I was on a firm path to recovery but then some other crap happened."

Sam inhaled, as if he were taking a breath for her, and scooted closer to her on the seat. He let his breath out slowly, then said, "Take a minute, Julia. That's a lot of shit."

She let her breath out with a whoosh, looking straight ahead. "I suppose it is."

He clasped her hand again and stared ahead. After a pause of silence, he murmured, "I have a daughter."

She turned her head quickly, studying him. "You do?"

He nodded, slowly. Appeared to be thinking. While she was grateful for this pause from her story, she wondered if he was really ready to share with her yet.

"The shoes?"

"Yes."

"The pictures on the wall in the hallway?"

"Yes. And the name of the boat."

Julia hadn't put that together yet. "Her name is Hannah?"

"It is."

Now she supposed it was her turn to be the listener. "Tell me about her? Where is she?"

He hesitated, then said, "Albuquerque. She grew up there with her mother, whom I never married. It was a brief fling when I was on leave years ago. We gave it a try but honestly, we were estranged for most of Hannah's life, which meant that my daughter never really got to know me. The school pictures came every year, but that was about it."

"She never visited?"

"We tried visits once she was older, at my insistence. After I'd retired. She was moody, resistant, cranky, and at times, out of control. I didn't know what to do with her. Last time I saw her she was fifteen. She's twenty-one now, and just graduated from college."

"Fifteen is a funky age."

Sam shrugged. "Well, I was largely unavailable most of her life, off in the Middle East fighting ISIS and al-Qaeda and the Taliban, so she didn't know me. I'm sure it was difficult for her too."

"Well, yes, in her defense. And in yours, those early teens years are difficult for girls even under normal circumstances, whatever normal is —most parents don't know how to handle it."

"Yeah, but I'm sure I handled most everything badly."

Julia squeezed his hand. "Sam, I'm so sorry. That's rough."

He shook his head, then met her gaze. "Not compared to what you've gone through. We both lost our daughters but in different ways, I guess. At least I have pictures."

And I have a headstone. Julia closed her eyes, the vision of Caroline's grave flashing into her mind. She tried to press her eyes shut tighter to stop the tears but could feel them coming anyway.

"Ah shit. Sweetheart. I'm so sorry." His arms went around her.

"No, it's okay. I know what you were saying."

"Come here." He tugged her closer, her head resting on his shoulder. Sam stroked her hair with one hand and pulled her snug up against him with the other. "One thing I never want to do is make you cry."

Something tugged at her heart then, drawing her to him. She slanted back, looking into his eyes. Sam brushed a few hairs back from her forehead and peered into hers. Slowly, he leaned in and kissed away the tears from one cheek, then the other. He held her gaze for a moment and Julia felt her soul crack open a little.

Slowly, Sam leaned in and gently pressed his lips to hers.

"This isn't a good idea," she whispered after a few seconds.

"No. Probably not." His lips feathered over hers.

Julia sighed. "I'm really not in a good place."

"I know. But we're both fucked up. Right?"

Pulling back slightly, she searched Sam's eyes, finding warmth, caring, compassion, and perhaps, her soulmate there. "Fucked up as they come."

"Then it's all good."

Sam teased her lips again with his. Her arms went around his neck as she deepened the kiss.

Twenty

Beach week, day 1,
 Saturday morning,
 25 days sober

SAM HADN'T BEEN SURE IF HE'D SEE JULIA THAT MORNING.

He'd pondered whether the kiss had been the right or wrong thing to do after she'd left his house the day before, and throughout the night. The last thing he wanted, other than make her cry, was to push himself on her or make her uncomfortable.

Hell, relationships with women were never his strong suit and at fifty-nine, he didn't suppose he'd get any better at it. The awkward way that Julia had left within minutes of arriving back at the dock told him she was questioning the sanity of letting him kiss her.

But she had kissed him back. Hadn't she? Definitely.

Pulling into the parking lot in front of the beach access, Sam tried to push the yesterday scenario out of his head and concentrate on a relaxing morning of fishing, whether Julia would be there, or not. Gathering his pole and bucket and chairs, he headed over the path and wove through the dune fence to the resort beach.

And there she was, sitting in her chair in the normal spot, drinking a cup of coffee and watching the surf.

A sigh of relief exited his lips then, and his chest immediately felt less taut.

Sauntering closer, he dropped his gear, crouched beside her chair, and with his forefinger, turned her head so he could look into her eyes. She gazed back, searching deep into his.

"Good morning, Fisherman," she said quietly.

"Morning, College Girl."

"Quiche?" she asked.

"Now, sweetheart. You know real men don't eat quiche."

She grinned. "I heard that somewhere."

Straightening, he looked toward the surf, studying the water. "You getting fancy on me?"

"No. Just had a lot of eggs and cheese."

"I see. Homemade crust?"

She shook her head. "Naw. Store bought."

"You're slipping College Girl."

"I'm also lying. I didn't make quiche. Just wanted to see your reaction." She laughed, standing. "I made burritos."

"Sausage and cheese?"

"Yes. Want one?"

Sam glanced about but didn't see any burritos. "No."

"No?"

"Not yet." Leaning in, he grazed her lips with his, lingering over her mouth for several seconds. "Okay, now."

She grinned. "I was afraid you were going to quit me."

Slowly, he shook his head. "You should probably quit me, though."

"I don't want to."

"Good. Me, either." He reached for her hand. "Not sure I want to fish this morning."

"It's a bit rough, windy."

He nodded. "It is that."

"The burritos are at the cottage."

He looked at her. "Oh?"

"Her eyes grew rounder. "They were hot. Steaming. Scorching."

"Perhaps we should do something about that."

"I think so." She pulled in her lower lip and bit it.

Good God, woman.

"But my girlfriends are coming around noon, so...."

He glanced at his watch. It was barely seven a.m. "So we better get breakfast over with sooner rather than later?"

She gave a half nod. "I hate to rush things but...."

"Nothing worse than a cold burrito."

"True."

"Sometimes hot things are good eaten fast."

"Holy fuck." Julia stood and reached for his hand. "Come on, Fisherman."

He stood and tugged her closer. Leaning closer, his lips a breath away from hers, he whispered, "I'm right behind you, College Girl."

Leaving the chairs and gear on the beach, they walked hand-in-hand toward the cottage.

About halfway there, Julia halted, jerking his hand. "Wait."

Sam narrowed his gaze. "Cold feet?"

"It's just that... It's been a while since I've, uh, had a burrito."

He couldn't stifle a burst of laughter. "Let's jump back in together, sweetheart."

JULIA STRAIGHTENED THE PILLOWS ON THE BED AND RAN HER hand over the comforter. Glancing about, she saw no sign of Sam in her bedroom. Good. Maggie was her roommate this week, and she had the nose of a bloodhound when sniffing out sex. She'd probably smell it as soon as she walked into the room.

She grabbed the air freshener from the bathroom and sprayed over the bed and throughout the room.

Sex. With Sam. Oh, my God.

Anxiety rushed over her from out of the blue. She'd wondered if kissing him was a mistake the night before. Now, what the hell was she doing making love with him? This wasn't good. The timing wasn't right for her. She couldn't risk a relationship while she was in recovery. It was one of those things they talked about in AA. At the time, she hadn't paid much attention to the discussion because it didn't seem to apply to her. Her relationship with Mark was already on the skids and she'd pushed him away enough to realize she couldn't entertain thoughts of starting something back up again.

Plus, the divorce was all but final.

"Shit." The divorce. Or maybe she should say, the non-divorce. She'd lied to Sam, unintentionally, and supposed she was going to have to correct that miscue sooner rather than later. The last thing she wanted was to start off a relationship with a lie.

Is this a relationship? Or the start of one?

The panic that welled up inside her forced her to sit on the edge of the bed and clutch her stomach. She'd let her guard down. Again. Twenty-five days sober and she thought she was okay? What the fuck? She'd acted like things were normal. Hadn't she?

Stupid.

Her life was not normal and hadn't been for some time.

She stared out the window at the ocean. "At least I told Sam the truth about drinking. That I was an alcoholic. Admitting that to him was sort of like reminding myself. That I knew what I was doing."

Then why do I feel so on edge?

Because it was a mistake.

"Shit, shit, shit."

Reaching for her phone on the bedside table, she scrolled for Bill's number in Louisville. He picked up the call within a few seconds.

"Julia?"

"Hey Bill."

"You okay?"

She paced beside the bed. "No. Yes. I screwed up."

"Are you drinking? Where are you?"

"No," she said quickly. "No. I haven't had a drink since that night. I'm still at the beach. But I think I broke an AA rule or something."

"Rule? How so?"

"I've been seeing someone. A man. And this morning, we had sex."

Bill chuckled and that made Julia a little angry. "Don't laugh at me. I'm serious!"

"Julia, AA doesn't make strict rules about dating or sex, for that matter. We do have recommendations, but that is all they are—recommendations. Some people can't handle a growing relationship and everything that goes with it while in recovery. The point being that this is time to focus on yourself, not someone else."

She figured as much. "But what if he's screwed up too?"

"Is he an alcoholic?"

"No, no. But he has PTSD."

Bill paused. "Julia, do you want a relationship with this man?"

Did she? "I think so. I'm not sure. It's so new."

"How do you feel around him?"

"Relaxed. Carefree. But also, safe."

"Those are good things."

Thinking of Sam and their interactions while fishing made her feel warm and less anxious. "He makes me feel good about myself, Bill, and I forget about the other crap in my life."

"That's not a bad thing either—unless you forget to focus on the fact that you are still dealing with the crap in your life."

She thought about that. "And that I'm still in recovery. Okay. You're right."

"Just don't exchange the temporary bliss of a relationship for doing the hard work. Remember that relationships take work, too."

How well she knew that. "And working on myself should come first."

"That's the idea behind the AA recommendations."

"I get it."

Bill paused for a moment, then added, "Look, Julia. Think about this. He has PTSD. Don't think you can fix him. Don't make him your project and ignore yourself. Enter into the relationship because of how you feel when you are with him. How he makes your life better, and how you make his better. How you are better together than alone. Is that possible?"

"It could be. Needs time. But Bill, I just don't want to slip again."

"Have you felt like you were slipping?"

"No. Just anxious earlier because I was afraid I'd screwed up, broken a rule, and because of that, feared I might slip."

"No rules, Julia, except when it comes to drinking. When do you go to meetings out there?"

"Wednesday mornings."

"Maybe find a meeting sooner. Or call me anytime. You know that."

"I will."

Bill hesitated, then asked, "By the way, have you heard from Larry?"

She hadn't, but she hadn't expected to. A twitter of panic raced across her gut. "No. Is he okay?"

"Not sure. I've not seen him since Gretchen's funeral."

Not a good sign. Should I text him? "Maybe he just needs a break."

"Maybe. I hope that's all it is."

"Me, too." She sat again on the side of the bed, glancing at the clock. "I will let you go, Bill. My girlfriends are coming for the week and will be here soon."

"Beach week? Are you ready for that?"

"Yes. I have a plan and they already know what it is. I worked through it with Melinda."

"Good."

"Thanks for listening, Bill."

"Call me. I'm serious. When are you coming home?"

That was a good question. "Not sure. I'll let you know." *At the moment, I'm not certain I even want to.*

Since Lia and Julia were already at the resort, and Alice lived just across town, the plan was for the three of them to meet at The Sandcastle at noon and wait for Maggie—Maggie, whom no one knew for certain was even going to show up.

To be honest, Julia didn't expect her. And if she did show? She fully expected Maggie would not stay long.

Julia found Lia sitting at a table overlooking the beach and joined her. Alice swept in a few minutes later—on her lunch hour—leaned in to hug each woman, and then sat across the booth from Julia and beside Lia. "Gosh, you and Zach have done a great deal of work on this place, Lia. It's fabulous."

"I keep telling you to come by. We have a new chef, too. Try the clam chowder."

"Sounds yummy."

Julia closed her menu. "I think I'm going for fried and greasy today. Fish and chips."

"Oh, those are great too," Lia offered. "Zach gets those all the time. Have you all noticed he's put on a few pounds lately? Sampling new menu items is his favorite pastime."

The girls all laughed.

"So, let me make sure I have this right," Alice said, opening her menu. "The last bit of communication any of us has had with Maggie was over a week ago."

Lia nodded. "As far as I know."

"And what was it she said again?"

Lia sighed and picked up her phone. "Here are her exact words: *I'm in. Will send details.*"

"Well, that's odd," Julia said, looking at her own phone. "I never got that text."

Lia studied Maggie's message. "Hmm. Looks like she sent it just to Alice and me. I didn't realize that."

Rolling her eyes, Julia shook her head and turned her attention to the menu. "Figures."

Alice leaned toward Julia. "You and Maggie still at odds?"

She huffed. "I suppose. But that's not my story to tell."

"Oh boy." Alice sat up straight and glanced over the restaurant. "Seriously, Julia, if there is something we need to know, please tell us."

She shook her head. "No. Any conversation Maggie and I had is privileged because I was her attorney at the time."

"But she fired you," Alice said.

"Doesn't matter."

"I just worry about her," Lia interjected. "It's been a year since I've seen her, and I can still see the defeated look on her face when she left Tequila Sunrise with Max last summer. In fact, I don't think there's a day gone by that I haven't thought of her, worried about her and the kids, and wondered how she was coping."

Julia huffed. "She's fine. Park your worries elsewhere."

"God. You don't have to be so callous," Alice muttered.

Julia swallowed a *very callous* retort. Instead, she sucked in a breath, let it out slowly through her nose, and stared at the beach.

Alice must have realized she'd hit a nerve because she didn't utter another word.

After a minute, she looked back, eyeing both women across the table. "Maggie has figured out how to cope with Max and her life. I may not agree with her methods, and you may not either, but that's as far as I go with the conversation. Anything else has to come from her. Now, let's change the subject until she gets here."

Alice agreed. "Fine. That's fair."

"Good."

Silence settled over the table while they all perused their menus. Lia closed hers and crossed her arms over the table. "I'm going for the shrimp and grits."

"Sounds good," Alice said. "I'm trying the chowder."

A pause settled over the table, then Lia asked, "Julia, how was your date yesterday?"

Shit. She met Lia's gaze. "Not a date. Just a boat ride."

Alice perked up. "Oh please, do tell. I want to know all about this non-date."

This was the last thing she wanted to discuss—but perhaps she should get it over with before Maggie arrived. Discussing her personal life with her was not an option. Right now, she didn't trust how Maggie would perceive her friendly relationship with Sam.

Which you know is more than friendly, Julia Salinger. "It was fine. Let's discuss another time."

She avoided eye contact with both women.

Lia broke the silence first. "I didn't realize the subject was off the table. I'm sorry."

Immediately, she felt apologetic. And a little weird about it all. "No, it's okay. It's just so new, and I'm prickly and a little on edge right now because the last time I saw our friend Maggie, it didn't go so well. Let me just say this—the boat ride was fun, and we talked a lot."

"Who? What boat?" Alice grinned and reached for Julia's hand on the table. "Hey, I'm happy for you but... But what about Mark and everything?"

Julia pushed back from the table, her chair squeaking a little. "See? This is the conversation I don't want to have yet with anyone because I don't know any of the answers. Right now, I'm just living one day at a time. I had fun. I don't know anything else. Please, let's drop it, okay?"

Alice took a breath and held it. Julia wondered if she was going to explode before she exhaled. Finally, she said, "I'm sorry, Julia. I jumped way too far ahead—"

A shadow fell over the table. "Well, hello ladies."

All three looked up. Maggie stood there, grinning wide, looking happy as a clam at high tide.

"Maggie! Thank God." Lia's chair screeched against the floor as she pushed away from the table.

Alice squealed and both she and Lia jumped up, hugging Maggie, hopping up and down, and chattering about Maggie's shorter hair and her outfit. Julia sat in her seat and avoided looking at them for a moment, then lifted her gaze.

Maggie, caught up in the excitement, hugged the women back and giggled until she made eye contact with Julia over Alice's shoulder. Her grin faded and Julia looked away.

Twenty-One

Beach week, day 1,
   Saturday afternoon

AFTER LUNCH, LIA AND JULIA WALKED TO GULL COTTAGE while Alice and Maggie headed for their cars in the main parking lot, to move them closer to the cottage.

"She looks good, doesn't she?" Lia remarked.

"She does."

"Her shorter hair is cute. Is it darker?"

Julia hadn't really noticed. "I think it might be."

"And her outfit? Wasn't it—"

"A little slutty for her age? I thought it was just me." Julia glanced sideways at Lia's profile and grinned.

But Lia chewed on her words for a minute. "It was a little youngish. The skirt was really short."

"And the top lowcut."

"Plus, I think she's wearing false eyelashes. I've never known her to do that."

Julia shrugged. "Maybe it's all the rage with middle-aged women trying to look younger."

"You think that's what she's trying to do?"

"I think she's trying to boost her self-confidence." She'd said enough.

But Lia wasn't dropping it. "Do you think everything is really okay with her and Max? To hear her talk, they've patched things up."

"I'm sure he's riding her long and hard and often and she's living her life for the thrill of it."

Julia halted a few feet from the cottage steps and looked at Lia. Yes, Maggie had been boastful at lunch about how well she and Max were getting along, and the sexual discussions had gone far beyond innuendo —almost to the point where she'd been uncomfortable. But Julia had silently called bullshit on her every word. Sex doesn't make everything better. Still holding Lia's gaze, she added, "What I think is that Maggie is fooling herself and it's going to come back to bite her in the ass."

Lia blinked and stared for a few seconds. "She appears happy."

"Appears. Think about the meaning of that word," Julia snapped. "The mere fact that you chose that word implies that you don't really think she is happy."

"I don't know what to think, Julia. I'm trying to reconcile what I see about her—her physical appearance and demeanor—with what I know about her personally, and her history with Max. I just want her to be okay, so I guess I'm hoping she is, and has found some common ground with him." She sighed. "Or something."

"Or something is more accurate." Julia climbed the three steps to the porch, then glanced down the narrow road. "Here they come."

Lia ignored that, moving up the steps beside her. "You know something. What's going on?"

Julia nodded. "Yes, I do. But like I've said before, it's not my place to tell Maggie's business. You know she can't keep a secret, so she'll blurt it out sooner rather than later, I am sure of it."

She stood and watched the two cars move into the parking spaces beside the cottage, next to Julia's car. "Besides," she added. "I'm really pissed at her for looking so damn good."

Lia angled herself closer. Julia could feel her staring. "Why?"

She met Lia's gaze. "Because, dammit, it's been a whole fucking year and we all have been worried about her, afraid that Max was hitting her, and maybe the kids, and she doesn't communicate with us *at all—then*, she prances in with rings on her fingers and bells on her toes, like every fucking thing in the world is right."

"And we know it's not," Lia said.

"And we know it's not. Yes." Julia echoed.

They looked to the small parking lot as car doors swung open, trunk lids popped, and Alice and Maggie babbled about while retrieving their luggage and other belongings. As they approached the cottage, Julia stepped aside, ushering them across the wide porch.

"Here, let me take a bag," she said to Maggie, making direct eye contact. "You're staying in my room. Alice, you and Lia are in the second bedroom. And bonus! Each room has its own en suite, but of course we have to share that."

"No problem!" Maggie eyed her and smiled sweetly. "I'll follow you."

"Super," Julia mumbled, and took the smaller bag. *God grant me the serenity... Give me strength and please do not let anyone have bourbon in these bags.*

Neither she nor Maggie said a word as they moved through the cottage.

Alice and Lia followed, casually chatting.

"I'll bring my stuff over later," Lia said. "I still have a few things to tie up at the office this afternoon—not a lot, will take me about thirty minutes, hopefully—then I'm here for the duration."

Julia silently wondered if they would get through the week. The duration could be the entire week, or just a couple of days. Remained to be seen.

They entered her bedroom and Julia put Maggie's small bag on the bed. "This one's yours. Hope that's okay. I've been here for a bit, so I've already claimed the bed by the window." She pointed.

"No problem." Maggie glanced about. "The cottages are nice, aren't they? Isn't Lia so lucky to have found Zach again and this incredible place?"

She had to agree. "Actually, it is quite amazing. I've loved staying here."

Maggie studied her. "You've been here for a while?"

"Yes. Taking a break from the Louisville life."

"I see." She paused, biting her lip. "Julia...?"

Julia stepped away from Maggie's bed and moved toward the window, anticipating the upcoming speech. "We don't need to go there, Maggie. It is what it is."

"What do you mean?" Maggie followed her.

Turning, she glared. "Face it. We left things rather uncertain between us the last time we saw each other. There's bound to be tension."

Maggie put her hands up, palms out. "Stop. I know. Can we let that go for the week?"

"I can. As long as you're honest with me, and everyone else. Can you?"

"Honest? In what way?"

Julia grasped both Maggie's forearms and shook her a little. Then immediately, she regretted that, looking into Maggie's startled face. She let go and stepped back. "Look. We are all worried about you. We've barely seen or heard from you in a year, since Max took you away last summer in an angry fit. We didn't know if he was beating the shit out of you or fucking you silly, whatever. You need to communicate with all of us. We care about you, Maggie. Now buck up and do the right thing."

"Yes. Okay. I get it." Maggie stepped away. She hoisted her larger bag onto the bed, staring at it. "It's just that sometimes it's difficult for me to call."

"And text? That only takes a few seconds."

"But Max is always under foot. He's working from home now."

Julia studied her. "So, I imagine that makes it a little difficult to rendezvous with the 'Bama boyfriend. You're still seeing him, I assume?"

Maggie looked away and sat on the edge of the bed, staring at the wall. "I don't want to talk about it."

Avoiding eye contact, my friend? Avoiding telling them that you're fucking a redneck cowboy on the side?

"See? There you go." Julia sat beside her. "Tell me."

"Yes."

"You're still seeing him?"

"When Max is out of town, which is often."

Julia nodded. "I see."

Shifting to face her, Maggie asked, "Have you told the others?"

She shook her head. "Not my place."

"Thank you." Maggie stood and unzipped the bag on the bed, throwing the top back, and pulling out a stack of folded clothing. "I have some things to reconcile and am not sure what I am going to tell anyone. But I hope to figure it out this week."

Julia went back to the window, and looked out over the beach, frowning. She sure wished Sam was out there—she could use some of their carefree banter about now, but he was long gone. He knew her situation this week, that she might be more scarce than usual, and he understood. She'd likely be the one begging away to catch him when she could, wanting—no needing—to see him.

She'd had it easy the past few weeks, dealing only with her own issues. Was she ready to tackle Maggie again?

And honestly, should she?

Taking on another human's problems and postponing her own was not a good idea. Bill had more or less said that about Sam the other day. Maggie could also fall into that category.

Glancing quickly at her bed, she caught an image of the two of them together there, naked, tangled sheets, bodies intertwined....

Was that just a couple of hours ago? Seemed like an eternity.

She jerked that thought away and looked back at Maggie. "Well, beach week is good therapy. Right? We've always said that. Maybe it will help. But Maggie? You have to tell Lia and Alice about your cowboy lover because I don't want to be the keeper of your sordid secrets."

Maggie met her glare. "Okay. Let me choose the time. All right?"

"Fine." Julia headed for the bedroom door. "I'm going to check on the others and let you get settled."

Maggie said nothing for a moment. "Wait. You're drinking again? I read the text."

She whirled back. "Oh, you care? You didn't say anything when I sent it. You never do and we're never sure you even read them."

"I'll do better. Promise."

"And no, I'm not drinking again. I'm sober."

Maggie put some T-shirts in a dresser drawer. "I'm glad. But you relapsed or something? What do they call it?"

"That's right. Relapsed. And yes, I did."

Maggie peered into her eyes. "I'm sorry. I hope you are okay."

"Ditto." Swallowing a dry lump in her throat, she added, "I'm sober nearly a month and plan to keep it that way."

"Well, good."

Tension ebbed and flowed between them for a moment. Julia wondered if Maggie was truly being compassionate and sympathetic or just throwing her a bone.

Abruptly, Lia and Alice burst into the room.

"So," Alice said. "What are the plans for this afternoon? Beach? Shopping? Naps?" She laughed. "I swear, with the week I've had, I really would like a nap this afternoon."

"I'm up for a nap too," Maggie said. "With getting everyone out the door this morning, plus the drive, I'm exhausted."

Lia moved closer to Maggie. "Oh? Are Max and the kids going somewhere?"

"Yes. Max is taking them down to Hilton Head. He has a golf tournament, and we figure Carol is old enough to watch the younger kids while he's gone."

Julia had to swallow her tongue to keep from blurting out words she didn't want to say. Carol was a scheming little teenage bitch, and unless she had matured a whole helluva lot over the past year, Julia questioned the sanity of Maggie's thinking.

It's none of your business, Julia.

"Wow," Alice said. "I forget how old Carol is. They grow up so fast." Her gaze skittered from Lia to Julia.

"She's sixteen. Seventeen in November. Definitely old enough to care for the little kids." Maggie's tone was defensive.

All Julia could think about was the stunt Carol had pulled last summer during beach week, when she and her siblings were staying with

George and Ella, and pulled a disappearing act, lost for hours, only to find out she'd called her dad to come get her.

"Is she still close to Max?" Lia asked.

Was Lia thinking the same thing?

Maggie turned her way, her expression frozen. "They get along very well."

Shit. She wished Alice and Lia would just let it go. *Change the subject.*

"Well. Since the two of you are taking naps, and Lia, you need to do a little work, right? I think I'll take a walk on the beach and burn off the fish and chips."

"I'll walk with you toward the hotel," Lia said. "You two take naps and let's all meet back here in what, say, an hour or so?"

"Perfect." Maggie grinned, then yawned. "I'll be perkier by then."

Julia wasn't sure she could stand a perkier Maggie.

She took a longer walk than intended, strolling north on the beach for an hour, and then another hour back to the cottage. She even managed to navigate the crowd of people on the beach, pretending they weren't there and keeping her head down, scanning the surf for treasures.

Part of her worried that the others would be mad she was taking so long getting back. The other part of her—the *fuck you* part—didn't give a flying leap. While she wasn't upset with Alice and Lia, her increasing frustration with Maggie was winning out over everything else, and obviously coloring her mood.

Dammit.

Get a grip, Julia.

During the stroll, she contemplated a number of things— mostly about Maggie—but she also ruminated over her budding relationship with Sam. She should probably put time into thinking about what she was doing with him, but this week that would be impossible. One thing she knew for certain, Sam was an off-topic subject of discussion with the girls—she had a lot of soul-searching to do for herself and didn't need girlfriend opinions messing up her head.

Mother Hen Alice would have a strong opinion. *Are you sure you know what you are doing, Julia? What about Mark?*

Maggie would be the opposite. *If the sex is good, I say go for it. You only live once.*

And Lia? She'd be non-committal. *Whatever you think is best, Julia.*

None of that was helpful, so why even go there?

Once again, she longed for Willow's non-bullshit opinions. She was a straight-shooter, and Julia respected the hell out of that. Wren could be too but was slightly more cautious.

Damn. She missed those women!

When she got back to the Gull, to her surprise, the cottage was strangely quiet. Lia wasn't there yet either, it seemed. She peeked into the bedrooms and saw that both Alice and Maggie were still sleeping.

The scene brought a brief smile to her face as she headed back to the porch and settled into a comfortable chair to watch the ocean, kicking off her flip-flops and propping her bare feet up on the porch rail. Twenty-some years ago, naps during beach week happened because they were either hungover from a night of drinking or were baked from an afternoon of sun and marijuana.

At the thought of weed, Willow burst into her head again. She'd always been their ticket to finding a weed man on the island, especially when they were in college. Julia supposed this year there would be no weed because there would be no Willow.

Frankly, she didn't think her smoking pot was a good idea. Bill hadn't recommended it, and truthfully, she'd never been particularly attracted to the substance—let alone addicted. Yet again, prior to her binge-drinking episodes after the baby, she'd not been addicted to alcohol, either.

However, a little weed at the end of the day during beach week had always mellowed her out, particularly if the girls were arguing—which they frequently did. They loved each other but fought like sisters.

Probably best to steer clear. But she seriously doubted weed was even going to be a thing, anyway, because of the absence of the twins.

She wished to hell and back that one of them would surface soon, or she was going to have to pull some strings with a few law enforcement agents she knew who might be able to dig into their disappearance.

And the only reason she hadn't done that before now was because she'd wanted to respect their wishes and privacy. Obviously, they didn't want to be found. For some troublesome reason, she sensed the women were in danger, and her poking around into their affairs might cause a domino effect of investigation.

The last thing she wanted was to rat out her best friends.

Sometime later, Lia called out, rushing up the cottage steps.

Did I drift off?

"Julia! I'm so sorry I'm late. I got caught up in all kinds of fires that I simply had to take care of."

Startled a little, Julia set up straight, attempting to orient herself. "No problem. What time is it?"

"Nearly six o'clock."

"Damn. I guess I slept. Are Maggie and Alice up?"

Lia shrugged. "Haven't a clue. I just got here."

Pulling her feet from the rail, Julia stood, stretching her arms toward the porch ceiling. "After we all shower, it will be time for dinner. I suppose we're going out tonight?"

"We could do The Sandcastle again, if everyone wants, since it's day one and people are tired. We can go into town tomorrow."

"I'm fine with that. Let's get them up."

They headed inside.

Lia immediately halted, looking toward the kitchenette. "The back door is open. Maybe they are on the deck."

"Well, let's hope they are. Otherwise, we have intruders." Julia teased.

Lia rolled her eyes.

They pushed through the open door and the smell of pot met Julia's nose. It was like her earlier musings had manifested into real life. Alice and Maggie were stretched out on deck chairs, sharing a joint.

Lia rushed toward them. "What the holy crap, girls? This is a family area. Who brought it?"

"Well, I did," Maggie said, holding out the joint. "Want a puff?"

"No!"

Stepping forward, Julia glared at Maggie. "Since Willow's not here, you thought you'd take it upon yourself to find a weed man?"

"No. I brought it with me." Maggie sat up and handed the joint to Alice. "I have connections at home. Besides, it's private back here, right? —with the dunes and sea oats and those scrub trees surrounding the deck. No one can see us."

Lia paced. "Well, put it out. We worked hard to make it known that this is a safe place for families and children. The smell of pot doesn't give that impression. Besides, it's still illegal in North Carolina." She turned to Alice. "And frankly, I'm surprised at you, given your job and all."

"And the fact that she's a goody-two-shoes and the mother hen of the group," Julia added.

Alice laid the joint on a small plate they were using as an ashtray. "Look. I've had a week. Besides Marilyn's campaign heating up, she's been getting a lot of flak from the press about some city issues. I needed something to take the edge off."

"Yeah," Maggie added loudly. "And she's not so much a goody-two-shoes any more now that she's fucking the mayor!"

Julia huffed out a breath. *Another tangled mess....* "Good God, Maggie."

Alice stood. "Fuck. Shut up. Do you have to yell?"

"Hold on, ladies." Julia took a breath and met Maggie's gaze. She lowered her voice in an attempt to lower the temperature of the conversation. "So, it's okay for you to blurt out about Alice's affair with Marilyn—which we already knew about anyway—but it's not cool for you to come clean to everyone about your side action?"

"What?" Alice and Lia shouted the word simultaneously.

Maggie's eyes grew big and round, glowering at Julia. "You promised!"

"Yeah. And you all promised not to get shit-faced around me."

"We promised not to have alcohol in the cottage. That's different. And it's weed, not bourbon," Maggie said. "We thought it was okay. Hells bells, it's beach week!"

"It's illegal and it's addictive. And apparently, I have an addictive personality. What the fuck? Besides, can't you see how this is upsetting Lia? This is her business, her livelihood—don't risk that. And frankly, we aren't twenty-somethings any longer. We're grown women in our forties and perhaps we should all start acting like it." She turned, heading toward the cottage.

"Pot calling the kettle black?"

Julia whipped back. "Yes, indeed. I'm putting myself into that scenario too. It's time some of us faced the music and got our shit together."

"Fuck off, Julia. You're spewing a lot of bullshit, and you know it."

Moving closer, she peered deep into Maggie's eyes. "At least I'm up front and honest with my shit. You could take a lesson." She rotated and rushed through the back door.

"It's none of your business, Julia!" She heard Maggie's words and halted. Tempted to head back out on the deck and wring her friend's pretty little neck, she stopped herself.

Walk away.

Fine.

"Enjoy your dinner," she called out. "I'll see you whenever. Don't wait for me." Walking straight through the cottage, she left out of the front, the screen door slapping closed behind her. Grabbing her fishing chair leaning against the porch, and a large beach towel she'd tossed over the rail earlier, she headed for the fishing spot.

It was going to be a long night.

DAY 1, SATURDAY EVENING

JULIA LAY BACK IN HER BEACH CHAIR, FACING THE SURF, watching the tide slowly lick higher on the beach. The moon was nearly full, and a few people milled around closer to the hotel. The Tiki Hut Bar was lively though, and she listened to the partiers laughing and talking loudly. Normally, that didn't bother her. She could hear them most nights from the porch cottage but tonight, she was craving peace and quiet—*needed peace and quiet*—and the lull of the waves to calm the unruliness in her headspace.

Bits and snatches of conversation with Maggie and the girls.

Throwbacks to dialogue with Mark.

Melinda's guidance ringing in her ear and Bill's candid advice setting her straight.

It seemed odd that for more than three weeks, she'd felt so collected and together. Everything had changed when Maggie stepped into The Sandcastle earlier today.

What that said, she still had to uncover—or perhaps, simply face head-on.

She was best alone.

When dysfunction entered her life, that's when she felt challenged. So, it seemed she had a choice—either learn how to cope with the dysfunction or spend the rest of her life by herself.

Or maybe, with someone who was just like her?

Her phone pinged and when it did, she wished she'd left it back at the cottage. It was Lia.

Lia: *I have your dinner. Should I bring it to you?*

Julia: *Thanks, but no. Stick it in the fridge.*

Julia: *I don't want to see anyone right now.*

Lia: *Are you okay?*

Julia: *I'm working through some things in my head. Yes, I'm fine.*

Lia: *Maggie is sorry.*

Julia: *Fuck that. If she was sorry she'd apologize. To me.*

Lia: *About the weed I mean.*

Julia: *Did she not think?*

Lia: *I don't know. I think she's caught up in her own world.*

Julia: *You think?*

Lia: *Yeah. Obvious, huh?*

Julia: *Hey. I'll be fine here tonight. I need the waves.*

Lia: *I'll worry about you.*

Julia: *I'll text.*

Lia: *Good. That works. Sweet dreams.*

Yeah, right.

Julia: *Good night.*

The phone lay silent for a moment, then Lia texted again.

Lia: *The girls want to go to Ocracoke tomorrow. Will you come? Please?*

Julia: *Don't know. Check with me in the morning. Maybe.*

SHE ACTUALLY SLEPT PEACEFULLY MOST OF THE NIGHT. USING the towel as a blanket, she'd kept warm enough. The nights were still pleasant, but humid, anyway, in late August. The waves had lulled her into a state of peaceful bliss, taking her troubles out with the tide—at least temporarily.

She blinked herself awake just as the sun peeked over the distant horizon, a chain reaction of oranges and pinks and yellows drifting into the day.

Movement off to her right caught her eye as the orb drifted higher. Sam ambled her way, a surprised look on his face. "Morning College Girl. You're up early."

He halted by her chair and dropped his things.

"I've been here all night."

"Seriously?"

"Yes."

He glanced up at the cottage. "Trouble at the sorority house?"

Julia laughed. "Something like that. Women are fucking crazy." She pointed. "Stick that chair in the sand and talk to me, Fisherman."

He eyed her for a moment, and she let him study her. Looking up, she could feel the warmth of the rising sun on her cheeks. Or was it his stare that heated her face? After a moment, he unfolded the chair and sat, all the time focused on her.

"You seem a little tense. Agitated."

She imagined she was. "I suppose the waves didn't work their magic like I was hoping. Yes, I'm a bit on edge."

"I've never seen you like this."

"I've been thinking about how much I love bourbon—and how much I hate it at the same time."

He stared. "Do you want a drink?"

"No. And that will always be the answer to that question."

Nodding, he said, "Okay, sweetheart. How can I help?"

"Get me the fuck out of here?"

"Really?"

"I don't know. I should be here with them, but my friend Maggie is driving me crazy. We've argued too much already, and I honestly can't see spending the rest of the week with her unless she gets her act together...or I learn how to ignore her."

"What is she doing?"

Julia shook her head. "It's a long story."

"I got nothing but time."

Her phone pinged but she ignored it. Then again.

"Someone trying to reach you?"

Julia rolled her eyes. "They will go away."

Another text notification sounded.

"Really?"

Lia called out then from the cottage porch. "Julia! You coming? We're leaving in thirty minutes."

"Jesus." She looked back at Sam. "I suppose I should go with them. They want to take the ferry down to Ocracoke Village."

"That's a fun trip."

"It's been years since I've been."

"Good fishing."

She smiled. "Can Hannah take us there sometime?"

He nudged her with his shoulder. "Anytime you want, sweetheart."

"Hmm." Julia studied him. "I should be with them, as much as I want to escape with you. I need to resolve this issue with Maggie sooner or later, because I can't keep thinking about my love/hate relationship with bourbon." She peered into his eyes, leaned a little closer, and whispered, "Can you rescue me later tonight? After dinner?"

His grin went sideways. Kinda sexy. "Sweetheart, I can rescue you any damn time you want. How about a midnight boat ride?"

She fully leaned in then, her lips nearly grazing his. "I love the sound of that."

"We can even sleep on the boat, out in the sound, if you want."

"Oh, even better. Under the moonlight?"

"Where else?"

"I can't wait until midnight."

"How about if I meet you right here. Supposed to be a full moon tonight. I'll come and get you, so you don't have to drive."

"Good plan. I'll sneak out. I already have goose bumps."

"And I'll be here to whisk you away." He leaned in and brushed his lips over her mouth.

Julia savored the light touch and whispered back, "Perfect, Fisherman."

Twenty-Two

Beach week, day 2,
26 days sober

THE ONLY THING WORSE THAN BEING TRAPPED ON A FERRY for forty-five minutes with bickering girlfriends, was being trapped in the car with them for the hour drive south to Cape Hatteras. Why had she agreed to this?

Because it's beach week and this is the kind of stuff we do during beach week.

She should count her lucky stars. At least the ferry was open-air, and she could get out of the car, stroll around, and watch the water for fish.

The squabbling had started before they left the cottage. They'd settled on taking the vehicle ferry over from Hatteras, rather than the passenger ferry, because Maggie insisted she wanted her car to drive around the island.

"Besides," she'd said. "We might want to check out the beaches."

Alice narrowed her gaze. "Maggie, we have a beach right out our front door here. We're going to Ocracoke for lunch, shopping, a bit of sight-seeing, and a relaxing afternoon."

Smiling widely, Maggie picked up her beach bag. "And maybe skinny dipping on one of the more secluded beaches?"

"Oh, good grief, Maggie," Lia said. "No."

Maggie grinned wickedly. Julia sensed she was intentionally trying to get Lia and Alice's goat. "Or we could do something tamer, like shelling."

"Any shells that washed up last night are gone by now," Alice mused. "Tourists and locals alike know to get out early."

Maggie shot Alice a sneery look. "Oh, come on. What's the big deal anyway?"

"Well, parking, for one," Lia told her. "Goodness, it's been years since I've been down there. Things have changed and probably not like you remember. Ocracoke Village is still a quaint fishing town, but it's a lot busier than it was twenty years ago. Besides, the new passenger ferry drops people off at the town harbor now, and we can walk everywhere. If we drive, we have to worry about finding a parking space."

Maggie batted the air. "Oh pooh. I've never had any trouble before."

"Like Lia said, how long has it been since you've been down there?" Alice asked.

"A few years."

"I rest my case. Things have changed."

Squaring herself at the door, Maggie stared at her friends. "Well, I want my car. I'll drive separately."

At that, Julia had had enough. Picking up her crossbody bag, she slung it over her shoulder. "Let's get the fuck going. If she wants her car, she wants her car. I can drive the rest of us." She headed for the porch.

"Well, shit, Julia."

Swinging around, Julia glared at Maggie. "What?"

"You all just come with me. No use taking two cars. If anyone wants to take the passenger ferry when we get to Hatteras, then go for it."

"We might need reservations for that," Lia offered feebly, pulling her phone from her bag. "I'll check."

"Then let's get going and take care of that in the car. Can we get out the door please? It will be past lunch time before we get there at this rate."

Their banter continued in the car, alternating with bouts of silence.

Julia sat in the back seat with Lia—most of the time her right knee bouncing up and down with nervous energy—while she watched the sea oats and sand dunes whirr by as Maggie traveled south on Highway 12.

Now, on the ferry, she could see Ocracoke Island ahead. *Thank God.*

Maggie stepped up behind her. "Time to get in the car. We'll be exiting soon."

Julia huffed out a breath and followed her friends, taking her place in the back seat. They waited, windows down, for the ferry to slip into the dock at the terminal. She sat behind the passenger seat and glanced at Maggie, who was gripping the steering wheel tightly with both hands.

"Girls, I have a confession," she blurted out. "I need to tell you something."

Julia glanced at Lia and clamped her lips shut tight. *Here it comes.*

Alice, sitting in front of Julia, reached out and touched Maggie's arm. "What is it, honey?"

Maggie looked straight ahead. "What Julia said last night was true. I've been spreading a lot of bullshit. Things are not good at home and I'm probably making things worse."

The cars on either side of them started their engines.

Maggie nervously fiddled with her car keys in the ignition.

Lia leaned forward. "Maggie, if you are upset, why not let me drive?"

"No." She shook her head, still looking ahead. "I'm not upset. I'm sort of mad at myself for a lot of things. Let me get this car off the boat and find us a place for lunch. Let's talk then. Okay?"

"You're sure you are okay to drive?" Alice asked.

Lia and Julia exchanged glances.

"I'm fine. Let me drive for a few minutes, if that's okay with all of you. I need to think a few things through."

Is that because you are not sure you want to tell us everything, my friend?

Julia almost uttered that question then held her tongue. Maggie was opening up. It was not her place to stop her, whether whatever she was going to say was reality or the Maggie version of reality.

"Whatever you need to do, honey," Alice cooed. "We're not going anywhere."

Damn right. We're held captive in Maggie's car. Was this her plan all along? No place to go when seat-belted in a moving vehicle.

Less than fifteen minutes later, Maggie pulled the silent car into the parking lot of Jason's Restaurant, located just on the edge of Ocracoke Village. No one had said a word while Maggie drove. Julia found the atmosphere in the car a little stifling so was happy to open her door and head toward the restaurant entrance.

Once inside, Maggie took control again. Julia simply stepped back and let her, as did the others. Maggie asked the hostess for a table for four, rather than a booth, and Julia supposed that the table seating avoided having to sit right beside someone. Plus, it was easier to make eye-contact with a group. It was a tactic she had also used at times when meeting with clients in a public place.

They settled into their seats and perused the menus. Shortly, the server came back with water glasses. "Are you ready to order?"

"I am," Julia said. "I'll have the crabcake sandwich."

"Me too," said Alice, closing her menu.

"I want the fish sandwich," Maggie added.

"The Hippie Wrap for me," Lia said.

Julia stared at her. "What the heck, Lia? It's beach week. A veggie wrap?"

Lia shrugged. "Zach isn't the only one in the family who has put on a few pounds."

Alice leaned toward her. "But it's beach week, Lia...."

Glancing around the table, Lia made eye contact with each of them. "Oh hell. Bring me a crabcake sandwich too."

The server smiled. "Coming up ladies. Anyone want anything other than water to drink?"

"Got tequila?" Maggie said.

Julia shot her a look.

"Sorry. Just wine and beer here," the server said.

"I think we're all good with water," Alice told her, smiling. When the server left, Alice whipped around and glowered at Maggie. "What the heck was that? Tequila? Are you trying to make us mad at you?"

THE SPACE IN BETWEEN: A NOVEL

Maggie bit her lower lips. "It slipped out."

Julia waved it off. "Good God. Forget it. The last thing I want any of you to do is change your habits or do something different because of me. Even though I sort of asked you to. Order some wine or beer if you want. It is fine."

"But we don't want to add to your issues."

"I get that," Julia admitted. "And you won't. But look, we all have issues, right? I'm a drunk. Maggie's a sex addict. Lia thinks she's fat. And Alice is..." She looked at Alice. "Damn, what are your issues? Do you even have any?"

At that, Alice burst into laughter. "More than you know. I just don't talk about them."

"Tell me one," Julia goaded.

Alice rolled her eyes. "Goodness. I don't know what to say."

Lia leaned closer to Alice. "Come on. Something little?"

Alice closed her eyes momentarily, then without opening them said, "I'm addicted to porn."

Maggie waved her hand. "Phew. That's all you got?"

Alice glared. "When George is away... I watch porn. Lesbian porn. On my lunch hour, I watch porn on my phone." Her eyes flashed open then, and she laughed again. "Yeah, that's all I got, Maggie."

The other girls burst out giggling too.

"Oh, good Lord," said Lia. "Alice the Rebel"

Alice shrugged. "What can I say? That's pretty wild for me."

The women all burst into laughter.

Then after a moment, the table fell silent. Maggie began talking, her voice lowered. "I've been lying to you all."

No one immediately responded. Maggie looked around the table. "I hate every minute with Max but I'm kissing his ass because of the children."

Julia reached out a hand toward Maggie. "Sweetie, there are women all over the world who do the same thing every single day."

"I know that. But it has my head all twisted up."

"Tell us," Lia said.

Maggie closed her eyes and slumped in her seat a little. After a moment, she opened them and straightened her back. "I'm a pretty good actor. You know, all those plays in high school and college. Right? I've learned how to become someone else and there are times when I'm not sure who I am anymore."

She made eye contact with everyone around the table. No one said anything.

"I've literally become Max's sex slave," she said, lowering her voice. "I mean, it's not as bad or as degrading as it sounds because, you know, I've always loved sex with him. I've pretty much resigned myself to the fact that the only relationship we will ever have is in bed."

Lia cleared her throat. "So, Maggie, how is that different now, than before?"

"For one, he's not hitting me. And he hasn't raised a hand to the kids since last year."

"Well, that's a blessing," Alice said.

Julia remained silent.

Maggie fiddled with her napkin and shook her head. "The difference is that the stakes have escalated, in a way. The more I give him what he wants, the more I—and the kids—get in return. It's like payment for sex."

"Just like a hooker." The words were out of Julia's mouth before she realized it.

Maggie swung her gaze around. "Except we're married."

"In a legal sense only," Julia added. "Correct?"

Slowly, Maggie eased in a breath. "It's true that our marriage is open for Max. I don't have a clue what he does when he's away from me and I don't ask."

"Well, let's hope he's taking the necessary precautions because we don't want you getting something nasty." Alice reached out and touched Maggie's hand resting on the table. "And for you? Is the marriage...?" She let the question hang in the air.

Julia listened and waited, wondering how Maggie would respond.

The sigh slid out Maggie's throat. "Of course it's not open for me. At least not in Max's mind."

"But in yours?"

Maggie jerked and stared at Julia. She held the glare between them for several seconds. Julia didn't move or break eye contact. Finally, Maggie blinked and glanced around the table.

"All right. You all might as well know. I'm having an affair and I have been for the past six months. It's dangerous, I know that, because Max will leave me penniless and take my kids from me if he ever finds out. Hell, he will probably kill me."

"Why would you risk that, Maggie? If the sex is good with Max, then what in the hell are you doing?" Alice asked. "I'm frightened for you."

Maggie blew out a thin breath, her lower lip trembling. Maggie was more frightened by this entire situation than she was letting on.

"What I get from the affair is more than sex," Maggie responded. "You're right. I get plenty of that from Max. What I get, in this forbidden relationship, is sex plus affection. He cares for me. And believe you me, right now, I need that more than anything."

"Oh goodness, Maggie." Lia sucked in a breath and leaned closer to her. "Of course you need affection. Everyone does. But is this really the right thing?"

"I don't know. I tried to quit him once. I couldn't do it. Besides, he says he loves me."

"Oh, shit." Julia's leg shook again, her knee bobbing up and down.

Alice still held Maggie's hand on the tabletop. "I'm not sure what to say right now. I'm worried about you on the one hand, and happy for you on the other. I hope you let us talk you through some of this while you are here this week."

Nodding, Maggie gazed at Alice. "I want to, if you all are okay with it."

"Pretty sure we all are." Alice glanced around the table.

Lia leaned forward, glancing at Julia, then settled her gaze on Maggie. "Look. This could be a good week to make the break, Maggie. I mean, we'll be busy all week and you'll be distracted from the situations at home. Maybe you can relax and give yourself some downtime."

Maggie smiled at Lia. "You are always so thoughtful. Yes, you're right. I need the time away from them both."

Julia cleared her throat. "So, you know what that means, don't you? No texting him, no calling him. Give yourself a break."

Maggie pulled in her bottom lip and bit it.

Julia knew that mannerism all too well. "Don't think too hard about it, just do it."

"Okay. Fine. You're right."

"Beach therapy. Right?" Julia smiled then. "Isn't that why we are here?"

"Yes. I suppose." Then Maggie said something Julia hadn't anticipated. "Julia, why don't you tell us exactly everything that is going on with you, too? Why did you suddenly start drinking again? Why did you leave Louisville and come here early? I'm not the only one who can benefit from some beach therapy, you know? Spilling your soul is cathartic for everyone, sometimes."

Julia damn well knew Maggie was right—and she should probably come clean with them. But could she?

"Who gets the fish sandwich?" The server balanced three lunch plates on a tray, the fourth in her other hand.

"That's me." Maggie raised her hand. "I try to avoid crabs."

Alice choked back a giggle.

The server settled the remaining dishes on the table, and everyone dug into their lunches like they hadn't eaten in days. Julia was grateful for the temporary silence.

THE REST OF THE DAY WHIZZED BY—SHOPPING, A WALK TO the lighthouse, watching the fishing boats come into the harbor. Julia had to admit the afternoon was relaxing, and reminded her somewhat of their younger, more carefree days. Perhaps they all needed a taste of that. They headed back to the ferry in the late afternoon, and after a dinner in the coastal town of Frisco on Hatteras Island, they were back at the cottage by early evening.

"Let's take chairs to the beach and watch the waves until the sun goes down," Lia said. "I haven't done that in ages."

"I'm up for it." Julia stepped off the porch. "I have one chair here and there are others stacked up at the side of the cottage by the outside shower."

"I want to change first," Maggie said.

"Good idea." Alice followed her into the house.

Within thirty minutes or so, they settled into beach chairs near the water line, casually chatting, as waves lapped closer to their toes with the rising tide.

After a lull in the conversation, Julia decided to take Maggie up on her earlier suggestion.

"I owe all of you an explanation. I've talked with Alice occasionally, but Lia and Maggie, the two of you haven't been privy to everything going on in my life. If I can ask Maggie to come clean and share what's going on with her, it's only fair that I do the same. Besides, in AA, honesty is stressed—at least in my group—so I need to practice that as part of my healing."

She was sitting at the end of the row of chairs. Lia sat to her left. Alice beside her. And Maggie at the other end. She angled her chair slightly so she could see all their faces.

Another lawyer tactic she'd acquired a while back.

"I've been going to therapy and AA for over a year since I got back from the beach. You know I checked myself into a recovery center in Louisville. When I got out, I set myself up with a strict regimen of things to do every single day to get my life back in order. My first goal was to get healthy. The second, to get the B&B up and running."

"And you did that, right?" Lia looked concerned.

"I opened the B&B for the new year. I had a few good months in the winter and spring. And I was getting healthier, for sure. Then things started unraveling."

Suddenly, the three other women pulled their chairs up closer to Julia, making a semi-circle around her. Alice reached for Julia's hands, and without hesitation, Julia laid hers in her palms. "Tell us."

At that moment, Julia realized how she'd ignored for far too long some of the most important people in her life—probably the only people who truly understood her and could help her heal.

"There were a lot of small things that escalated, a domino effect in a way."

Her gaze bounced from one girlfriend to another.

"My dad was pressuring me to come back to work. The baby was haunting me—Melinda kept saying that I hadn't properly grieved—and for some crazy reason, at times I could hear a baby crying in the house. That part I don't want to go into yet."

"This is your story to tell in your way, Julia." That came from Maggie, and Julia appreciated that comment from her, likely more than Maggie realized.

"I found myself leaning on Mark more, which made me anxious. I wondered if that made me weak, to lean on him and others. The divorce papers still sat in a drawer in my desk, unsigned by him. In a weak moment one night, I called him, and he stayed the night."

"You had sex?" Maggie asked.

"Well, yes."

"Oh, shit." Lia touched her forearm.

"Yeah. That sort of messed with my head. I had to see Melinda."

"And how was Mark about it?"

"Oh, he says he still loves me. Has never stopped saying that. But I just...can't."

"God, Julia. I'm so sorry." Alice squeezed her hands tighter.

Julia nodded. "I became more disconnected with life every time I thought of the baby, or someone mentioned the baby, so I increased my AA meetings. I had two good friends at my regular meeting, Gretchen and Larry. Then, one night, Larry calls and tells me Gretchen died. Heroin overdose. She may have killed herself. I sort of spiraled. Then the baby was crying again, and...."

She stopped talking and looked out toward the ocean for a moment. With a deep inhale and sigh, she turned back to face her friends. "At some point along the way I had bought a bottle of bourbon. That night, I opened it, and drank half the bottle. The next morning, Mark gave me an ultimatum to get my act together or he was taking the B&B away from me."

She paused, studying the sand. "I need the B&B. There are answers there for me, I know it. I just need to find them. I can't let him take it away. So, I made a deal with him to come out here, to Tuckaway Bay, to get my head back on straight. He made it clear that I am not to come back home until I know what I want—the B&B, him, a life without booze, or none of the above—or don't come back at all."

Maggie blew out a breath. "Wow. That's quite the ultimatum."

"Yes. But no more difficult than what you are dealing with."

Shrugging, Maggie went on, "I've resolved my fate. You still need to decide yours. Just know that I'm with you."

"We all are with you," Alice said.

"Absolutely," Lia echoed.

That was the moment Julia realized that depending on friends was helluva lot more beneficial than depending on strangers who were sort of like friends, but not really. Not that Larry and Gretchen weren't friends—they were in so many ways. Losing Gretchen was painful because they *were* friends, and because they shared something that her girlfriends would never totally understand. And Larry, while he was a friend, was now apparently AWOL.

Bill and Melinda were doing their jobs.

Pam, while supportive, was also doing hers.

And Mark? Mark was there because he was always there.

Should she give him a second chance?

Her head spun just thinking the words. *Not thinking about it today.*

And Sam. What about Sam?

Not thinking about him, either.

You're dodging things again, Julia.

That's right. I am. At least for tonight.

Hadn't Melinda accused her of avoidance? And Mark had too, the night they had sex. Obviously, she needed to bring this back up with Melinda in her next session.

Or, perhaps, she could bring it up in beach therapy.

She'd gone through more shit with her girlfriends than any of them likely wanted to admit. They wouldn't abandon her. And they'd shoot straight, mostly. Above all, they were well-meaning.

And no matter what, she wouldn't abandon them, either. Even Maggie.

Especially Maggie.

Maybe she needed her girlfriends now more than ever.

"I MISS WREN AND WILLOW." JULIA SAID LATER, STUDYING the gently rolling waves.

The sun had set behind them now, over the sound. The full moon rose above, washing the beach with a golden hue. The women still sat at the shoreline, covered in their beach towels now against a slight breeze. The tide inched higher, easing closer to their chairs.

"Good gracious, so do I," Lia said. "I wish we knew where they were, or at least that they are okay."

"Same. No one could liven up things like Willow." Maggie smiled and glanced off, and Julia watched her reminisce for a moment. "Or put things into perspective like Wren."

"Both true."

"Is this the first year since college that they've not been to beach week?"

Julia thought back over the past couple of decades. "You know, I think it is. Jesus, I wish they would surface."

"I just wish I knew what happened." Alice looked thoughtful.

"I have ideas about that," Maggie said. "Willow's business was a bit shady. We all know it. High-end escort services are nothing less than high-end prostitution. She made a shit-ton of money and lured Wren in to keep her books. I think they were in trouble with the government."

Lia gasped. "Good Lord, Maggie. Wren wouldn't do anything illegal."

"Willow would. We all know it. She was the risk-taker when we were in college and I'm pretty sure that hasn't changed," Maggie pulled her towel up around her chest. "Brr. That breeze is getting chilly."

"But Willow wouldn't do anything to hurt Wren," Lia added. "Besides, their dad left them with buckets of money when he died. They were already rich. I can't believe Willow would put her business before her sister's welfare."

"Maybe not." Julia stood and gathered her towel around her shoulders. "But then again, nothing would surprise me. Maggie could be right. With all the stuff that happened last summer with Willow, it would surprise me if the government wasn't looking into her business practices—but I also wouldn't be shocked if it was some underground crime organization."

"Like the Mafia?" Alice's eyes went big and wide.

Julia nodded. "Something like that. If she was cutting into their profits in some way, they'd want her gone."

"Shit. Shit-shit-shit." Maggie stood too. "I didn't think of that."

"No wonder they disappeared."

"Oh fuck." Maggie suddenly looked horror-stricken.

Oh, fuck is right. Julia blew out a healthy breath and strolled toward the surf. She stood there for a moment, letting the foam tickle her toes in the wet sand.

The group fell silent behind her, then Lia said, "We should probably move to the porch."

"Good idea." Julia turned.

They quietly gathered their towels and chairs and took a few steps toward the cottage.

"Wait," Julia said. "Let's take a selfie and send it to them, in the group text where we still have their numbers. I know we won't hear from them, but it will at least make us feel like we are including them. What do you think?"

"I think it's a great idea," Alice said, "but is it too dark?"

"My phone does great night pictures," Lia said. "Let's use mine."

"Super." Maggie waved them all closer. "Over here!"

They dropped their things in the sand and gathered close together, smiling broadly and waving, the ocean and moon in the background.

"Here we go," Lia said, holding her cell phone out and up. "Cheese!"

"Cheese!"

"There." Lia took a glance. "It's great. I'll send the text. What should I say?"

"Just say we miss them, we love them, and we hope they are safe," Julia said.

"Perfect." Lia typed the message, attached the picture, and sent it.

All their phones pinged simultaneously.

"Well, that's that," Alice said. "Let's get up to the cottage." She picked up her chair.

Julia and the others did the same. She slung her beach chair over her arm and threw her towel over her shoulder. They chatted as they headed toward the cottage, mindful of the ghost crabs poking their heads out of their holes and skittering across the sand.

At once, each of their cell phones rang out with a notification.

The women halted, looked at each other, and grasped their phones.

Julia saw the picture first. "What the fuck?"

"Oh, my God," Alice blurted out.

"What the hell?" Maggie said.

"Is that Wren or Willow?" Lia pinched the picture to make it larger.

Julia sucked in a breath. "It's Willow. Pretty sure. But she's very thin."

"Yep."

"It's Willow and a baby. A little baby."

Julia felt like her throat might close up. *A baby.*

"Do we text back?"

She didn't really care at the moment, but just knew that she couldn't. "Go for it," she said to Lia. "I doubt if we get a response."

And she was right. Another text from Willow never came.

Hold it together, Julia. You can do this.

"I can't believe Willow has a child. I can't imagine." Alice turned toward the cottage.

Lia nodded. "You're sure it's her and not Wren?"

"She doesn't look well, does she?" Maggie said.

"No." Julia couldn't utter more than that. Her heart had seized in her chest a little at the first glance of Willow's baby. Not fair. She never wanted a child.

And I did.

The women shuffled toward the cottage in silence then, each lost in their own thoughts.

"I'm heading to bed." Alice yawned as they reached the porch.

"Same here." Maggie smiled at the group. "It was a good day. Thanks for listening to me."

"It's what we do, Mags. Right?" Lia gave her a hug. "I'm so tired I'm not even going to wash my face or brush my teeth. See you all in the morning."

Julia didn't say anything, just nodded.

Seeing Willow with a baby in her arms was a shock on one hand.

But on the other, a comfort. If anything could settle Willow down, it might be a child—even though it was something she professed to never want.

There are women who want babies and never get them. And there are women who don't want them and spit them out like pumpkin seeds.

Life is strange.

Suddenly, she felt surprised that she was not as upset as she felt she could have been. In fact, she was glad Willow had a baby, and she honestly didn't feel any pangs of regret because of losing her own child. Her Caroline.

Am I finally getting better?

Several minutes later, she sat on the side of her bed, looking out the window toward the beach, wondering where in the world the twins had landed. Would she ever see them again? It was interesting how life had changed for them all in the past couple of years. She supposed that was normal.

Glancing at Maggie, who was already asleep, Julia hoped she would get her act together and live a safe life. The fact was though, there was nothing Julia could do to make that happen. It was all on Maggie.

Looking at the clock, she saw that she had an hour until meeting Sam at the fishing spot.

She pulled out the drawer of the nightstand and removed Veronica's journal.

It was time.

THE PRIVATE LIFE OF VERONICA MILLS
September 30, 1872

I mourn. Every day. I mourn.

I mourn not only for the loss of my baby boy, but also for the loss of the nursemaid's companionship. She came at a time when I was out of my wits, a young mother with no clue how to handle the baby—any baby—nonetheless, this baby. Not in the way that he needed to be cared for... All day long and into the night. Why, I had responsibilities as the lady of the house; my husband had impressed this upon me. Insisted. I had a reputation to uphold, a place in society to keep.

And then Matilda appeared that day with a scrap of paper in her hand that she'd torn from a newspaper back in Pennsylvania. It must have taken every penny she could scrape up to leave Philadelphia and travel west, and then to hire a driver to bring her to our home in Louisville.

Small, frail, pale... I knew in an instant she would do well, although Herbert was not convinced she could do the job.

She did. That and more.

She not only served the role as the baby's nursemaid but that of my friend.

Matilda. As I stare at a single lilac bud popping out of the wall I think of her. Why did she do such a thing at Lakeland? Why did she sacrifice...?

Curling deeper into my pillow, I pull the quilt up over my body in an attempt to ward out the chill of the fall afternoon. The day. And the lilacs. All thought.

Melancholia. Hysteria.

That's what they call this. My women friends. The physician my husband forced me to see. But they don't understand.

I am sad. I am in mourning. I am....

I sit straight up in my bed, tossing the covers away from me. I am angry! And full of hate for the man I vowed to love and cherish forever.

I am full of hate.

I know not how I shall live with him.

I know not how I shall live without my child.

Twenty-Three

Julia set off for the fishing spot fifteen minutes before midnight. She stole away leaving a note on the kitchen island for Lia, telling her she was with Sam, and not to worry if she was not back by breakfast. She would understand. Maggie and Alice were usually late sleepers during beach week, and if she knew her friend, Lia, she'd be up early to check in with her family, and perhaps the office, before the start of beach day number two.

The day had been long. She was tired but at the same time energized because she was heading off to see Sam. It was exciting and felt a little wicked, her insides tingling like she was a hormonal teenager sneaking out of the house to see a boy. She smiled at the brief thought of their lovemaking earlier that morning.

She couldn't break away every night, she knew that. Her obligation was to spend time with her girlfriends. But tonight, she needed Sam, and she hoped he needed her too.

Smiling, she kicked off her sandals and carried them as she shuffled through the sand and hurriedly made her way to the spot—where Sam stood, waiting for her, bathed in the mellowing moonlight.

Waiting for her.

Seeing him there nearly took her breath away.

She rushed forward.

He swept her up in his arms.

"Take me away, Fisherman," she whispered, right before his lips seductively nibbled hers.

"That's my plan, sweetheart," he murmured.

THE BOAT HAD SLEEPING QUARTERS IN THE CABIN, BUT SAM gave her another option.

They'd sailed away from his dock several minutes earlier and anchored the boat in the middle of the sound—or so it appeared to Julia. She truly had no idea where they were—and frankly, didn't care. She trusted Sam to keep her safe.

The water gently lapped at the boat while Sam headed to the back, adjusting a light at the rear—or the stern, she thought they called it. Lights at the front—*is that the bow? I need to learn these things*—were on too, so they could easily see each other and everything on the boat.

And other boats could see them, he'd told her. "We don't want to get T-boned in the night."

"That definitely would not be good," Julia said. "If that happened, I would begin to question your expertise, Fisherman."

He stopped what he was doing and peered at her, then grinned. "Well, *College Girl-with-all-the-smarts,* good thing I've got you around."

She nuzzled closer to him, peering up into his face. "Good thing." Leaning in, she teased his mouth with hers. His arms settled around her, pulling her against his chest. He was warm and strong, and she felt safe and adored. Imagine that, someone adored her!

Had this man captured her heart?

Or was she just desperate for some affection—like Maggie?

"Whoa," he said after a minute of kissing. "Any more of that and I'll likely lose all my senses."

Julia laughed and pushed away, looking out over the water. "So what's the plan?"

"It might be a little cramped, but we could make a pallet on the deck with blankets and a comforter, and sleep under the stars. It's a calm night, so it should be nice. Or, we could sleep in the cabin. What do you think?"

Julia bent a little to look past the cockpit and into the cabin, several steps below. "I had no idea that was even there. The doors were shut before."

"Most of the comforts of home," he told her. "Bed, shower, toilet, a small kitchenette. What else does one need in life?"

Julia didn't respond until he looked at her. "I can think of at least one thing." She flashed a saucy grin.

After a moment, the corner of his mouth turned up, and he held her gaze a little longer. "You are going to be the death of me."

"Oh, I doubt it."

"Well, I don't know about that."

She moved closer into the cockpit. "The cabin is nice."

Sam nodded. "Yes. I rarely use it because I normally go on day fishing trips. Haven't slept on the boat since...." He paused.

Julia turned at his silence and studied the frozen expression on his face.

"Since...?" *Since your last fishing trip? Since you brought another woman here?*

He met her gaze. "Since Hannah was here. That was a disaster."

"Oh. I'm so sorry Sam."

"It's okay. Forget it." He shoved the small cooler aside, pushing it up against a bench seat. "So, what's the verdict? Under the stars in the open or private and cozy below?"

"Does cramped mean I get to snuggle closer to you?"

"Sweetheart, that's a given, even if there was a California king-sized bed here."

She tossed him a grin. "I like the idea of sleeping under this big full moon."

"Then that's what we'll do." He headed down the steps into the cabin. "Let's grab the blankets and get comfy. Shall we?"

"We shall." She followed him down the steps and wasn't surprised at all when he turned and tugged her closer, kissing her soundly on the lips again until they fell lazily onto the bed.

It was an hour or so later before they dragged the blankets to the deck.

THEY LAY HUDDLED TOGETHER ON A THICK COMFORTER, covered with a lighter blanket and bathed in moonbeams. A light warm breeze drifted over them, and Julia was more than comfortable, settled into Sam's arms. It was late—or rather very early morning—but she wasn't sleepy. Sam, however, appeared to be dozing.

Running a hand over his shoulder and down his arm, she loved the way his muscles were hard and taut under her touch—he was in great shape, even pushing sixty. Smiling inwardly at that, her thoughts returned to their earlier lovemaking. Age certainly hadn't restricted his sexual prowess.

Closing her eyes, she burrowed in closer, savoring the warmth his chest offered and the sense of security he emitted. Safe. Yes. She felt so safe with him.

Abruptly, Sam jerked and moaned. Julia pushed back, looking into his face. His eyes were closed but his facial expression tense, his features pulled into a tight ball, almost. He shouted then, louder, and twisted slightly away. She leaned forward and put her arms around him as best she could.

Dreaming?

PTSD?

"Sam," she whispered. "Sam, wake up."

He sat straight up and yelled, eyes open, expression blank.

"Sam!" She sat up too, running her hands up and down his arms. Then she whispered calmly. "Sam. Wake up, Fisherman. You're okay. It's me, Julia. College Girl. We're on the boat and you're okay."

He looked at her then and finally saw her, a flicker of recognition in his eyes.

"Goddamnit. I'm sorry." A long breath whooshed from his lungs.

"It's okay. I'm here."

Without hesitation, he pulled her closer. "Damn night terrors."

"Was that a bad one?"

"Not by a long shot. I think you helped me get past it quicker."

"Good."

His arms tightened their grip. His breath fanned warmly against her cheek. "Seems like the longer I dream the worse they are sometimes. I'm glad you were here."

"I'm not going anywhere," she whispered.

"Good," he echoed, holding her tighter.

JULIA DIDN'T REMEMBER FALLING ASLEEP. SHE DID REMEMBER waking up to Sam's kisses, with him rolling over on top of her to rouse her awake—the sky behind him a misty gray with pink tinges.

"Morning sweetheart," he mumbled.

"Morning Fisherman. Sleep better?"

"Um. Like a log. You?"

"Best night in ages."

"Great." He scooted to her side and glanced toward the east. "Sun's coming up."

"And we're not at the fishing spot to see it."

"But this is nice too. Isn't it?"

Julia leaned in for a kiss. "It's perfect."

"Agreed." He paused, watching the sky. "What time to you need to get back?"

She thought about that. "No rush. An hour or so? The girls sleep late."

"I like the sound of that. We'll head that way in a bit."

"You're not getting frisky again, are you?" Julia winked and pushed up, smiling. She trailed her forefinger down his face, over his chin, and down the center of his chest.

"Sweetheart, do you remember when I said you were going to be the death of me? Remember that I'm almost sixty. Okay?"

Julia threw her head back and laughed. "All right, Fisherman. There's always tomorrow."

"And the next day," he added. "Besides, we never have trouble filling the airspace with talk. Truth is, I love learning more about you."

"And I, you." Julia searched his face. "Tell me something."

"Like what?"

She shrugged. "I don't know. Anything." She paused, thinking. "Tell me about Hannah?"

"Hannah? Why?"

Julia shrugged. "You mentioned her last visit a couple of times. Sounds like it wasn't pleasant. But that was years ago. Right? Have you reached out again?"

"I contact her at least once a month. I call but she never picks up. She responds to texts occasionally if she has a reason to do so." He paused, looking up into the night sky. "I texted her a couple of weeks ago after I sent a graduation present, wanting to know if she'd received it. She replied that she had, said thanks, and then told me the gift wasn't necessary."

Julia frowned. "Why would sending your daughter a graduation gift be unnecessary? That's a normal thing for a father to do. I don't understand why she would react that way."

"It's just what she does. Like I said, it's not an easy relationship."

She suspected there was a lot Sam didn't know about his daughter. How could he when he rarely saw her? "Tell me more about her, Sam."

He looked a little uneasy but responded. "What would you like to know?"

"Anything. What does she do for fun? What was her major in college? What's her favorite food? Did she like the beach?"

Sam stared, blinking. "She liked the beach, yes. I have to admit I can't answer the other questions."

"You don't know what her major is? Did you ever ask her?"

"I... To tell you the truth, I'm not sure. I didn't go to college. I don't know what that life is about."

Julia sat up. "Sam. Not being critical here, but she's your daughter. Ask her!"

He turned onto his side and faced her, propping his head up. "It's a difficult relationship. Even when she was very young, she accused me of never being there for her, doing the things that other dads do. I'm sure she heard a lot of that talk from her mother, who frankly, liked to complain. Even though I supported them financially—never missed a child support payment, took care of their health insurance, and paid my half for college—it was never enough. In her mother's eyes I was a deadbeat dad because I chose to stay in the military rather than marry her and live with them."

Julia searched his face. "Did your ex understand that had you quit the military, the benefits you provided would likely diminish?"

"Oh, she didn't care. 'Just get another job,' she'd say. Like I said, she liked to complain. She had a habit of telling me that I chose my job over my family. Hannah fell into the same bitter pattern."

"Hannah deserves to know the truth. Does she realize you were doing your part?"

"She believes only what her mom tells her. I tried to explain things when she was here, but she wouldn't listen."

"You do have rights, you know."

"She's twenty-one, Julia. The time for that has passed. Besides, she'd just accuse me of calling her mom a liar—which she is—trying to make her look bad."

How often had Julia heard this same kind of rhetoric in her family law practice? "Then my advice is this—start treating her like an adult, not like a child. Invite her for a visit and see how it goes. It's been years, right?"

"Yes. About six or so. I'm sure she's ready to set out on her new life, new career, and all that."

"And maybe she'd like to explore a different relationship with you—an adult relationship."

Sam looked surprised at her advice. "I don't know, sweetheart."

"You know I'm a family law attorney, right? I have dealt with a lot of divorce and custody issues. Hannah sounds troubled, at least she was when she was younger. Probably confused, too. Teenagers lash out with their emotions. She might surprise you now."

He studied her. "Maybe." Laying back down again, still on his side facing her, he traced her profile with his forefinger.

His soft touch melted her a little. "It couldn't hurt to try."

He nodded, glancing off. "I do have regrets. She grew up so fast. But I was older than most fathers with a young child, and the military was all I knew. It was the only way I had to support her. I wasn't ready for a kid.

Hell, or marriage. Thought that scenario would never be a part of my life. I didn't want to commit even though I tried."

"Is that a SEAL thing?"

He shrugged. "Maybe. Some guys want to have someone waiting for them at home, a family to fight for, to come home to. Others want to go it alone. If they die, they die, and not as many hearts are broken."

Julia moved closer, gazing into his eyes. "Are you the latter one?" she whispered.

"I guess I was."

"And now?"

"Now is different. I'm not off fighting a war."

At least not a physical war. But Julia sensed there was still one going on inside him.

"In some ways, Gena, Hannah's mom, was right," Sam added. "I may have used my job as an excuse not to do the family thing."

"We all make excuses when we are uncomfortable with whatever life throws at us and can't get a grasp on how to handle—most of the time, that is. I've done my fair share of that the past few years."

He studied her. "Oh? How so? The drinking?"

"Yeah, sure. That and more."

Julia flopped over on her back, staring up at the sky. Lacing her fingers over her chest, she waited for a couple of heartbeats before responding. "I hid the drinking problem for a long time. Told myself I could stop any time I wanted, that it was a temporary break from the pain and heartache and grief. I lied to myself and my husband and my parents about being depressed. At all their insistence, I found a therapist to help me deal with the trauma of losing the baby...grief that apparently, I had never appropriately suffered through, or dealt with. I'm still working on that. I'd pushed my misery so deep into myself that I couldn't stand it, until the only way I could cope was chasing the bottom of a bottle of bourbon. I lied about that for a very long time—until I couldn't get out of bed for days on end."

Sam stayed silent beside her, and she closed her eyes briefly, listening to his breathing. After a minute, she looked his way—he'd rolled onto his back too, also gazing into the morning sky—and watched his chest rise, then fall, with a long exhale.

"Somehow," he murmured, "I feel like I experienced all that pain alongside you. You've had to deal with a lot of shit, sweetheart."

"More than you know. And more than I've shared with you, Sam. It's a lot."

"Then tell me." He faced her again, propped up on his elbow. "I want to know everything."

Julia wasn't sure she was up to telling the story again today. She'd already unloaded on the girls. "Let's just say that besides dealing with the baby's death, my divorce, the drinking, I had a friend who died, a father who was pressuring me to come back to the firm, and a ghost living in my house."

Sam arched a brow. "A ghost."

"Apparently so."

"And how do you know?"

"Because I hear her baby crying in the attic. And I've read her journal. Her name is Veronica and she lived in my house in the late 1800s."

Sam blinked. "Wow."

"You think I'm crazy."

He shook his head. "No. I think you are incredible. Why do you think her spirit is still there?"

She shook her head. "I don't know but I think I need to find out. I think she's calling out to me." Glancing off, she lost herself for a moment in Veronica's words. "I think, maybe, that she understands me —we both lost a child—but I don't think she wants me to end up like her."

Abruptly, she looked at Sam. "That's odd. I hadn't thought of that before."

"Perhaps her spirit wants you to be happy. In her journal, is Veronica troubled?"

Julia nodded. "Yes. Very much so. In fact, how I have felt at times almost mirrored how she described feeling."

"Do you know what happened to her?"

"I don't. I need to keep reading."

"I think it's important you find out," Sam said. "Believe it or not, I think when the spirit world reaches out, there is a reason."

Julia stared at him. "You believe me."

"I don't doubt any of it for a minute."

"Why?"

He shrugged. "When you deal with a lot of death, things happen. You see things, feel things."

He believes me. I'm not crazy. She rolled onto her side, too. "Sam, it's a lot. I'm a lot. And if you feel like you need to run, and run away fast, then do it now, before...." She couldn't say the rest, but presumed he got the idea.

Sam snaked his arms around her and tugged her closer. "Sweetheart," he whispered, then kissed the tip of her nose, "I'm not going anywhere. Nothing you do or tell me can change that. I'm not a young man. My decades are limited. And for the first time in my life, I'm not running away from a relationship. In fact, I want to run toward it."

"You're sure?"

"I'm totally enamored with you, sweetheart. I'll be honest. I'm not sure whether to be thrilled or scared shitless but there is one thing I am sure of—I'm staying put. I want you in my life."

He wants me in his life? "Well," Julia began, "I can honestly tell you that I'm scared to death right now."

"Talk to me, College Girl."

"I'm in no way prepared to share my life with anyone. I have issues with the booze. Yes, I'm working hard to control that but there are no guarantees. Please know that. I need AA and I need therapy and I need to resolve the reason why the ghost in my house is calling to me."

Sam didn't hesitate with a response. "And as you saw earlier, I can be a handful as well. But I will also tell you that waking up with you next to me, with your arms around me and your soft voice waking me from my nightmares—well, something like that could heal a guy pretty damn quick."

What are you saying, Sam?

She searched his eyes, trying to gauge his emotion. In them she saw concern and compassion and patience—and perhaps more. Love? What she didn't see was resentment and ultimatums and doubt—unlike what she'd seen in Mark's eyes the past year or so.

"Sweetheart, what if being in a relationship—a healthy relationship with someone who supports you unconditionally, and cares for you unconditionally, and gives you back as much as you get—is what you really need? Isn't that a healthier option than going it alone?"

"Oh, Sam. I'm a lot to handle."

"And you're not alone in that. What if we work on our issues together? Support each other. What if we are good for each other in a healing way?"

A lump formed in Julia's throat and for the first time in a very long time, she felt like crying tears of joy, not sadness. Happy tears. Maybe even tears of relief. The sensation was foreign, yet welcome. And slightly overwhelming.

With his thumb, Sam brushed a wayward tear from her lower lid.

"Damn you, Sam Watters," she said. "You are going to make me go and fall for you."

Grinning widely, Sam tackled her and pinned her to the deck.

JULIA SAT CLOSE TO SAM ON THE BENCH SEAT OF HIS TRUCK, feeling a little like a teenager again. Her hand rested on his thigh as they drove toward the resort, and she liked the intimacy of feeling the sinews of his leg move beneath her fingers as he braked and accelerated.

"Just take me to the parking lot. I can go through the hotel to get to the cottage. No need to sneak in from the public beach access this morning since we're not fishing."

"That works for me."

Her phone sounded abruptly, shifting her thoughts, and she rummaged for it in her bag. "It's Lia," she said. "Let me see what she wants."

"Okay, sweetheart."

Lia: *Hey. Where are you?*

Julia: *Heading back. All ok?*

Lia: *No. Maggie is missing.*

Her chest tightened. "What the fuck?"

Sam braked a little and glanced her way. "What is it?"

"Maggie is missing." She typed furiously into the phone.

Julia: *What do you mean? How long?*

Lia: *We don't know. Was she here when you left last night?*
Julia: *Yes. Asleep.*
Julia: *Her car still there?*
Lia: *Yes.*
Julia: *Then she can't be far.*
Lia: *Meet me at my office? Alice is here.*
Julia: *Sure. Almost there.*
She slipped her phone back into her bag. "Well, crap."
"Trouble?"
"Maybe. Not sure yet. Maggie left sometime in the night."
Sam drove on, staring ahead. "Does she make this a habit?"
It was true that when they were younger, in college, Maggie had gone AWOL a few times. But they always found her, usually in some farm boy's pickup truck on a country road somewhere.
Sam pulled into the resort parking lot and found a space up front. "Mind if I go in with you?"
"Of course not. I don't mind."
"I've been meaning to check in with Zach about something for a while now. I'll see if he is around."
Julia grinned. She liked the easy way between them. They got out of the truck, and casually glanced behind them. Immediately, a big pickup truck with Alabama license plates caught her eye.
"Holy fuck."
"What?"
"I think I know where she is."
Sam glanced back at the truck. "Trouble?"
"Probably."
"Clandestine lover?"
She nodded. "It's very likely. Let's just hope her husband doesn't find out."
Sam rubbed his chin. "Now, that could be a problem."
"Exactly."
They climbed the outside steps to the first floor of the hotel, turned the corner and entered Lia's office. Her phone pinged again as she stepped across the threshold, and she fished it out to look at it. Another text.

Pam: *Call me, Julia. ASAP.*

Sam leaned in. "Everything okay?"

"My manager at the inn. I'll call her later. Probably needs a recipe or something."

Lia sat behind her desk talking with Alice. Julia glanced about and saw Belle, Lia's daughter, talking on the phone at her desk on the opposite side of the room.

"Thank God." Lia stood, then looked at Sam. "Hey Sam. How have you been?"

"Good. Thought I'd see if Zach was around."

"He's off running errands but should be back soon." Lia tossed Julia a questioning glance.

"It's okay. I already told him."

Alice stepped forward. "We have to find her."

Julia let go of a long breath. "Well, we won't need to look very hard."

"Why?" Lia rounded her desk and moved closer.

Huffing out a quick breath, Julia blurted, "Because the cowboy's truck is in the parking lot."

Alice and Lia just stared straight ahead. Suddenly, their facial expressions shifted from concern to anger—like someone had flipped a switch.

"Yeah. Just what I was thinking," Julia told them. "Lia, who took care of reservations this week."

"Well, Belle, starting yesterday. But I did them up until then."

"Do you collect license plate information?"

"Yes. So many tourists try to use our parking lot, so we have a camera on the lot and try to keep track."

"Can you search for someone with Alabama plates and what room he is in?"

Lia looked stunned.

"We don't have to search." Belle hung up the phone and joined them. "I know what room he's in."

"What do you mean?"

"He came in late yesterday," Belle added. "Big guy, cowboy hat, Wranglers, boots, and all that. He looked so out of place. Asked for a room on a low floor with an outside door, away from others, if possible.

Of course, it's August, and we're booked solid, but we had a family leave early yesterday morning and the Sand Piper cottage was available."

"So, he's in a cottage." Julia crossed her arms over her chest and paced a little. She could feel her anger rising and wasn't sure whether it was a good idea to approach Maggie right now, or not.

"He's just three cottages down from yours, Julia."

"Well, shit."

Alice stepped closer. "And of course, that's where Maggie is too."

Julia had to bite back her words. She glanced at Sam and then the girls. "I'm going to ring her fucking neck!" She briskly turned and headed for the door.

Sam grasped her arm.

She whirled back. "Don't Sam. Let me go."

His expression remained deadpan and steady, and he kept his grip on her arm. "Slow down a minute, sweetheart. Okay? She's not going anywhere soon, I imagine, and you're too worked up right now."

Julia pulled away, jerking her arm back. "See? I told you I was a lot to handle."

"And I told you that we would tackle our issues together. Remember? I'm here for you, Julia. Right now, I think it's time to take a breath. Get yourself together before you go off half-cocked."

All Julia could do was meet his gaze head on.

"You don't know anything about this Sam. About Maggie's history and her impulsive behavior. We've been keeping her out of trouble for over twenty years."

"Then maybe it's time you let her make her own mistakes and live up to them. At some point she must figure things out for herself. You can't own everyone else's problems, Julia. You're not her keeper."

How many times have I been told that? When is it going to sink in?

"Right. Yeah."

The phone on Belle's desk rang and she trotted off to answer it. "Sea Glass Inn at Tuckaway Bay."

Sam continued. "I'm not saying you shouldn't approach her. I'm saying take a pause."

"He's right, Julia." Alice said. "We know she's safe so let's just wait until she comes back to the Gull."

Julia closed her eyes and turned away. Huffing out another breath, her shoulders relaxed a little. "Fine. I'm too wound up."

Belle called out. "Mom, there is a call for you. Urgent. Can you pick up at your desk?"

"Sure."

The tone of Belle's voice made Julia turn back. She glanced from Belle to Lia, who took a few steps and reached for the desk receiver. "This is Lia."

Something is wrong. God, please don't let it be Zach.

"Yes. She's here."

Oh, shit. It's Max.

"No. Let me do it." Lia looked straight at Julia and held her gaze. "Yes. Please keep us informed. I'll let her know to call you right away."

Julia stepped closer. "What is it? Max?"

"No." Lia shook her head.

"Zach okay?"

"He's fine."

A shiver of panic raced over her gut then. It was sharp and icy, like a premonition she couldn't avoid. "Who...?"

Lia moved closer and took Julia's hand. She looked briefly at Sam, standing next to her. "It was Pam, back at the B&B. You need to call her."

"I know. She sent a text earlier. She..." *Oh shit. Has something happened? Caleb? The house on fire. No. Of course not.* A shaking breath shot from her lungs. "I'll call after we're finished with the Maggie thing. Probably some question about the books, or something."

Lia gripped her hand tighter. "No, Julia, you need to call her now. You need to go home."

Her body felt stricken, like the icy fissure of panic in her gut she'd been avoiding was now holding her hostage. "Why?" Her voice was weak, the word barely escaping her lips.

Lia took a breath. "Mark was in a car accident, honey. He is hurt real bad."

Suddenly, Julia's breath came involuntarily in short, shallow, and frequent breaths—hyperventilating, she guessed—and she was light-headed. Nauseous. "Accident?"

"It's not good, Julia. He may not make it."

Julia grasped the back of a nearby chair and sat. "Oh fuck. No."

She looked up at Sam, her vision fuzzy. "I'm so sorry," she whispered.

He held her gaze steadily. "I'm almost afraid to ask this question... But who the hell is Mark?"

Julia knew she had to tell him the truth. He'd been good to her. She cared for him. And she couldn't lie to him. They could have had something but.... "He's my husband, Sam. I'm sorry. For everything." She got up, glanced at Lia and Alice, then rushed toward the door. "I have to go now."

Louisville

Twenty-Four

*Mid-September,
40 days sober*

FISHERMAN: *TALK TO ME COLLEGE GIRL. TELL ME WHAT'S
going on.*

JULIA DELETED THE TEXT AND SET HER PHONE TO VIBRATE.
She didn't need reminders of what she'd left behind in Tuckaway Bay.

Crossing the parking lot to the Catholic Church, she entered the side door of the building. She'd arrived intentionally late and found an unoccupied metal chair at the rear of the semi-circle in the basement meeting place. Bill sat across the way, talking to a man she didn't know, and nodded as she sat. She tossed him a quick head-jerk.

She'd told no one she was coming.

Not Bill. Not Larry.

She did mention it to Gretchen, who she'd talked with a lot lately—in her head, of course—discussing things like coping with death, grief, depression, sadness... Why she'd made her choices and how deep her desperation must have been in order for Gretchen to do what she'd done. They'd never know if her overdose was intentional or an accident —but the one thing Julia knew was that her pink-haired friend had to have been mighty desperate to shoot up again.

While she'd known her own desperation, she'd never considered suicide an option.

Julia also talked to Veronica on a regular basis, mostly at the house, up in the attic. She felt closer to her there, like she could sense her spirit milling about in the dusty old room.

Goodness. All my friends are dead. I have to get out more.

But these days her hours were pretty much eaten up at the hospital. Mark was her priority, not herself. Thank God for Pam running the inn and that she was good at it.

Quickly glancing about, she didn't see Larry, and reminded herself to ask Bill if he'd heard from him lately. She hoped to meet with her sponsor privately after everyone was gone—if it worked out that way. She was sneaking away from the hospital now, as it was.

In fact, she wasn't sure she would even make it, which was why she'd not made a definitive plan. She wasn't sure how long she could stay, either. If the nurse texted, she might have to leave right away.

It wasn't that Mark necessarily wanted her there 24/7—but she'd discovered early on in the two weeks since the accident, practically living at the hospital, that no amount of monitoring from the nurses was enough. The staff was short-handed, busy, stressed, and a couple of times, had made mistakes. Minor ones, granted, but she'd pitched a fit and dug in her heels. She felt a whole helluva lot better being there than not being there.

Mark couldn't do much for himself, and she'd be damned if she'd let him lay there waiting for someone who wasn't going to come immediately. Truth be told, the nurses probably wanted her gone. She'd become a bit of a pest.

"Welcome everyone." Bill leaned forward, looking around the semi-circle. "It's good to see you."

This was her first AA meeting since she'd been back in Louisville. She had reached out to Bill though, by phone, a couple of times. Fortunately, the church was located just a few blocks from the university hospital where Mark was, and she could walk over.

Bill continued and she tried to focus on his words. "For those of you who are new to our meetings, welcome. Those of us who are lifetime members," he chuckled, and a few others did too, "be sure to welcome our new folks and make them feel at home. Take a minute to introduce yourself to your neighbor if you would."

Julia smiled at the woman next to her, who said her name was Penny, and introduced herself. To her left, she shook hands with an older gentleman named Frank. She didn't linger over conversation or getting into anything personal with either of them, because she knew she didn't have the capacity right now for small talk or creating new friendships.

Maybe in a few weeks.

"Before we get into our topic tonight, would anyone like to share?"

Julia stood, knowing her time there was limited. "I would."

Bill nodded. "It's good to see you, Julia."

"You, too." She hesitated, glancing at the floor for a few seconds, back to Bill, and finally around the circle. Blowing out a cleansing breath, she started. "I'm Julia. I'm forty days sober. I relapsed last summer after a difficult time. I was 283 days sober before that when I fell off the wagon, and prior to then, I was drunk for most of a couple of years."

Pausing momentarily, she watched a few heads bob around the circle. They knew exactly what she was talking about.

"Welcome, Julia," a woman down the row to her left said. "We're glad you are here."

"Thank you. I've not been here since the relapse because I've been spending time in North Carolina with friends—beach therapy, you might say—where I attended meetings every week. It's not been easy, I'm here to tell you. But it's doable away from home. Honestly, getting away from the environment here was healing in so many ways." She glanced about. "Thanks for listening."

She sat, and a woman down the row leaned forward. "Has coming back to your home environment been difficult? I ask because I'm sort of in the same situation. I left home and moved here to get away from friends who partied too much. They seem to go-with-the-flow with their addictions, but I don't want to live like that. I have to go back home soon to take care of my mother."

Julia studied her and exhaled. "It's not easy, for sure. I feel for you. Perhaps focus on your mother and not your friends. Or, can you move your mother here? Remember that you have to take care of yourself, too, so you can take care of her."

The woman nodded. "That's good advice."

And advice I should heed myself.

Someone else stood up to share but Julia got lost in her own thoughts, his speech drumming along in the background. She was right. The past two weeks she'd put a lot of effort into Mark. If she didn't learn to focus on herself, how would she ever take care of him?

Sam had said something similar to her, hadn't he? About Maggie? *You can't own everyone else's problems, Julia. You're not her keeper.*

But Mark was different. Mark was her husband and truth be told, she owed him.

So be it.

Her phone vibrated silently, and she glanced at it. The nurse.

Glancing up at Bill, she pointed to her phone. Nodding, he understood that she had to leave. She rose and slipped out the back door as quietly as she had entered.

The walk was only a couple of blocks but by the time she got to the hospital, she'd decided to change course. She read the nurse's text: *Mark is back from therapy. Should I order dinner for you too? He wants to know if you are coming.*

Though the nurses thought her a bit annoying, the hospital had been great to see to her needs, as well as Mark's, all the days she'd been there. But tonight, she was tired. Exhausted, if she'd admit it. And rather than having dinner with Mark, what she really wanted to do was take a long hot bath and go to bed early.

Should she?

You can't take care of others unless you take care of yourself first.

She texted back to the nurse: *I'm tired and heading home. Tell him I'll see him tomorrow.*

Twenty-Five

Mid-September,
41 days sober

FISHERMAN: *GOOD MORNING. FISH ARE BITING TODAY. RED drum.*

SHE'D SLEPT LATE—LONGER THAN SHE'D SLEPT SINCE SHE'D been home—and it felt heavenly. The phone vibrating on the nightstand had jogged her partially from sleep. She'd check messages later, but likely knew who had texted. It was becoming a regular thing with him.

She never answered.

Rolling over, Julia groggily stared at the wall. Her gaze followed the ripped rose wallpaper up to where the lilacs showed from underneath. Sitting straight up, she sat on the side of her bed, her brain rolling over an impromptu thought.

Yes. She knew exactly what she was going to do today, after she checked in on Mark.

With renewed energy, she showered and dressed, then headed down-stairs. She met Pam in the dining room, clearing the buffet of the morning breakfast spread.

"Good morning, Julia," Pam said and smiled. "I'm glad you got some sleep. Breakfast?" She lifted a casserole from the buffet and headed into the kitchen. "I can pop a plate into the microwave for you."

Julia reached for a basket of croissants and another of muffins and followed her. "I can get it," she said. "Wow, the croissants look heavenly. Did you make them?"

Pam set the casserole dish on the island. "I didn't. I hope you aren't mad but there is a new bakery downtown that is to die for, and I special order them. They deliver by seven a.m. It's saved me a ton of time and the guests love them."

Julia studied Pam. "Why would I be mad? I think you've made an excellent decision, as you've obviously done for the past several months." This wasn't the first time she'd realized what a gem Pam was. She'd been single-handedly running this place for a couple of months now. Julia was more than pleased.

Pam's face brightened. "Really?"

"Absolutely. You're doing a great job. I appreciate it and I know Mark does, too." She pulled a plate down from the cabinet.

"How was he yesterday? I was thinking of visiting him, if you think he's up for it."

"In a word, cranky." She sighed. "I'm sure he'd love a visit."

"Well, I suppose that's natural. He was such an active guy."

He was, and his paralysis was going to be a test for him, both mentally and physically. "I'm hoping when he gets to rehab they can work on his attitude, as well as wake up his muscles. If he had the slightest chance of walking again... Well, that might help but...."

"I'll throw up a few more prayers."

She hadn't known Pam was a religious person. "I suppose I should do that myself, but I'm not sure I remember how."

"I just talk to a higher power and ask for what I want."

"Does this higher power ask for anything in return?"

Smiling, Pam touched her hand. "Gratitude?"

She supposed that was the thing. *Maybe I should practice gratitude occasionally.*

Turning away, Julia fished for a large spoon in the utility drawer and dipped into the casserole. "Yum. My favorite. Green chilies, goat cheese, and sausage." Immediately, she thought of Sam, then pushed that thought out of her head. No use torturing herself.

"Your recipe, of course."

Julia took a bite. "Oh my God. Heaven on a fork." She put another scoop of the casserole on her plate and plucked up a croissant too. "What are your plans today?"

Pam scraped a couple of plates into the garbage, then set them aside. "The usual. Clean the kitchen. Change the beds. Dust. Laundry."

"Do you have time to go shopping with me this afternoon? I'd like your opinion on something."

Pam faced her. "Shopping?"

"Yes."

"I'd have to be home by three when Caleb gets off the bus."

"Perfect." Julia pulled off a bite of the croissant and popped it in her mouth. She chewed, then added. "I'll go see Mark this morning and will be back by ten. I can help you with the chores and then we'll set out. Maybe we'll even have time for lunch. That work?"

Pam's face held a hint of question. "Sure. But what are we doing?"

Julia smiled. "Buying wallpaper. I'm redoing my bedroom."

Hospitals weren't her favorite place in the world. She often avoided them, just like she avoided funerals and open-casket visitations. And after two weeks of daily jaunts to be with Mark, to make sure he was well taken care of, her opinions hadn't changed.

The smell. The clinical atmosphere. Often, the chaos. People admitted, people leaving, people in trauma, people dying. It could take its toll on anyone.

I could never work in the medical field.

The door to Mark's room was partially ajar when she got there. She knocked lightly before peeking inside. Mark's doctor and a nurse stood beside his bed.

They turned. "Come in, Julia," Dr. Matthews said. "We were just discussing Mark's release."

A sliver of panic raced across her gut. "Already?"

"To rehab, he means," Mark said. "They think I'm ready to get out of here. Honestly, I think they really want to get rid of you."

Julia ignored that comment and rounded the foot of the bed. "You don't think you are ready?"

"I suppose it doesn't matter what I think," he said, his voice laced with cynicism.

That attitude, of course, wasn't unusual. Mark was skeptical and doubtful of everything these days. But who wouldn't be in his situation?

"These people are pulling the strings. I'm just a puppet. Except, of course, my legs don't move."

Julia reached for his hand. "I'm sure you will be fine." Glancing to the doctor, she asked, "Are we rushing things?"

"No." Dr. Matthews shook his head. "He's been here fourteen days. The typical stay for spinal cord injuries like his is around ten to twelve days before discharge to rehabilitation and continued therapy. I imagine he'll be there for a month or longer."

"But his progress? Is it on track to do that?"

The doctor nodded. "Yes.

"So, what is the plan? What exactly will rehab do for him?"

Dr. Matthews studied Mark—who met his gaze with a blank stare. "We were having that discussion when you arrived." He faced her then, and not Mark. "As you know, his injuries involved the L1 and L2 lumbar spine region. It's complete paraplegia, and fortunately, doesn't affect the chest and abdominal muscles, or his upper body. I know I'm not telling you anything new. Therapy can take on many forms and the therapists and doctors at the center will create a plan for him... And *with* him and you. It could involve physical therapy, neuromuscular stimulation, occupational therapy, and more. Exactly what depends on further evaluation once he's admitted to the center."

Mark huffed. "You didn't mention treadmill, swimming...."

Dr. Matthews met his gaze. "That's up to the experts at the center to determine but I'll be frank—your legs and feet are paralyzed. As we've discussed, it's doubtful you'll walk again. I wish the news were better, Mark."

"Yeah, well," Mark spat out. "You know what they say about wishes —they only come true in fairy tales, and I guarantee you my life has not been one of those. Especially the past few years."

Closing her eyes briefly, Julia squeezed Mark's hand. At least he could feel that and knew she got that message, loud and clear. The room fell silent.

"Thank you, Dr. Matthews," she said, looking at him now. "Anything we need to do to prepare for tomorrow?"

The nurse stepped forward. "Come with me. Let's get started on the paperwork."

Julia glanced at Mark. He turned away, looking at the wall, pulling his hand out of her grasp.

———

THE WALLPAPER SHOP HAD AN INSANE NUMBER OF CHOICES. Eventually, Julia settled on a subtle coastal theme with an aquamarine color and eddies of abstract waves. It didn't scream beach—no shells, no sailboats, no anchors—just the swirls of waves that reminded her of Tuckaway Bay nights, sleeping with her windows open.

"I'll need new drapes, too," Julia said, placing her menu aside. They'd decided so quickly on the paper that they had time for a late lunch at a Cuban restaurant on the east side of town, near the shop.

"And probably a new comforter, sheets."

She nodded. "Why not?"

Pam closed her menu too. "Are we going to put it up or will you hire it out."

"Oh, hire it out. Definitely. Neither of us have time." She snapped her fingers. "That reminds me, when we get home, I need to call the contractor."

Pam frowned. "Do we really need a contractor to put up wallpaper?"

She shook her head. "No. We need to finish the downstairs suite. The plan had always been to make it handicapped accessible. Remember? But with everything that happened, we never did those upgrades. We need to do that now."

Pam met her gaze and didn't say anything for a minute. "That room is booked solid for the fall. When do you want to have it done?"

Julia exhaled a sigh. "Four weeks. Mark may be released from rehab around then."

"He's coming to the inn?"

"Where else?"

"I don't know." Pam looked puzzled. "I hadn't thought about it, actually."

Julia stared. "Mark doesn't think it's the best idea, but I'll convince him it is."

Pam slowly nodded. "I see."

There was something odd about how Pam responded. "You don't think it's a good idea? Mark staying at the inn?"

"Oh no. I don't think that at all," Pam said quickly, averting her gaze. "I was just thinking about the logistics."

"Logistics?"

"You know. Everything that has to happen."

Julia agreed a lot had to happen in a short amount of time. "I want to make sure he has access to everything downstairs. We need to check the doorways, making sure they are all wide enough to accommodate a wheelchair. His bathroom will need a total overhaul—shower, lowering the cabinets, grab bars and such..."

"Do we need a ramp into the house?"

Julia nodded. "Yes. I was thinking in the back. But honestly, I'll need to do a little more research about exactly what we can do since the house is on the historic register. I know there are regulations for that and ADA compliance."

Pam glanced about the restaurant. "A lot to do, for sure. What about the guests booked for that suite?"

Julia leaned closer. "Move them to my room. We'll get it done first, guest ready, and move my things to the first-floor suite. It's big enough for both Mark and me, even if we have to move in a special bed for him. I don't know yet but will find out. We'll probably need to call and confirm that the switch will work for the guests but honestly, it shouldn't be an issue—unless, of course, one of them is Mr. Kelley."

"He's booked for a week in October."

"Okay. Well, we'll have to do some moving around. He can't climb two flights of stairs, so my room is out for him. I'll call him this afternoon. We'll look into the other reservations over the next few days."

Pam looked a little worried, but Julia dismissed it. *She'll come around.*

She drummed her fingers on the table while waiting for their server. Glancing about the crowded restaurant, she noticed a familiar face looking back at her from a booth against the wall. Larry? Across from him sat a woman and she wondered if it was his wife. He looked away quickly after catching Julia's eye. Her gaze fell to the table where two half-empty glasses of Margaritas sat.

Oh, Larry. No wonder neither she nor Bill had heard from him for weeks.

And while her heart ached for him, she also knew it was not her place to intervene. He'd seen her. It was up to him to reach out—if that was what he wanted to do.

LATE SEPTEMBER,
52 days sober

FISHERMAN: *SLEPT ON THE BOAT LAST NIGHT. GUNNER AND me. Wanted you beside me.*

JULIA GLANCED DOWN AT THE PHONE SITTING BESIDE HER leg on the cushiony sofa. *I have to stop this.*

The text reminded her she'd not shared anything about Sam with Melinda yet—and she had to wonder about that. Was she avoiding the obvious? Focusing on Mark so she could push Sam out of her head and her heart?

Did she fear Melinda would give her advice she didn't want to hear?

"You know, Julia. I'm really pleased with your progress the past few weeks." Melinda flipped open her steno pad and jotted down a couple of notes on the paper. "You appear more levelheaded and calmer than I've seen you in quite some time. Which, with all you are doing for Mark, seems rather remarkable."

Julia slid the phone under her leg, so she didn't have to look at it, and sat firmly against the back of the pillowy sofa, trying not to slink down into the downy fabric and get too comfortable.

"I think it's because I'm not running all over the place trying to be a hundred different things to a hundred different people. I may have learned that lesson."

"How so? Tell me more."

"Well, before the relapse, I was running the inn, working for my dad, trying to help Maggie, and Larry, and Gretchen..." She paused, thinking. "Simultaneously dealing with grief—or maybe not dealing with it—and then the crying baby and Veronica. Shit. That's a lot."

"It was a lot." Melinda uncrossed her legs, shifted in her seat, made another note on her pad, then recrossed them the opposite way. "And it could continue to be a lot—if you let it. Are you taking care of yourself? Your mental and physical health has to come first."

"I am. I'm doing a lot of walking, which is good for both. And if I've learned anything through all this so far, that is it. No matter what, self-care just isn't a thing people say, it's a thing we all should do."

"Excellent." She paused and glanced back down at her steno pad. "Have you come to any conclusions with everything that has happened?"

Julia shifted her position and crossed her own legs. She'd walked to her session, so she'd worn her favorite cross-trainers and yoga pants—as opposed to Melinda's stockinged legs and heels. One foot bobbed up and down while she thought. "I don't need to be everything to everyone. I can't be the pleaser or the fixer. I have to work on myself first, so I can be there for others."

"That's good." Melinda smiled broadly. "Progress."

"I truly think I'm moving forward in a good way," Julia said.

"Have you talked to Bill lately?"

"Every week at meetings and a few texts in between. I feel so much stronger. I rarely think of drinking these days."

Melinda nodded. "Let me ask you something that I've been wondering about. How does it feel giving up control of the inn to Pam?"

"You know? Surprisingly good," Julia responded. "To be honest, it has felt so much like such a natural progression that I haven't given it much thought. She is a godsend."

"The regimen of running the inn—getting up on time, fixing breakfast, doing all the housekeeping tasks on a daily basis for the guests—all that was your salvation for a while."

Julia agreed. "It was."

"And you don't need that now?"

She exhaled slowly. "I don't. I loved cooking for guests and trying out new recipes. It energized me. It's what got me up in the mornings. But now, I'm motivated in other ways."

"Like, Mark?"

"I suppose. Yes."

Melinda studied her. "Julia, why are you prioritizing Mark right now?"

"Why? Because he needs me."

"Does he?"

"Of course he does. He's paralyzed."

"Has he asked for your help?"

Had he? Not in so many words. What was Melinda getting at? "Mark is having a difficult time handling everything. His attitude sucks, honestly. I know him like I know the back of my hand. He's really scared about his future, and I get that. But he won't ask for help. I'll be there anyway."

"Like he was for you when you were at your lowest?"

Julia glanced off, staring at the bookcase behind Melinda's desk. "What do you mean?"

"Was Mark there for you a couple of years ago? When you truly needed him?"

He wasn't, and Julia knew that. Melinda did too. They'd talked at length about how she'd felt abandoned, with no one to lean on at times. "At first, yes. He was supportive. But once I started drinking heavily, we both grew distant. Neither of us was there for the other. Mark was frustrated as hell with me, and I think he simply gave up. That's my fault."

"Is it?"

Julia was surprised at the question. "Isn't it?"

Melinda shrugged. "That's for you to decide. Is it your fault Mark was frustrated? You don't control his reactions or responses to anything. Do you?"

"Well, no. But perhaps I provoked it."

"I repeat. You don't control his reactions. How he treated you was not your fault. That's on him. How you treated him? Now, that's a different story."

"Yes. And I treated him badly."

"Is that why you feel you need to be there for him now?"

"Melinda, he's my husband."

"Is he?" The therapist met her gaze.

Julia didn't know exactly what to say, how to respond. "The papers... I've signed them but Mark hasn't. You know that. I've been meaning to tear them up."

Melinda sighed and reached for Julia's hand. "Don't. I would rarely give this advice but Julia, you should pause on that. The ball is in Mark's court. Destroying the papers takes that choice away from him."

"But—"

Melinda interrupted. "Don't do anything without thinking it through, Julia. Mark has little else right now, don't take away his ability to make his own decisions."

The clock on the mantle chimed and they both glanced toward it.

"Guess it's time," Julia said, pushing to a stand. Melinda's words had nearly taken her breath away. She'd ponder them on her walk home, she was certain. In fact, she might need to take a longer route.

"I have one more question on my list, if you don't mind." Melinda stared down at her steno pad then looked up to meet Julia's gaze.

"Of course."

"You've not mentioned the crying baby—have you had any more occurrences since you've been home?"

"Actually, no." She glanced toward the hallway. People were chatting outside the door. "It sounds odd, but I've not thought about the crying baby the past couple of weeks. I did, however, change the wallpaper in my bedroom."

Melinda smiled. "More progress." She rose and faced Julia. "This may seem from left field, but I have a friend who is a medium. If you have any need for her expertise... If you want to explore the situation with Veronica and the baby a little deeper, spiritually... Let me know."

That could be interesting. "Thanks. I will give it some thought."

More to ponder on the way home.

EARLY OCTOBER,
  59 days sober

FISHERMAN: *THE MORNINGS ARE COOLER HERE. HOW ARE you, College Girl?*

THE HAMMERING DOWNSTAIRS WAS GETTING ON HER nerves, interrupting her nap on the twin bed in the attic. One might think it wouldn't be so loud, three floors up, but apparently sound traveled through wood and pipes all the way up.

She and Pam had cleaned the attic room the previous week, providing Julia a private place since both her room, and the first-floor suite, were under renovation. They'd stored boxes and old furniture in a large attic closet, removed cobwebs, washed walls and floors, and cleaned and painted the old bed. A new mattress and linens, and Julia was as comfortable there as anywhere else in the house. Sometimes, she napped there in the afternoons, read a book, or contemplated life and other things.

For weeks, she spent most of her waking hours with Mark. Since he'd gone to rehab, she'd not needed to be there 24/7—and with his afternoons devoted to therapy, he'd made it quite clear he did not want her there for that—which gave her personal time.

She was grateful.

Gratitude, yes. Like Pam said a few weeks earlier.

She was stronger every day, mentally and physically. More clear-headed and focused than she'd been in months, about most things in her life. She had a purpose now, and that purpose was Mark. Melinda's advice was ever present in her mind, however, and she was cautious not to overdo that purpose.

Mark didn't know about the first-floor renovations. She'd not told him. He assumed he was going back to his townhouse—the one he'd leased when she'd told him she wanted a divorce and to get out of the house.

She'd made her argument that the townhouse wasn't handicapped accessible. No ramps. His bedroom and bathroom were upstairs. He'd need a chair lift. The bathroom was too small for a wheelchair, the shower was a tub, the counters too high. And while he'd argued that he had arrange for accommodations with the landlord, she argued fervently that it wasn't the best choice.

Initially, he wasn't buying it.

The lawyer in her was at her best, while at the same time leaving space for discussion. Again, Melinda's advice was in her ears. *Don't take away his ability to make his own decisions.*

But that continued debate with Mark would not happen this afternoon. Another day.

THERE WERE TIMES THE ATTIC FELT LIKE THE ONLY PLACE she was at peace. Other times, she seemed to absorb the turmoil of the past that had once occupied the room—Veronica's space, hers and little

Jimmy's. And perhaps Matilda's. If she ever renovated the space for guests, she'd name it Veronica's Room.

But for now, that was her private getaway.

Today, she felt at peace. She'd been back in Louisville a month. There was only one aspect of her life that felt unsettled—and that was with Sam.

She knew she should respond to his texts. He'd been religious in sending them daily. Just a brief message, always positive, usually mentioning her in some way. She just didn't know how to respond, or if she should. She didn't want to encourage him, did she?

Their lives held no future together. That was obvious now. Best to put it to bed. But how could she, when he was there, every single day? How long could she ignore him, or put him off?

Maybe she shouldn't.

JULIA: *I'M FINE, SAM. BUSY. HOPE YOU ARE WELL.*
Fisherman: *Talk to me.*
Julia: *No Sam. We can't.*
Fisherman: *I'm not giving up on you.*
Julia: *There are things I need to do.*
Fisherman: *You know where I am.*

SHE REACHED FOR VERONICA'S JOURNAL LYING ON THE small bedside table. She'd not opened it since the beach. Hadn't needed to, perhaps, because she'd had so many conversations with Veronica the past several weeks. The journal entries were also extremely personal, and often somewhat disturbing, and Julia hadn't been certain if she wanted to read more—until now.

Melinda's mentioning of a medium had intrigued her.

Julia stared down at the faded leather cover.

The Private Life of Veronica Mills

She leafed through the pages, finding the last passage she'd read and turned the page. No words. Blank. In fact, all the remaining pages were blank.

"No." As much as she'd feared reading what came next in Veronica's life, she now felt cheated that she would never know.

With a frustrated sigh, she tossed the journal aside. It landed cock-eyed on the bed. A folded piece of yellow, brittle paper jutted out from a slit in the back cover.

Carefully, she pulled the paper from its hiding place. A letter.

Dear Mum,

I pray you are well, although I know you are not. I am writing on this, our first day, at Lakeland.

At first, I found the quietness of this place strangely soothing. I love to look out the tall window in little Jimmy's room, high above the lawn. While it is relaxing and calm, it is also tremendously strange and eerie.

Whatever the world is here, it matters not to me. My job is to keep the boy safe. Care for him. I stayed when you could not. Yes, it was a lifetime sacrifice, but my life is unimportant. The boy is mine...or like mine, anyway, caring for him since he was a wee babe. I will ensure he is safe.

The day I stepped onto Kentucky soil from the paddlewheel ship that brought me from the east, I knew my life would be forever changed. Now, it has changed again. I journeyed to this river valley from Pennsylvania, where I'd lived for a short time after we fled Ireland,

to the bend where the growing city of Louisville sat
perched like a jewel.

My Irish eyes missed the hills and the cliffs of
my homeland. This city and valley were a welcome sight.
There were gentle hills to rest my eyes upon, and
although a river is no substitute for the ocean, it is
water all the same.

Before I came to Louisville, I spent a few months
in Boston with a family that abused me in horrible
ways, and then threw me to the streets like a soiled
handkerchief. Returning to my family in Pennsylvania
was a mistake; it was soon made obvious I was a
burden.

That's when I sought other employment and found
your notice in the local newspaper. I was nineteen and
too old to marry. I was thin and hungry. No dowry.
Plain. I came to you, seeking a place and you gave it to
me. That, and the only other thing I held most dear—
little Jimmy.

And the Mister was about to take him away from
me, too. Away from us.

I could not bear it. Seeing you so distraught was
horribly painful. I did the only thing I knew to do. I
stayed, for you, and for the little man, but mostly for
me because I love him so. You have a life to live, now,
Mum. An important life with your husband and in your
high society. A life like that would never be afforded
to me.

279

I am destined to live my days here, in the asylum. With little Jimmy.

My life is devoted to our baby, Mum. No worries. I will take care of him. I will keep him safe. Always.

With affection,

Matilda

Twenty-Six

Late October,
*   70 days sober*

FISHERMAN: *ORDERED HATCH CHILIES FROM A PLACE IN NEW Mexico. Casserole recipe?*

"YOU'VE BEEN QUIET THE PAST COUPLE OF WEEKS, JULIA. Is everything okay?" Lia sounded concerned. "Is Mark better?"

"Everything is fine, Lia," Julia put her on speaker phone while she organized the bills from the contractor on her desk. "I've just been so busy with the renovations and getting ready for Mark to come home in a week or so."

"Are they finished?"

"Almost. The first-floor suite is now fully handicapped accessible, and the downstairs is wheelchair safe. They are finishing the ramp outside today or tomorrow."

"What does Mark think about all this?"

Julia looked up and stared out the window. "I don't know. Argumentative. I haven't convinced him yet that he's coming here."

"Should you do that though? I mean, is that really a good plan for the both of you?"

Probably not. "I'm determined to at least see him through for a while. I'm still trying to figure out my own future—but for now, I want to see him settled."

"In your bedroom. In your house. In your life? There are other ways for you to be there for him, you know."

Julia pushed her chair back and stood. "I don't want to talk about that right now, Lia."

"I get that," Lia said, "but I'm just worried you're taking on too much and you'll...."

"I'll what? Fall off the wagon again? Invest in a distillery? No, Lia. I'm not heading down that path and have no plans to do that in the future. Please trust me on this. Okay? I need to do it."

"Sure." Julia heard Lia's frustrated exhale through the phone. "I do trust you. I love you like a sister, remember? I want you to be okay."

"Thanks, Lia. I'm more okay today than I've been in years." She shuffled a few more papers around, then added, "Have you heard from Maggie?"

She'd talked with both Alice and Lia not long after she'd returned to Louisville and the immediate crisis with Mark had passed—but she'd not spoken with Maggie at all since the night at the cottage when she'd stolen away to be with Sam, and Maggie had slipped out to meet the cowboy.

"No, I've not talked with her. You know that Alice and I decided to leave her alone until she returned to the cottage. That was when Alice lit into her like a bug to a flame—I think she was taking over your position, honestly—and Maggie fought back. They argued. Maggie packed up and went back to the cowboy's cottage, and none of us have heard from her since. I wish I knew what was going on in that head of hers."

"I don't think we'll ever know, Lia. I hope to hell she figures it out before Max knocks the shit out of her."

"And divorces her, taking the kids away."

"I don't know if that could happen one hundred percent, but you never know."

"We have screwed up friends," Lia said. "And considering that, I suppose you've had no word from Wren or Willow?"

"Of course not. I'm assuming you haven't either."

"No."

"I've about given up hope. Goodness, I miss them all. I miss the 'us' we all were in the past." She paused, her mind drifting to how much they all had changed over the past twenty years. Even Alice was iffy, with her boss lover and potential separation from George. Thank God Lia was solid. "How are things in Tuckaway Bay?"

"You mean, how are things with Sam?"

She closed her eyes. "That's not what I said. How are things with you and Zach and Belle?"

"Eh, okay. We've had a bit of a challenge here lately, but in the end, things will be fine."

That alarmed her a little. Lia was never one to put her problems out there for girlfriend consumption unless she wanted or needed advice. "What's going on?"

Lia sighed. "I almost don't want to say. I don't want to upset you."

"Why would it upset me?"

"It's Belle, Julia. She's pregnant."

Wow. That was a surprise. "I didn't know she was seeing anyone?"

"She isn't. It was a one-night stand early summer with a tourist and she has no clue how to find him."

"Did he stay at the resort?"

"Yes. With friends and they aren't cooperative."

"Well that's a bummer."

"Yes."

"Is Belle okay?"

There was another pause. "She's getting there. Motherhood at twenty-one was not her plan but who of us gets to carry through our plans? We all have to cope with what life throws at us. Right?"

That we do. "I hope she'll be okay."

"She will. She has Zach and me to make sure of it."

"Tell her I love her."

"Will do." Lia fell silent for a minute. "Julia, does it bother you? All the babies? Willow, and now Belle?"

She didn't hesitate to respond. "You know? It doesn't. I'm happy for them both."

"I'm glad."

"Me too."

Julia thought she could hear wind through Lia's phone. Or maybe it was the waves. "Where are you right now?"

"I'm on my deck looking out at the beach. It's a blustery morning."

Julia closed her eyes and imagined what it might look like. Dark and gray, white caps on the waves. "Anyone fishing today?" The words caused a ripple of panic to roll across her belly.

"Just one person," Lia said.

"Oh?"

"Yes. Do you want to know?"

She bit her lip. "Sure."

"It's Sam, Julia. He's still here every morning."

"Alone?"

"Well, yes."

"Thought he'd have picked up another woman from the cottages by now."

"No." Lia paused for a moment, and Julia heard more waves. "Sam never picked up women. Just you."

She swallowed the hard lump in the back of her throat. "How is he?" It was the first time she'd inquired about Sam—not that she didn't think of him often. How could she not, with his daily text messages.

"He seems sad, Julia. I think he misses you."

"But he hasn't said that to you. Has he?"

"No."

Then you're just speculating. "I'm sure he's fine."

"Maybe."

"I imagine he's really angry with me."

"I don't think that's it, Julia."

"Then what is it?"

Lia hesitated. "Sometimes he talks to Zach. He's hurt. He really cares about you. I think he's worried. Maybe you should call him when you get a chance."

And I really cared for him, too. "Not a good idea."

---

72 DAYS SOBER

HER NAME WAS BETTY MARTINDALE. JULIA WAS SURPRISED by that. When she'd called Melinda to ask for the referral to her medium friend, she'd expected a name like Aurora Starshine, or something similar. Showed how much she knew about the psychic world, didn't it?

While her analytical lawyer brain made her somewhat skeptical of communication with the spirit world, she also knew that there were times when mediums had solved complex cold cases. Of course, her own personal experience with the crying baby and her connection with Veronica were evidence of something otherworldly going on.

Betty wanted to meet her at the inn—where the occurrences had happened. Julia scheduled an afternoon time when guests were generally out of the inn—sightseeing, shopping, or working. She'd also given Pam a heads up to be out of the house that afternoon. Pam mentioned she thought she'd give Mark a visit.

"Should I tell you now? About what's been going on?" Julia asked over the phone when scheduling the appointment.

"Oh no. I prefer to work in the place of the happenings. I have your address. I'll see you tomorrow afternoon."

Short and to the point. Betty hung up before Julia could say another word.

In the meantime, she thought she'd pursue another avenue, and logged onto her computer and the Louisville Free Public Library website. Her goal was to find out whatever she could about Veronica Mills and the house they'd both occupied in the Central Park area of Old Louisville.

Something Veronica had written in an earlier journal entry had nagged at her, so she started with the historical archives of the local newspapers in Louisville.

It is what I do. My husband stole my writing world from me years ago when we married. No reputable married woman writes for a newspaper, he had said. And that was that.

It didn't take her long to find several brief articles telling of the social happenings within the city, penned by Veronica Mills in the Weekly Courier-Journal. The pieces were newsy and chatty, about people in the city who had died, or had hosted a party, or had opened a new business. Julia gathered that Veronica had been all about writing the society news.

Just as she was about to leave the website for the evening, an obituary notice caught her eye.

VERONICA ELLEN BIXBY MILLS. WIFE OF HERBERT CALHOON MILLS, PRESIDENT, BANK OF LOUISVILLE. MRS. MILLS, A FORMER WRITER FOR THE WEEKLY COURIER-JOURNAL, PASSED AWAY UNEXPECTEDLY ON OCTOBER 2, 1872, AT HER HOME. SHE WAS 28 YEARS OLD. SHE IS SURVIVED BY HER HUSBAND OF SEVEN YEARS, HER PARENTS, ELEANOR AND FRANKLIN BIXBY, AND A SISTER, VICTORIA EILEEN, OF CHARLOTTSVILLE, VIRGINIA, AND WAS PRECEDED IN DEATH BY HER INFANT SON, JAMES HERBERT MILLS. SERVICES ARE PENDING.

JULIA PUSHED OUT A LENGTHY SIGH. "THAT EXPLAINS THE blank journal pages." Still, she had questions. She hoped Betty would come tomorrow and find answers.

SHE GREETED THE MEDIUM AT THE FRONT DOOR AT EXACTLY two o'clock the next afternoon.

"The veil is thin here. Did you know that?" Betty said as she entered Julia's home. "The atmosphere is porous between the physical world and the spiritual worlds. Old Louisville holds many secrets of lives past."

"I have heard that," Julia told her. "This way." She and Betty climbed the stairs to the third floor and entered the attic room.

"This is where things happen?"

Julia stepped further inside. "Yes. My bedroom is across the hall. It used to be part of the attic, but we renovated it to create a primary suite, leaving this side, where we are now, for storage. Recently, we cleaned up the clutter to provide a private space, since we are renovating. That bed," she pointed, "was here when we moved in, along with the cradle on the adjacent wall."

"They are in their original spots?"

"Pretty much, yes. Would you like to have a seat?"

Instead of responding, Betty roamed the room, touching objects, closing her eyes briefly at times, appearing to be thinking or perhaps conjuring. Julia knew not which. Slightly unsure what to do with herself, she sat on the edge of the bed.

"There is energy here," Betty said, then turned. "Definite energy." Scooting a ladderback chair closer to the bed, she sat across from Julia. "What do you want to know?"

"Do you want me to tell you what happened?"

Betty shook her head. "No. I want you to ask me a question. What do you want to know?"

That was not what she expected, and Julia had to think for a minute.

"Take your time," Betty added.

Julia nodded, closing her eyes. An image of Veronica—or how she envisioned Veronica—came into her mind's eye. "A woman lived in this house in the late 1800s," Julia said, "and spent time in this room. Something happened to her."

"Do you want to know what?"

"Yes, I want to know what happened. I want to know how she died."

Here eyes flashed open, and she met Betty's stare.

The medium took a deep breath, reached for Julia's hands, and closed her eyes.

She watched her face. Her eyeballs moved beneath her eyelids, fluttering beneath the thin skin. Jumping back and forth. Betty's breathing fell even and steady but slowed.

"I feel their energy. The women who spent time in this room. Two women, actually."

Two women.

"One older, perhaps a mother. The other woman quite younger. Maybe her daughter."

The clairvoyant exhaled then, blowing out a breath from deep in her lungs, then inhaled slowly. A low hum came from her throat.

Julia didn't know whether to say anything or just sit.

"Both cared for a child. A child that was taken away. Both mourned and slept in this bed—but one woman, perhaps the younger of the two, left. Perhaps, with the child."

Immediately, Julia thought of the journal entry. The nursemaid? Matilda. She stayed with little Jimmy.

"And the other woman?" Julia whispered.

Betty paused, not saying anything for a few minutes. The hum vibrated in her throat. Finally, her eyes slowly opened, and she looked at Julia with a blank-eyed stare. "She has a message for you."

"A message?"

"Yes." Betty nodded.

"Her name is Veronica, and her message is this: *Live your life. Do not waste your days.*"

Julia pulled her gaze away from Betty, glancing at the journal on the bedside table. "Are you able to answer my question?" she finally said, looking back.

"How did she die?"

"Yes."

Betty stared hard into Julia's eyes. "Some answers may be difficult to understand."

"Please tell me."

Again, Betty exhaled long. When she spoke again, her voice was softer, different, formal and with a deep South dialect. "My name is

Veronica. My life was very sad near the end. All the joy was taken from me, and I did not want to go on living. I ended my life in this room. I climbed onto a stack of wooden crates, swung a rope over the attic rafters, tied a noose around my neck, and jumped. I do not want you to suffer the same fate, Julia."

"Oh, God."

"Yes. God was there to catch me, sweeping me off to a better place. I am fine."

Julia gazed intently at Betty, but in her mind, could only see the image of the woman she knew was Veronica. And while she was happy Veronica was fine, she needed to know more. "And little Jimmy?"

"Ah, my sweet boy. He joined me sometime later. Matilda too. We rock him to sleep every night in the cradle, along with the darling girl you sent ahead."

Julia blinked rapidly, taking in those words. "Darling girl?" Her voice was hoarse, raspy.

"Oh yes," Veronica said. "We will keep little Caroline safe for you, until you join us. But no rush, Julia, it is not yet time, and your sweet girl is safe and happy."

LONG AFTER BETTY LEFT, JULIA TUCKED VERONICA'S journal back into the wall and nailed the board back in place. She left the cradle and the twin bed exactly where they were. As she left the attic room, she padlocked the door from the outside, never intending to go back inside again.

Veronica and Matilda deserved their quiet sanctuary. And should Julia ever hear a crying baby again, she would simply smile, knowing that the women were rocking the babies to sleep in the cradle.

---

75 DAYS SOBER

. . .

MARK GLARED AT HER FROM WHERE HE SAT IN HIS wheelchair. She'd arrived before he'd finished an occupational therapy session and had waited for him in his room.

"What are you doing here now? You usually come in the mornings." The physical therapist aide, the PTA, rolled him closer to the bed. Mark glanced up. "I can do this."

"Let me lower the bed a little."

Julia stood back, watching while the bed was lowered, and Mark angled the wheelchair closer to the side of the bed while the aide watched.

The PTA turned toward Julia. "His upper body strength and arm muscles have been doing a lot of work and will only get stronger. Part of his therapy has been how to safely transfer from wheelchair to bed, and vice versa. He's made good progress."

"That's great news," Julia said. "Thanks for sharing that."

"I'm in the room here, you know," Mark said. "I'd appreciate it if you talk to me and not around me."

"Duly noted." Julia moved toward the foot of the bed, watching what the PTA was doing. "Could I come in next week—with Mark's permission of course—and get some instructions on how to support him with these kinds of transfers? I want to make sure I'm doing it right."

Mark glared. "Like I said, I'm not a child, Julia. I can tell you what to do, if needed. You don't need to come in. Besides, you're not going to be around all the time."

She opened her mouth to speak, then decided not to. Smiling at the aide, she simply nodded and waited.

With the help of a sliding transfer board, Mark successfully moved himself from the wheelchair to the bed, adjusting his legs and scooting back against the pillows. With the remote control, he adjusted the part of the bed behind his head to sit more upright.

"See? I'm a quick study."

"He really is." The PTA laid the board against the wheelchair and moved it slightly out of the way. "In fact," he caught Julia's eye, "I believe the team is discussing his discharge to home in the morning.

He's checking off all the boxes. I'd say he'll be home by the weekend. Good news, huh?"

"Yes, of course."

Mark glanced at her. "Peachy."

"I'll see you tomorrow afternoon." The guy waved at Mark and headed out the door, shutting it behind him.

Julia met Mark's glare. "Don't start with me," he said.

"We need to come to an agreement, Mark."

"I'm not staying at the inn."

It was time to tell him all she'd done. "Look," she approached the side of the bed. "Everything is ready for you there. We now have a ramp at the back of the house. The first-floor suite is handicapped accessible. Everything is ready for you to come home. Truly, Mark, I want no arguments. Do you hear me? This is for the best."

His gaze narrowed. "What the hell, Julia!" he shouted. "I know what you've done. Do you think my brain is paralyzed too? I talk to people. What I don't understand is why? Why spend the money when I've not even agreed to stay there? My townhouse is fine."

"Your townhouse is shit for a person in a wheelchair, Mark. Face it, this is the better decision."

"I'm not a child. And I'm not even your husband."

"Oh really? I beg to differ."

"Really? The thing is, Julia—"

The room door swung open, and Pam stepped inside. "Hey! Oh. Julia."

Julia blinked and watched her abruptly halt, stepping more slowly into the room. "Pam? What are you doing here?"

Mark interrupted. "She visits occasionally, Julia. Back off."

She whirled. "Back off? What am I doing?"

"Being bossy as shit is what you are doing."

Pam coughed. "I'm intruding. I'll come back later."

"No," Mark said. "Come here."

Julia watched while Pam hesitantly stepped closer to the bed. She watched the interplay of the two of them, exchanging glances. Mark reached for Pam's hand, and she put hers in his.

Julia blinked, dumbfounded. "What the fuck?"

"You've not been listening, Julia. I've tried to tell you coming to the inn was not a good idea. It would make things too complicated. I know you feel like you owe me, or something. That you need to make up for when our lives were shit. But seriously, that's all in the past. You don't need to do that."

Pam edged closer to Mark, looking adoringly down at him. He caught her loving gaze and smiled back.

Realization clutched at Julia's gut. "Holy fuck. You two are in love. How long?"

Mark nodded. "There were sparks while you were gone—but this last month, well—things have escalated. We didn't know how to approach you with it. Neither Pam nor I wanted to make things worse for you."

"I'm fine. Seriously. Both of you. I'm fine."

"I feel responsible for your drinking."

"Well, don't," she said. "Seriously, Mark, that was all on me. Not you."

He held her gaze. "If that's true, then perhaps it's time."

"Time?"

"I signed the divorce papers weeks ago, while you were at the beach. You'll find them in the top drawer of the wooden filing cabinet in the office. All you need to do is take them to the courthouse and have them processed."

She looked from Pam to Mark. "You're sure this is what you want?"

"I'm more than sure," he said.

"All right then." She took a moment to study them both, holding hands, sharing a quick glance. "I'll just say this before I leave. I care for you both. Mark, you've been my best friend for nearly a lifetime, and Pam, you've become a very good friend, too. I wish you both a world of happiness."

She headed for the door.

"Thank you, Julia." It was Pam who uttered those words.

Quickly, she turned back. "Oh, and just so you know, I'll be heading out of town by morning. I'll get with dad before I leave, Mark, and the two of you can discuss how to sort out the loans. The inn is yours. I'm assuming you two want it?"

"Yes, we do," Mark said. "Thank you."

"Good."

She left the room then, her step lighter than it had been earlier.

Free. She was free of it all. At last.

She was no longer stuck in-between.

Tuckaway Bay

Twenty-Seven

November,
77 days sober

Julia: *Recipe. See attachment.*
    Fisherman: *How do I open a damn attachment?*
    Julia: *Hold on.*
    Fisherman: *I'm holding. I've been holding. How long do I have to hold?*

Julia moved down the three porch steps of Gull Cottage, a plastic container of green chili casserole in each hand. She wore a hoody and her yoga pants and tennis shoes because it was spitting rain periodically and the wind was atrocious. *Must be a storm off the coast.*

Maybe she'd have a fire tonight in the cottage fireplace. That would be nice.

If she were lucky, maybe she'd have someone to share it with.

But she was getting ahead of herself. Seriously ahead of herself.

What if Sam wanted nothing to do with her?

She'd never know unless she got her ass down there to the fishing spot.

Moving quickly, she approached him from behind, then slowly rounded his chair. He sat there, wearing a heavy windbreaker with a hood, which shielded his face a little, looking down at his phone like he was waiting for a text message.

"Green chili casserole?" she said loudly, hoping he'd hear over the wind and through the hood.

He glanced up and met her gaze. "Hatch chilies?"

"Of course."

"You make that this morning?"

"Last night, actually. I got in late."

He stood and looked over her shoulder. "You staying at the Gull?"

She nodded. "Booked indefinitely."

"Is that so, now?"

"It's definitely so."

He took a container of casserole from her hand. "It's cold already."

"Hm. We could warm it up in the cottage."

One of his brows arched, and that sexy sideways smile slid across his face. "Fair warning, but there might be more than a casserole that needs warming up."

Julia grinned. "I was thinking earlier about lighting a fire in the fireplace." She paused. "Or, perhaps elsewhere, depending."

Sam laughed a little. "Now, that's something to ponder."

"I suppose we have all day to ponder... And maybe talk?"

He nodded. "You take care of all your business in Louisville, College Girl?"

"Yes, sir. All tied up in a bow."

Sam took her arm and led her toward the cottage. "Now, I like the sound of that. Can't wait to hear more."

"Wait." Julia glanced back. "The poles."

Sam kept walking. "They'll be there when we get back. Let's go heat some things up."

"The casserole, you mean. Right?"

"Whatever happens, sweetheart. I'm open." He leaned in and nudged her hoody away, planting a soft kiss on her cheek. "Oh, by the way," he added, "Hannah's coming for Christmas. You'll still be here then?"

Julia faced him, moving in closer, her chest against his and her arms around his shoulders. "I'm not going anywhere, Fisherman. I'm here for the duration, flaws and everything."

He grinned. "I wouldn't have it any other way, sweetheart."

Leaning closer, their lips finally touched, and Julia knew she was home.

Dear Mum,

The Missus.... *Mum* as she called her... Would scant make it through this, Matilda was certain. Scant make it through. She would lie in bed for days on end, perhaps partake of too much laudanum. She wondered if the Mrs. would take her life over this. She prayed she would not.

"God be with you," she said, staring out over the green-treed hills, the rolling fields, and the lake that went on forever. "Take care, Mum," she whispered.

She tucked the letter into an envelope she'd found on the desk, printed the address on the front, and wondered who she should see to have it posted.

The boy clucked behind her, lying on the bed in the cramped, dark room. The coverlet was dingy and stained. The walls, once pretty and bright, she imagined, with their floral paper, were faded and ripped in many places. It didn't bother her. She could deal with this, had dealt with much less before.

Jimmy played with his toes while she looked upon him. Rosy cheeks, eyes wide-set and a little off, one askew too far to the left. She'd known early on that there as something especially wrong with the child... Had known in a few months what the

301

Missus could not see. And the Mister, aye, he had seen it all too… Probably before any of them, because he had shunned the boy from the beginning.

The arguing late at night was all she'd needed to know, and understand, about how the birth of this odd child was tearing the couple apart. She might not be a smart and educated woman like the Mum, but she knew children, had nannied many a family back in Dublin, and had thought she would nanny many more here in America.

She'd been wrong. Jimmy, as she liked to call him, would be her last charge and she would have him until he was grown and beyond. She would love and protect him. Care for him. Keep him safe. He would be hers—and together they would finish their years here. Safe. Protected. This fine roof over their heads, food to eat, a warm bed to sleep in each and every night.

She would cuddle and rock him to sleep as she had done since he came into this world.

A brisk knock sounded at the door, and she turned, glancing over the bed and the boy to a woman in a black dress who entered. Her lips were set in a thin, firm line, her eyes black and small, her hair pulled severely back into a bun. A nurse in dingy, bloodstained white stood beside her.

Matilda bowed her head slightly.

"That is him. There is the boy," the woman in black said.

The nurse reached for him.

Matilda stepped forward.

The woman in black raised her hand, palm out, and slapped her across the face. "Stop, girl!"

Matilda's blood froze in her veins, her heart thumped inside her chest, her mind not making sense of what was happening. A hand went to her cheek. Her eyes glazed over with tears.

"But where…."

The sister moved toward the door, taking Jimmy with her. He cooed in her arms, glancing back and giving Matilda a crooked, unknowing smile.

"He is our charge now, and well placed. We will keep him with the others who are like him. Better all the way around."

"But I am to care for him. That is my job."

"No."

"But—"

The hand went up again, and the stern, strict voice called out. "No."

Everything Matilda thought she knew suddenly spun on a coin. What was happening? She needed her Jimmy. What was going on?

"But you do not understand, Ma'am, this was the intent of my staying. The Mister, I heard him tell you, give you money. The reason I am here, to take care of the child... The child I have cared for since...."

"Enough. Hamilton!" She yelled the name, and a large dark man came running. He looked her over and Matilda did not like the way his gaze traveled her body.

"Find her some clothes for working. She can either clean or do laundry, or perhaps put her in the kitchen washing dishes. I care not. Move her to the servant's quarters. Find her a place, work her hard, keep your eye on her at all times, and do not let her near that child."

Shock riveted her. *What had she done? What had she done?*

Thank You!

Thank you for reading **The Space in Between, Julia's Story**. I hope you are enjoying meeting all of the girlfriends of Tuckaway Bay, and diving deeper into their personalities.

I would love your feedback so please consider leaving a review wherever you purchased this book—or on my website at www.maddiejames books.com. I'd love to hear what you think of this story!

Are you ready for **Christmas at Sea Glass Inn?** Spending the holidays at the beach with the girlfriends and their families sounds lovely. Right? What could possibly go wrong?

Christmas at Sea Glass Inn

Christmas at the beach anyone?

Having survived their first year running Sea Glass Inn, Zach and Lia Allen decide to celebrate the holidays by inviting their friends back to Tuckaway Bay for Christmas.

Wait. Correction. Zach reluctantly agrees. He really wanted a quiet Christmas at home with Lia.

Of course, there is plenty of room at the inn for Lia's girlfriends—even though half of the inn is shut down for deep cleaning and painting—but is there enough room for children and significant others, and perhaps an ex-spouse who pops by? And what about Zach's friends from New Hampshire who crash the inn after a storm cancels their winter fishing expedition?

As if space is the only issue... Is the resort large enough to handle fluctuating family dynamics, teenage angst, giddy girl crushes, pregnancy hormones, and perimenopausal women?

Can Sea Glass Inn, and its occupants, survive the mood swings and hot flashes?

Fa-la-la-la-la. Let the reindeer games begin!

Tuckaway Bay

2024 Releases

Beach Therapy: A Novel
The Space in Between: A Novel (Julia's Story)
Christmas at Sea Glass Inn: A Novella

2025 Releases

The Me I Left Behind: A Novel (Maggie's Story)
The Flip Side of Now: A Novel (Alice's Story)
Anywhere But Here: A Novel (Wren & Willow's Story)

And more....

About Madeleine Jaimes

Madeleine Jaimes is the women's fiction pen name for bestselling romance author Maddie James.

While Maddie dabbles with cowboys and small town happily-ever-afters, Madeleine explores the real-life, complicated relationships of women, men, and families, and tackles those problems through story. She figures she's lived long enough to bring some of her own life experiences into the mix.

Maddie also writes mainstream romantic suspense as M.L. Jameson.

Maddie James and pen names have published over 70 romance titles worldwide, and in a variety of formats (ebook, print, audiobook, and more). Affaire de Coeur says, "James shows a special talent for traditional romance," and RT Book Reviews claims, "James deftly combines romance and suspense, so hop on for an exhilarating ride."

Learn more at www.maddiejamesbooks.com

www.ingramcontent.com/pod-product-compliance
Lightning Source LLC
Chambersburg PA
CBHW050527110726
47899CB00005B/1622